HOPELESS ROMANTIC

HOPELESS ROMANTIC

MARINA ADAIR

THORNDIKE PRESS

A part of Gale, a Cengage Company

GALE

A Cengage Company

LIBRARY OF CONGRESS CIP DATA ON FILE.
CATALOGUING IN PUBLICATION FOR THIS BOOK
IS AVAILABLE FROM THE LIBRARY OF CONGRESS.

ISBN-13: 978-1-4328-8840-4 (hardcover alk. paper)

Published in 2021 by arrangement with Kensington Books, an imprint
of Kensington Publishing Corp.

Printed in Mexico
Print Number: 01   Print Year: 2021

To the best plotting ninjas a girl could ask for. Skye Jordan, Jill Shalvis, and RaeAnne Thayne, thank you for your friendship and guidance. I'd share peanut brittle with you three any day!

To the Sacramento Autistic Spectrum and Special Needs Alliance (SASSNA), Autism Speaks, and Autism Society, for spreading awareness and enhancing the lives of individuals and families living with autism spectrum disorder.

CHAPTER 1

According to town legend, Beckett Hayes didn't believe in romance. It couldn't possibly be that she was actually a hopeless romantic who'd spent practically a decade living in — and trying unsuccessfully to leave — Rome. Looking for romance in Rome was as cliché as wishing on shooting stars or chasing rainbows, both of which had about as much chance of success as swiping right in the pursuit of everlasting love.

Nope, Beckett had never put much stock in Cupid. Now, a laundry fairy? That was a mythological creature she could get behind.

She was never much interested in dreaming about "The One" or "The Dress" worthy of a resounding yes. There were far better ways to spend her sleeping hours — sadly, sleep being at the top of her list. So what if people believed she was too practical for love? That was far less pathetic than

7

the reality.

Beckett didn't have time for love. That was the ugly and embarrassing truth. Life seemed to consume her every waking hour. Anything more complicated than no-strings dating and the occasional *petite morte* provided by someone who didn't require a battery wasn't in the cards right now. Which made Bruce the perfect Man of the Moment.

Like her, Bruce was insanely busy, liked to spend his downtime bicycling up the coast, and, as an added bonus, didn't disappoint in bed. He wasn't a big hitter by any means, but he got the job done. Unfortunately, he was also a bit boring.

And late, she thought, glancing around the bar. Okay, that was a lie. She pretended to search for her date while taking in a long drink of Levi Rhodes and all his testosterone-dripping glory as he carried a keg of beer single-handedly from one end of his bar to the other — earning the attention of every female patron in the joint.

It was one of the few times Beckett reacted in accord with the ladies' night crowd. But a glimpse of Levi was worth lowering her standards. Not that she'd let him know that. It would just make his day.

And if there was one thing Beckett hated

more than being cliché, it was making Levi's day.

Levi applied the same fierce dedication to running his family's bar and marina as he did cementing his status as Rome's Most Unattainable Romeo. Not that there was a large pool of sexy and single men under sixty-five in Rome. Because the Rome in question was not known for its Sistine Chapel or romantic fountains. No, Levi was a born-and-bred Roman from Rome, Rhode Island, a small beach community that was home to the world's largest clam dig.

It was hard to get romantic about clams.

Levi was another story. Which was why Beckett made sure to stay on the hate side of their love/hate relationship. When she walked into the Crow's Nest, a former fish market that had been expertly repurposed into a sleek, high-energy bar and grill, she was always combat-ready, prepared for what was sure to be the cockfight of the century.

So it didn't surprise her when her entrance was met with curious, and a few flabbergasted, looks. Or when Levi took time out of his very busy schedule to lock those stormy blue eyes on hers and mouth, "You're trouble."

It was nearly five, so he was fielding requests from all sides as the after-work crowd rushed to get their happy hour orders in under the wire. But there he stood, casually filling up mugs in a pair of boat shoes, blue cargo pants slung low on his hips, and a white long-sleeve Henley that was stretched to the limit over his broad shoulders and six-pack.

Guys like Levi didn't rush — for anyone. They were too busy playing Peter Pan to be bothered with the concept of time. Even the way he took orders, chatting up the patrons while tossing around good-natured laughs and flirty winks as if he were one handshake from announcing his candidacy for Rhode Island's next governor.

"Trouble?" Beckett mouthed back, making a big to-do about looking over her shoulder, then clutching a hand to her chest. "Me?"

He pressed his lips together, looking handsome in a pissed-off way that made her heart feel like breaking out in song.

Beckett smiled her best smile and walked over to the bar, unsnapping her bike helmet and sitting on a stool.

"It's that kind of hospitality that keeps me coming back," she said to Levi, although his eyes were trained on her co-worker of sorts, Gregory, who took the stool next to hers. She'd met Gregory at Fur-Ever Friends, a nonprofit dedicated to training emotional support companions for people with emotional or neurological disabilities.

Gregory was fun and guaranteed to keep things entertaining, should Bruce choose to forget his sense of humor at home again. Or Levi choose to be nice to her. The love/hate line always got a bit fuzzy when he was nice.

There wasn't much chance of nice happening tonight, though, because while fun, Gregory was also a honey-colored silkie chicken nearing the end of his ESA training.

Levi pinched the bridge of his nose. "Come on, Beck, we've gone through this. No pets allowed in my bar."

"He isn't a pet. He's an emotional support companion and my latest trainee. He also happens to be from a long line of silkie chickens who have provided support for humans with PTSD, autism, social anxiety, and seizures. Isn't that right, Gregory?"

"*Cluuuck cluckcluckcluck.*" Gregory's little beak peeked over the lip of the countertop when he squawked a very loud affirmative.

"Gregory?"

"Gregory Pecker," she clarified, and the rooster in question flapped his wings to get on the bar. Beckett caught him in mid-flight and set him back on the stool with a stern

11

wag of her finger.

His response was to peck Beckett's nail — *hard.*

"Hey, no biting."

"Pa-cock," Gregory sassed.

"This is why I need to bring him out in public more," she said to Levi. "He tends to misbehave in front of a crowd. It's the whole mine-is-bigger-than-yours BS — he needs to show the other guys just how impressive his wingspan is. Hens are so much easier to train."

Levi's lips twitched, but he kept his not-on-my-watch expression firmly in place. "You got papers for Pecker and his wingspan?"

"He prefers Mr. Pecker or Gregory, and he has a vest." Beckett did her best game-show-girl impression to showcase the adorable SERVICE COCK vest that Mable, one of Beckett's most loyal customers, had knitted as a Christmas gift.

The vest was red, which matched Gregory's wattle and really highlighted his beautiful white feathers, and had holes big enough to accommodate his wings.

"So is that a no on the papers?" Resting his forearms on the bar, Levi leaned in as if stressing the seriousness of Gregory's working animal status. "Then, I'm sorry, but unless Pecker is a licensed *service* animal, he's against health code, so he can shake his tail feathers in some other guy's establishment."

"While I understand your rules, surely you can make an exception?"

"Nope."

"But we're celebrating. Tonight we completed hug training. He even got a little diploma, which means next week he gets to spend bonding time with his fur-ever companion."

"Hug training?" he challenged. "That's as bad as the dog-ate-my-homework excuse."

"Watch." Beckett patted her chest, and Gregory moved into action. He hopped on the bar and waddled to Beckett, his head rising like a periscope. She sent a *whoopsie* grimace Levi's way, then leaned forward and patted her chest twice. Gregory walked to the end of the countertop as Beckett moved in close for a hug. The moment their chests touched, Gregory tilted his head and, resting it on her shoulder, delivered one of the sweetest hugs yet.

"See how he's pressing against my chest? The gentle pressure and soft cooing is proven to lower anxiety."

"Impressive. But he still has to go."

"There's something else." She looked around as if about to impart her deepest,

13

darkest secret. "He's training to be a companion for a vet with PTSD." Which was pure fabrication. "It's quite a sad but heroic story."

"Not my problem." He pointed to the sign: NO SHOES, NO SHIRT, NO SERVICE, with a hand-scrawled AND NO PETS in Sharpie at the bottom that had been added when Beckett brought in her client's llama, Larry, for lunch.

In addition to training emotional support animals, a hobby that had begun when her younger brother was diagnosed with Autism Spectrum Disorder and they couldn't afford a companion, Beckett was also a professional odd jobber.

Pet sitting and picking up people's dry cleaning wasn't exactly living the dream, but when her family moved to Rome nine years ago, there weren't a lot of career opportunities where specializing in "getting shit done" was the only qualification necessary. Beckett worked hard to find jobs flexible enough to accommodate her unique family situation, but over time her unpredictable schedule tried the patience of even the most understanding bosses. Which was how she found herself the favorite former-employee of nearly every mom-and-pop business in town.

So odd jobs became her livelihood. She could set her own hours, choose her tasks and, most importantly, choose compatible clients. Being a glorified errand girl wasn't glamorous but what she did was meaningful. Making people's crazy lives a bit more manageable mattered. But there were days she felt like nothing more than a pizza delivery driver.

Today happened to be one of those days. So she'd braved the end-of-winter temperatures to come to the Crow's Nest, looking for a cold beer and a fun night out, and she wasn't about to be cock-blocked by a bartender with rooster envy.

"To be clear," Beckett said, loud enough for the bar to hear, "are you anti–people with special needs, or anti–war heroes? I just need to clarify your stance, so I know whether or not to support your *establishment.*"

Levi hitched a brow. "My dad was a vet, my grandfather was a vet, and you know damn well the only thing I object to is your menagerie of bizarre pets shitting in my bar."

"So, Gregory is being persecuted because he wasn't born with four legs and a tail, or what society deems as more service-companion-like traits?"

"Your service dogs have never shit in my bar," he said coolly. "Your other animals don't have the best track record."

"That only happened once, and it was because one of your customers fed Larry buffalo wings. Everyone knows llamas are vegans."

"Once was enough." He extended a hand, palm up. A big, masculine hand that looked strong and capable. "Show me papers or find another place to haunt."

"You're a species elitist." She snapped her fingers, having an *aha* moment. "Unless. . . . Are you one of those guys who's intimidated by a prettier cock?"

"No."

"You sure? Because Gregory isn't your everyday, ordinary cock. He's got more up here" — she tapped a finger to her temple — "than most males. In fact, he's living proof that a cock can be house-trained. I know, shocking."

His lips curved into a reluctant grin. And, man, when he grinned, that love/hate line went from fuzzy to forgotten. "Beck, everyone knows a pecker can be trained. Now, a cock on the other hand?" He shrugged. "If you were hoping to see one of those in action, you could have just asked for my number."

Beckett squirmed, a little flustered by the sexual banter. Because while he was giving her one of his double-dimpled smiles, something in his eyes hinted that he wasn't joking.

"Noted for next time," she said, wishing she were wearing anything other than two-day-old jeans and helmet-hair from zipping back and forth across town on her Vespa.

Levi didn't move an inch as his eyes tracked down to her mouth and lower, taking in everything he could before making the slow trip back up. And if her nipples hadn't given him a high-five on the descent, then they sure as heck did on his second pass.

"Are you intimidated by a pretty cock?" was all he asked, but his voice was pitched low and sexy, making Beckett's heart race frantically.

"Not much intimidates me," she said as casual as can be.

Looking unconvinced, he rested his elbows on the bar, his biceps flexing under the weight as he moved in until their cheeks were nearly touching and his breath teased her earlobe. It teased a whole lot of other places, too. Places that the Bruces of the world could only locate with the help of a hand-drawn map and satellite-powered GPS tracking. Levi did it with a single look. "Noted for next time."

She laughed. "You're awful cocky."

"It's called confidence, Beck," he said, and she ignored how much she liked it when he called her that. "Something you wear well."

A little thrown by his compliment, she let her gaze drift down to study the bar top. Levi flirted with everyone, but he never flirted with her. "Last time, you said I was stubborn."

"Did I mention I happen to like stubborn?"

No, but her heart was never going to forget it. Neither was her head, because stubborn was one of those qualities, like smart, that men always found sexy until it was focused on someone other than them.

Levi was a born charmer, with a laid-back and easygoing way about him, not to mention he was pretty easy on the eyes. But while he was busy getting to know everyone, she noticed he never gave away anything of himself.

Beckett recognized his particular form of evasiveness. She saw it in the mirror every day when she brushed her teeth.

"No. You also didn't mention the drink specials," she said.

"I don't serve anything in a trough or sip-per bottle. But if you want to take your friend home and come back alone, I'll serve you anything your little heart desires."

Too bad her little heart always desired things that were not good for her. Like flirting with Levi.

"Sorry, no can do. I'm picking up a to-go order for the Harpers." Which she would deliver on her way to the movies with Bruce. He was easy that way.

"The Crow's Nest doesn't do to-go orders anymore."

"Sure you do." She stretched her arm across the bar, hand inches from his face, and pointed to the ink scribbles on her palm. "Crab cakes. Two bowls of chowder. Salmon burger." She mimicked the bouncing ball over the words as she read. "To go. It's all right there."

A tiny grin played at the side of his mouth.

"Oh, and Mrs. Harper says to go heavy on the fries. I guess last time the portions were a little stingy."

"Gus shouldn't be taking to-go orders," Levi said, referring to his chef. "We are an in-dining establishment only."

"Gus and I have an arrangement." She winked.

"How did you manage that?"

"A month or so back, Annie was working

19

a double at the hospital. Emmitt was in New York and wanted to make sure she had a hot meal, so he called me." Annie was not only Emmitt's new fiancée; she was also *Beckett's* best friend. "It became a thing. Whenever he was out of town, he'd place an order; I'd deliver it to the hospital. What can I say — love makes people do crazy things."

"Yeah, like completely ignore bro code," he mumbled. "And Gus went along with this?"

"Gus is an excellent head chef. Accommodating and pleasant, which is why I decided to offer the service to all my clients. Gus thought it was a great idea and we formed a system. Customer calls me, I call Gus, Dean meets me at the back door."

He ran a hand down his face. "You have my waitstaff in on this?"

"Just Dean."

"Why am I not surprised?" He groaned.

"He thinks I should make an app. You know, really streamline the process. I'm considering it."

"An app," he repeated, but he didn't sound angry. Oh no, the laid-back bartender grinned as if he found this entire thing amusing. "What am I going to do with you?"

Beckett could think of one million and

one delicious things he could do to her. Since all but one landed in the "inside thoughts only" category, she said, "How about some crab cakes, two bowls of chowder, and a salmon burger to go? Pretty please."

"Not even with sugar on top. No matter how appealing that might sound coming out of your mouth," he said, and Beckett froze. When it came to Levi's opinion of her mouth, appealing was never a word he'd used. Smart, loud, dirty at times, but never appealing. "Last time you had an arrangement with my restaurant, I spent my first night off in months serving two hundred mini crab cakes and six seafood platters at the fire chief's retirement party. Not to mention the identical order we had to trash because it went bad waiting for pickup."

"That was an unfortunate situation." Which only managed to reconfirm Levi's — *totally bogus* — opinion that Beckett was a flake.

Oh, she'd provided him with a dozen reasons to fuel that belief — and that was just in the past few months. But the old saying about withholding judgment until walking a mile in someone's shoes? People would rather dance barefoot over glass shards and rusty fishhooks than even put on one of Beckett's shoes. But she'd learned long ago that she didn't have to justify her reality to anyone — no matter how sexy he might be.

"And it won't ever happen again. I promise." She almost cringed, because she'd also learned long ago never to make promises she couldn't keep — even if she meant them in the moment.

"Can't happen again, since we no longer do to-go orders," he repeated. "And before you remind me how ludicrous, futile, and shortsighted my rules are, know that I'm not in the mood."

She leaned on the bar, which brought her way past up close and personal. "You forgot moronic, asinine, and a bad business decision."

He smiled. "My decision to make. In fact, if I wasn't already overbooked and short-staffed, Gus would be looking for a new job. He's struggling to keep up with the volume of orders from the bar and dining area. He doesn't have time to be running orders for takeout. And don't even get me started on Dean."

"No running involved, because lucky for you, I was a state champion sprinter." Which would come in handy, since she'd given herself four months to transform her little errand-running business into a lucrative company with a steady income.

That was two months ago, and there was no backup plan.

Beckett was too old to babysit or deliver papers, too controversial for office politics, and way too smart to participate in another clinical trial. Giving a temp agency a percentage of her hard-earned cash was also out. So eighteen months ago, she'd done what any self-respecting, mature woman with only a high school diploma and strong work ethic did when faced with acute, recurring unemployment syndrome.

She'd become her own boss.

According to the writers at *Us Weekly* and the mastermind team who wrote the "Your Next Career; You're Welcome!" quiz, Beckett had four perfect matches for future employment: portable-toilet cleaner, landfill operator, adult entertainer, and becoming her own boss.

With the support of her friend Heineken, she quickly ruled out the first and second options — confined spaces gave her the willies, and vehicles with four wheels were a waste of resources. Option three had merit, but when it came to mastering tassels, she learned that she didn't have the right skill set. Which left her with six empty bottles and a single option.

She'd filed the necessary paperwork for Consider It Done, Rome's top personal concierge service, the next day and never looked back.

With years of odd jobs under her belt, establishing a steady base of regular customers hadn't been hard. But convincing the town that hiring a personal concierge wasn't the same as hiring a teenaged neighbor to mow the lawn? She was still working on that.

"I'm expanding my services to include select local businesses that could benefit from my expertise and experience. I can help with staffing, overseeing small projects, and bulk food delivery. I'm working with a law firm in town, handling all their employee relocations for intra-office transfers, and they're willing to put me on retainer to be their lunch delivery service. We're discussing which restaurants will be included on their list."

She unzipped her favorite kick-ass leather jacket, which made her feel like a tough girl, and flashed Levi the new, personalized NO MATTER HOW BIG OR SMALL THE TASK, ALL YOU HAVE TO DO IS ASK, THEN CONSIDER IT DONE tee she'd had printed up.

"Catchy." He straightened. "Now I know how you got Dean to go along with you,"

24

he said — to her chest.

"You're such a guy." But his suspicions had merit.

Dean was a twenty-year-old marine science major, on the six-year track at the local junior college, who embraced Van Life in his upcycled mustard colored, '67 Volkswagen Deluxe Microbus. Catching waves and women were his way of life.

"How'd you get Gus to agree? The guy's as rigid as his starched apron."

"Dean went along for the tips." She looked at the crowded waiting room, studying the new arrangement of the tables, which made room for three more tabletops but placed the hostess stand too far from the bar, making it impossible for people waiting there to hear their names being called. "Gus went along because he values my insight. Look around — you have more interest than seats available. And no matter how many different ways you try rearranging this place, there are always going to be more hungry customers than seats."

"Not such a bad problem to have," Levi said, but he didn't sound as confident as he had a moment ago.

"Maybe. But kind of dumb to have a problem at all when the solution is sitting in front of you."

Levi looked at her shirt again, then to the chicken who'd hopped into her lap.

"You're right. I'd like to hire you to solve a pressing problem." He took a folded bill from the tip jar, straightened it, then slapped it on the counter. "Here's twenty bucks for you and your chicken to go anywhere but here."

And to think at one time, she'd considered him sweet.

"No can do. I'm already on a job. Plus, you wouldn't deny Gregory a celebratory drink for passing his empathy test, would you?"

"I'll give you a paper cup and you can make him a trough. Outside."

"Sorry. I'm meeting someone for a drink. *Inside.*" She took off her coat and leaned back, making herself comfortable.

"I hope this someone is human."

Gregory took the moment to flap his little misbehaving butt onto the bar top again. Levi leveled a glare at him and then pointed a threatening finger.

"Oh, be careful, sometimes he . . . bites," she trailed off, completely in awe when, instead of pecking at Levi, Gregory hopped back down into his chair, his clucking quickly morphing into a soft cooing.

"Wow, how did you do that?"

He leveled her with the same glare and, *oh boy,* those intense blue pools had her body cooing in no time. That's when she noticed that his eyes looked almost turquoise in the light, with a sky-blue ring around the pupil.

As if he could sense exactly how her body reacted to that look, his lips curved. "Now, do me a favor and either take him home or leave him in the car. At least during prime serving hours."

"What kind of person leaves a living being in their car?" she asked, horrified.

A familiar sadness welled in her gut. She knew firsthand the exact kind of person who would do something so selfish and inhumane. Which was why, over the years, Beckett volunteered her time connecting animals with human companions, because no one should have to face their fears alone.

"Plus, I drove my scooter tonight." And every night, since she didn't own any other vehicle. When absolutely necessary, she'd borrow her dad's truck. But to her, a car was nothing more than a giant steel cage on wheels.

"I'll give you a pass tonight, but starting tomorrow, this is a fowl-free zone."

"That I can agree to."

"Are you meeting Software Engineer

Steve? Isn't like him to be late. He usually shows up a half hour early for your dates. Sits in the corner booth right over there." He pointed. "Then you show up, and he stands so he can pretend you both arrived at the same time. It's kind of cute, in a lapdog sort of way."

She was a little speechless that he'd paid enough attention to know not only that she was dating, but also *who* she was dating. Her dad, family, and friends called her dates The Boy to simplify matters. And yet, Levi remembered.

Which was as startling as it was sweet — for a jerk.

Even though Beckett had lived in Rome for almost a decade, and Levi was of the born-and-raised variety, they didn't really know each other all that well. It was only recently, after his best friend began dating her best friend, that they'd shared words beyond, "Your largest margarita, please" or "A pint of whatever IPA you have on tap." Beside a few run-ins at Annie's house, they'd never spent any time outside of the bar together. Their time in the bar had led to some fun banter and arguments about animal rights, but they'd never talked about anything personal.

Then again, he *was* Mr. Personal — with

every person who sat at his bar. His interest in her was nothing more than a necessary skill of the trade.

"No, Steve is now engaged to the love of his life," she said, smiling at how happy Steve had been when she'd last spoken to him. He'd wanted the whole white-picket-fence fantasy, and he'd found it. "They're getting married this summer. I'm meeting Bruce."

His eyes lit up with humor. "Is Bruce a biologist?"

"No."

"A bus driver?"

"No."

"How about a beauty consultant?"

She considered this. "He does have great pores. But no."

He snapped his fingers. "I got it. A bailiff."

"No," she said, then buried her face in the curve of her elbow. "He's a banker."

Levi burst out laughing, and she shushed him with her hand. "It's a fluke. I promise you, name and career alliteration isn't a requirement in my dating prospects."

"Thank God for that." With a tummy-flipping grin, he slid a frosty mug across the bar. "Although, I was once a junior life-guard. In case you're taking applications."

Her cheeks burned. He noticed, then

winked. And, *lord have mercy,* it did funny things to her. Like make her lean closer and consider walking back and forth across *the line* as if it were a tightrope and she had the balance for such things.

"Cock-a-doodle-doo." Gregory ruffled his feathers, his neck straining up as he screeched. Then pooped on the barstool.

Beckett stole a guilty glance at Levi, who silently handed her a towel.

"How does Bruce feel about sharing you with a rooster?" he asked, while reaching under the bar with one big, manly hand to retrieve a frosty mug and fill it with her favorite local IPA, impressing her with his memory and his mean multitasking skills.

"Not much bothers Bruce," she said, noticing that while Levi looked relaxed and laid-back, his hands never slowed down, leaving her to wonder what other kinds of things those hands could accomplish.

"Is that a good thing?" he asked, right as her phone pinged with an incoming text.

Frustration tugged at her lips. She didn't need to read the text to know exactly how her night was going to end. History had taught her as much. History had also taught her what to expect if she didn't respond.

With a heavy sigh, she dug through her purse — aka her filing system for taxes —

dumping two years of receipts, a Ziploc of pellets, and a sorry-looking banana on the counter. When it pinged again, she was working her way through the outside pockets, finding six baseball cards, make that seven, and no phone. Then the pinging started to pick up, one after the other, and she knew, just knew, her one free night this month to enjoy some polite and casual sex with sweet but boring Bruce was about to come to a premature end.

"Looking for this?" Levi reached into her jacket and pulled her cell from the exact pocket where she'd placed it so as not to lose it again. She was a mess.

"Thanks." She looked at the phone but didn't reach for it, knowing that the second she did, the clock would strike midnight on her fun and she'd turn back into a pumpkin — the most overrated vegetable ever to grace a caffeinated drink.

"Hey, you okay?" he asked in a gentle, caring voice that had her melting. "If you need me to punch some dickhead, just let me know?"

"Maybe next time." She took the phone, their fingers brushing for a moment longer than polite, and the screen flashed, confirming both her suspicions.

One, sex with Levi would be anything but

nice and polite, and while that excited her, it also terrified her. Two, if she couldn't find a way to fix her life, sex with any man wasn't ever going to happen again.

She took a big swig of her beer, closing her eyes to enjoy what might possibly be the last moment of adult fun for a while, then stood. She dropped a few bills on the counter. "I gotta run."

"Is Bruce seriously canceling this late?" He sounded offended on her behalf.

"Bruce!" *Oh my God!* Her hands went to her head. "I almost forgot about Bruce."

"Sounds like you guys are the real deal," he deadpanned.

Bruce could be the real deal — for someone who had time for such luxuries. Beckett was not that someone and didn't have a clue as to whether she'd ever be in a position to be a forever-someone.

"Nah, we're just friends with common interests. And I'm about to be a really shitty friend." She could already feel anxiety creep up her spine. "Would you tell him I'm sorry, that something came up? He'll understand."

She had turned to leave when Levi's hand came to rest atop hers, holding her in place. "Beck."

"Right." She met his concerned gaze, which only added fuel to the stress-induced fire. "You've never met Bruce. He lives in Westport. Just look for a guy in a suit and loafers with tassels who's super sweet, but likely boring the person next to him with stories about his bird-watching excursions. Did you know there are over fifteen types of doves in the Americas?"

"Beck," he said again, this time in a calming tone that wrapped around her like one of the seven weighted blankets she kept in the house. The real problems started when she looked into those blue orbs watching her in that quiet, assessing way of his that made her squirm. "You okay?"

"I'm fine." Or she would be, as soon as she got home.

It wasn't often that Beckett allowed the things out of her control to get to her. But this summons had more than gotten to her. It had knocked her so off balance, she'd begun to forget reality. Or maybe that was Levi's fault. Either way, she needed to get out of there.

"Hey, Beck," he called after her. "Next time you find yourself short a partner for Hug Training class, give me a ring. I don't violate any health codes. Plus, I know some great techniques to reduce stress." He patted his chest twice and slid her a teasing wink.

Beckett didn't dare engage because, while Levi might come off as the King of Cool, something told Beckett that beneath the calm surface lay some seriously deep currents. If she wasn't careful, they would suck her in and drag her right out to sea.

CHAPTER 2

Levi was fluent in four different dialects of chick-speak, and decent in two others, so he knew that the simple phrase, "I'm fine," had exactly twenty-seven different, complex and hard-to-decipher translations, ranging from, "Hold me and tell me I'm beautiful" to "Do I look fucking fine?" And his all-time personal favorite, "Do you have a penis? Yes? Then crawl down into a deep, dank hole and stay there."

For all his experience with women, and he'd had a lot, Levi had never been on the receiving end of Beckett's particular variety of "I'm fine," but it gave him the knees-to-the-nuts feeling he got whenever someone mentioned his sister's passing. Usually, the best course of action was to smile through it, then escape at the first opening. Only she'd done the escaping, which should leave him feeling relieved.

The kitchen was backed up, the dining

room an hour wait, and the red light flashing on the phone made his left eye twitch. He'd managed to turn his dad's small fish-and-chips stand, which catered to fishermen and guests docked in their family's small marina, into a full-scale bar and grill.

Now, with thirty-five tabletops overlooking the crystal still waters of the bay, an additional patio with beachfront access, and an exclusive member's club on the top floor for guests docked in any one of the two hundred berths, it didn't take an expert to tell him he'd exceeded his goal.

Fan-fucking-tastic, had his goal been to run his dad's business for the rest of his life. Once again, he'd hard-worked himself into a corner. Like tonight. He'd been so focused on getting one of those sweet smiles from Beckett, he'd overlooked the most important thing.

"Cluuuck cluckcluckcluck cock," Pecker said, and Levi rubbed his forehead. Because in Beckett's rapid exodus, she'd left something behind. Maybe that had been her plan all along. Regardless, he was not happy.

Levi glared at the chicken sitting on his barstool and sighed. Pecker's head bopped up, his neck stretching like a slinky, to peer over the countertop. He didn't look, or act, like any chicken Levi had ever seen.

36

The guy had feathers everywhere. There were so many on his feet, he looked as if he were wearing boxy white trainers. On top of his head sat a wild crop of feathers that stood out in all directions, making him look like a Muppet collided with Einstein on the set of a rap video.

"Cluuuck. Cluck. Cluckidy, cluckcluck." Pecker's tone sounded irritated.

"I'm not happy about this, either," Levi said.

"Man, the past five minutes was worth braving the storm to get a cold beer," put in an amused voice from beside him.

"I'd have walked all the way here in the rain without an umbrella to see that," another, even more annoying voice said.

He looked over as Emmitt and Grayson, the two people he'd most want by his side in a fight, appeared from the kitchen. Both carried platefuls of food piled high, and both wore matching shit-eating grins.

"This isn't a soup kitchen," Levi said.

"Add it to my tab." Emmitt Bradley, his best friend and constant pain in the ass, took a stool three down from the one Beckett had vacated faster than a fisherman in a hurricane. Gray plopped down next to him.

"Add mine to his tab, too." Dr. Grayson

Matthews, the town's favorite pediatrician and Levi's brother-in-law, leaned over the bar to grab a frosty mug. He placed it under the spigot right as Levi snatched it away.

"Do I walk into your office and touch your things?" Levi asked.

"Bad form, Gray," Emmitt scolded. "You know how pissy Levi gets when someone touches his spigot."

"You guys should take this act on the road," Levi said, but poured them each a beer. "Why are you even here?"

The look his friends exchanged was a familiar one. Something was up. He glanced at Emmitt. "Shouldn't you be at home with your pretty fiancée?"

"Annie's covering a shift for Lynn. Won't be home until eleven."

Great. Five uninterrupted hours of Emmitt interrupting Levi at work.

Early on, Levi had taken great joy in watching the self-proclaimed ladies' man, who'd spent most of the past decade photographing and covering world events from the opposite side of the globe, mutate into a house-trained and lovesick puppy. But when left idle, Emmitt acted like a sugared-up toddler, unable to sit still, entertain himself, or play well with others.

Whenever Annie worked late at the hospital, and Emmitt was between assignments, he quickly became bored. And if he couldn't find anything better to do, he'd pass the time by driving Levi crazy. Didn't matter if Levi was tending bar, managing the marina, or sleeping on his boat; Emmitt's pestering knew no limits.

Yeah, he was having a hard time finding the humor in the situation now.

"And why are you here, scarfing down dinner on a Tuesday night?"

"Paisley's at your mom's place," Gray said, referring to his stepdaughter — and Levi's niece. "She failed her driver's test."

"Again?"

"So much for third time's the charm," Emmitt said, glaring at Gray. "It's not often that nurture trumps nature, but this is all on you, man."

"The hell it is," Gray choked out around a mouthful of calamari burger. "You're the one who *insisted* on teaching her to drive. I'd put some heavy quotes around the drive part, but my hands are full."

"It's a rite of passage for a dad to teach his kid how to drive. Biologically, that's me." Emmitt pointed a fry in Gray's direction. "But nothing, and I mean zippo, nada, zilch, could make up for the years of bad habits she inherited from riding in the back

39

of your mom-mobile."

That's right. Emmitt was the birth dad, Gray the stepdad, and Levi was the guy who'd taken on the role the minute Michelle told him she was going to be a single mother.

The three men couldn't be more different, but one amazing little girl had cemented their connection — made them a family. Paisley wasn't so little anymore, and their tribe was down one member, but their bond was stronger than ever.

That's what love did, stripped away all life's baggage and BS until all that was left was family — vulnerable and pure, embracing each other's imperfections without hesitation or judgment. From that moment on, everything on the spectrum from bliss to pain, joy to loss, was experienced together.

In this case, it was three dads joining forces to give their daughter the fullest life possible — and pointing fingers at each other when the shit hit the fan.

"I'm an excellent driver," Gray said, leaning forward on his stool. "Not that it matters. Paisley said she wants to pick her teacher for the next round of driving practice."

"Smart girl. She gets that from my side of

the family." The moment his words hit the air, Levi realized the steaming pile of shit he'd just swan-dived into. Eyes wide open and headfirst.

"We agree. To the first part, anyway." Emmitt leaned over the bar to smack Levi on the shoulder — and *boom*! "So buckle up, Uncle Levi, you're the lucky winner."

"Oh no," Levi said. "No way. I'm still trying to fill the day manager's position as well as find someone to come on as a general manager." He needed someone qualified to oversee Levi's entire operation.

Plus, there was the task of finding an experienced harbor master. His current harbor master, who'd come with the marina when his dad had purchased it back in the seventies, was great at charming the guests and keeping the dockhands on their toes. But making sure the marina ran smoothly — and in the black — had become Levi's second full-time job.

Levi's captain's chair would be hard to fill. But if he didn't fix this mess soon, his trip down the coast would have to go on the back burner again. And this time, Levi was afraid his dream would catch fire and go up in a midlife puff of smoke.

"How does it feel to be the favorite for once?" Gray asked, then revved air-handlebars. "Vroom. Vroom."

"*Cock. Cock. Cock-a-doodle-doo,*" Pecker squawked from his seat.

Levi loved spending time with Paisley. She was so much like her mom; it was like being with his niece and sister all at once. But Levi had lived through Michelle's intro to driving; he didn't think his heart could make it through Paisley's. So yeah, he was about as excited to be a driver's ed teacher as he was to have a chicken in his bar.

Cute women made him do stupid things.

"I'll take her one day after school," he said, secretly touched that Paisley had chosen him. And moved by the idea of his sister looking down on him and laughing her ass off. "As for you . . ."

Levi eyeballed Pecker, who was eyeballing him back. Then the chicken gave a couple of hostile clucks and flapped his wings, catching enough air to get him bar-bound.

Levi reached out, grabbing the little clucker right before his creepy looking talons touched the counter, cutting his high-pitched rant short so it came out more, "*Cluck-cock!*"

Pecker dropped a load on Levi's floor.

"And you wonder why she left you be hind," Levi said, tucking the rooster under his arm like a football.

42

"You asking yourself the same question?" Gray said, shoving a fistful of fries in his mouth like he was at the fucking movies. "Because with skills like yours, it's a wonder you ever got laid."

"Seriously, the born-again virgin is judging me," Levi snapped. It had been nearly a year since the car accident that left Gray a widower, and he hadn't even looked at another woman. "Plus, I was just being friendly."

Emmitt choked on his beer. "Is that what the kids are calling it these days? You've been chasing Dr. Dolittle ever since my engagement party."

Curious? Yes. Chasing? Nope. His friend may have unsubscribed to the bachelors-till-the-end take on relationships, but not Levi. Between helping his mom after his dad's passing, and helping his sister raise Paisley, Levi had done the whole "live together, raise a kid, honey-do lists" thing, and he was ready to get back to being that guy with the world at his fingertips and the wind at his back.

According to the giant countdown clock that hung above the bar, the alarm on his phone, and the screen saver on his laptop, Levi had exactly seventy-one days, five hours, and twenty-six minutes left until his life was his again. Which meant he also had seventy-one days, five hours, and twenty-six minutes to help his mom find closure with his sister's death, get his niece college-ready, and renovate his dad's old yacht so Levi could take the trip down the coast and around the southernmost tip of the Americas that he and his dad had always dreamed about.

That didn't mean he wasn't open to a little fun while he was docked in Rome. But the kind of fun he was looking for didn't include a woman who couldn't even commit to a single drink with a boring banker.

"Watch the bar for a minute," he said, tossing a bar towel Emmitt's way.

"You can't help yourself, can you?" Emmitt laughed. "The redhead at the end of the counter wants to climb you like a tree. Her friend looks ready for you to sail your boat into her horizon, and you're running after the only woman within a mile radius who doesn't give two shits about where you drop your anchor."

"I'm not running after anyone. I'm giving her back her damn rooster," Levi said, ducking his head when Pecker started flapping his wings as if he were a matador and Levi was the bull.

"You just don't like being upstaged by a

cock in a raincoat," Emmitt said, and the two dipshits shared a high-five.

"You little clucker!" Levi jerked his hand back and out of the way of Pecker's beak, which was quickly making Swiss cheese out of Levi's knuckles. Pecker went airborne, nothing more than a blurring flutter of white feathers and red yarn heading straight at Emmitt's face.

Emmitt shot up out of his chair and took two defensive steps back, his hands covering his head. Levi and Gray both laughed. "Did you throw him at me?"

"No." Levi smiled. "Looks to me as if he doesn't like you much. Maybe the chicken's got something up there after all."

With a satisfied *"Cluccccccck,"* Pecker fluttered gracefully to the floor, working his wings as he did some kind of victory dance at Emmitt's feet. Two complete circles around Emmitt and a couple of head bops later, Pecker nudged the handle of his leash, then looked up at Levi as if trying to say, "Come on, human, pick up my leash so we can go find my mistress."

Rolling his eyes, Levi took the very pink and rhinestone-studded leash, not caring about the opinions voiced behind him, and ignored the click of Pecker's talons as he toddled his feathered ass straight out the

45

front door.

The sun had long since set, and Mother Nature was in a mood, blasting the East Coast with a March rainstorm.

Levi squinted into the mist as a stiff wind came off the coast, slicing through his clothes and adding a moist layer to the already drizzly night. A thin sheet of water blanketed the streets, reflecting the red tail-lights of the passing cars and shimmering over Beckett as she straddled her Vespa.

A car sped past, kicking up a fine spray of droplets, dotting the faded denim of her second-skin jeans, which were soaked through in the ass region. And, man, what an ass. If ass-sculpting were an Olympic sport, she'd take the gold every time.

What a sight she made, the streetlamp encasing her in a soft golden glow as she stared out at the horizon, her dark hair spilling over her shoulders and down to the middle of her back, wavier than usual and looking shower-fresh from the drizzle. Her jacket was zipped tight, molding to her gentle curves, while those legs of hers, which started at the South Pole and stretched all the way to Santa's Workshop, stood astride a bright orange scooter that had CONSIDER IT DONE painted on the front fender.

"I think you forgot something." He lifted Pecker.

She blinked at him as if only now aware that she was sitting in the rain, minus one co-pilot.

"Gregory! I can't believe I forgot you." She hopped off the bike, raced over, and picked up the bird. "I am so sorry," she cooed, pulling a space-pod-style backpack with a plastic dome-shaped view-bubble from the storage under her scooter's seat. With a kiss to the beak and a few more heart-tugging apologies, she gently ran her hand over the lucky little Pecker's back before placing him inside his pod and slinging the pack over her shoulders.

Finally, her gaze met his. "Thank you. I've been a little scrambled lately."

He understood completely, because he knew that the smart thing would be to wish her a goodnight and disappear back inside the bar. But it was too late to play this smart. Her sweet smile, paired with that tough girl exterior, did stupid things to his brain. Although he blamed another part of his anatomy for what he did next.

"If you give me a minute, I can grab my keys and give you a lift home."

She blinked as if that were the most ludicrous statement she'd ever heard. "You

47

want to drive me to my home? Why?"

He had to laugh. "Because it's raining, and you're driving a scooter. I mean, Pecker's got a sweet setup, but you'll be soaked through by the time you reach the highway."

"Then my bike would be here, and I would be home. That makes zero sense."

Levi looked over his shoulder through the window and had to agree. The longer he stood there flirting with a woman who clearly wasn't interested, the more backlogged the orders would become. His life had gone from putting out one fire to another, and he was working with an extinguisher that was so empty, it wasn't even blowing fumes.

"I can drive you back to grab it tomorrow morning," he offered, wondering why he was so intent on adding one more responsibility to his already suffocating list. He told himself it was because of Michelle's accident. But he knew better. This was all about pheromones — and Beck had the right kind.

It was cute how she pretended to consider his offer, but her eyes remained wary and nervous, a response that wasn't new when it came to him. Neither was the way his heart softened every time he saw it.

"I'm good. Plus, I don't tell guys where I

48

live. Dating 101 for the modern woman."

He believed that she didn't invite men home, but the reason she gave was complete BS. Which made him all the more curious. "Dating? Wow, we skipped right past the uncomfortable coffee meetup to dating. Admit it, Beck, you like me."

"Like isn't the word I'd use to describe how I feel about you."

"Before you offer me your final rose, I think we should explain things to Boring Bruce."

She rolled her eyes, but he caught a twinkle of humor. "Banker Bruce, and there isn't anything to explain, because your time and all this" — she circled her finger to encompass his face — "is wasted on me."

"Beck, time with you could never be time wasted."

She leveled those chocolate brown eyes on him. "I've seen that grin, witnessed the aftermath, and I'm telling you, I'm immune. So, I don't need your kind of help."

She knew his moves. Interesting.

"I don't know what kind of help you think I'm offering, but have you ever thought that a ride home can be as simple as a ride home?"

"Until it's not." Her tight smile had him easing off. "I can get home on my own."

And Levi realized right then he'd pegged her all wrong. Beckett wasn't stubborn so much as suspicious. For a woman who was always so free with her smiles and time, she was clearly uncertain about him, careful to hold her cards close to her chest.

"I just don't want to see you ride home in the rain," he admitted honestly.

"I've got my jacket."

"It's the first big downpour of the season, which means the roads are slippery. To-night's forecast said the worst of the storm will pass over in the next hour or so."

Levi used to love a good storm. The way the wind would whistle off the ocean and send rain dancing across the wood hulls. On a good night, the choppy waves crashed into the sides of his boat until the current stopped fighting the flood of the changing tide. It was chaos and power colliding, as unpredictable as it was thrilling. Now it just made him think of unjust loss and how unfair life's curveballs could be.

Grief unwound in his chest, followed by an irrational urge to keep Beckett close, where fate and happenstance weren't a factor. And where he could keep this conversation going, because he liked talking to her. A little too much.

"Maybe just wait out the storm." Levi

50

stepped out into the rain to stand by her bike. "I've got a hot bowl of clam chowder in the back with your name on it. I'll even let Pecker have a seat at the bar."

Her smile went warm and her eyes sympathetic as she reached out, her slender finger resting on his crossed arms. "I'm sorry about your sister. I didn't really know Michelle, but everyone says what a great person she was."

"She was better than great," he said with quiet reverence.

"How are you doing with all that?" she asked, and Levi cleared his throat, unsure how to respond.

She was the first person to ask him that question. He'd heard the words a thousand times over the past year, but they were always coming from his mouth. He'd been so busy helping his mom, and his niece, and even his brother-in-law deal with Michelle's death, there hadn't been a lot of room for Levi to deal.

"I mean, it's none of my business." Her fingers slid away. "I just know how hard it can be to fill the emptiness left behind when you lose someone you love."

Oh, he knew firsthand the pain that came with recovering from a loss that significant. He'd done it a decade ago, after his dad's passing. And his sister, just last year. But he was interested to know her experience. Because up until this moment, he hadn't realized she'd lost someone, which made him even more aware of how little he knew about his favorite customer. From the bits he had pieced together, she was generous and funny, but kept her private life pretty damn private. She never dated anyone for any length of time, and besides her few close friends, she didn't socialize much. He often saw her riding around town on her mango-colored cruiser with the white basket on the handlebars, taking care of an errand or delivery for her customers. But even with a job as Rome's most beloved personal concierge, which forced her to interact with people, no one really seemed to know *her*.

Even Levi. And it wasn't for lack of trying on his part. There was a reason she kept people at a distance. And damn if he wasn't determined to inch his way closer.

"Every day's a little easier," he said, repeating the empty platitudes people had offered him in the wake of his sister's accident.

"One day you'll wake up and that won't be a lie," she said softly. "It never really goes away; instead it becomes woven into every part of you."

Her phone pinged, and she closed her eyes. "I really have to go. My dad misplaced his pills. Again. But I don't live far from town, and I promise I'll be safe."

He was about to ask her to promise to give him a call when she got home, when Dean pushed through the front door, takeout bag in hand. "Oh, I thought I'd missed you. I have your takeout order."

"My dad called and I . . . I'm so sorry."

Levi noticed the heartfelt apology was directed at the guy who'd walked a plastic bag fifty feet — not the guy who would have been out the money had the order sat under the heat-lamp all night. No warm appreciation for the guy with chicken shit smudged down the front of his favorite shirt who was standing in the rain, offering to give her a ride home. She trailed off, implying Dean knew her well enough to fill in the gaps in her story.

"We're cool." With some kind of a boy-band hair flick, he let the bag dangle from his fingers while flashing a cocky *Come and get it* smile Beckett's way.

Oh, hell no. With a glare that had Dean choking on air, Levi snatched the bag right out of the horny little prick's fingers. In a blink, Beckett snatched it out of Levi's. And her glare was icy enough to cryogenically freeze his nuts.

"The Crow's Nest doesn't do takeouts, Dean," Levi said, but nobody was listening; they were too busy double-checking the order and inspecting the fry-to-entrée proportions.

"The Harpers are on my way home." She stored the bag in a heater box strapped to the back of her bike, then smiled his way. "We should talk more about that app. Rome's food delivery shouldn't be limited to pizza and Chinese."

With a wave, she pulled into traffic.

"She has a good point, boss," Dean said as they both watched her drive off. "You should consider it. She's smart."

"Sexy, too," Levi admitted.

Dean gaped at him. "She's got frizzy hair, her jacket's tucked into her pants, and her socks don't match. Most guys wouldn't think that was sexy. Adorable, maybe, but not sexy."

"I'm not most guys," Levi said, thinking it was a good thing Beckett was such a loose cannon and therefore off-limits. Otherwise, he'd find himself in trouble. Never a good position to be in, especially now that Levi's closest buddy and Beckett's best friend were engaged. Levi owed it to Emmitt not to go sniffing around his fiancée's friends. Regardless of how adorably sexy they might be. "Plus, who's been sneaking her takeout orders for the past few months?"

Chapter 3

Beckett hadn't even entered her dad's house, and she was ready to call it a day. Her hands were frozen solid, Bruce had taken her canceling harder than expected, and Levi was right — she looked as if she'd driven her scooter through an automatic car wash while still sitting on it.

Oh, and she just might, kind of sort of, like him. Which was why she'd never let him drive her home. Because a grown woman still sleeping in her childhood bedroom, under her Ryan Gosling HEY GIRL poster, was too embarrassing to share — even for Beckett.

But when your father made Beethoven look grounded, and your teenaged brother preferred to play video games in his underwear, embarrassing was bound to happen. Not that Beckett regretted her decisions. For her, family always came first.

She glanced up at the one-story, brick

federal-style house and smiled as her brother, Thomas, paced the porch from end to end, wearing cleats and a Yankees parka and holding a Wiffle Bat. Diesel was one step behind him the entire time.

Diesel was Thomas's emotional support companion, a French bulldog with a sweet tooth, who looked like a potato with tater tots for legs. After flunking out of cadaver dog school for having too big a heart, Diesel had become Thomas's best friend. Beckett had trained him to be Thomas's companion, his practice audience, and the first barrier between Thomas and the rest of the world.

If only men were as easily trained.

With a sigh, she grabbed the insulated bag from the back of her scooter and headed up the walkway.

"You're late," Thomas said, his flattened words and unorthodox rhythm both signs that he had autism spectrum disorder. "You said you'd be here in thirty minutes. It's been thirty-seven. You're seven minutes and —" His head bobbed in time with the changing numbers on his satellite watch. He waited until it reached a prime number. "Twenty-three seconds late."

"Sorry," she said. "Tiki Tiki Thai forgot to make your curry without peas, so I had to wait while they remade it."

"I don't like peas." Gaze running the length of the wood porch, he resumed his pacing. "I'm glad they remade it. But next time, tell them you have to be home in thirty minutes."

"They did their best, Thomas."

"No." He shook his head. "Their best is eighteen minutes and twelve seconds. They advertise hot and home in thirty minutes or less. Thirty-seven minutes and" — he consulted his watch again — "fifty-nine seconds is not less. It's more."

Beckett wanted to reach out and comfort him, but he didn't do well with intimate touch. A firm handshake, a clap on the back, he could tolerate. But any soft touch might result in an outburst. So Beckett had come up with their own "hug" of sorts, which allowed her to feel as if she were offering comfort and allowed Thomas to participate in the act of greeting or connecting with others.

Beckett flexed her right foot and stuck it out, knee bent, sole facing down, and waited. Eyes still on his watch, a sweet smile curving his lips, Thomas mimicked her stance. She tapped the side of her foot with his, he repeated the motion, they tapped together, and after locking their heels together, they hopped together clockwise while Diesel went up on his hind legs.

Tongue dangling, ears perked, Diesel did his best circus-bear-on-a-box act, snorting as he struggled to get oxygen past his smushed nose. He didn't bark or lick or exhibit any of the typical dog behaviors that would set Thomas off. Diesel had been selected and trained specifically for Thomas. He wasn't only an emotional companion or furry wall between Thomas and the touch-happy public at large. Diesel had worked hard to become her brother's best friend.

Moments like this made the thousands of hours of training, extra shifts to cover specialized trainers, and heartbroken tears when the first two dogs weren't a fit, all worth it. Before Diesel, Thomas lived on an island of one, too sensory-sensitive to make it through a full day of school or interact with other special needs kids. Diesel had opened up a whole other world for Thomas and given him the support to walk into it.

Swallowing back emotion, Beckett said, "Mrs. Darian already felt bad and sent you an extra helping of mango sticky rice."

"Ooh," Thomas said, his voice going higher with excitement, his hands clapping together. "I like mango sticky rice."

"I know you do." Beckett bent down to

kiss Diesel on the head, then handed Thomas the backpack, which the dog eyed warily.

Thomas wasted zero time, unzipping the pack enough so he could stick a finger in to scratch Gregory's wattle. A soft cooing came from inside the backpack, and within seconds, Gregory's head and back emerged, his eyes closed in ecstasy. Her brother might lack certain people skills, but when it came to animals, he was gifted.

"Why don't you put Gregory in his cage until after dinner," Beckett said, thankful that her feathered friend was going to meet his companion next week. A chicken was the perfect match for this particular client and situation, but in the future, Beckett would stick with four-legged creatures who didn't molt and welcome the sun with such vigor.

"Okay," Thomas said and headed for the house.

Beckett tugged the back of his jacket. "Cleats off in the house."

"I know," he said, dropping them in the mudroom and disappearing inside.

"Dad? I'm home," she called out, even though she'd seen his shadow bolt across the family room and into the kitchen when she'd pulled up. Fifty bucks, she'd find him with hands on hips, forehead furrowed in contemplation as he stared into the fridge to appear as though he were about to prep a nutritious family dinner.

Like Thomas, Jeffery was on the spectrum, only he would be classified as high-functioning. In fact, his symptoms often went unnoticed by others, or they assumed he had OCD or was just a bit quirky.

Get him talking or working on his music, and the world around him disappeared — including his family. Beckett's mom used to joke that his studio could be ground zero for a zombie uprising, and he wouldn't even notice. His ability to hyperfocus had made him a renowned musician, holding multiple awards for his movie and television scores. It also made him a scatterbrained father and neglectful husband.

Which was why Beckett's mom had relocated to Florida alone — leaving Beckett to pick up the pieces. Which she had. Most days, it didn't bother her. But on nights like this, when the week had been particularly challenging, she needed time outside the house. Time with a nice, normal guy to pretend she was a nice, normal girl. She wasn't avoiding reality, just trying to carve out a little space of her own.

With a sigh, she wrung out her hair, left

her jacket and boots in the mudroom, then made her way to the kitchen.

"I brought dinner," she said, hiding a smile when Jeffery's head popped up from behind the fridge door. His vintage, gold circular glasses were finger-smudged, his curly salt-and-pepper hair spiraled every which way, and his denim button-down and velvet sports coat made him look every bit the crazy studio musician.

"You didn't have to do that, kitten," Jeffery said, kissing her cheek. "But I love it when you do. Did you happen to swing by and pick up my beta blockers?"

"Right here." She lifted the bags and motioned to the white bag peeking out of her jacket pocket. "The pharmacist said she's called five times for you to come pick them up."

"I got busy." He grabbed the bag, tore it open, and popped two orange pills in his mouth. Swallowed them dry. "Then I forgot. You know how my mind works."

Oh, she knew better than most neuropsychologists how his mind worked. She'd spent almost a decade looking after her dad and brother, often feeling more like an in-home medical assistant than a family member. But there wasn't much she wouldn't do for her family.

"If you'd let me handle your prescriptions, you wouldn't have to worry about it."

"You already have enough to cope with," he said, grabbing some paper plates from the cupboard. "How was your date with The Boy?"

"He's a man, and we had to reschedule."

Jeffery looked concerned. "That's too bad. You were looking forward to tonight. You need to get out more."

Reminding him that he'd called her home wouldn't help, so she said, "Working on it." Beckett placed a few bowls on the table, dumped the takeout in them, careful to leave Thomas's in its carton, and called it dinner. "But about your pills — if you just let me know in advance, I can make sure they get picked up on time."

"Nah, you do enough around here. We've got it handled. Don't we, kiddo?" he said as Thomas entered the kitchen.

"My name is Thomas, not kiddo."

"Dad, you know he prefers Thomas," Beckett gently reminded him.

"What kid doesn't want to have a nickname from his old man?" Jeffery reached for Thomas's shoulders, but Thomas shrank away.

"I don't," Thomas said, sitting down and taking the remaining carton, which he handled as if preparing to make a surgical incision. He pulled his chopsticks out of the paper wrapper and went about the process of cleaning them of splinters. When done, he picked up each and every piece of chicken and vegetable individually, arranging them on his plate so there was an equal balance of colors, all separated, none of them touching the rice.

Beckett gave her dad a pointed look when he started to argue. Jeffery held up a surrendering hand, then started shoveling food into his mouth, barely taking breaks to breathe. When he spoke, it was with a full mouth. "This is great."

Not as great as flirting with Levi, but the food did smell delicious. Taking a seat, Beckett allowed her body to slump in exhaustion, relaxing for the first time since she'd left the house earlier that day.

"How's the song coming?" she asked Jeffery, the bowl blocking the lower part of his face.

"It's a score," Jeffery corrected, licking his chopsticks. "And I've still got the entire strings section to record."

Her dad wasn't just a musician, he was a musical savant, playing a total of twenty-eight instruments — one more than Prince, he liked to say — and fiddling around with

64

another nine. When he was a child, music was the way he communicated with, and participated in, the world around him. Over the years, he'd turned his passion for music into a flourishing career. And after his wife left him, music became his excuse to avoid anything that made him at all uncomfortable.

Beckett had once overheard him say that every minute he was kept from his music was like a minute blindfolded and gagged for someone else. Beckett had been five at the time, waiting for him to tuck her in with a bedtime story. The following day, she taught herself how to read.

Jeffery poured a helping of pad thai onto her plate, a signal for her to start eating. "Before it gets cold."

It was still steaming, but she picked up her chopsticks anyway. She dug in just as Jeffery reached across the table to fill up Thomas's plate. Because while Jeffery ate as if the world were ending, Thomas moved at a sloth's pace, cutting, measuring, and weighing each and every bite.

"Dad, he's got it." But Jeffery wasn't listening; he was too busy thinking of what project or piece he'd left unfinished in his studio down the hall.

Beckett leapt into action, her hands shooting out in alarm. But all the flirting had left her distracted, weakened her Olympic-worthy reflexes, so she was forced to watch in horror as Jeffery scooped a huge portion of pad thai out of the bowl and onto Thomas's perfectly arranged plate.

The plop of the noodles on ceramic echoed through the kitchen and, as if sensing her distress, Diesel whimpered from beneath the table. Sauce splattered all over the separated curried vegetables and chicken with no peas, while a noodle flopped from the seven to the two o'clock position, a chunk of sliced green onion dangling from its end.

"Oh no." Thomas stood, his gaze shooting from his plate to the upper corner of the ceiling, where it locked. His hands pressed into the front of this pants, smoothing from thigh toward knee, over and over. "It's ruined. You ruined it. The sauces mixed, and there is green on my plate. Green and red don't go together unless it's Christmas. Only then do green and red go together."

Thomas was pacing, and Jeffery — sweet, impatient, always-got-it-wrong Jeffery — looked around the table with an earnest helplessness in his eyes that went a long way toward soothing Beckett's frustration.

"I was just trying to help speed things

along," Jeffery admitted.

"I know, Dad," she said softly. "Why don't you grab a clean plate, and we'll see if we can fix him up a new plate."

"No." Thomas stopped, his head shaking like the Hermione Granger bobblehead figure on the handlebar of her Vespa. "It can*not* be fixed. The sauce is touching the curry. It's ruined."

"It's not ruined." Beckett moved the pad thai with the offending green onion slice to her plate, then used her napkin to soak up the remaining dots of sauce. "It's just a few splatters."

"No!" Thomas was back to pacing, eyes glued on the space where the wall met the ceiling. "A few means three. There are more than three, and some mixed with the curry, so we will be unable to separate those." He stopped and faced Beckett. "We need to call Mrs. Darian and reorder."

"We're not reordering," Beckett said softly. "We can make you a new plate. Free of splatters. Deal?"

Thomas's lips thinned as he considered. With a smile, he took his seat, perched on the end, hands on his knees. "That is a deal. A new plate made from items that did not touch the irreparably damaged plate will be fine."

Beckett should have finished her beer before heading home.

Ignoring the seed of a headache that had formed behind her right eye, she gave Jeffery an encouraging smile when he set down the new plate, then carefully remade the dinner. As she scooped out equal bits of chicken, peppers, onions, potatoes, and baby corn — Thomas's favorite part — she patted herself on the back for saving dinner. She reached behind her for a clean napkin to wipe the edges of the plate and then paused.

She double-checked the carton and re-counted the items on the plate — twice. She was one baby cob short of a Thomas-approved dinner.

A familiar scratching came from the chair beside her. She located the source of the noise, and her head spun, because Gregory had staged a breakout to join them for dinner. Based on the little yellow bits of kernel speckling his beak and white feathers, he'd started with a chicken-sized cob of corn.

"Pa-cock."

One more male to add to Beckett's Problematic Pecker list.

CHAPTER 4

Moving heaven and earth would be easier than convincing Thomas to walk into the grocery store. It was the hum of the fluorescent lights, the overwhelming choices, and tightness of the aisles, especially during peak hours, that made it challenging. Which was why Beckett picked downtimes, kept her lists small, and included items that Thomas enjoyed.

Today, he wasn't having it.

"I do not want to go," he said, twisting his upper body to face the parking lot.

"Today's Tuesday morning," Beckett said. "What do we do on Tuesday mornings?"

"We go grocery shopping. But I do not want to go grocery shopping. I will wait here until you are done."

"That's not an option." And neither was skipping their weekly shopping trip.

Shopping was one of the crucial skills Thomas needed to master if he were to have the kind of future he deserved, which was why Beckett had started her day before the sun. She'd met with clients, brought Diesel to the children's hospital for his weekly visit as Dog Wonder, and managed to make it back in time to pick up Thomas. Cutting it close to lunch hour, she hadn't taken the time to change her clothes, afraid that the market would become overcrowded.

They'd made it — barely. Now came the familiar but never fun process of coaxing Thomas inside. To help ensure a positive experience, they'd gone over their list in the car, paying special attention to the most important item — a bag of peanut M&M's to reward a job well done. But none of her tricks were working.

It didn't help that the market was busier than normal. The storm had passed, leaving behind blue skies and an unusually warm morning, which tempted people out of their houses and into town. Including two of Beckett's clients, who'd stopped to say hello, unaware that the simple social norm of chitchat ate into Thomas's daily decision-making quota.

"If you help eat the food, you help replace the food. That's the rule," she gently reminded him.

"Then I will not eat."

70

"Wow, that's too bad." She kept her voice animated and light. "Tonight, for dinner, we're having barbecue chicken kabobs with cornbread and honey butter."

"I like cornbread and honey butter."

"I know, but it will take everyone pitching in to get it done. Dad said he'd barbecue, I'm baking the cornbread, and you need to help shop for ingredients. That's how families work. Everyone participates."

"Unpacking the groceries and putting them in their correct place is participating." He smiled as if he'd just reasoned his way out of shopping. "I *can* have cornbread and honey butter."

Beckett bit back a groan. Her world ebbed and flowed in direct proportion to the kind of day Thomas was having. The more cornered he felt, the higher his anxiety rose, the narrower Beckett's window for life outside of home became.

She grabbed a cart, cleaned it with a wet wipe, then presented it. "You can push the cart or walk beside me. Which would you prefer?"

"I would prefer to go home."

"I'm partial to holding hands, if that's on the table," a deep and sexy voice said from behind them.

Beckett looked over her shoulder to find

71

the last person on the planet she wanted to encounter when wearing pink go-go boots, black leggings, and a pink GirlWonder cape.

It was the guy who'd starred in last night's steamy, sensual, and embarrassingly inappropriate sex dream — everyone's favorite flirt of a bartender, Levi Rhodes. Only instead of wearing nothing but a tan and a ball cap, he had on faded jeans and a soft gray sweatshirt with his bar's logo on the pec, flip-flops on his feet, and a smile that obliterated her brain cells.

He looked laid-back, windblown, and ready to break some hearts. Thankfully, her heart was too busy breaking for Thomas to notice.

It still bugged her that Levi always managed to catch her in her most vulnerable moments. She couldn't think of a single time she hadn't looked frazzled, tattered, or just plain run-down in front of him. Even when she'd dressed to impress at Annie and Emmitt's engagement party, she'd managed to come off like a crazy lady.

Today was the cherry on top of that humble pie à la mode. She was dressed like a superhero, negotiating with a ninja, and all her edges were one thread from fraying.

Ignoring Levi, she went back to using hostage negotiation tactics on her brother.

"Your M&M's are at the register, so we have to finish shopping in order to get your reward."

"We could order from Amazon Prime," Thomas said. "And it is rude to ignore a question when asked. Answering with a 'yes' or 'no' or 'I'm not sure' are all appropriate comments to use to express interest in what your friend says."

Embarrassment pulsed hot and deep in Beckett. A normal reaction when being called out in front of a sexy guy by her kid brother — using her own words.

"Are you interested, Beck?" he asked on a soft laugh.

She snorted. "No." *Maybe. Yes.*

Gah! The way he said her name made her head spin. "Can you stop smiling like that?"

Out came the dimples. Both of them. "Like what?"

"You know what." She turned to Thomas. "And he's not my friend."

"Yes, he is." Thomas dipped his chin into the curve of his neck. "He is in your personal space bubble, and you are not yelling at him to back off."

"Give her a minute to warm up," Levi said with a grin. "I'm Levi Rhodes, Beckett's very good friend." He extended his hand.

Thomas curled his hands into himself. "I

am Thomas. Thomas Hayes. Beckett's brother. I do not like to shake hands. Or fist bumps, high-fives, or any other kind of touching hands." He lifted his leg and flexed his foot. "But I will tolerate a foot bump."

Before Beckett could launch into an explanation, Levi lifted a foot, acting for all the world as if a footsie hello were a normal way to greet someone when meeting for the first time.

"Smart kid," Levi said in a warm voice filled with acceptance and understanding. "I wouldn't like shaking some old guy's sweaty hand, either."

"Three percent of the population experience sweaty hands. The most common causes are hormones, stress, nervousness, and excitement," Thomas informed everybody within a one-block radius. "Which one are you experiencing?"

"I'd say a mix of the first and last," he said, but Thomas had already turned away to pet Diesel. Leaving Beckett alone to handle the full force of Levi's attention. "How about you? What's putting so much color in your cheeks?"

The same thing that had her lady parts flipping that OUT OF BUSINESS sign to an optimistic APPLICANTS WELCOME. Hormones. Sex-starved hormones.

74

Now, Beckett would be the first to admit her morning-after etiquette could use some brushing up. Which was why she kept dating to the occasional movie night out, followed by casual, polite sex that ended with a goodnight kiss on her way out the door. There had been nothing casual or polite about Sex-Dream Levi.

Oh no, Sex-Dream Levi liked it fun and a little dirty. He knew when to take and when to give, and he'd give all night long if it meant getting the job done. A thought that she found as thrilling as she did terrifying, because Sex-Dream Levi would never settle for a goodnight kiss on the way out the door. There was no doubt in her mind that in real life, Levi would not, either.

And wasn't that the problem? While most men could never live up to their dream selves, Beckett had a feeling that In Real Life Levi would make Sex-Dream Levi look like a bumbling amateur.

"Beck?"

She tore her gaze off his lips to find him watching her. "I'm sorry. What?"

"I didn't catch your answer."

"To which question?" Whether she was interested, or if her hormones made her want to do crazy, sexy things with him? To him.

"Lady's choice." He winked, a glimmer of amusement in his expression.

"All signs of exasperation," she said, and he laughed.

She failed to see the humor. Or maybe she was too tired to see it. Thomas was pacing back and forth, his hands flapping by his sides; four more cars had pulled into the lot, and Levi frazzled her. If they waited much longer, this excursion would end before the cashier could ask, "Paper or plastic?"

"Where's Pecker? Couldn't find his cape?" Levi asked, and she barely resisted the urge to pull her own cape over her head and disappear.

"No, he's at home." She held up her list and pointed to the third item down. "Chicken. We're having kabobs for dinner, and bringing Gregory along seemed a little insensitive, given his species."

"I serve chicken at the restaurant."

"Range-free. There's a difference," she lied.

Part of the reason Beckett brought her companions-in-training with her to the Crow's Nest was that they were great conversation starters. While Beckett might appear to be outgoing, in reality, she was an introvert hiding in extrovert's clothing.

Lessons in social interaction were quite different from the norm in the Hayes household. Her parents had had a hard enough time communicating with each other, let alone the patience to host playdates or sleepovers. By the time Beckett turned five, the fairy tale her mother had constructed around marrying a musical genius had crumbled, and her parents separated. They tried, on and off, to fix things, but Beckett had few memories of living under the same roof as her mom.

Thomas was the product of one of those "on" times, and she'd hoped he'd be the catalyst to bring her parents back together. And for a while, he did. Thomas was developmentally on target as a toddler. Then, almost overnight, the symptoms appeared, and her mom shut down. By his next birthday, she had moved out and moved on — leaving Beckett and the rest of the family behind.

All these years later, Beckett still wasn't any better at social situations, but she could fake her way through them. So yeah, last night she'd wanted a reason for Levi to talk to her, and Gregory was her wingman.

He gave her a complete visual assessment, then asked, "How are you feeling?"

She glanced down. Her leggings were

covered in dog hair, her shirt had smudges of leftover frosting from the doughnuts she picked up at the mini-mart, and she could only imagine what her hair looked like.

She patted her head, only to be reminded she'd twisted and secured her hair into two space-girl buns on top. "How bad is it?"

"Hottest Girl Wonder I've ever seen." She waited for her BS meter to blare as he took a slow inventory, from her boots all the way back up to her space-girl buns, but that stark look of male appreciation couldn't be faked. "I asked because a moment ago, you apologized to me. Uncoerced."

"Oh," she breathed.

"Yeah, oh." Levi brushed his knuckle over her cheekbone, scattering her thoughts. It was the gentleness of such large and work-calloused hands, she decided, that knocked her off balance. "So question two, how can I make today easier for you?"

The sincere offer was so foreign, Beckett was uncertain how to respond. Or how to feel, for that matter. She couldn't recall the last time someone had offered to take some of the load. That it was someone she barely knew extending the lifeline made her question just how bad her poker face had become.

She moved to step back, but he'd already

dropped his hand and given her a little breathing distance. With oxygen depletion no longer an issue, she went about gathering all the thoughts that didn't include him naked, him kissing her, or him naked and kissing her.

"Thanks, but we've got it." She gestured vaguely toward Thomas and Diesel.

"We do not have it," Thomas said. "You want me to go inside. I do not want to go inside."

Beckett let out a sigh that was half exhaustion and half ready to call it a day. She didn't have enough bandwidth left to take on Levi, Thomas, and a market full of people who would insist on talking to them. She dropped her head forward. Her plan was to count to ten, then head home without even a pint of mint chip to take the sting out of waving the white flag. Only before she got to three, a pair of flip-flop–clad feet came into her field of vision.

"How about I stay here with your brother while you get whatever you need from inside," Levi offered.

"He won't stay with anyone but me or sometimes my dad."

"Okay. Then how about you two hang here, while I pick up the things on your list?"

Astonished, she said, "I can't ask you to

do that."

"You didn't ask. I offered." He gave a playful tug on her cape, then looked at Thomas. "Does that work for you, Tommy?"

"He doesn't like to be called anything but Thomas," she began.

"He can call me Tommy," her brother interrupted. "I like Tommy."

"You hate Tommy."

Her brother stopped pacing, and Diesel bumped into his calf. "Not anymore."

"If only Girl Wonder was as easy to impress." Levi plucked the list out of her hand and headed toward the store.

Men finding an excuse to leave after getting a small taste of her reality wasn't out of the norm. A man finding a reason to come back? He would be the outlier. A refreshingly unexpected — and completely unsettling — outlier.

"You need money," she called after him.

"Normally, I'd request payment in the form of cornbread and honey butter. But you're in luck. Today I'll settle for a smile."

Hard not to when he said things like that. She knew he was watching her for a reaction, so she schooled her features, hoping not to look too eager. The apples of her cheeks burned from trying to tame the smile from a *My hero* to an acceptable *Thanks, friend.* He wasn't fooled.

The corners of his mouth lifted. "Be back in a minute, Girl Wonder."

With a wink that had her squirming in her go-go boots, he strolled into the market, leaving her by the line of shopping carts, completely flustered. To say he'd slid past her walls was like saying an F-5 tornado was a tad windy.

What surprised her the most was that he hadn't played her with his trademark charm and flirt. He hadn't been playing at all. And that was a problem.

Charming, flirty, behind-the-bar Levi she could handle. It was In Real Life Levi who brought a whole new level of complication to an already complicated situation.

Behind her, someone was counting down. Beckett turned to find Thomas staring at his watch, and she didn't fight her smile this time. Not one bit. She embraced the pure and innocent moment. With Thomas, there were no games, no lines to read between, just an honest and open-minded take on life.

Resting a hand over the face of the watch, she said, "He meant it as an idiom. Even Girl Wonder couldn't make it in a minute."

"Okay." Thomas dropped his hand.

"Why did you say he could call you

Tommy?"

"He wears soft shirts with no buttons and flip-flops. I like him. Can I have a pair of black flip-flops?"

"Winter's still hanging on. Your toes would freeze."

"I can wear socks."

She stopped to look at her brother. "You don't like things that go between your toes."

Tommy shrugged. "I can start."

She could start to like a lot of things, too, if she wasn't careful.

Levi was in a hundred different kinds of trouble. Who knew seven little letters could make a grown man sweat as if he were standing atop an active volcano, ready to tee off? He hadn't been this uncomfortable since finding lacy panties, which belonged to his too-young-to-own-a-thong niece, in the laundry.

His first instinct had been to call Michelle, who would've taken pleasure in Levi's current situation. It wasn't until he'd scrolled to her name that he remembered his sister was gone. He considered calling her anyway, just to hear her voice on the voice mail, which Gray still paid to keep active. Only Levi didn't dare risk bumping into someone he knew while bawling his eyes out and

82

clutching a box of tampons. So he called Annie.

"It's really a personal choice." Unlike Michelle, who would have been laughing her ass off, Annie was calm and comforting. Living with Emmitt had clearly given her loads of experience when dealing with clueless and incompetent men.

"That doesn't help me," he explained, picking up a box. "And what the hell is a pearl applicator? Is that referring to the color?"

"Google 'pearl applicator.' I'm sure there are a dozen videos that can explain it better than I could. Although some of the results may cause you to go blind. Or you can just call Paisley."

"They, uh, aren't for Paisley," he admitted miserably.

"Who are they for?" Annie's curiosity was clearly piqued.

He considered his next step carefully. "You have to promise not to tell Emmitt. You know how he and Gray gossip like little girls."

She snorted. "Emmitt can sense a cover-up from the other side of the world."

He closed his eyes. "It's for Beckett."

"My Beckett?" Her shock was clear. Which was fair, since he was pretty shocked, too.

Not only by Beck's willingness to accept his help, but by how incredible she'd been with her brother.

Maybe he'd been a little hasty in judging her a total flake.

"It's nice to know she has a keeper," he joked. "And yeah, I ran into her and her brother at the market. They seemed to be having a difference of opinion over just how badly they needed groceries. Tommy was partial to Amazon Prime, and Beckett looked ready for a nap."

Annie found this amusing. "And you, being you, offered to help a pretty lady out."

"I guess I took a note from your man's playbook," he said, chuckling. "Only I must be more out of practice than I thought, because I asked for her grocery list instead of her number."

"I told Emmitt there was something between you two at the engagement party!" she squealed. "You both disappeared right around midnight."

Oh, they'd found a quiet corner together. Chatted a bit, flirted even more. Then she excused herself for a moment, making the champagne-toasting ceremony nothing more than a party of one.

"I'm not giving her the key to my boat. Just buying the lady some groceries."

"A man offers to do a busy woman's shopping? That's pretty much foreplay."

"Aw, come on, Annie. I can never unhear that." Levi cringed. "I'd rather google 'pearl applicator' than hear you say the word 'foreplay' ever again. All I need is her number — then I can get out of here and burn my phone."

Annie read off Beckett's number, laughing the entire time. Levi jotted it on his arm, then thanked Annie and disconnected before she could list off more domestic favors that turn women on. Not that he wasn't interested in the inside knowledge; he just didn't want to hear it from his best friend's fiancée.

He dialed and was convinced it was going to go to voice mail when Beckett answered. "Who is this?"

Her accusatory tone said she already knew who it was. "Miss you too."

"How did you get my number?"

"Annie. I needed to know, uh, what kind of tampons do you want?"

"Playtex is fine." And she was gone.

Levi found the Playtex section and — *holy shit* — there were even more choices than in a mattress store. When he didn't see a "ribbed for her pleasure," he considered getting a multipack and calling it a day. But he'd said he'd take care of her, and he wasn't about to be taken down by something called *gentle glide.*

He redialed, and she answered on the first ring. "I forgot to ask. Applicator, no applicator, pearl applicator?"

"Any applicator is fine."

"Just curious, what do you do without an applicator?"

"Oh my god, just get going!" She hung up, but he could tell she was smiling.

He plucked the first box he saw, then froze and immediately called her back.

"Jesus, they come in sizes," he said by way of greeting. "Am I allowed to ask you your size, or is it like asking a guy if he wears Trojan XXL?"

"Normal is fine."

"Huh." In his world, no guy would ever admit to normal. Not that Levi had that problem. But, shit, what if she now thought he had that problem? He was about to assure her that he did not, in fact, have any problems down there, when she spoke.

"Any more questions?"

He had so many, he didn't know where to start. Beckett was quirky and cute, and one big, hot mess. A sexy one, he'd give her that, but flaky people drove him nuts. And she was flakier than the box of frosted cereal in his basket.

Levi liked uncomplicated and casual. Which brought him to the next problem: There wasn't a casual bone in that tall, willowy, smoking-hot body of hers. When he watched her with her brother, it was clear — when Beckett loved, she loved hard. That tough-girl act provided armor to protect her from future heartache. But any guy lucky enough to breach those walls was in there for life.

And standing there with a box of tampons, playing the part of some damn hero-to-the-rescue, he wondered how it would feel to be that guy.

Sadly, his life would soon set sail in a different direction, so he simply asked, "Scented or unscented?"

CHAPTER 5

Beckett was feeling accomplished.

She'd managed to make it three days without running into Levi, had finished with her last regular for the week, and had picked up two orders of takeout — pizza for her family and Thai for the Carmichaels — which left twenty minutes to give Gregory a bubble bath and Brazilian blowout.

Today was to be Gregory's first overnight with his fur-ever family. Beckett's job was to ensure that her feathered friend was primped and peacock-ready for his big moment. Like any successful first date, crafting the right initial impression was imperative. It was the first and most important opportunity for Gregory and his prospective companion to bond, and it would determine when the final rehoming would take place.

Everything had to go smoothly.

After a bath that left Beckett covered in suds, and an uneventful session with the blow-dryer that left Gregory a little damp under the bustle, Beckett quickly crafted a bow tie out of an old bra-clasp and one of her dad's unused ties. Except her client had flown the coop.

"You get back here," she called as his feathery butt disappeared down the hallway.

Beckett followed him to the front room. After a quick search, she decided that Gregory was either hiding or MIA. It was hard to tell with the detritus of the day scattered throughout the room.

Clean clothes were strewn over every piece of furniture, as if expecting a visit from the laundry fairy. An army of empty Red Bull cans lined the coffee table. And someone must have fed the pile of tightly wadded paper balls, because they had multiplied to cover most of the north side of the room and were quickly gaining territory in the east.

And situated in the middle of the room, blocking all paths to freedom, sat Jeffery and his drum set. Number two pencil between his front teeth and oblivious to the chaos, he played as if headlining at the Greek. His face glistened with perspiration, his shirt sweaty and stretched out of shape. His art deco dinner jacket was rolled at the sleeves and hung open, as if buttons were too much of a commitment. A pair of studio-grade headphones in place, his hair swaying with every beat played, he banged away.

He looked like a missing member of the Rolling Stones.

On a rare patch of bare hardwood flooring sat Diesel, looking distressed and out of sorts. And walking around him was an agitated and overstimulated Thomas, with his hands pressed against his ears.

"It is loud. Very loud," Thomas explained, as if Beckett had somehow missed the jam session in progress. "The noise has exceeded the ambient level by ten decibels for more than five consecutive minutes. That is a violation of Noise Ordinance 2014-b, which states —"

"I know what it states." Thomas quoted it so often, she could recite it word-for-word. Not that anyone would be able to hear her if she did. The music was so loud, every beat vibrated against her sternum. "Dad, plug in your headset."

Jeffery didn't budge. Thomas's pacing became more frantic.

Tired of shouting, she crossed the room and pulled back Jeffery's right earpiece. "Dad, you need to plug this in for it to work." He didn't even slow down as she inserted the plug in the corresponding hole on the drums, and the room plunged into immediate and blessed silence.

"I don't like drums," Thomas simply said, then sat on the couch. Diesel plopped on top of Thomas's shoes and released an exhausted snort.

"I know you don't."

A light tap sounded from the front door, and Beckett turned to find her friend Annie on the other side of the screen. Dressed in suede boots and matching skirt, with a winter-white sweater, and carrying a pink box that made Beckett's mouth water, she stood with her knuckles poised to knock again.

Annie gave an uncertain smile. "I wasn't sure if I should knock again or come back later."

"And eat whatever's in that box all by yourself?" She ushered her friend in.

Annie barely had one foot in the door when Gregory decided to come out of hiding from behind the curtain. Eyes on Annie, he made a direct line for the swinging white string that dangled from the box.

Feathers out, head bobbing, he released a battle cry and, as if she were to blame for the offending noise — he rushed the door.

With a squeak, Annie lifted the box and

stepped back outside, barricading herself behind the screen. Undeterred, he flapped, flapped, flapped . . .

And went airborne.

Like Michael Jordan, Pecker sailed through the room — only to collide with Diesel's rump.

There was an uncharacteristic yelp, and Diesel's little potato legs moved at alarming speed as he retreated under the end table on the other side of the couch. A moment later, he bounded out of hiding, with Pecker hot on his stub of a tail.

"We don't chase in this house," Thomas informed Pecker, who didn't give two shits about the rules. "We pet and snuggle and respect boundaries. We don't corner, yell, or chase."

Gregory kept chasing. Thomas started yelling. Annie took another step back. A tornado of feathers and angry clucking whirled around Beckett, over the couch, and between the drums.

Jeffery lifted his left leg to grant passage, then took a moment to pencil in a few notes on his music sheet.

On the third lap, Beckett scooped up the chicken, his alien-looking legs still moving as if trying to gain traction in midair, and tucked him under her arm. With a few cooing sounds, she calmed Gregory. Aware that the danger was over, Diesel skidded to a stop beside Thomas, sniffing to make sure he wasn't in distress. Then he plopped down on his big belly, panting and snorting, his disdainful eyes locked on Gregory.

"I can totally come back," Annie assured all of them, but her attention was directed at Gregory.

"He's just had a day; plus, he knows something's going on," Beckett said. "Let me put him in the kitchen."

"The rule says no chasing," Thomas informed Annie as Beckett disappeared into the kitchen. Even through the closed door, she could hear him. "Diesel isn't a pet, he's a working companion. Never chase, distract, or touch an emotional support animal when they're working."

Beckett lifted Gregory so she could kiss his beak. "You're just scared and letting me know. Don't worry, you're going to love Katie. She needs a friend and loves to cuddle. A perfect pairing, if you ask me."

"Cluuuck cluckcluckcluck," Gregory cooed softly, his bug eyes sliding closed when Beckett held him tight against her chest.

"Out of all the baby chicks at the ranch, Katie picked you. And she's been waiting patiently for you," Beckett whispered, surprised at the tightness in her throat. Gregory's time here was almost up, and Katie was going to be one lucky little girl.

It didn't make the departure any easier or mean that Beckett wouldn't miss him when she said her final goodbye. She missed every one of the animals she'd trained over the years. Had an equal number of little cracks in her heart to prove it.

After a long hug, she dabbed her eyes and carefully attached the red-and-white polka-dot bow tie around Gregory's neck. She set him on the floor, and he practically preened, strutting back and forth.

"Don't you look dapper. Katie will take one look at you and never let go." She had to get out of the kitchen before she lost it. "Now, why don't you show me what a good, house-trained rooster you are and wait here while I handle business in the front room."

Cluuuck cluckcluckcluck.

Beckett walked into the family room, not surprised to find Thomas still talking.

"It was very loud," Thomas relayed.

"I thought you were having a concert," Annie said.

Thomas silently contemplated for a beat, then smiled. "That was a joke. Our house is too small to hold a concert, so you must have meant it as a joke."

Annie tapped her pointer finger to her nose and winked at Thomas, who began laughing and flapping his hands. His laugh was unfiltered, unexpected, and beautifully unapologetic — just like him.

Last year, when Emmitt had his head up his own ass, a heartbroken Annie had crashed on Beckett's couch. She was there only a week, but her warm spirit and patient nature made quite an impression on all the Hayeses — most especially Thomas, who'd formed his first crush.

What could she say? The kid had good taste. Annie was stunning, smart, funny, and had this way about her that made even the most skeptical people believe they could find love. After watching Annie and Emmitt fall deeply and madly, and seeing how happy they were, Beckett believed one hundred percent that it could happen — for other people.

"I've never been to a concert," Thomas said. "I don't think I'd like it."

"Why go to a concert when you have a real-life musician in the house?" Annie said. "You get your own private concert every day."

"I like video games better. On mute." Thomas sat down on the couch, picked up the remote, and the television flashed to life.

"We can play together. You on the chair." He pointed across the room. "And me on the couch."

"You have art class today," Beckett said, shutting off the television. "So why don't you take Diesel downstairs and hang out in the Batcave for a bit."

Made from blackout curtains and extra-soundproof foam from Jeffery's studio, the Batcave worked as a sensory deprivation room, where Thomas could decompress from the noisy world around him. Access was by invitation only, and instead of superhero gadgets, this Batcave was all about baseball.

"Can Annie come?" he asked.

"Wow. Me?" Annie asked, her surprise genuine. Invites to the Batcave were rare, and usually reserved for immediate family only. That he was extending the offer to Annie was a big step for him. "Thank you for inviting me into your cave. That means a lot."

"You are welcome," he said, and Beckett looked down to find her brother wearing black flip-flops — with matching athletic socks to keep his toes from freezing. She hadn't a clue as to where he'd acquired any of these.

"Where did those shoes come from?" she

asked, wondering if Jeffery had Primed in his sleep again or if Thomas had purchased them without her consent.

"They are OluKai flip-flops, not shoes. And they came from Amazon," he explained.

"Did you order them?" she questioned, working hard to keep accusation out of her tone.

"No. But they are mine. The box said so." He squeezed his toes, and the left sandal flipped against his heel with a snap. "I sprayed them with hair spray to create more friction and prevent blistering. They only bother my toes a little."

"You'll get used to them," Annie assured. "And I'd really like to see your cave, but I only have a short time today," Annie explained gently. "Maybe next time?"

Instead of pushing the issue and explaining all the ways they could make today work, Thomas turned to Annie and said, "Lady's choice." And with a wink, he headed into the basement, his hundred-dollar flip-flops clapping against the floor and down the steps.

The door clicked shut behind him, and both women burst out laughing. Amusement and something a little reckless pinched at Beckett's ribs until her sides hurt from giddiness.

"What was that?" Annie asked.

"Don't ask." Because then Beckett would have to explain how many times she'd pictured Levi in those butt-hugging jeans and flip-flops. And the flutters that took flight over the mystery of the Amazon flip-flops.

"You're blushing," Annie pointed out.

"Just warm is all."

"Your house is an icebox, and you're in a tank top and damp jeans." Annie studied her through assessing eyes. Beckett smiled casually. Annie wasn't buying it. "I'll find out." She lifted the pink box and wafted it under Beckett's nose. "I have my ways."

Beckett took in a whiff of the sweet treat hiding inside. A quick glance at the pink box and then her friend's smile, and every one of her approach-with-caution bells went off. "What's in the box?"

Beckett would be able to determine what kind of visit this was based on Annie's answer. Together with their friend Lynn, they made up Ride or Pie: a girls-only, got-your-back, pie-mandatory kind of posse that meant as much to Beckett as her family. They also used to be a Man-Free Living club, but Beckett seemed to be the last man-free friend standing.

"Sorry, no pie. Lynn's working." They had a strict no-pie-partaking rule unless all members were accounted for. "I was walking by Holy Cannoli and thought you could use a little chocolate in your day."

"Chocolate? You're buttering me up."

"You know, sometimes a treat is just a treat." She waved the box enticingly.

"There's never a *just* when chocolate is involved."

"I guess you'll just have to see." Annie laughed, plucking a feather out of Beckett's hair. Then she stepped inside, too polite to comment on the chaotic nature of the Hayes's family home.

Beckett was no Marie Kondo, but she did her best to keep a tidy house. Some days were better than others. Today fell into the "others" category. But there were only so many hours in the week, and only one Beckett.

While stressful and sometimes overwhelming, it was her reality. And she owned it like a grown-assed woman. "Let me grab Gregory's carrier, and I'll meet you in the kitchen."

In the two seconds it took to fetch Gregory's things, Jeffery had disappeared into his studio, the rooster had barricaded himself under the table, and Annie had dropped to all fours, her butt in the air, clicking her tongue as if calling out to the neighborhood cat.

"What are you doing?" Beckett asked.

"Trying to love Gregory." Unashamed, Annie wiggled until the rest of her body disappeared from view under the kitchen table.

"Peeee-cock cock cock cock," Gregory warned. Sadly, Annie wasn't fluent in Fowl.

"Ouch," Annie cried. "Why won't you let me love you?"

"It has to be on his terms." Beckett placed the cage on the floor, taking a baby carrot out of the fridge.

"Typical male." Annie came out with a tuft of feathers in her grasp. Beckett raised a brow. "I swear, I didn't pull them. He's just trying to make me look bad."

"Mission accomplished. Now toss those out before Thomas catches you and repeats all the rules for handling a support companion."

Footsteps came toward them, and Annie threw the feathers in the air, then ran to stand on the other side of the room.

"Don't worry, it's just my dad," Beckett said, putting the carrot on the floor to tempt Gregory out.

Annie sagged with relief into a nearby chair. "Hi, Mr. Hayes. How are you?"

Jeffery walked right past Annie as if she didn't exist and peeked in the to-go bag on the kitchen island.

Beckett batted back his hand and glared. "That's for the Carmichaels. The pizza is for you and Thomas. And this is where you say, 'Hi, Annie. I'm doing great, and how are you doing this fine day?'"

Jeffery looked almost childlike when he was sheepish. "Sorry, I'm working on a new song. It's a short piece for a national commercial. Pork. You might think short equates to easy, but it's actually much more difficult to tell a short story than long, especially when the topic is an interesting one."

Annie bit back a smile. "Pork is interesting?"

"Oh, sure," he said, sounding every bit the crazy composer. "It's the other white meat and tends to be overshadowed by its better-known counterpart, chicken. It's one of the greatest underdog stories in history, and I get to be its narrator. Put a voice to the centuries of misinformation and, frankly, the misrepresentation the pork industry has suffered."

As if aware that his species was being defamed, Gregory ran out from beneath the table to peck at Jeffery's untied shoelace. Jeffery ignored him and sat next to Annie.

101

"Just take the children's movie, *Babe,* for instance. A two-hour propaganda piece on how —"

"Dad, don't get comfortable. You have to take Thomas to class in a few minutes," Beckett said. "Plus, you still haven't said hi to Annie."

"Oh my, you're right. Sometimes my mind runs away from me, and common courtesy goes right out the . . ." He turned to Beckett. "I thought you were taking him."

"No. I'm taking Gregory to the Richardsons' for their first bonding session," she said, ignoring the ache forming behind her ribs. "You're taking Thomas to class as specified on the family calendar, your personal calendar, and the sticky note I hung on your studio door this morning."

Jeffery blinked in rapid succession, his lips curling down in distress. He looked as scared as a lost kid in a closing amusement park. "If I have the truck, how will you get the chicken, his cage, and the Thai food to the other side of town?"

Beckett froze. She'd been so focused on her emotions over Gregory's overnighter, she hadn't thought through an actual game plan for getting him to the sleepover. When she'd scheduled the rehoming, art class had been on Tuesday. But when the new semester began last month, the class was moved to a new location and night. "I'll call an Uber."

"Nonsense," Jeffery said, his relief palpable. "Why don't you take the truck?"

"Because Thomas needs to socialize. Next week is the class field trip to the museum. Tonight's assignment and talk will help prep him for what to expect."

If anything, that should get Jeffery's attention. He detested surprises so much, he'd once checked himself into the hospital, feigning a heart attack, because he caught wind his then-wife had a surprise birthday party waiting for him at home.

"What about the rooster?" Jeffery asked. "He needs to be placed with his new family as soon as possible, before he becomes too attached to this one. The longer you postpone this sleepover, the longer he's here, and the harder it will be to say goodbye."

The soft look he sent her made her eyes sting. Her dad wasn't worried about Gregory so much as Beckett. She played it tough, but every pet that passed through their doors brought its own heartbreak. It was why she maintained a strict three-month policy when it came to her fosters. Any longer, and she wouldn't be able to let go. And since there was only room enough for one full-time companion in Casa de Hayes, Beckett did what she could to maintain a professional distance.

"I've got it," Annie said. "Beckett can take my car. You can drop it back by my place later."

"I can't do that." Beckett stuck her hands behind her back when Annie dangled her keys enticingly. Not the most mature of moves, but effective.

"You can. Just stick out your hands." When Beckett did no such thing, Annie pried them out and forced her to take the keys. "And look at that." Annie clapped in delight. "Now, Jeffery can take Thomas, you can take Gregory, and all is worked out."

"How will *you* get home?" Jeffery asked Annie.

Annie shrugged, unconcerned. "I'll call Emmitt. He loves to drive me around. It gives him the impression he has a say in matters."

Both women looked at Jeffery, who gave a noncommittal smile.

Beckett sighed. "You've got this, Dad?"

"Sure he does," Annie encouraged. "To art class. Home from art class. Easy peasy, Mr. Hayes. Beckett was so sweet, she even brought home pizza, so you don't have to worry about fixing dinner when you get home."

Jeffery pushed his glasses farther up on his nose. "Right. Pizza. That was nice of you."

"Dad?"

Beckett's stomach churned as she waited for him to respond. Nothing about this arrangement left her feeling confident. Left to his own devices for a minute, Jeffery would squirrel, and Thomas wouldn't make it to class. No class meant no field trip. And Beckett had double-booked clients that afternoon, knowing Thomas would be in good hands.

"I'll cancel," Beckett said, knowing she should have rescheduled Gregory's re-homing for a day when it didn't conflict with her brother's class schedule.

She pulled out her phone to deliver the bad news to Katie, but Jeffery snatched it away.

"No need to cancel when I've got tonight covered," he said confidently. "In fact, Thomas and I could use some guy time. There's a ball game on tonight. So why don't you go out, honey. Relax, have dinner with Annie here."

Beckett looked him over skeptically. He was completely dressed, his hair brushed, and there was a chocolate stain down the front of his shirt, proof he'd eaten at some point in the past six hours. "If you're sure."

"As sure as Beethoven's Symphony Number Five." Jeffery handed back her phone. "I'm going to put on my hashtag-like-a-dad shirt before we head out. How's that for handling my business?"

With a double thumbs-up that had Beckett rolling her eyes, Jeffery made his exit.

"You still never said hi to Annie," Beckett hollered after him.

"Hi, Annie," came from the back of the house. "Have a good day, Annie."

"You too, Mr. Hayes," Annie hollered back.

The day her mom walked out for good, leaving a sixteen-year-old Beckett in charge of her brother's care, she'd stopped feeling the need to excuse her family's eccentricities. Especially around someone as unjudgmental as Annie. But sometimes, when she looked at her life from an outsider's perspective, it was hard not to cringe.

"Thanks for lending me your car," Beckett said, uncomfortable with the sudden onslaught of emotions. "I can drop you off on my way."

"Perfect. You can tell me about Gregory's

new companion. I heard he's a military war hero."

Beckett snorted at the idea of just who had spread that incorrect tidbit. She liked the way Levi's dimples peeked out, even when he was trying to be a hard-ass. Liked even more how soft his touch had been when he followed her into the rain to make sure she was all right. In fact, she liked him a little too much for her own good.

"What else did you hear?" she wanted to know.

"Only that he's former military." Annie waggled her brows. "And I know how you have a thing for guys in uniform."

"Had." Beckett grimaced at the reminder of her ex. One of Rome's finest, whose protect-and-serve mentality didn't extend to Beckett's heart. "You know when the uniform comes off, they're just regular guys. With the same commitment, house training, and wandering-dick syndrome as every other man out there."

"There are a lot of great men out there. You just need to know what to look for. And yes, some just need a little more patience than others, but look at Emmitt. All he needed was love, understanding, and someone who called him on his shit." Annie sighed as if she'd just told Marc Antony and

Cleopatra's story. "Now, I'm the luckiest girl alive."

"Emmitt's transformation was all you. Ask anyone. You found the lone unicorn in a herd of jackasses."

"All I can say is birds of a feather."

Beckett laughed, loud and hard. "I don't know what kind of flock you're envisioning, but unless it's peacocks, I don't see Levi fitting. He's boastful, feral, vain, and acts like Rome royalty."

"He *is* Rome royalty. His family owns most of the wharf and harbor district. And he's not bad on the eyes."

"They call them an ostentation of peacocks for a reason. And he still doesn't have a domesticated bone in his body."

Annie waved a dismissive hand. "Agree to disagree. I'm more interested in Gregory's new man. Is he single, hot? Skip to the 'without uniform' part. That sounds interesting." Annie's expression said she was expecting pictures and diagrams.

"*She* is an eight-year-old girl who suffers from a horrific stutter and acute anxiety," Beckett corrected. "The stuttering started after her grandmother had a heart attack while babysitting her. It worsened when she was asked to read aloud to her classmates. Now, it's reached the point that she doesn't talk at school anymore."

Annie's hand covered her heart. "Poor thing. I can't even imagine what her parents are going through."

"No matter how hard they try, nothing has worked. Her psychologist hopes that maybe practicing on an audience who won't judge her will help." Beckett's hope was that Gregory would work his magic and love all the fear and shyness right out of Katie.

Animals possessed a unique ability when it came to healing the human spirit. Beckett had seen, firsthand, the impact animal therapy had on her patients, sometimes helping patients when medication and traditional treatments alone had failed.

Many times, Beckett had taken shelter in the love of an animal when life's storms knocked her over. She was a late bloomer in the art of winning friends and influencing people; as a child, she'd been painfully shy, making it doubly hard to form meaningful connections. In elementary school, her loneliness became so painful, it began to cause more harm than her anxiety. She was desperate to belong but lacked the skills and confidence necessary to approach people and make friends.

When she was around the age of ten, her luck changed when a five-foot-long garden snake slithered into her classroom. The girls looked on in horror, and the boys in cautious interest, as Beckett caught the snake in her backpack. Her teacher said that as long as she kept the backpack outside and promised to release the snake far from school, she could keep it. School ended, and Beckett started for home with the snake around her neck like a scarf. She hadn't even made it to the curb before she was surrounded by her classmates. Even the scared ones wanted to pet Chewbacca — named after the best sidekick in history — or ask questions.

Instead of walking home alone as usual, Beckett laughed and joked with a group of kids from her neighborhood and had more playdate offers than days in the week. Beckett never outgrew being a quiet homebody who would rather spend time with her pets than other people, but Chewbacca gave her the foundation she needed to form friendships.

"Bring on Gregory," Annie guessed.

"Yup. He's the perfect companion for Katie. Patient, sweet, adores cuddles. And most importantly, he loves being talked to."

"Sounds like the perfect match."

"I hope so." Beckett took a box of baby corn on the cob from the to-go bag and placed it in Gregory's bag. It was her gift to Gregory and Katie. A little treat to help speed up the bonding process. "That's why I need to spend as much time as I can with them tonight. Katie has gone through so much. She needs this sleepover to go smoothly." So did Beckett. "Then Fur-Ever Friends can sign off and make it a permanent placement."

"What project will you take on next?" Annie asked.

She stared at Gregory, cuddled on top of her foot, and her chest ached. Bringing lost animals into her home, training them, loving them, breaking down all their walls, only to send them off to live with another family, was becoming too hard. She invested all her heart into each foster she took on. The more deeply she bonded with the animal, the better companion they'd become, and the harder it was for her heart to heal. Lately, she'd begun to fear that too many pieces of her heart were floating around for it to function properly.

"Honestly, I don't know if I can handle a 'next.' I've considered just focusing on my business after Gregory goes to Katie." Being a personal concierge came with its own set of issues and headaches, but it left her heart in the clear.

"You know I'm here for you, right?" That was Annie, offering a compassionate ear and a helping hand to fix Beckett's problems.

"After watching you balance a new position at work, a new fiancé at home, and a soon-to-be new stepdaughter" — who was sixteen, testing every limit, and dealing with the recent death of her mother — "I think I can handle a single chicken alone." She glanced at the pink box. "Is that why you brought me sugar? You didn't need to. Because you know I've been doing this since I was a teenager."

"That doesn't mean it isn't hard. And who says sugar-parties only happen for bad reasons?" Annie slid the pastry box across the table, positioning it directly in front of Beckett. "Maybe I'm here to celebrate."

"I could use some good news."

Annie steepled her hands. "It's great news. Amazing, really. Now that I know there's an upcoming opening in your calendar."

Suspicion tingled. "An opening that requires a family-sized box of bribes from Holy Cannoli?"

"A box of celebration," Annie said with barely contained excitement. "Emmitt and I want to hire you."

"You want to hire me?" They'd hired her to fulfill some pretty bizarre requests in the past, including tailing Paisley after the winter ball and transforming a canoe into a gondola to take the couple down the river when he proposed. None of those had required a chocolate bribe. "Is this one of those 'drop your keys in the fishbowl' kind of offer?"

"Nope." Annie tapped the lid but made no move to open it. It was like staring into Pandora's box. Once opened, it would unleash chaos into the world, and that was the last thing she needed right then.

"Then what's with the bribe?"

"No bribe. Just something to help celebrate our partnership," Annie said with a smile sweet enough to cause a bellyache. "After you agree to be our wedding planner."

"What?" Gregory squawked at Beckett's high pitch, then fluttered to the ground to peck at a dust bunny that had caught his attention. "You want to hire me, Cupid's kryptonite, to plan your wedding?"

"Absolutely." Annie sounded so confident, panic wove its way around Beckett's chest.

Planning a wedding was a huge commitment. Planning the wedding of a perfectionist was asking for trouble. It took someone with an open schedule and no other distractions, someone who could be available at a moment's notice. Not an errand girl who disappeared at the ping of a text or walked around with chicken feathers in her hair.

Bottom line, Annie needed someone with an eye for detail, a gentle touch. Beckett was more of a sledgehammer-through-Sheetrock kind of operator. Shit got done, but it wasn't always pretty.

"Not only do I lack the necessary style and qualifications to plan a wedding, but the last wedding I attended included me sneaking out the bathroom window of a church in a borrowed dress."

It hadn't helped that she'd attended the wedding with a guy who'd made her believe that one day they might be the ones walking down the aisle. That even though her life was chaotic, she was worthy of a man who would go that extra mile. Pete was winded by lap one. He'd started dragging his heels shortly after, then tapped all the way out before they'd even had a chance to hit their stride.

Turned out she was only worth the extra mile if it wasn't uphill or riddled with any of life's speed bumps. And Beckett's life had more obstacles than a preschool parking lot at pickup time.

"I disagree," Annie said simply. "I need help finding vendors. You are the walking equivalent of Rome's yellow pages. I work most days. You've been trying to get more daytime clients. I need a wedding planner I can trust. You want to expand your business and take on bigger projects."

"Not by using my friend's wedding as a trial run!"

"You have to start with someone's event. Why not mine?"

"I was thinking more along the lines of working with a few smaller hotels in town. Assisting their guests, arranging for transportation, things like that. Not picking out centerpieces."

"You can assist my guests, arrange for transportation, and this is a centerpiece-optional kind of wedding," she said. "I'm already so wound up about weddings, I'd rather give up pizza for the rest of my life than go through this process with a stranger. You know me, know what I like, and who else would I want by my side if Emmitt reneges?"

"No way would Emmitt ever stand you up," Beckett reassured her.

"Because he loves me, or because you'd kill him?"

"Both."

Annie laughed, but Beckett was feeling too apprehensive to join her. Mixing business and friendship rarely turned out well. Especially when said friend was a perfectionist.

"You don't even need a planner," Beckett pointed out. "You've been planning your wedding since you were a kid. You have a twenty-pound binder of pictures and magazine clippings. It's literally the perfect wedding."

"And someone else walked down the aisle in a knockoff of my dream dress."

Right. There was that.

Annie's ex-fiancé didn't only dump her a few months before the wedding. He repurposed the venue, the date, the honeymoon, the entire wedding, all the way down to the carrot cake. He only swapped out the bride.

"Whenever I think about planning my wedding, I break out in hives." Annie pulled up the sleeve of her sweater. Little red lumps dotted her forearm. "I'm not worried about getting married. Only the planning part."

"Have you thought of eloping?"

"I don't want to elope. I want a wedding."

"I'm not a planner. I'm a personal concierge. Who doesn't believe in fairy tales, by the way," she reminded Annie. "I book tables at restaurants, assist people with relocations. You don't need to hire me. I will help you with anything you need. Limo service, lodging for out-of-town guests, endless errands — I'm your girl. Planning a wedding is way above my pay grade."

"We don't want the fairy tale. We want a small, intimate celebration with close friends and family." Annie rested her hand over Beckett's. "You're my best friend, Beck. That more than anything makes you the perfect person for the job."

Or the perfect cause for alarm.

There was a reason Beckett could count the number of her friends on one hand and have three fingers to spare. Her life was as unpredictable as it was complicated — which was why she ran errands for a living. Turn down a few invites, split in the middle of one too many girls' nights, and people stop calling.

Not Annie, though. She was one of those see-the-best-in-people kind of friends who never gave up — even when they'd been given a zillion reasons. Annie knew Beckett was more or less a sold-as-is kind of person, but she loved her anyway. No matter how many times she canceled plans at the last minute.

She couldn't bail on an appointment with a wedding venue or stand Annie up when picking out floral arrangements. Then there was the pathetic, but all-too-real, truth.

"I don't believe in love," she said, and —
wow — admitting it aloud was a million
times worse than thinking it. But now that
it was out there, no way would Annie still
want to hire her.

"Sure you do," Annie said softly. "You love
your family."

"That doesn't count. It's a result of shared
DNA and forced proximity. Hashtag science. Look it up."

"You love your animals." The box slid
toward her — again.

Beckett slid it back. "They don't care if I
shave my legs."

"You love me. You love Lynn."

"Against my will. You decided I was going
to be your friend, and you were relentless,"
Beckett teased, when in reality, it had been
Beckett who'd sought out Annie.

She hadn't walked up and said, "Want to
be besties?" But she'd gone out of her way
to put herself in Annie's path. There was a
barely contained joy about Annie that drew
people in. People like Beckett who needed a
little light in their lives.

Friends like that were as rare as a man
with emotional maturity. And Beckett was
terrified of disappointing her.

Taking the job would be like walking

through a minefield of potential disappointments with her eyes closed, while wearing clown shoes. One wrong step and the wedding would go up in smoke. Then again, refusing would result in one-hundred-percent certainty of letting Annie down.

There was no way she'd do that to the one person who always had her back, no matter what.

Looked like Beckett needed to invest in one of those wedding-planner books and find a backup sitter for Thomas in the very likely event that Jeffery decided to go Jeffery during one of Annie's appointments.

"Don't say I didn't warn you," Beckett said.

Annie squealed and leaned all the way across the table to give Beckett a hug, which Beckett endured.

"Is that a yes?" Annie leaned back to study Beckett's expression. "Oh my God, it's a yes!"

"I'm going to open the box; just promise not to strangle me again."

Annie promised, and Beckett opened the box. Inside sat an enormous eclair with white icing piped over the top. It read, SHE SAID YES!

Beckett reached in to pick it up, but Annie stopped her. "One last thing. I don't want to know any of the details."

"What does that even mean?" Beckett's hearing must have malfunctioned. "You're the bride. You have to know the details."

"Actually, I don't." Annie pulled out a piece of paper. It was small and bridal pink with little check boxes in the margin. "These are the musts. The rest is up to you."

"What do you mean, 'The rest is up to me?' " Beckett flipped the list over, and — that was panic she was choking on. "There are only six items on this list. What do you want me to do, plan you a surprise wedding?"

Annie smiled. "Exactly!"

CHAPTER 6

Levi was in his back office, no closer to finding the root of the problem. Overnight, a thousand dollars of inventory had up and walked away. He hoped it was a clerical error, but his gut said it was more of an error in judgment.

He'd been teaching Paisley the finer points of parallel parking when a delivery of high-end wine arrived. With his one manager working nights and the position for day manager still vacant, the responsibility of signing for and unloading the order had fallen on the new lunchtime chef.

There was a rap at the door, and then it opened. Sounds of the kitchen staff prepping for the dinner rush drifted in along with Gray.

"What's the point of knocking, if you don't wait for a reply?" Levi asked.

"It's not like I'd be interrupting something." Gray dropped onto the couch and

121

sprawled out. "I doubt you've been laid since Vikki dropped her anchor in some other guy's marina."

There were a lot of things he hadn't done since Vikki left. Sex wasn't one of them. Not that he needed a sock for the doorknob, but he'd dated. Some. Then again, he hadn't met anyone who'd made him want to take things beyond the morning after. Lately, even the casual hookup had lost its appeal.

Sadly, he didn't have time for anything more.

"You're one to talk."

"I'm an out-of-practice single dad with the gray hairs to prove it," his brother-in-law said, and they both knew he was lying. Gray hadn't looked at another woman since meeting Michelle nearly fifteen years ago. That fact hadn't changed since her death.

"Your patients call you Dr. Doable — I think you'd do all right."

Gray deflated with the labored sigh of someone who was circling the drain. "I'm not ready. Plus, Paisley needs all my attention right now. Studies show that emotionally, teenagers benefit more from a stay-at-home parent than pre-adolescents. Between Michelle and me, we arranged our working hours to make sure there was always someone around to help with homework, friend issues, things like that."

"Between you, me, Emmitt, and now Annie, that kid has more eyes surveilling her every move than a mob boss under investigation." Levi leaned his elbows on the desk. "I think you could find the time for a date here and there."

"Says the guy whose must-do list is getting longer instead of shorter, even though you spend every spare minute working on that boat. *Rhodes Less Traveled* has been ready to set sail for over a year, yet she hasn't left Buzzards Bay. Why's that?"

First, he'd postponed the trip because his dad was gone, and he couldn't stomach taking it alone. Plus, he had to help his mom and Michelle run the family's marina and fish-and-chips shack. Then Paisley came along, and just when she was becoming her own little person, Michelle died, and he hadn't felt like leaving at all. But enough time had passed, Paisley and his mom had worked through the worst of their grief, and he still couldn't bring himself to leave.

Levi could say that he was waiting for Paisley to head off to college. But that would be a lie. He hadn't a clue why his anchor was cemented in his hometown harbor. Hell, he didn't even know when it began to harden.

"Teenagers benefit more from a stay-at-home parent figure than pre-adolescents," he intoned, repeating Gray's earlier statement. "Look it up," he joked. Paisley wasn't the whole reason he was delaying. But until he could identify what was holding him back, parental duty was the best he could come up with. "And I'm as much her parent as you are."

"Jesus, we're pathetic." Gray laughed. "If Emmitt could hear us now, we'd never live it down."

"Only because he's getting some on the regular. Otherwise, he's the same guy who lost his trunks going down the Slip 'N Slide on a dare. He was trying to impress Jamie Olsen but failed to factor in that it was November and really cold water. Back then, his hair was more reddish than auburn, so let's just say he spent the better part of junior high finding his locker full of baby carrots."

"Is that why he hates carrots?" Gray asked, laughing.

"He didn't hit his stride with the ladies until senior year. In fact, where is he?" Levi checked his laptop for the time and saw the date. "Tonight's bowling. The fucker talked me into it, so I declared him the designated driver. At least I can enjoy a pint or two on his tab while proving my long-standing theory that prolonged exposure to lab coats negatively affects one's coordination."

Not even a chuckle from the Lab Coat sitting on the couch.

"Tonight, I will expand that theory, to see if it includes humor and all-around likability."

Gray continued his assessing stare and added a head tilt. In conjunction with a well-placed elbow to the knee, posture slightly forward — in a manner meant to convey capability and trustworthiness — it could only mean one thing.

Doctor Gray was officially in the house.

"Bowling was Tuesday," Gray said. "Tomorrow night is Friday, which means family dinner night at my place. You're bringing beer, dessert, and your mom. Do you need me to write down my address? Or your mom's, for that matter?"

"I've been a little busy holding together the family business. I've got more jobs to fill than people on my payroll. A stack of résumés that would take me a week to sift through. And the 'emergencies' from my mom are nonstop. I'm on fumes, man."

"How can I help?" asked the only other man on the planet who understood, first-hand, what it was like to be part of Ida's family. The fierceness with which she loved her children, the endless loyalty she had for her family, and the unparalleled devotion with which she ferreted out every single detail of every aspect of their lives.

It was relentless. Done with love, but he swore Ida could extract all the burial sites from a serial killer. Still, at the end of the day, she was his mom, and Levi's love for her was boundless.

"She's just lonely," Levi said, the familiar burn of injustice and anger beating in his chest. "Her meddling is how she stays connected when we're not around. And lately, I've been a pretty disappointing son."

"It's been a rough ten months." Gray's words were thick with emotion. "For all of us. Can we do better? Sure. But give yourself some slack."

"You taking your own advice, Doc?" Levi asked. "Because from where I'm sitting, it looks like you've taken on a little wear and tear since the last family dinner."

"The head of pediatrics is about to announce his retirement and wants to endorse me as his replacement. He came to me Monday to gauge my interest."

"That's great, man. You were born to boss people around," Levi said, and they both laughed. "What did you tell him?"

"That it's a great opportunity but terrible timing." Gray's head dropped, and he cradled it in his hands. "Thanks to you, Emmitt, and Annie, I've come a long way, but it hasn't even been a year." He looked up just enough to make eye contact, and the grief that lay there hit Levi square in the chest.

When his sister passed, Levi had made family his number-one priority — and that responsibility extended to the soul mate Michelle had left behind. To shield them, Levi had put his own loss and grief aside to ensure his loved ones came through the devastation and tragedy intact. That they'd emerge the same people they'd been before was as improbable as the missing wine suddenly appearing, but he prayed they'd come through feeling a new kind of wholeness, and happiness and joy would be possible again.

Had he been so caught up in his own mess that he'd missed something?

"We haven't checked in in a while. That's on me," Levi apologized. "How are you doing?"

"My therapist suggested I do something that used to make me happy when I was younger, so I started paddleboarding again."

"Is it helping?"

"Hell if I know." He laughed. "But everyone keeps asking if I ski, because my nose is constantly sunburnt."

"How did you leave it with the head of pediatrics? Because you essentially won the medical lottery with his offer. You do know that?"

"Oh, I know exactly what is on the line. But then I think of Michelle and everything she brought to my life, to our relationship, all the love she gave me every day. Doesn't she deserve a year of grieving?" Gray asked.

"A year doesn't even come close."

"That's what I realized. Nothing will." There was a desperate hopelessness in his words. "So I started thinking, there has to be some point where there is no option but to go forward. Not move on," he quickly clarified. "Never move on, because I'm going to make sure Michelle is with me every step of the way. But move forward."

Levi felt the weight of those words like a sledgehammer to the chest, beating harder and harder as if preparing for the final blow. He wasn't sure if it would take him all the way under or set him free, but deep in his soul, he knew it was necessary.

Worrying about the inevitable wasn't helping anyone.

"Whatever it looks like, it can happen

today, on the one-year anniversary of Michelle's passing, or ten years from now," Levi explained. "Either way, she would want you to take the promotion." Just as she'd want Levi to take that trip. Or at least take a risk, enjoy the life he'd worked so hard for. "In fact, I'd bet P's next driving lesson that she'd kick your ass if you passed on it."

"I might suck at poker, but I'd never bet against Michelle." Gray turned serious. "When Dr. Neuman offered me the position, there was this moment, not even a split second but so vivid, when I forgot she was gone. And I pictured the look on her face when I told her about the offer, thought about how she'd feel when she wrapped her arms around me and laughed with excitement." Gray lifted his head all the way, his eyes boring into Levi's. "You know, the laugh when she gets so excited —"

"She begs for you to say something boring, so she won't pee her pants," Levi finished, thinking back to all the ways he used to make her laugh so she'd say just that.

"I swear to God, when Neuman left the office, I could smell her perfume like she was there with me, kissing me on the cheek and telling me how proud she was, how proud my dad would be." His voice broke.

"Can you imagine the two of them sitting on a cloud, drinking whiskey sours, and screaming at me to run after Neuman. Tell him that, not only do I want the position, I'm going to rock the fuck out of that job."

"That's exactly what she'd say. Did you do it?"

"We both know I wasn't the ballbuster in the couple. But I did seek out Neuman and tell him I was more than interested; I just needed a little time to figure how my life would work with the added responsibilities that go with the position. He agreed to hold off on announcing for a few weeks."

"Don't wait. Take the promotion. I think I can speak for everyone when I promise we've got your back. Whatever slack needs to be picked up, just say the word."

"Thanks. I mean it. But I came here to see how you were doing. Some people think you need a keeper."

Levi knew how he looked. He was wearing yesterday's jeans and was sporting fell-asleep-at-my-desk hair. While he'd showered off in the employee's locker room and changed his shirt, he couldn't guarantee it was necessarily fresh. But he was handling business to the best of his ability. Loved ones breathing down his neck only added to the pressure.

"I'm working on it," he admitted, and he held up a stack of résumés to prove it.

"Work faster, because if you miss any more family events, your mom's going to move in with you to make sure her baby is getting enough food and beauty rest."

"Shit." Instantly alert, he sat straight. "She said that?"

"If I said yes, would it make you less picky about hiring some help?" Gray asked, and Levi sat back. "I didn't think so. Well, don't spend so much time putting out fires that you can't find the time to call a fireman."

"I wish it were as easy as dialing a number." He had a thousand dollars in missing alcohol to prove it.

"Sure it is. Place ad. Swipe right. Then right again. Before you know it, your problems will be solved. I'm only here a few hours a week, and even I can tell the place is suffering."

Levi rested his head in his hands. "I know. Things are slipping through the cracks. Mistakes are happening. Michelle handled all this shit." Levi lifted a stack of invoices and résumés. "I ran the bar, handled alcohol orders, and spent the rest of the time running the marina."

"I'm the last one who should be saying this, since I can't seem to take my own advice, but no one's asking you to replace Michelle," Emmitt said softly. "And she'd have your ass if she knew how stubborn you were being."

"Diligent. And I've got a new bartender coming in tomorrow, before opening, so I can start training him."

"You might want to be diligent a little faster. It's already filling up out front."

"Can you handle things for a few?"

"No can do. I'm picking up takeout, then headed right back to the free clinic. Paisley's helping Annie with filing to fulfill some of her community-service requirement, and we were all hungry for burgers and steak."

Levi crossed his arms. "Funny. We don't do takeout."

"Sure you do." Gray gave a shit-eating grin. "Just ask Beckett."

At the mention of her name, his pulse picked up. Which was all kinds of ridiculous. She hadn't stopped by to sweet-talk him into breaking the rules since Pecker-gate. "That was our official last takeout order."

"You might want to let Gus know that. He's been hooking Emmitt and me up with meals for months. Even gives me the friends and family discount."

"You didn't, by chance, *friends-and-family* yourself to a case of some hard-to-find

Syrah? Or know someone who did?"

"No, but I do love a good Syrah. I'll help myself to a bottle on the way out." Gray stood, smoothing down his bright blue, impeccably clean scrubs.

"Can you not wear your surgery gear to the restaurant? People look at you, and all they can think about is needles and oozing fluids. Doesn't really set the right mood."

"I'll try to remember for next time. Oh." He patted the pocket of his scrub pants. Then the other. "I almost forgot to give this to you."

He pulled out a piece of paper folded into a football, which reminded Levi of the paper football games guys used to play in high school to pass the time during detention. Gray didn't strike Levi as the kind of guy who'd served detention — he was too busy dropping SAT words to impress girls who read Jane Austen — but for a couple of years, Levi and Emmitt had called it a second home.

"Aw. I'm touched. Are you asking me to prom?" Levi joked.

"You're not my type. And it's from Annie. When I told her I was coming here for takeout, she asked if I could deliver a note."

He reached out his hand. "You can tell her the note was delivered."

133

"It's not for you. It's for Beckett." Gray held it up to the light, trying to read it. "And judging by the illegible scrawl, which I think is intended to be actual letters from the English alphabet, it appears Emmitt wrote it."

"This is where you deliver it."

Only Gray didn't hand it over. He secured the note between his thumb and middle finger and twirled it.

"Seriously?" Levi asked.

Gray flicked the note. "Did I mention that Little Miss Dolittle took a seat in your section right as I was coming in? And she brought her A game."

Levi's heart gave a little bump to the ribs at the thought of just how good her A game would look seated at his counter. "I work the bar tonight. I don't have a section."

"I figured wherever she decided to sit would be your new section." Another flick. "Annie attached a message for Beckett to the note. She got held up at work and won't be able to make it tonight." Gray held the note out. "Can you give her the note and message?"

"Why not just talk to her on your way out?"

"Because you look like you could use some help."

134

"I'm doing just fine on my own."

"That's either stupid talking or the eternal optimist in you. The way I see it, neither one of them has a clue how to handle a woman like Beckett."

"And what makes Beckett different?" he asked, even as a mental list of all the ways she was one of a kind tallied in his brain faster than football stats in Vegas.

Beckett was as refreshing as the way he felt when he was around her.

"You haven't tried to sleep with her yet," Gray said. "That's not your usual MO."

There was that. It hadn't been for lack of interest. When it came to Beckett, interest wasn't the problem. It was timing. They'd never been single at the same moment. He'd had Vikki, and she had a never-ending supply of boring bankers and software engineers. The only time they'd both been single and in the same place had been Emmitt and Annie's engagement party.

Holding the football upright with one finger, Gray flicked it through the air, nailing Levi in the chest. "You can thank me later."

Gray stood and exited the office before Levi could hand it back. Not that he was sure he would, because Gray had a point. When it came to Beckett, he was in desperate need of help. The fact that he was this excited to have a legit reason to seek her out was ridiculous.

It was rare that Levi allowed himself to become distracted. Once he set a goal, he zeroed in, relentless in his pursuit. A trait left over from his sailing days. It had served him well in the past, allowed him to carry his family during the worst of times, and helped him keep a laser focus on the business when the freedom of the open sea tempted.

Beckett was a temptation he both wanted to explore and needed to avoid, but no amount of focus seemed to be helping. A problem that kept him up nights — and under his BVDs come morning.

It had been that way since the grocery store run-in. He wasn't sure if it was the warm vulnerability she'd shown when accepting his help or those ass-hugging leggings she'd been wearing, but she had his full-on attention.

Now she was sitting in "his section," wearing a pair of black-leather biker boots and a case of helmet-hair that would scare a gang of Hell's Angels. She was looking as ruffled as ever, and Levi couldn't take his eyes off her.

Oh, she was looking his way, too. Only

warm and *accepting* weren't the first two words that came to mind. *Wary* and *apprehensive* were more accurate. Given the way her eyes darted everywhere but his way, his appearance was to blame.

Levi grabbed two frosty bottles of her favorite beer. Cracking his neck to each side and bouncing on his toes, he made his way toward the booth at the back of the bar, feeling better than he had in days.

Funny how the possibility of arguing felt a hell of a lot like foreplay.

He set the beers down, and she frowned. Her chin jerked at the extra bottle. "Who's that for?"

"Not the chicken you're hiding in that backpack," he said.

"He's not hiding." She clutched the pack close, and a string of clucks and flapping sounds erupted from inside the bag. "In fact, he refused to come out, because he doesn't like being in your bar."

"That's fair, since I don't like having him in my bar, either." More commotion, and it was as if a feather bomb exploded into the air. "Are you trying to get me shut down?"

"I wanted to go to Tipsy Pelicans, but Annie insisted on meeting here. Go argue with her."

"Pelicans sucks. They water down their

137

alcohol. And you're the one arguing."

She opened her mouth, then realized she was about to argue and snapped it closed.

Deciding the extra beer was for him, he slid onto the bench across from her and took a long pull. Her silence gave him the chance to study her over the rim of the bottle.

Her lips were as full and glossy as ever, her cheeks flushed, and the tip of her nose bright red — likely from riding her bike around town in the middle of March. Her eyes, though, were hooded, and extremely apprehensive. Her stress visible.

"What?" she asked, patting her head. "Do I have something in my hair?"

"I would have been worried if you didn't," he teased, then reached across the table and brushed some glitter from her hair. "Never took you for a sparkly kind of woman."

"I'm not." She undid her braid and shook her hair, scattering a few more sparkles on the table. "I was looking through paint swatches, and it must have hitched a ride."

"Repainting something?"

"Nope," was all she said.

"Redecorating, then?" He sat back and took a leisurely sip of beer. "Maybe I can be of assistance. I've recently spent a bit of time researching color schemes and how

138

they affect mood."

"Color schemes?" Her lips twitched.

"That's what Paisley called it. I finished refurbishing my dad's boat, and now I'm working on the inside. She's helping me paint and decorate the inside in exchange for driving lessons. She wanted to make sure to use calm, soothing shades, especially in my cabin. You should come check it out."

"Let me look at my calendar and see when I'm free." Instead of her appointment book, she consulted the countdown clock above the bar. "Sorry, it looks like I'm booked for the next sixty-one days, twelve hours, fifty-one minutes, and eleven seconds. Give or take."

Putting her next opening at the exact moment Levi was to set sail on his trip down the coast. "I'm touched. Is that your way of asking to be my skipper, Beck?"

"No." She did that cute squirming-in-her-seat number that gave away her nervousness. "That's my way of saying I will never, ever, *ever* visit your cabin, see your cabin, or inquire about your cabin. Amazing new paint job or not."

"Sure a lot of never-evers for someone who isn't interested in the goings-on inside my cabin." Elbows on the table, he leaned in and lowered his voice. "And amazing doesn't even begin to describe it."

"Don't you have a bar bunny to charm?"

"Free for the moment."

She snatched the bottle from his hand. "Well, you're in Annie's seat."

"She can't make it. She pulled a double at work."

"What?" She gasped.

"Yeah, Gray left a few minutes ago with dinner and my most expensive bottle of wine, neither of which he paid for. It's part of his big plan, which requires pampering your friend for the remainder of the evening." He slid the note across the table. "He said to give you this."

"Oh no," she breathed, backing away as if the note were made of radioactive paper. If he thought she'd looked stressed before, then she was in a sheer state of panic now. "I haven't slept since Annie gave me her note. I'm not sure I can handle one from Emmitt."

That shed some light on the zombielike state Beckett had adopted over the past week. Every time he spotted her around town, she appeared to be sleepwalking.

Oh, she hadn't slowed her pace any. Beckett still went about her business as if mainlining a cocktail of caffeine and jet fuel, much like an F-5 tornado, stirring up chaos

140

and taking out everything in her path. Watching her tackle a problem was a sight to behold, as impressive as it was sexy. But the ferocity that usually crackled and sparked with her every step was missing.

Levi would bet she couldn't even tackle a dandelion in her current state, let alone whatever was in that note.

"Maybe I can help," he offered, reaching for the paper. Beckett snatched it right out of his fingers. "Whoa, I was just offering to read it for you."

"My note. My problem. No help needed." Her voice was tight. She spun the note around and around between her fingers, never once attempting to unfold it. "I'm sure it's another list."

"I slayed your last list."

Some of the tension disappeared as a small grin tugged at her lips. "It was sweet of you, and I'll admit, without your help I likely would have gone home frustrated and empty-handed. But 'slayed' is a bit boastful, don't you think?"

"Lady, while I was in that grocery store, I asked my second-grade teacher what kind of tampons she used. If that isn't slaying some kind of dragon, I don't know what is." She didn't look convinced, but she also wasn't asking him to leave. "I'm a great problem solver and know all Emmitt's plays. Maybe I can help."

She considered this for a long moment, then said, "How good are you at the 'whole walk down the aisle and say I Do' thing?"

"You proposing, Beck?"

She snorted as if that were the most ridiculous idea in the history of humankind. And strangely enough, the dismissal stung a little. Especially coming from a woman who dated guys like Snore-fest Steve and Boring Bruce.

"I'll have you know that I am prime, grade-A husband material." Not that he was looking to put a ring on it anytime in the near, or distant, future. "I'm good with a hammer, great with problem solving, and even better at listening. We've already talked about my cabin-activity skills, I know my way around the kitchen, and am extremely business-savvy. I never leave the toilet seat up and can handle everything from diapers to teen drama when it comes to kids."

"Are you going to give me references next?"

"That might be a little tricky on the cabin-activity side. I'm not one to decorate and tell," he said, and she was back to looking stressed. "I can always say I forgot to give it to you."

She shook her head, then met his gaze. "Annie's really not coming?"

"Afraid not. Gray said she's helping Paisley with a filing project."

Beckett took a swig of her beer, nearly draining the bottle, then closed her eyes. "I'm pretty sure this is his addition to the Must Haves list for their wedding. They set a date."

"I heard."

She opened her eyes and — *talk about slaying* — those warm brown pools could make a man do stupid things. Stupid, dangerous things . . . like make a happily single guy consider how much happier he'd be with more Beckett in his life. Even though he was counting down until he could finally set sail, and she was anchored in Rome.

"Did you hear they hired me to plan it?"

"Emmitt left that part out." Levi wondered what else his friend had left out. From the stress lines pressing in on Beckett's forehead, he'd say a lot. "I would think that being asked to plan your friends' wedding would be a big honor."

"It is," she said softly. "It's also a big responsibility. Too big."

After the disaster with the fire chief's retirement party, Levi would have to agree.

It wasn't that Beckett lacked drive; she worked harder than anyone he knew. But when it came to follow through, she seemed to spread herself too thin. Then again, this was her best friend's wedding, not delivering a couple hundred crab cakes to the Moose Lodge.

Annie could organize a library in the middle of a hurricane and direct a parade of feral cats. If she needed help with her wedding, odds were, it was more emotional than logistical. Beckett might come off as flighty at times, but the way she cared for those closest to her was astounding. She was the self-appointed protector of her family and friends.

After the market and seeing just what she was dealing with in her personal life, Levi had a hard time passing judgment. He knew the level of selflessness it took to step in and raise another family member's kid, knew the sacrifices that came along with it, and he respected the hell out of her for how she'd handled the situation.

"Maybe you're just what she needs," he said softly. "Someone to stand between her and outside expectations. Someone to remind everyone that it's her day."

"The scary gatekeeper with a crowbar role is the easy part," she said, and he laughed.

"It's the rest . . ." She took a deep breath. "They want me, someone who hates weddings, to plan an elegant, intimate, perfect wedding for the perfect couple. Only they don't want to be bothered by details. *Any* of the details," she said, looking a bit hysterical. "As in, plan it all, and we'll show up."

"You hate weddings?" he asked, trying to name a single woman he knew who hated weddings. He couldn't think of one.

The women in his life were hardwired to weep, squeal, or burst into applause at the mere mention of a wedding. His mom had her wedding photo framed above the fireplace, the album on the coffee table, and her dress in a vacuum-sealed container, which would likely survive a nuclear blast. Michelle hadn't been any better.

When Prince Harry and Meghan married, Levi was forced to shut down his bar during a Red Sox and Yankees game to broadcast the royal wedding in a private viewing party for Michelle, his mom, and two hundred of their closest friends. Michelle had stuffed him into a tux and top hat so he could escort each lady to and from her car.

"That's your big takeaway?"

"No, I just thought all women wore wedding goggles."

"No goggles here. A benefit we fringe women experience," she said, heavy on the sarcasm.

Her posture told a different story entirely. Her eyes were downcast, her hand fidgeting with the beer label, and there was almost something fragile about the way she sat. Something similar to the way she'd hugged herself at the market. It made his chest hurt then. Made it ache now.

"I didn't mean —"

"I know," she interrupted, casually waving him off.

"Is that why you disappeared during their engagement party? An allergic reaction?" He'd meant it as a joke of sorts.

She didn't laugh.

"I left because of a personal issue, which I explained to Annie. She understood." Her chin was high, her eyes narrowed into two *back the fuck off* slits that had him doing anything but.

His heart warned him to pay attention to that glare, but his head couldn't let it go. The "hostess" might have had a solid reason for bolting before even the first toast was made, but it was clear she had zero clue as to the fallout she'd left in her wake.

Levi had noticed Beckett outside by the pool in a stunning teal dress, her hair swept up in a fancy knot, wearing a pair of strappy heels that became instant spank-bank stars. She had a box in her hand, her back to the party, and her face tilted to the sky, the moonlight casting a glow over her smooth skin.

He'd always thought she was beautiful, but that night she'd been stunning. And all alone.

Sensing his opportunity, Levi approached her and made a gentlemanly offer to get her a drink and place her dessert box inside with the others. She looked at him as if he were the devil incarnate. Told him she'd be right back, then disappeared.

Ten minutes later, Levi had heard the traditional tinkling of glasses. He headed back inside to celebrate one of the happiest moments in his best friend's life, only to discover the bride and groom in the kitchen, dusted in flour and anxiety, making appetizers for the sixty hungry guests in their front room. The hostess and her dessert were MIA.

"Maybe she did, but that didn't change the fact that Annie ended up hosting her own engagement party. She spent the night running around, catering to her guests, and didn't get to enjoy herself."

"I didn't know. She told me everything

got handled, and it was a lovely evening. I should have known it was Annie who handled everything." Her voice was thread-thin. Her cheeks flushed with embarrassment.

A devastating dose of guilt had Levi's heart delivering a painful *I told you so* pinch.

"It worked out," he heard himself say consolingly.

"This is their wedding!" Her voice was more than a little desperate now. "It can't just work out. It has to be perfect." She gave a nervous laugh. "Which is why I have a favor to ask."

"Are you asking for my help?" he asked, and she took a big breath that had Levi looking for the metaphorical oh-shit handle, because he had a bad feeling he was about to be dragged along for one hell of a wild ride.

"No. A favor. For Emmitt and Annie." She pulled out what he guessed was Annie's first note and handed it to him. A quick glance showed seven items, each with a check box next to it. "Read on."

A burst of caution rammed against his sternum. "Number one. Any cake but carrot. Two, wine and beer fine, no hard liquor. No fuss. No stress. And absolutely no exes of any kind." He eyed Beckett over the paper. "Does that just go for the bride and groom? Or wedding party as well? Boring Bruce will be heartbroken."

"I didn't tell you he was my ex. And just think of all the heartbroken bar bunnies there will be."

"The bar bunnies will be fine. And you didn't need to tell me. He isn't here helping you — that's all I need to know." He held up the list. "Shall I continue?"

"Yes." She squeezed her eyes shut. "You're getting to the good part."

"They want it on the summer solstice?" He glanced at the clock. "Two months to plan a wedding. Not a lot of time for a wedding." He looked at her over the paper. "How many people are they inviting?"

"Small and intimate, with just close friends and family."

"With Emmitt, that could be anywhere between twenty and two hundred."

"No exes, remember?" she said.

"That will eliminate the town's females between drinking age and menopause." He scanned the last two lines, and there was that bump again. "They want the wedding on or by the water."

"Which rules out Pelicans."

"And for the reception, a view of the ocean." He stopped, refolded the list, and laid it on the table. "There are only two

149

venues that meet those Must Haves."

"Yup," she mumbled, eyes squeezed tightly closed.

One was the Seaside Resort, which was under construction, and the other was the Crow's Nest. "I didn't know that the Seaside was reopened."

"It's not." One eye slid open, and she clearly didn't like what she saw, because it immediately slammed shut. She dropped her forehead against the wood top with a thud and groaned. "This is why Annie was supposed to be here. She was supposed to sweet-talk you. I'm no good at sweet talk."

"It wouldn't have helped. Hosting the wedding here is a nonstarter," he said, making sure to showcase the steel-cased absoluteness of his decision. "I don't have the staff for that, and with the piles of résumés on my desk, and interviews to be conducted, I don't have the time to oversee a wedding."

"That's where I come in." She sat up, a big smile plastered to her face. If it was supposed to make him feel better, it didn't. "I will oversee everything. All you have to do is say yes, and I will run with it. Annie and Emmitt can get married down on the marina, then move to the restaurant for the reception. Twinkle lights on the deck and buffet-style dinner, so we don't need a lot of staff. Or we can hire a few cater waiters. It's perfect."

"Except for the part where it's held here. Cater waiters, buffet, none of that matters." He softened his voice. "You and I haven't had the best track record when it comes to working together —"

"I know," she cut in. The sincere apology in her eyes slid right past that steel casing and into his soft underbelly. "There's no excuse for leaving you hanging with the retirement party, and I should have been honest with you about what happened. But whenever I bring up my brother, people look at me differently. Look at him differently. And I didn't want —"

"Beck." He took her hand in his and gave it a gentle squeeze. "I get it. You put me in a bad situation, but I get it. Probably more than most."

"It must have been tough being a dad to Paisley at such a young age," she said, surprising him with her astuteness. Most people who knew Paisley now saw a thriving sixteen-year-old with two dads and a soon-to-be stepmom, living with the town's favorite physician. But during the early years, the night-time-feeding and diaper-blow-out years, it had been just him and Michelle — barely adults themselves.

151

Michelle had had their mom as a resource, but their dad was gone by then, leaving Levi without anyone to ask how to be a good dad. He'd done the best he could and was finally hitting a confident groove when Gray came along.

Suddenly, Michelle was married, and the little girl Levi had raised as his own was calling another man dad. No more bedtime stories or chocolate-chip pancakes before work. It was just him and his boat — with an anchor he couldn't hoist up.

"There were moments, but I don't regret a thing." And he meant that. Yes, he'd missed out on the whole "college experience," and he'd only had one serious adult relationship, but he wouldn't give up those times with Paisley for anything.

With that chapter of his life shortly coming to a close, what came next would finally be up to him. He wasn't sure how he wanted those pages to read, but he'd be interested to see what they'd look like if Beckett made more than just a footnote. And while he knew he'd regret agreeing to this wedding, he was certain he'd regret saying no more.

"Okay, we can have the wedding here."

"Are you serious?" Her smile bright and so damn beautiful, she bounced in her seat.

"This is amazing. Annie didn't ask for much, and I was afraid I'd have to disappoint her only a week into my job."

That statement wrapped itself around his chest and squeezed painfully. It clued him in a little as to why Beckett worked herself ragged and, more importantly, the kind of childhood she must have had to be so certain she'd disappoint.

"I promise, you won't regret this," she said, taking his hand between both of hers. Her fingers were delicate, her skin warm and silky, and the gentle way she held on — well, he wasn't regretting a thing right then.

"I know. Between the two of us, this wedding will be smooth sailing."

"Two of us?"

He ignored her protest. "We'll need to meet weekly, of course. Make sure nothing falls through the cracks. Scratch that — twice weekly. I'd volunteer my place, but you made your feelings clear on my color schemes."

"We can't work together!"

"Why not?" The spark from simply holding hands told him they would work together just fine.

"Because," she sputtered. "Because, well. . . . Because they hired *me*. Yes. And you're short-staffed and trying to hire new management, remember? I'm sure that means a lot of time devoted to interviewing, hiring, and training. So much training. Plus, there's your countdown clock. I could never ask you to take time away from working on your boat."

"Oh, I thought it was because you're attracted to me." His gaze landed on their still-clasped hands; hers followed.

"It has nothing to do with that." She dropped his hand like a hot potato. "This is about Annie and Emmitt hiring *me* to plan their wedding. A wedding that needs to be perfect. Having too many cooks in the kitchen will only complicate things. Simple as that."

"Then why are you blushing?"

"I'm not," she lied. "And this is why we can't work together."

"Because you blush whenever I'm around?"

"Because we need to take this seriously, something you can't seem to do. So while I am so thankful you have agreed to have the wedding here, we all need to stay in our own lanes. I am the wedding planner. You are the venue owner, Mr. Rhodes."

If she meant for the title to establish a modicum of professionalism, she failed. In fact, the way his name slipped so easily from

154

her lips had more pillow talk about it than personal concierge. And the way she absently touched her lips said her mind had gone to the same steamy place.

As if sensing his gaze, she crossed her arms and sat back in the booth.

"Don't worry, Miss Hayes. It was good for me, too."

"Stop playing with me," she whispered, and the distress in her tone had him backing off immediately. She could handle arguing with him, bantering, even tolerating his humor. But when it came to flirting or compliments or anything remotely personal, she became uncomfortable — shy, even.

It was as if Beckett was not in the habit of talking about herself or being singled out for any reason other than her job description. Something he looked forward to working on with her.

"When I'm playing with you, you'll know it," he said with gentle honesty. "As for the wedding, closing down for a private event involves a lot of moving pieces, and I can't afford any surprises. So if the wedding happens here, then I need to be involved. Beyond just being the venue owner. I need to know the hows, whos, and whats of the event, which means you and I will be communicating and working together. That's my Must Have."

Emmitt was going to owe him big time. While having his best friend's wedding here felt incredibly right, Levi was going to lose some serious money on the event. His mom loved Emmitt. No way would she accept payment for use of the restaurant and marina. Ida would also skin Levi alive if he charged Emmitt anything over the cost for the food and alcohol.

Yup, this wedding was going to cost Levi a pretty penny. In return, Levi would get the opportunity to appease his curiosity about the stubborn and sexy Dolittle sitting across from him.

"I guess that's understandable," she agreed, but he could tell she didn't like it. "But when this is all over, and I prove to you how good I am at what I do, you will give Consider It Done a trial run as your exclusive delivery service. That's my Must Have."

She smiled, and the barely contained hopefulness radiating from her made it hard to say no.

"Deal." He reached across the table to shake, but she eyed his hand as if it were a venomous snake.

"Don't you want to know how long the trial will be and what the terms are?"

"We can talk about them Saturday. Anywhere that isn't here."

"As long as it's strictly a business appointment," she clarified, and *man,* she was the most suspicious and independent person he'd ever met. No doubt a result of constantly having to reshuffle the cards she'd been dealt.

"Until you say otherwise."

A quick handshake later and, look at that, they were planning a wedding.

CHAPTER 7

Over the next few days, Levi learned something troubling about himself. He had lost his touch with the ladies. Not only had Beckett mind-tricked him into throwing a wedding at his restaurant, but his driving-challenged niece had argued her way behind the wheel of his truck.

What had started out as an empty parking lot lesson on staying between the lines had jumped the curb, and Paisley was showing him all hundred-and-thirty-seven reasons she was a three-time-fail in the practical driving exam.

"You want to try to stay in the middle of the lane," he said, flexing his right butt cheek as if it could somehow keep them from sideswiping the parked cars, which were close enough to kiss.

"Okay. But then it feels like I'm too close to the oncoming cars," Paisley said, jerking the wheel hard to the left. The *thump-thump*

of the tires crossing over the yellow reflec-
tors and into the next lane matched his
booming heart rate. "Better?"

"Try to look over your shoulder before
changing lanes."

"Oh, right." With a beaming smile, Paisley
leaned forward and looked over her shoulder, but didn't change lanes so much as
swerve left.

Levi's phone rang, and he automatically
sent it to voice mail, but not before Paisley
glanced at the screen, causing her to drift
right, back into the slow lane.

"It's against the law to be on the phone
and drive at the same time."

She looked at him as if he were dense.
"My phone's in my backpack." As if to
prove her point, a muffled ring came from
the back seat.

"That was more of a reminder to keep
your eyes and focus on the road," he said.

"Gotcha," she said — to him.

His phone rang again. And again, she
glanced his way. Slapping her hand over her
mouth, she laughed.

"Eyes on the road," he said.

He disconnected the call, only to hear
Paisley's phone go off again. His niece
didn't look, but she did smile. "It's prob-

ably Grandma. She's calling to check on us."

"I'll call her back after I drop you off at home."

"You know she's just going to keep calling until one of us breaks and answers. And when that doesn't happen, she'll start calling my dads, which will freak Gray out. And since I'm driving . . ."

That left Levi.

He ran a hand down his face, wondering when his life had spun so far off course. Usually, he could deal with his mom, Paisley, and the other two guys who made up their unconventional family. It wasn't like him to avoid responsibility, especially when that responsibility was family. But lately, he'd been so busy, he was sending more and more calls to voice mail, missing softball practice with his city league. He'd even slept through dessert at the last family dinner.

It must be exhaustion, he thought. He'd pulled one too many hours at the bar. The guys had been bugging him to hire more help, but what he really needed was another Levi, someone who could run orders, work the bar, and help Gus out in the kitchen from time to time. Especially if he wanted to get his boat ready to set sail.

His phone rang, and Paisley laughed. Levi

sighed long and hard, knowing that a call was never just a call when it came to Ida Rhodes. It was a conversation, confession, and cross-examination. And that was if she'd had her second coffee.

He answered. "Hey, Ma."

"Levi. Are you okay?" Ida asked, her intonation betraying her Greek roots. "I've been sitting here worried out of my mind, trying to reach you all day."

"Told you," Paisley mouthed to him.

"Eyes on the road," he mouthed back, pointing two fingers in her direction, then out the windshield. "I'm fine, Ma. It's just been one of those crazy days."

"Too crazy to call your mother?" The worry in Ida's voice was as real as the guilt she was serving up.

"I was going to call you after I took Paisley home."

"The doctors tell me yours was the most painful birth they ever witnessed. Encouraged me to take the drugs, but I said no. No to the drugs. I will endure this for my son. And he doesn't even answer when I call, leaving a mother to imagine the worst," she said, and Levi could hear the fake tears Ida was working hard to produce.

Born on the island of Crete, Ida Rhodes took her oath as a Greek mother seriously.

She held advanced degrees in worrying, micromanaging, and extreme couponing. And when it came to her family, her love knew no boundaries. Neither did her nosiness.

"I'm with Paisley," he explained. "We are practicing for her driver's test and —"

"Don't tell her!" Paisley yelled, her foot more than tapping the brake.

Levi dropped the phone, his head jerking around at the cars swerving to avoid a collision. "Wide open road, kiddo. Wide open road. Remember, we go with the flow of traffic," Levi said, more calmly than he felt.

"Then don't tell people my business," Paisley said, accelerating to a whopping twenty-five in a thirty-five zone. "Gawd, now if I fail, Yaya will know I failed."

"Tell her she'll do just great," Ida said from the floorboard.

Levi picked up the phone. "Now's not a good time, Ma."

There was a beat. "Should I call her phone instead?"

"No." He turned to Paisley. "Grandma says you'll do great."

Paisley leaned over to yell into his phone, pulling the steering wheel with her. "Thanks, Yaya! Love you!"

"Love you too, Sweet P," Ida said, and

162

when Levi didn't relay the message, because he'd reached out and grabbed the wheel to angle them into the center of the lane, Ida got stern. "Tell her."

"Mom, she needs to focus on driving." On how close to the curb she was again. Or, perhaps, the guy behind them who kept flashing his brights.

Satisfied that Paisley had things under control for the moment, Levi turned and lifted an apologetic hand. The guy lifted a well-deserved finger their way.

"She needs to know her grandmother loves her."

"Grandma loves you," he passed along.

"Love you too!" P said, again with the swerving.

"Okay, really gotta go." The stop sign ahead of them was getting closer by the second, and he needed to make sure she stopped.

"Oh, okay." Which was followed by a long, impatient sigh. "I can tell you have your hands full — I didn't mean to be a bother. I'll let you go."

Knowing his mom was lonely and missing Michelle, he asked, "Did you need something?"

"Now that you mention it. Someone accidentally moved my pink craft box to the top shelf in the basement."

"I did. You wanted to make room for your holiday things and asked me to move it to that exact spot."

"Because it was Christmas. Now it's spring. What am I going to do with holiday-themed supplies in spring?" she wondered aloud. "My pink box has spring-appropriate supplies that I need before my scrapbooking class tomorrow." She let out a long-suffering sigh. "But I don't want to bother you, since things are *crazy* there. I'll find a way to reach it myself."

"No, Mom." God, the last time she got out the ladder, Levi spent three hours in the ER while she had her head stitched up. "I'll come over after I drop P off at home." Which would eat up any time he might have had to swing by his boat and change into a shirt that wasn't sweat-soaked before the dinner rush.

"If you feel that strongly about it, I'll wait. Be sure to drive safe and ask Paisley how her day was. When I dropped off her lunch this afternoon, I got a feeling something was wrong. And you know how accurate my feelings are."

After successfully predicting three Powerball numbers in a row, Ida began telling people she had "the sight." It didn't matter that she hadn't purchased any of the three lotto tickets, or that she hadn't successfully predicted anything since.

"Will do. And don't even touch the ladder," he said, ending the call before Ida could talk him into putting her on speaker so she could ask Paisley herself.

"What happened to the twenty bucks you got for lunch?" he asked Paisley.

"How do you always know everything?" she accused. "Are you on the dads' text thread?"

"Yes, but I was referring to the twenty I gave you last night."

"Oh, right."

"Who else gave you money?" And how long had she been fleecing him?

"No one. And how do you know I didn't spend it on lunch?"

"Because you're a terrible liar." She got that from her mom, since her dad was a world-class liar. "And Yaya told me she brought you a hot meal for lunch today."

Her eyes remained locked on the road. "I can't talk about this right now. I need to focus on the stop sign ahead."

Levi coughed "bullshit" into his hand, but her gaze never strayed. Even with her entire focus on the stop sign, Levi's body tensed as his truck jerked to a halt, practically bumper-kissing the car in front of them. The car moved, and Paisley shot forward, covering the six feet in the blink of an eye, before slamming on the brake.

The scent of burned rubber and barely avoided death filled the car. Levi sat back and let out a breath when Paisley took a cautious look to the left, and then —

Whoa, Levi was pushed back into his seat with the force of all nine hundred horses simultaneously activated as his one-way looker raced through the intersection, only to apply the brakes hard on the other side, dropping their speed by twenty before settling on a solid nine miles under the posted speed limit.

"Are you excited about the ski trip?"

"What?" She rolled her eyes. "No."

"Eyes on the road."

"What is up with everyone talking about the ski trip? Even Mrs. Kale stopped class to talk about the ski trip. She doesn't interrupt her lecture to let someone go to the bathroom, but Olivia Humbert talked for the whole last ten minutes of class about skiing."

"The parent permission slips are due Friday," he said, sitting on his hand so he wouldn't reach out and grab the wheel. "I thought you were excited to go?"

"I'm over it."

Fine with him. Levi was over it the minute he discovered the dog-eared article titled TOP TEN REASONS WHY SPRING IS A FITTING TIME FOR A FLING in her laundry basket. In fact, the moment his niece discovered boys, Levi and the dads started brainstorming how to get the trip canceled. He'd added it to next week's PTA agenda, Emmitt was working on gaining his mom group's support, and, in case all else failed, Gray had signed up to be one of the parent chaperones.

But Gray couldn't be everywhere at once, leaving unsupervised moments for girls and boys to sneak off and get into the kind of trouble that girls and boys have been getting into for centuries. So this news should have him fist-bumping the air. Only, his mom was right — something was up with Paisley.

He hated to admit it, but his sweet, rational niece had been taken over by hormones. There wasn't much she wouldn't do to get alone time with a cute boy. And she'd started planning for this trip freshman year when her best gal pal, Phoebe, asked her to be bunkmates. On her nightstand sat a journal with clippings of skiwear, makeup styles, and winter hair tips dedicated solely to this trip. She'd even blown a year's worth of babysitting on the new ski jumper hanging in her closet.

A jumper that was wholly and completely Emmitt's fault. Because when Paisley pointed to the glimmering gray-and-pink belted number in a store window, Emmitt had the genius insight to say that if she wanted a glorified skinsuit, she'd have to buy it herself. So Paisley, being the exact image of her mama, applied to be an after-school babysitter to every family in the neighborhood and was in such high demand, she charged more per hour than her friend Owen, who worked at the skateboard shop in the mall.

Her "being over" this trip wasn't possible.

"Do you even care why I don't want to go?" she asked.

While the female-aware male in him, who knew talking would lead to tears, wanted to say nothing and avoid being the cause of a nineteen-car pileup, the devoted uncle who'd held Michelle's lifeless hand and vowed to give Paisley a full and happy life knew his niece needed to talk.

"If you want to tell me," he ventured softly.

"No." She sounded appalled. "And why is everyone acting like this trip is the most important thing in the world?"

Last weekend, she had been the main one of those somebodies. Actually claiming, when Gray voiced his concern over her going on the ski trip when she'd never skied, that her life depended on going, and to not go would be social suicide.

"Hello?" she went on. "It's not the SATs or college essays. It's a ski trip. We've all been skiing, right? Or at least everyone in my grade has but me. How fun would that be? Me on the bunny slopes while my friends are doing black-diamond runs."

"Not everyone skis," he reminded her. "And I bet if you talked to Phoebe and Owen, they'd hang with you," he said, referring to the other two that made up Paisley's bestie trio.

"I don't want to ruin their time. Plus, they know me. Know that I don't even really like the snow. It's cold, and it gives the worst face tans."

"But it's also fun," he tossed out, noticing that the light a few hundred yards ahead of them had turned red. "I thought you were happy because you got on the same bus as Owen."

"He's on the boy's bus," she said, and Levi wanted to thank whoever had decided to divide the buses by sexes and not grades this year, only he was too distracted by the big, bright, red light directly in front of them.

"Plus, it's so deceiving. You know?"

"Boys, or the distance between us the red light ahead?"

"Snow." She laughed. "It looks fluffy and soft, but when it's been skied, it gets packed down and becomes unforgiving. So when you fall, it's like falling on cement," she said, as if she hadn't just announced she'd never been skiing. "And you know how easily I bruise. I just healed from soccer season, and I want to spend at least a month bruise-free, because once club soccer starts up, it's all jeans and pants."

The bumpers ahead of them got closer and closer, and Levi's foot pressed harder and harder into the floor, so hard his butt and thighs lifted off the passenger seat and he gripped the oh-shit handle with enough force to tear it off the ceiling.

"The soccer coach in me is happy you're already thinking about next season, but the uncle in me doesn't want you to miss out on the fun parts of high school." He rested a cautionary hand on her thigh. "Be aware, the light ahead is red."

"Even Owen is excited. And he hates school trips," she went on, paying neither him nor the light any attention.

"I remember my school ski trip. It was the highlight of junior year for your dad and me." Levi grimaced even as he said it, because — *Red light. Red light. Red light* — he knew exactly what had made it so memorable.

Senior ski bunnies. He and Emmitt had individually conquered several slopes that year. And that was before this swipe-right generation that considered third base casual dating.

"You might want to slowly start applying the brake —"

"Not everyone is going, so it won't be like I'm the only junior staying behind," she said. "Not that I'd go to school that week. I was thinking of using it as extra prep time for the SATs —"

"— The brake is the pedal on the left."

"Or maybe I should hang out with Daddy more. He still gets lonely missing Mom, and how can I go on a trip and pretend to have fun when I know he'll be back at the resort thinking about how Mom was supposed to chaperone, not him? And Mom was going to teach me how to ski, but now she's dead and can't. . . ."

Levi was torn between yanking her into his arms and yanking the parking brake when Paisley finally decided she'd stop for the light. Inches from the car in front, she found the correct pedal and pushed it down with enough force that he could have sworn his back two truck tires momentarily came off the ground.

Oblivious to how close they'd come to colliding, Paisley spun on him. Angrily wiping at her tears, she snapped, "So no, under no circumstances will I ever go on that trip. Stop asking me!"

CHAPTER 8

"At least it's better than being stood up at the altar," Cecilia, the owner of Holy Cannoli, whispered in Beckett's ear.

"I'm just early," Beckett explained, regretting her decision to leave Gregory home.

Her last client of the day had been a no-show, which placed Beckett at the bakery with an hour to spare — and no one to talk to.

Unwilling to commit to a dinner date, and unable to find an hour of free time, Beckett had agreed to meet Levi for coffee and a cake tasting.

He claimed the male perspective needed to be represented — she was sure it was an excuse to micromanage. Today's goal was to prove she was handling shit. That's why she'd chosen a location that would show how boring and girly planning a wedding could be. And while a cake tasting wasn't the worst way a guy could spend his after-

173

noon, looking through the cake designer's three-hundred-page portfolio was a bit more involved than ordering outdoor heaters.

Beckett glanced out the window at the slick road and passing cars, still wet from an earlier shower. She hadn't fared much better. On her way to the café, she'd been caught in the drizzle, and her jeans were damp and her hair frizzy — the exact wrong look when trying to appear put-together.

"Or is he late?" Cecilia said. "Seven husbands, I know the signs."

"Just looking for a refill, not advice."

"I know I may not look like much now, but at one time, men came from all around to be waited on by me. Even asked me to pose. Not just photos, either; real artists. Painters. Some of the greats."

"I thought da Vinci was rumored to be gay." When Cecilia turned to walk away, Beckett lifted her cup. "The refill?"

The woman glanced at one of the three dozen clocks lining the wall, all rimmed with antiqued brass and all set to Vatican City time. Her crop of red hair, a shade that didn't appear in nature, shook with judgment. "Maybe you should wait to see if the cake tasting is a go."

Time seemed to pass at sloth speed. While Levi wasn't technically late for their cake tasting appointment, Cecilia's puckered lips implied that Beckett was entering the groom-having-second-thoughts territory.

Not that Levi was the groom. This meeting was for two professionals to select a cake for their joint client. The jitters in her belly were in anticipation of cake before dinner. Nothing more.

"It's a go," she said, holding up her mug for another refill. Cecilia didn't look so convinced. "Really, my client should be here any minute."

Cecilia sucked on her teeth. "That's a lot of mascara for a client."

"That's a lot of coffee for just two customers." There was only one other person in the café.

"The place is empty because my soap is on. Everyone knows not to interrupt my soaps."

"Your posted hours should reflect that."

"New policy, starting now." The older woman dug a pudgy hand into her rotund hip. "Bottomless coffee and free internet starts when the cake tasting begins. So order up or sip slowly."

She lifted the pot, but before the first drop hit the bottom of the oversized mug, Beckett's cell rang.

"Do you still want a refill?" Cecilia asked,

as if it were a foregone conclusion that Beckett had been stood up.

"It's not him," she announced. "So yes, to the top."

Beckett waited until Cecilia was out of sight to check the name on her phone screen, in case it was Levi, which — *thank you, God* — it was not. The caller was her no-show client, Kevin Porter, a CPA whose company was moving him to New York to run the office there. Kevin was expected to start in less than two weeks, so his company had hired Beckett to assist with the move and make all the necessary arrangements for a relocation.

If all went well, Beckett could be looking at her first corporate client, responsible for all relocations in and out of the Boston and Rome offices.

"Kevin," Beckett greeted. "How are you?"

"Confused," Kevin said. "We have an appointment. You're not here."

"Yes, we did have an appointment at two. I rang your bell three times, but no one answered." Even though it was clear from the voices inside the house that more than one someone was home. "I also called to see if maybe you hadn't heard the bell and left a message." Then she'd waited twenty minutes, huddled under her raincoat on a cold stoop.

When the clock struck half-past, she called it.

"I was on a video conference with the office. As soon as it ended, I opened the door to find you gone."

"It's nearly three-thirty."

"Like I said, I was on with the office," Kevin explained, as if that clarified any confusion. "But I'm free now."

"Unfortunately, I'm meeting another client in a few minutes. But we can reschedule for Monday." Beckett opened her planner and flipped the page twice. Completely booked. So was Tuesday. And Wednesday was art class. "Actually, how about Thursday? Does three work for you?"

"No. Thursday doesn't work for me at all. How about tomorrow?"

"Tomorrow is Sunday." The only day of the week that was all hers. Although Beckett's business was growing so fast that she'd spent the last three Sundays dealing with overflow from the previous weeks. In addition to her regular clients, she'd organized spring inventory for a boutique in town, arranged transportation and lodging for a visiting team of doctors, and found a real estate company a new office manager.

Being busy was a good problem to have,

but also exhausting.

"I can't. But maybe I can swing by your place after my last client on Monday. It would be late, around seven."

"I prefer tomorrow," Kevin said, obviously not giving two shits about Beckett's availability. "There's a lot of hours in a Sunday. I'm sure you can find a slot for me or rearrange your schedule."

"I rearranged my schedule to fit you in today." Which had knocked one of her regulars to Monday.

"Well, I'm free now. Or you can come tomorrow after your last client."

Beckett could practically hear the guy writing in his calendar. "It's not that. I try to keep Sunday reserved as my family and personal time."

"What exactly happens during this 'personal time' of yours?" a different, much sexier male voice inquired.

Beckett looked up from her planner to find Levi. A damp blue Henley clung to his I-lift-kegs-for-fun shoulders, and his hair stood up in wet spikes. The man even wore rain well. Instead of resembling a drowned cat, he looked like Aquaman rising out of the ocean.

"Asking for a friend," he added.

Beckett covered the mouthpiece with her

178

palm and whispered, "I still have five me-time minutes left, so can we not do this now?"

"Excuse me?" said Kevin, who apparently had the owl-like hearing.

"Not you," Beckett apologized. "Some guy was trying to get my table."

"Some guy?" Elbows on the table, he leaned in and whispered. "We're planning a wedding, Girl Wonder. You can call me Levi. Unless you prefer something more personal. Maybe a nickname? I like Babe, Sugar, or Sweets, but I must admit I'm a little partial to Hott Stuff — with two Fs and two Ts." All smiles and easy confidence, he picked up her mug and took a leisurely sip. "The only no-go is Boo."

"Get your own!" she mouthed, unable to concentrate on what Kevin was saying.

"You mean, 'Get your own, Hott Stuff.' And it's sweet of you to treat."

Before she could tell him to buy his own coffee, he was gone.

"And I will need all that on a spreadsheet," Kevin continued, as if Beckett had been listening and taking thorough notes. "As for the boxes, I want each one numbcrcd and tagged with easy-to-read labels. Lct's just make that printed labels, to be sure."

"Of course. All these things can be discussed at our next meeting. I'm afraid that over the phone, I might miss an important detail," Beckett said, reminding herself of the big payoff if this move went well. "So did you decide Monday at seven or Thursday at three?"

"I decided on Sunday, but you don't seem to be listening."

Beckett closed her eyes and counted back from three. It was a trick she'd learned during a support group for caretakers that she belonged to. It was meant to clear the head and lower stress levels. When she reached one and opened her eyes, she found Levi watching her. And next to her planner was a long white plate with eight mini slices of cake.

"You already picked out the cake flavors?" she whispered.

"You seemed a little hangry," he said. "I got you some protein."

"Kevin, I'm going to have to call you back. My next meeting just walked in."

"This is a team effort, Beckett. We all need to do our part, sacrifice what needs to be sacrificed to make this new position possible," Kevin said, as if she were benefiting from his promotion. "You came highly recommended, which is why my boss hired you to begin with. It is also why he is paying you so much. Can you meet tomorrow, or do I need to notify work that we need a concierge with the time to dedicate to this project?"

Kevin was 5'5", balding, and as excitable as a Jack Russell at the dog park. When he felt slighted, his words spiked, and his voice traveled farther than a carrier pigeon. So it wasn't a surprise when Levi lifted a brow, which translated as *Do you need me to punch someone?* No doubt he could hear every word.

"That won't be necessary, Kevin. I can swing by tomorrow morning." That would still give her the afternoon to herself.

"I have an early tee time, so eleven would be better."

Not for Beckett, it wouldn't. By the time she addressed all his needs and answered his questions, she wouldn't get home until after two, leaving her little time to relax before starting dinner. She'd been thinking more along the lines of eight, but Kevin had already disconnected.

She penciled in eleven on the next day's page, even though she might as well have used pen, since she doubted she'd be able to get Kevin to agree to an earlier time. God forbid he should miss his tee time.

"Do you always let your clients speak to

you like that?" Levi asked.

"Yes, when he stands between me and a potentially huge corporate client," she shot back, hoping the surge of shame she felt for giving in to a bully didn't show on her face. "Plus, right now, he's my only corporate client."

"It still doesn't give him the right to talk to you like that."

No, it didn't, but honestly, she hadn't noticed the level of disrespect until Levi said something. And wasn't that embarrassing.

When had people started speaking to her like that? More importantly, when had she started allowing people to speak to her like that? And it wasn't just clients. Her dad and brother were no better. Jeffery never raised his voice like Kevin, but his constant dismissal of her efforts was equally troublesome. And even though Thomas had a hard time controlling his emotions, there were times he knew better and dismissed her anyway.

What was most concerning, though, was how angry Levi looked. Not at her, but on her behalf. Which was new to her. She was comfortable with her role as protector. Shielding her family, her friends, her animals-in-training, and the families she worked with. Even her job placed her as a caretaker.

"Maybe you need to find some new prospects," Levi suggested, as if she hadn't had the same idea a dozen times over the last ten minutes.

"I'm working on it." She held up a stack of papers that had to do with the wedding. "Kind of have my hands full right now."

"Does the bride-to-be know you're stretched thin?"

Beckett's hackles came up. "Annie doesn't have to worry. There's no way I'd let her wedding suffer."

"My concern is for you," he clarified. "Most brides struggle to plan a wedding and keep life together without dropping any balls. You're trying to do both *and* grow a business."

"I've juggled more in the past."

"You shouldn't have to."

The concern in his voice made it hard to maintain eye contact, so Beckett studied the plate of cakes. "Is that carrot cake?" she asked, pointing to the first cake in the lineup. "Annie hates carrot cake."

"Yes, but I happen to know that you love carrot cake." He slid her a fork. "After that call, I figured a selfish slice was in order."

When she didn't immediately dig in, he cut off a big bite, then handed it to her. Her belly growled loudly, and he chuckled.

She wasn't trying to be stubborn, but being cosseted by Levi was as unfamiliar as it was unsettling. It left her feeling vulnerable. And she hated feeling vulnerable. Thankfully, right then, she was too hungry to feel anything more than cream-cheese frosting with a hint of nutmeg hitting her mouth.

"So good," she said, licking the frosting off her fork.

"I would have asked what Pecker's preferred cake of choice was, but" — Levi made a big deal of looking on the surrounding chairs and under the table — "it appears you don't bring pets into other people's establishments?"

"Nope. I save them just for you."

"See, I knew you liked me," he said, making her smile on what had become a shitty day.

"I wouldn't go as far as like, but you're not pissing me off at the moment."

He laughed. "Forward movement. Alone time. I'll take it."

"Don't get used to it. Gregory's at home because I'm on my scooter, and there aren't enough chicken-sized sweaters in the country to protect him from the giant mud-slushie that exploded over downtown."

"You drove on your scooter?" He shrugged

out of his coat. "Here. You must be freezing."

"It's actually hot in here," she lied, because she was afraid if she took his coat, her walls would no longer be strong enough to protect her from Levi's charm.

Locking gazes with her, he coughed loudly into his hand, and it sounded a lot like *bullshit.*

She ignored this and took another bite. "I hope the other flavors are even better, or I'm going to have a hard time justifying not picking this one."

"Wait until you try the lemon cake with limoncello buttercream frosting," he said. "It's my mom's favorite. She had it at her wedding. So did Michelle. And Paisley asks for it every birthday and Christmas."

"I guess I know what you'll be having at your wedding."

"Oh, I don't know if I want a wedding," he said, his admission catching her off guard. She knew why *she'd* ruled out marriage, but she'd always imagined Levi to be a married-with-kids-and-white-picket-fence kind of guy. "Why do you look so surprised?"

"You were the one who insisted you were good husband material."

"I'm fantastic husband material. But I've

185

already raised my kid; I'm getting ready to send her off to college. Another commitment is the last thing on my mind. What's your excuse?"

"Besides the sexist vows and patriarchal traditions?"

"You're trying to tell me a garter toss scared you off?"

"I'm not scared," she said, scratching a spot on her arm. "I'm realistic."

Marriage required unwavering trust and unconditional love. Even a mother's love had buckled under the conditions Beckett's world brought to the table. If she ever did find love, she'd be foolish to believe it would last forever.

"Realistic?" He laughed. "You wear a cape and talk to animals."

"That's different."

"How?"

He gave her an expectant look, and she blew out a breath. "What can I say? Marriage isn't for everyone. And I've learned it isn't for me."

He leaned forward on his elbows, his expression serious. "What kind of asshole taught you that lie?"

"What makes you think it's a lie?" she asked.

"Because I've watched you with Tommy,

with your friends." He shook his head. "You love to love. And your heart's too big not to have wanted someone of your own to love at one point. I'm sorry that whoever he was took that from you."

She drew in a deep breath. "It wasn't one someone. But wouldn't that simplify things."

One someone could be a fluke. Two some-ones, a little spell of bad luck. But Beckett's life had been a revolving door of someones who left at the first sign of trouble. Which made secretly wishing for someone to stick all the more ludicrous.

Around them, the rain continued to trickle down the pitched roof and against the glass panes. He tilted his head, his deep blue eyes searching hers in that assessing way that had her wondering how much he saw; how much she'd already given away.

"Was yours?" she asked after a few mo-ments. "One someone?"

"Nah." He shook his head. "Three some-ones."

"All at once?"

"Actually, yes." He laughed. "But not how you're thinking. It was a mom and her two sons. Vikki, Jaden, and Cole." He cleared his throat and glanced briefly away.

"How long were you with them?" she

asked, because a guy like Levi was all or nothing. If he was dating a single mom, he'd view it as dating her whole family.

"We were together three years. Two of those sharing a house. She trusted me with her kids, so I took that to mean she trusted me with her heart. Turned out, I was only half right."

Three years was a long time to love two kids, only to lose them. She'd worked with enough grieving families at the pediatric hospital to understand that kind of loss went bone-deep, tunneling through until it reached the soul. With time, those holes healed, but the person was never the same.

"What happened?"

He looked at her, his eyes guarded, his tone careful. "I made it too easy."

She blinked. "What?"

"I know, crazy. But that's what she said." He sat back and gave a humorous laugh. "I guess in her mind, when someone doesn't have to work for things, they become unimportant. I became unimportant. So she found someone who made her work every day for a spot in his life."

"Are you kidding?" She gasped. "That, right there, is why I don't date. Life's already hard. Why would she want someone to make it harder?"

"It's a mind fuck, that's for sure." He lifted a big shoulder and let it drop, that easygoing twinkle in his eyes. But beneath it, she could sense a longing and a loneliness, which resonated deep within her. He was playing it cool, but the loss still clung to him like barnacles to an unmanned vessel, increasing surface drag and hindering momentum.

"Do you miss them?" she asked.

"Vikki? No. The boys?" He released a big breath. "It's been three years since I've seen them, and I still hang their stockings, just in case they come to visit their grandparents. It's been so long, I don't even know what they're into, but I can't help myself. Eternal optimist, Gray calls me."

"That must be hard," she said. "When my mom left, Thomas was too young to remember her. But every Mother's Day, he still wants to make Judy a card and mail it."

"Do you?"

She snorted. "No. But I keep them in a box, tied with a white ribbon, in case . . . hell, I don't know why I keep them."

"Because beneath your tough-girl exterior and superhero armor, you're a romantic, Beck," he said, without an ounce of judgment in his voice.

Her phone pinged, rescuing her from the

189

conversation.

"Sorry. I need to check this." She glanced at the screen, and it was Kevin, wanting to remind her about the printer labels. She texted back that she'd bring them.

"Was that Bruce?"

"God, no. We broke up by text while I was bathing Gregory Pecker," she challenged. "You still think I'm a romantic?"

"Sorry. The only words I heard were 'you,' 'bathing,' and 'pecker,' " he said, a slow smile curving at his lips. "It doesn't get more romantic than that."

"You're hopeless," she said.

"And you're single," he pointed out. "I happen to know a great guy, if you're looking."

"Definitely not. Looking."

"I get it. We have to work up to peckers and bathtubs." He took a bite of a chocolate cake with raspberry filling and ganache frosting. "You have to try this."

She did, and it was delicious and decadent. "So good. Have you tried the peanut-butter caramel cake?"

Her phone pinged again. It was Kevin. Again. He wanted to remind her that if he wasn't home at exactly eleven, she should wait. She didn't text him back.

"I made a few calls to some contacts,"

190

Levi said. "Got some quotes on extra lighting, outdoor heaters, and a temporary dance floor. If you'd rather go with your contacts, no biggie. Just thought I'd get some ideas on paper."

He handed her a spreadsheet, a very thorough spreadsheet that contained the names, contact info, quotes, and details on delivery and pickup, for more companies than just lighting and outdoor heater rentals.

"This is great," she said. "But it must have taken you hours."

He shrugged. "I had some extra time. Plus, I've worked with most of these guys before. I didn't look into flowers or decoration or companies that handle the aesthetic side of weddings, but I can if you want."

"No, you've done plenty. And I have a lot of contacts on the aesthetic side." She smiled at that.

Her phone pinged. This time, it was her dad, asking when she'd be home and if it was his night to cook dinner. She quickly texted back that yes, in fact, it was. But all he had to do was throw a frozen pizza in the oven.

She set her phone down. "I made a few calls of my own. I have notes scribbled down in here somewhere. But I was wondering if you've thought about my proposal."

"You mean, when you blackmailed me into giving you a trial run."

"I didn't blackmail you. I just said it was a condition of your micromanaging this wedding."

He sampled another bite of cake and took his time chewing. She took her time watching the way his throat worked, how he licked his lips after each bit. The man was as mouthwatering as the cake.

"It's called overseeing, and for me to be comfortable moving forward with using your company as a delivery service, I'd need to be involved in that, too."

She loved how straightforward he was. There was no guessing involved when it came to Levi, which meant she always knew where she stood. And if she knew what was expected, it was less likely that she would disappoint.

"I understand that," she said. "But I want to make sure you know that what happened before, with the crab cakes, won't happen again."

"Glad to hear it." He forked up another piece.

"It was bad timing," she felt the need to explain. "My dad had just started on a big project, and my brother had been switched to a new classroom at school. Instead of staying with Thomas, my dad dropped him off at the curb. Thomas went to the wrong room and panicked. When the school couldn't locate him, they called me."

"Beck," he said gently. "You already apologized. I accepted. You don't have to explain anything."

"I want to. I know how put out you were by my decisions that day, so I need to make sure you know that I didn't bail because I was having fun or didn't feel like going to work. It took six hours and three search-and-rescue teams to find Thomas."

"I'm glad you found him and that he wasn't hurt."

"I was so caught up in all the what-ifs that I completely spaced on calling you or the firehouse until the next day. And even though it was an emergency, my behavior was still unprofessional."

"It's hard to keep from drowning when you're struggling to keep everyone else afloat," he said, and something old and rusty shifted inside her chest.

"That's exactly how I feel," she admitted, wondering how someone, a man she assumed she had nothing in common with, could understand things even her closest friends didn't. "How did you know?"

"Personal experience," he admitted. "Between my family, the restaurant, and the marina, there are times I barely have time to sleep, let alone deal with the piles of résumés and hire new staff."

"That's one of my specialties, you know, facilitating hires for small business owners. I could help you," she offered.

"Okay, Consider It Done, what would you do different from what I'm doing now?"

"I'd recommend that instead of trying to fill all the openings, you place an ad for a senior office manager who knows the managerial side of a business. That person would conduct interviews, train new hires, manage the schedule, and make sure bills go out on time and product arrives before you even know you're low."

"Are you applying?"

"To run your office? Not my calling. I'm offering to familiarize myself with your company, so that I can see what is needed. I'd place a new ad for an office manager and then narrow down the candidates. Only when I've narrowed it down to the top three will you meet with them. After you hire one, who I guarantee will be highly qualified, your new manager will take care of filling out the rest of your staff and making sure the office runs smoothly." His expression had her pausing. "What?"

"I never imagined a personal concierge could do that."

"Do you think I'm just some glorified delivery girl?" she asked, pissed that those silly words had the power to hurt. "I have been hired to do the exact thing I described for a few shops and one of the hotels in the area. Do you want references?"

Her chin high, her eyes two narrow slits, she was making it clear that she did not like to be underestimated. Especially by him.

"I wasn't surprised, Beck. I was impressed. You impress me," he said.

Beckett couldn't be sure whether it was heartburn from her three cups of coffee on an empty stomach, but warm flutters filled her chest. That was one of the nicest things anyone had ever said about her.

Her cheeks went hot at the unexpected compliment. "I'm not sure how to respond. Most days I'm barely holding it together, which is a far cry from impressive."

"Then you don't see yourself the way I now see you," he said, and when he didn't laugh, Beckett knew he believed what he said. "We're all just holding it together. I've let things, important things, fall through the cracks. Treaded water more times than I'd like to admit."

She thought about the heavy responsibilities placed on his shoulders — some by choice, and most, she was learning, not — and wondered how he would manage to pull off a six-month sailing trip. "When did it get easier?"

"For me? When I admitted I needed help."

Accepting help, as far as Beckett could tell, took the ability to let go and trust others. Two things her childhood hadn't allowed for. The only way to keep her world spinning was to maintain control of all the moving pieces. One wrong move, and it was checkmate. As for trust, that meant being vulnerable and opening herself up to the possibility of disappointment. Which brought her to the third thing she didn't do.

She'd rather go it alone than suffer through any more disappointment. But she was beginning to understand that planning this wedding alone was no longer a possibility. Annie had enlisted Beckett's help, and Emmitt had asked for Levi's, so it didn't matter that Beckett preferred to work alone. Her clients' wishes always came first.

And right now, Annie and Emmitt were her clients. So when her phone pinged, she set it aside and asked, "About this cake . . . Emmitt give you any thoughts on what flavor he's leaning toward?"

"Nothing more than happy wife, happy life."

"Smart man." Her phone pinged. She ignored it. It pinged again.

"Want me to handle that dick for you?" he asked.

"No. I handle my own dick."

"I believe you," he deadpanned, and they both laughed. "I also believe that I need to try a few more cake flavors before deciding. How about you?"

"I'd better not. It's almost dinnertime, and I have to make a few calls to prepare for my meeting with Kevin tomorrow morning."

"After a client like him, you deserve a little more of life's icing before returning to reality."

She wanted to agree, but having her icing and eating it too wasn't a luxury her schedule afforded. And even though this was her last appointment of the day, she still had a million-and-one things to do — just as she knew Levi did. Not that you could tell that from the laid-back way he reclined in the chair, his long legs sprawled out under the table, taking up more than their share of space.

"Icing doesn't pay the bills," she teased.

"You deserve a hell of a lot more than icing," he said with a soft protectiveness that took her by surprise, made her believe that maybe she did deserve more. Tempted her into ordering *two* more platters of cake, because with him, she didn't have to have all the answers.

She could just breathe. Which was as unfamiliar a feeling as it was refreshing.

"What could a little more cake hurt," she said, and Levi smiled as if she'd made the right call. It shouldn't matter to her how he felt about her decisions, but today, it did.

"That's the spirit, Girl Wonder." Levi waved to Cecilia, who took her sweet time walking around the counter and across the café. Her red hair arrived before she did, and her irritation at being pulled away from her daily soap opera would linger long after she took their order.

"This the husband?" she asked Beckett.

"He's just a client," she said, although she was quickly learning that Levi could never be *just* anything.

Cecilia's gaze did a little Wimbledon action, back and forth between her two cake tasters. Beckett refused to elaborate on principle, since she'd explained the situation when she first arrived. Which left Levi to take the full force of Cecilia's glare.

"Does your mom know that you're tasting

with intentions? Because she was in here yesterday and didn't say a word about your getting hitched."

"We're here for Annie and Emmitt's cake tasting," Levi explained. "And we'd like a second platter." He named the seven new flavors they'd like to try.

Cecilia pulled the stub of a pencil from behind her ear but didn't write anything in her notebook — which was still securely in her apron front. "They know you're hijacking their tasting?"

"They know," Levi assured her.

"Because it's only twenty-five percent off on the first tasting. I don't reward stupidity," Cecilia said, clearly immune to his charm.

Must be nice, Beckett thought, wondering what the woman's secret was. "Remember, they hired me to plan their wedding? They know I'm here."

Cecilia jabbed her pencil at Levi. "And what about him?"

"He's along to make sure the male point of view is represented in all wedding decisions," Levi said, sending a wink Beckett's way.

Beckett winked back. "He can't pass up the chance to mansplain about his vast knowledge of wedding planning."

"Last I heard, this was your first wedding," he said.

"You two sure you're not a couple?"

"Absolutely not," Beckett said at the same time Levi said, "Working on it."

"We are not," she said to Cecilia. Then, to Levi, "We're not."

"Not a couple or not working on it?" Levi asked sweetly.

Beckett's face immediately heated — damn her Irish heritage — and her stomach went into a spin cycle.

"Huh." Cecilia was back at Wimbledon. "Well, like I said, one tasting per wedding, so if the real bride and groom come in asking for a tasting, they're going to have to pay full price. They know that?"

"They know," Beckett and Emmitt said in unison, which then had them laughing in unison.

Cecilia recited their order verbatim. On Levi's approval, she licked the tip of her pencil and wrote down the order. Pencil back behind her ear, she asked, "I suppose *she* wants a refill as well."

"*She* does," Beckett said, and as if the universe were proving a point, her phone vibrated with an incoming call. Levi watched Beckett watch her phone. Cecilia watched them suspiciously, as if they might

200

be dine-and-dashers.

A part of her itched to answer. Another part, though — the part she rarely let out to play — told her Levi was right. There was nothing wrong about winding down with a friend after a particularly difficult week.

She ignored the call. "Make that a refill with a heavy shot of grappa."

"I'll have to bill you extra for that. And we're not talking happy-hour prices, either." Cecilia eyeballed the clock over the cookie display. "Unless you want to wait eleven minutes?"

"No need to wait," Levi interrupted. "And make that two caffè correttos."

"Big spender, this one," Cecilia said, returning a few minutes later with the two adult coffees. "Cakes will be up in a minute."

Beckett took a sip and groaned as the Italian brandy went to work on her knotted muscles, the mug warming her hands. Levi did a good job of warming the rest of her. She appreciated his laid-back approach, perfectly timed humor, and the way he pushed her out of her comfort zone while never making her feel cornered.

"You ready to look at cake designs?" he asked, then did something unexpected. He opened the binder, which Cecilia had placed on the table when Beckett had first been seated, and gave careful consideration to each photograph.

This left Beckett with two options: Let him get lost in the bible of cake designs, many of which went out of date when Reagan was in office, or flip to the three she'd marked earlier, which she was sure Annie would love. The first option would keep them occupied until they finished their coffees and go a long way toward proving just how boring wedding errands could be. The second would wrap up the business for the day, leaving room to get personal.

Beckett avoided personal. Professional was more her speed. Even when she dated. But this meeting had already turned more personal than any date she could remember.

"I found a few I knew Annie would love." She flipped to the first one, an all-white cake with orchid blooms made from sugar and a floral cascade delicately iced on each individual tier.

"The first thing Emmitt would say is that orchids look like —"

"Moving on." She flipped to the second one. "This is a naked three-layer cake —"

"You remember, this is Emmitt we're talking about." He turned the page and stopped. "How about this one? It's simple and elegant. Annie will like the old-world romance of half-iced sides, and Emmitt won't feel emasculated by flowers and frills."

Beckett didn't know how to respond. The rustic cake, topped with fresh berries and a wreath made of forest greenery, was the third option, and hands-down her favorite. For all the same reasons Levi had articulated.

"I think it's perfect," she said.

"Don't sound so surprised," he teased. "I was raised by women, so I do have some taste. And as Michelle's man of honor, I made it through my share of tastings and dress fittings."

"Not so much surprised as impressed." It was a side to Levi that she hadn't expected. Yes, he was a flirt. And yes, he tended to focus on the humor in situations. But Beckett was so focused on that could-careless, life's-one-big-Jimmy-Buffett-song vibe he had going on, she'd completely missed the caring guy who put his family first and paid close attention to the small details in his loved ones' lives.

She'd come here expecting to prove to him that she was more than the chaos that surrounded her; instead, he'd been the one to show her a new and endearing Levi who was hard to resist.

"Your mom would be proud," she said. "She raised a good man."

Their eyes remained locked, and neither spoke as a meaningful silence, and something Beckett wasn't ready to admit, passed between them. They remained frozen in place, too afraid to speak and too afraid look away. Remembering how to breathe became difficult.

A loud buzzing came from her cell. She could answer it or stay in the moment. Either way, she'd be letting someone down. Indecision churned in her stomach.

"You know, it's okay to put yourself first sometimes," he said, as if reading her mind.

"Even when it feels selfish?"

"Think of it as self-preservation." He set his fork down. "You fight so hard for everyone else — don't forget to fight for yourself."

The phone wouldn't let up, Annie's wedding was a few weeks off, and it was nearing dinnertime. "With so much on my plate, it's easy to forget about me."

"Then I'll remind you." His voice was whisper-soft, his expression even softer, as he took a forkful of cake and held it out to her. "Open up for me."

They both knew he was talking about more than cake. Maybe it was the grappa, or maybe it was the small, hopeful smile he gave her, but she did.

She was too nervous to eat from his fork, but she did send the call to voice mail. Then, using her own fork, she tapped his as if in celebration. "To carrot cake."

"Is that what you'd do if you were putting yourself first? Sit here with me and share cake?"

Her first instinct was to look him right in the eyes and lie her little butt off. But he'd been so open with her, and if this was about learning to put herself first, then she didn't want to start off fibbing. So instead of shying away, she pushed through the uncertainty and discomfort of his open and honest interest, and even managed to return some of her own.

"Surprisingly, yes," she said honestly.

He seemed pleased by her admission, and that made her ridiculously happy.

"To you," he toasted and, *holy moly,* the look he sent her — heavy-lidded and heavy on the innuendo — while licking his fork clean made it clear that he'd rather be licking the icing right off her lips.

She swallowed her piece whole, then nearly choked on the growing sexual awareness between them. There were a dozen reasons she could list as to why crushing on

Levi was stupid, but she decided to save them for later. Right then, she wanted to pretend she was the kind of woman who regularly met sexy, single men during work hours to share cake and intimate conversation.

It had been a long while since she'd done that. Even longer since she'd felt this way.

"How about you?" she asked.

"This," he said, reaching across to give her hand a squeeze. She didn't squeeze back, but she didn't object to the contact. "Only instead of here, I'd have arranged for the tasting to happen a mile out, at dusk, on the deck of my boat. You, me, the sunset, and cake for two."

"Does cell service exist a mile out?"

"Beck, if that's what it takes to get you on my boat, just say the word, and I'll dismantle whatever satellites need dismantling."

Oh boy! Not only did she believe him, but she was just one of his double-barreled grins away from asking when it was anchors up. She couldn't remember any Steves or Bruces being so interested in getting to know her — like, really know her. In fact, Levi had asked more personal questions than all her past dates combined.

This was the most intimate first date she'd ever been on. And it wasn't even a date!

Beckett could only imagine what a real date with Levi would look like. She wasn't sure if she wanted to find out.

"Too bad I swore never to set foot in your cabin," she reminded him.

"I believe it was never, ever, ever. Lucky for us, my deck is reachable without having to pass through the master cabin. Although, I'm up to give you a tour belowdecks whenever you're ready."

Beckett was about to tell him that if he kept ticking off boxes like he was, she might not be able to resist a full tour of his boat, when the phone rang — again. This time, it was the shop phone.

"That was your daddy," Cecilia hollered, and every one of her warm flutters turned cold. "Said he tried calling you, but it went to voice mail."

Her heart thumped against her chest — no longer in a good way — as she looked at her cell. Seven missed calls from her dad. Three texts from Thomas.

"He wanted to know when you were coming home," Cecilia continued. "Said something about Thomas letting his pecker out and chasing it in the yard. Your dad tried to cage it when it got aggressive with the neighbor. From Karen's shouting in the background, I'd say he failed."

"He's referring to an emotional support rooster," Levi clarified.

"Whatever you kids are calling it, you better get home before Karen goes after him with her pistol. Chased off the last pecker to wrong her with a single shot. It's why Mr. Kipper walks with that funny limp."

That was what Beckett was afraid of. Last time Gregory found his way into Karen's garden, she chased him off with a pitchfork. "Can you call him back and tell him I'm on my way?"

Without waiting for an answer, she began collecting all her papers, which were haphazardly spread across the table, and shoved them into her bag. A pile of them fluttered to the floor.

"Dammit." She dropped to her knees, the tiles chilling her still-damp denim as she attempted to sweep the papers into a pile.

Levi crouched down, balancing on the balls of his feet. In one simple maneuver, he easily organized all the papers into an orderly stack and handed them over.

"You okay?" he asked.

No, she was so far from okay that she felt tears burning at the back of her throat. She cried when she was frustrated. And right then, she was frustrated as hell — at herself. For ignoring her responsibilities and pretending that she could play hooky without consequences. Pretending she was the kind of woman who could flirt with a sexy sailor over adult coffee.

She shoved the papers into her bag and stood. "No. Karen's made her feelings about Gregory clear." In a loud and harsh manner, which had Thomas listing all the rules of EMAs. "I am so sorry, but I have to go."

"Here, let me pay the bill, and I can drive you." Now he was standing, too.

"No. You enjoy the rest of the cakes. I already know that Annie would love the limoncello one. So if you think Emmitt would agree, then we'll go with that."

"At least take some of the cake home." He was flagging Cecilia as if they were on a sinking ship and she was in a rescue boat in the distance.

"I don't have time." Her heart was racing, her palms sweating. If she didn't get home in time, Thomas would likely call the police.

"Beck." He took her hand, and she spun around. "It's going to be okay."

"No, it's not. If I don't get home before Karen goes for her pitchfork, then Thomas will call 911 to report an assault in progress, and I'll be looking at another fine." The third this year.

Unless Thomas called his favorite man in

blue, Officer Pete Richards, who a few years back had responded to a 911 call Thomas placed after losing his 1993 Derek Jeter rookie card.

With his shiny badge and fully loaded smile, Pete located the card, made a superfan out of Thomas, and charmed Beckett into dinner — which led to a walk on the beach and, eventually, a sprint toward Happily Ever After.

If there were any chinks in his armor, signs that her knight with a shining badge wasn't up to the task of dealing with her family, Beckett didn't notice until it was too late. She wouldn't make the same mistake again.

"Look," she said. "I know you're trying to be understanding, but there is no way you can understand this."

"Then explain it to me so I can help." He took both of her hands. "I want to help you, Beck."

She believed him. Just as she believed that any more help from this strong, capable, and oh-so-incredible guy would leave her with more trouble on her doorstep than the police. And she didn't have the time or the heart for another disappointing attempt at love.

"You can help by stop being so damned nice to me."

Because when he was nice, she forgot she had to be the tough chick. His intentions were good, but intentions didn't matter if the end result was disappointment.

Without another word, she headed for the door, texting Thomas to say she was on her way home and not to call the cops. The rain pelted her skin as she hit send and sprinted across the parking lot. By the time she reached her scooter, she was dripping from head to toe, so it didn't much matter when she straddled the wet seat.

Helmet secured, she cranked the key, but the engine sputtered before turning over. She tried again with no luck.

"Are you shitting me?" She tried one last time and got enough spark to realize she'd left her front light on, and it had drained the battery. "Come on!"

"Someone need a ride?" Levi asked, standing over her, looking like a hero for hire with his leather coat, umbrella, and stack of to-go boxes. "I've got a heater that will leave you feeling tumbled dry in no time, and I'll even let you eat the rest of the cake in the car."

Never in her life had she been this close to a public display of tears. That it was in front of a guy who gave her tingles only made it worse. But she was stuck between a pecker and a pitchfork, and Levi's smile was warm enough to melt through every ice wall she was hiding behind.

"Only if you promise not to be nice," she said quietly. "I can't handle nice right now."

"No nice. Got it," he said, then reached out the umbrella to shelter her from the rain.

CHAPTER 9

After a series of crazy days, Levi began to see Beckett's point. Finding quality me-first time was only as easy as his family and schedule allowed. He'd never questioned his decision to take over running the Crow's Nest after Michelle passed, but if he wanted any kind of personal life, something had to give.

In addition to running the restaurant, he'd helped his mom install a new bathroom vanity, handled rent from marina tenants, and lived through another death-defying driver's lesson with Paisley — who sideswiped a pylon, burst into tears, and claimed her life was officially over. And it was only Wednesday.

His first day off in weeks. With the bar and grill in Gus's capable hands, Levi planned on spending some of that desperately needed me-time on his boat, which had always been his happy place. He could be himself there, get away from family obligations and the problems at work, and relive the simpler times he'd shared with his dad on the water.

Nothing about today had turned out simple. Between fielding calls from the restaurant and a never-ending string of texts from family, Levi hadn't even left the marina.

The only person he wanted to talk to, he hadn't heard from. Beckett had been radio silent since he'd dropped her off at her house. She'd put on a brave face, but he could tell she was worried about her family; she'd looked ready to cry. Surprising, since Beckett was not prone to display water-works, no matter how bad the situation.

And by the time they'd pulled into her drive, bad didn't even begin to describe the situation. Thomas was circling the drive, Karen was waving a pickax from her yard, and the only thing standing between Diesel and a beheading was Officer Daniels, whose presence seemed to upset Beckett more than the pickax.

When Levi insisted on staying, Beckett said the best way to help was to leave. Which he did, right after Officer Daniels apprehended the ax and sent Karen inside to cool off. By the time he'd dropped off her scooter, any evidence of the near-miss altercation had vanished. So had Beckett.

When she didn't answer the door, he dropped her keys into the mailbox, texting her on his way home — and a few other times — to make sure she was okay. She'd only responded to the texts regarding the wedding.

Levi considered using the wedding as an excuse to see her, but Gus called first thing to report another case of missing wine, this one from a different distributor. With some serious housekeeping issues of his own, he left Girl Wonder to fight her own battle and launched a quiet investigation into what was going on at his bar.

His first calls had been to the wine companies, to track down their delivery guy and discover who had signed off on each of the orders. To Levi's surprise, he had. At least according to the signature on the delivery slips. Odd, since he had no recollection of receiving either case and had iron-clad alibis for the time of the deliveries.

While his wine search failed to locate any missing wine, it did uncover a charge for an eight-hundred-dollar bottle of scotch, which Levi had not ordered or authorized. After cycling through several customer-assistance reps, who offered jack shit in terms of assistance, he finally got through to a manager, who claimed that the order had originated from Levi's personal email and was charged on the company account. Since he couldn't prove otherwise, and the scotch was already in transit, he wrote down the tracking number — hoping it would aid him in trapping whoever was living large on Levi's dime.

Eyes gritty from lack of sleep, and feeling as if he'd made all the progress he could for the day, Levi decided to salvage the last couple hours of his day off and watch the tide roll in while figuring out his next steps in Operation Making Plans with Wedding Planner.

By the time he reached the stern of the boat, the sun was already making its descent into the distant horizon. And when the last bit of day disappeared beneath the waterline, and the blues slowly turned all the colors of a mai tai, Levi called it.

Somehow, his entire day off had passed without Levi gaining a moment's peace.

Grabbing a beer from inside, he threw on a winter coat and brushed off the cushion of a deck chair before plopping down. Damn if he was moving before the stars became visible.

He took a pull from the bottle and listened

to the rocking of the boat, doing his best to match his heart rate to the gentle rise and fall of the water beneath him. Seagulls flew overhead, circling a rock a hundred yards out, squawking as they dipped down only to circle back up after their feet touched the water.

Levi learned how to swim before he could walk. Was still in diapers when his dad took him out on his first sail. Levi grew up on the ocean; it was more a home to him than anywhere else. But sitting here by himself, watching the most beautiful sunset, with a fridge full of beer, he couldn't help but wonder how it would feel to have someone by his side, to share the moment with.

His phone vibrated across the glass-top table, and a small thrill sped through him at the possibility that it was Beckett on the other end. He looked at the screen and — well, shit.

"Hey, Mom," he said by way of greeting. "You watching this sunset?"

"With a margarita in hand." Her voice was wistful. "Nights like tonight always remind me of your daddy."

"Me, too." Pulling his coat around him, Levi took in a deep breath of sea air, the mixture of brine and seaweed bringing him back to a simpler time. "People who romanticize summer sunsets will never know the beauty of the rare winter one."

Those were the words his father swore by. Hector had believed that the most beautiful treasures in life lay hidden beneath the surface. Then again, he fancied himself an amateur treasure hunter. He never did find any chest filled with gold bullion, but Hector loved the hunt.

"Gray was over today. Brought some old photos of Michelle from when they first started dating. Some I had never seen," she said. "I'm making a scrapbook of her life and asked him if there were any favorites he could part with. Showed up with a whole box of photos and keepsakes. I was hoping you could go through your stuff, too."

"I stored a few wine crates of Michelle's stuff in the office." Just some of the many things Michelle had left behind. After she died, Levi hadn't known what to do with them, so he carefully put everything in some wooden wine crates and placed them in the corner.

He was waiting for the right time to give them to his mom and Gray. He hadn't been sure he was ready to part with them yet, but it seemed the right time had arrived.

"Oh no." Ida gasped. "Give them to Grayson. Whatever he and Paisley don't want, I'll take. But Michelle's things should go to them first."

"I'll drop them by Gray's later this week."

"I was hoping you could hand them to him tonight. At bowling."

Christ. He dropped his forehead against the table. He loved his family and had a great circle of friends, but honest to God, he didn't have the energy to peel himself away from the sunset to rifle through his dead sister's belongings before handing them off in the parking lot of the Bowl-A-Rama.

"I'm not sure how Gray will deal with getting that kind of material in public," Levi said, knowing that his brother-in-law was barely holding on. If Paisley wasn't living with him most of the time, Gray would fall deeper into the hole of his misery.

"Then drop everything by his house on the way."

"His house isn't on the way. In fact, it is a half hour in the exact opposite direction from the bowling alley."

"I know he'll appreciate it, and since you'll be only a few minutes from here, you can swing by and look at the front porch light," she said, completely ignoring his previous statement. "It's on the fritz again. Can barely make out the keyhole when I get home from scrapbooking class at the Y."

"Can the light wait until tomorrow? Today's my day off, so I'm not even at the bar to get Michelle's boxes."

"Then put your sneakers on and walk the hundred steps to the bar, Levi." Her tone implied she'd just solved global warming.

"It's not walking over there that's the problem. It's getting back to my car," he tried to explain. From the minute he'd set foot in the Crow's Nest until he got into his car, Levi would encounter a half-dozen employees, each with a dozen questions that only he could answer. "It will take me forty-five minutes just to get on the road. Another thirty to drop by Gray's, then fix your light." Then there was the trip back across town to the alley.

"That's okay, it took me forty-five hours to push you out," Ida said, effectively winning the argument. No man wants to be reminded that he once came out of his mom's vagina. No one.

"Maybe it just needs a new bulb. Is Owen around?" Levi asked, referring to Paisley's best friend, who happened to live down the street from Ida. "Maybe he can try replacing the bulb. Or maybe it just needs tightening." The *again* was silent.

The last time a light was "on the fritz," it

turned out someone had loosened the bulb enough to make it flicker. They could never prove it, but the whole family was confident the someone in question was Ida.

When she was lonely, rather than admit she missed her kids, she'd create a reason for a visit. Levi would bet the boat that Ida was the most creative mom in town. She once tossed a box of nails in the washer, ran it, then called to say her washer was making a strange sound. Last month, she required assistance taking her garbage can to the curb. When Levi discovered her garden bricks lining the bottom, she accused neighborhood kids of pulling pranks.

"I couldn't bother Owen." She was aghast. "I'm sure he's busy doing schoolwork."

Over the years, Levi had babysat Owen enough to know the kid was next-level smart. With video games and cells removed from the equation, he could accomplish a week's worth of homework in under two hours. When properly motivated, let's say with easy money, he could do it in less.

"Tell Owen I'll pay him twenty bucks, plus the cost of a new bulb, to screw it in." He'd consider doubling it since, by his calculations, to hit all the destinations on Ida's approved itinerary and still make it to bowling, Levi would have to abandon his me-first time and leave now.

"I will not! Emmitt dropped Paisley off a few minutes ago for a study group. I won't be responsible for distracting them."

"Emmitt was there? He could've checked the light."

"He's not my son," she said in a tone that usually ended with her calling Levi by his full name. "And he was in a rush to get home and start dinner. It was Annie's night to cook, but one of the players on Annie's bowling team was put on bed rest until she delivers, so Annie spent all afternoon trying to find a replacement on such short notice."

"She's short a player?" he asked, wondering if this was his out. The last thing he wanted to do was bowl, but he couldn't leave his team short a player. However, according to the week's lineup, it was nurses versus physicians, which put Gray's team against Annie's. So if the nurses were down a member, and Levi told Gray he wasn't coming, it would even up the two teams.

Maybe he'd get some of that me-first time, after all.

"No. Thankfully, Annie found a friend of hers to fill in, which was a relief."

"And while Emmitt was explaining all that, he couldn't reach up and twist in a bulb?"

"You know what, Levi James. If it will cause you that much trouble, I'll fix it myself."

Normally, it'd be no problem for him to visit. She'd call, he'd drive over, fix whatever needed fixing, then stay for whichever meal came next.

Tonight, he didn't have the spare energy or time — not if Annie's team was full and he had to make it to bowling. Then again, what was a measly hour of me-first time when compared to forty-five hours in labor?

Fixing his mom's light was the least he could do.

"I'll be at your place around six, but there will only be time to fix the light. Dinner or anything else will have to wait."

"But I made moussaka," she objected. "Your yiayia's moussaka. Ero's was having a special on lamb, half off your second pound. I said I'd take three pounds if he'd honor the half off on the third pound. When Ero said it only applied to the second half of each two-pound order, I reminded him how much you loved moussaka and how it was the only way I could sneak eggplant into your diet," she said, as if Levi were still six, and it was completely normal for her to talk about her children to the butcher. "He agreed to apply the deal to two of the three pounds. What kind of Greek mother would I be to pass on that?"

"Not a good one," he answered, because when it came down to meat, there were a few hard and fast rules that, according to Ida, all real Greek mothers followed:

1. Only serve lamb 2–3 times a week.
2. Always fresh, never processed.
3. A good deal on lamb is a good deal on lamb.
4. Buy from a trained butcher.
5. Who is Greek.
6. And who learned the trade from his Greek father (or grandfather, if the father turned his back on the family business).
7. In order to trust his meat, you must know him, his wife, kids, and extended family. (Relatives still living in the Old World are exempt.)

"Yiayia's moussaka sounds great, but I have bowling."

"How long will it take you to sit down and have a few bites? There's enough here to feed a family of six. It will go bad if you don't come to dinner."

Levi looked skyward for divine intervention. He hated the idea of his mom eating alone. He worried about her more and more, knowing that Michelle was no longer a few blocks over. Gray was great with Ida, and Paisley dropped by a few days a week after school, but he knew his mom was lonely. The kind of lonely only her children could heal.

"Maybe I can grab a few bites. But no salad, no sides, no dessert. A few bites while I fix the light. Then I'm gone."

"But I made my galaktoboureko, and you know it doesn't keep well."

"Mom," he warned.

"I'll package some to go," she said, and he could sense her excitement. Hear cabinets slam open and shut as she puttered around her kitchen, setting the table, getting out the good china, probably even crystal wine glasses, even though he'd only have water. "I'll also make a care package for Emmitt, since he was so sweet as to drop off Paisley."

"He's her dad. That's his job."

"You know how Annie loves my galaktoboureko," she said. "And after all this fill-in business, I imagine she could use a little mom-made dessert."

As long as it didn't come out of his share, Levi didn't care.

His phone buzzed. He held the phone back and glanced at the screen. It was

225

Emmitt, texting on the DADS text thread.

**2night won't be an easy win.
Annie recruited a ringer.**

Two texts came through, one after the other. Both from Gray.

Annie told me!

**Might want to bring
that A-game, L**

Gray knew that there was only one person worth Levi's A game. And a night with Rome's most adorable-sexy animal advocate was the exact kind of fun the good doctor ordered. Suddenly, Levi wasn't only optimistic about tonight, he was damn near hopeful.

"Mom, did Emmitt mention which friend of Annie's was filling in?"

"Of course, Levi James," she said, and Levi couldn't help but smile. "The sweet girl you took wedding cake tasting before bringing home to meet your mother!"

CHAPTER 10

Beckett had tried on every item in her closet, and everything was now strewn around her bedroom, making it look like a sorority house before homecoming. And the best combination she could come up with was a pair of jeans, a T-shirt, and a heavy cardigan.

It took rifling through her dirty clothes hamper and all six drawers of her chifforobe, but she'd managed to find a pair of matching socks. That was as good as it was going to get.

"This is all your fault," Beckett said loudly enough to be heard on her speakerphone as she tugged the shirt over her head.

"It's not like I held a gun to your head." Annie's voice was muffled beneath a pile of clothes.

"You drugged me with dark chocolate cake, then gave the 'it's for the kids' speech." Beckett ruffled through a pile of discarded underwear — did she have a single pair not resembling granny panties? — to locate her phone. She picked it up and gave the screen a hard look. "You know I can't be rational when chocolate and kids are involved."

"I was desperate." Annie looked bowling chic in a two-tone faded blue top with a matching blue knit cap and her smart-is-sexy black-rimmed glasses. "Our chances of making it to the next round are slim to none, so this is the last game of the season. And it's for a good cause."

Lucky Strike, a charity bowling league that raised money for local nonprofits, had selected the pediatric ward of Rome General as this year's beneficiary. Annie, who couldn't say no to save her life, had drafted every friend and family member to fill the empty teams.

Fortunately for Beckett, her schedule was so unpredictable, she'd only been able to sign up as an alternate for the alternate. Unfortunately, their alternate was incapacitated, and Beckett had to fulfill her duties to the team. It didn't hurt that tonight was nurses vs. physicians, a game that would decide who went on to the semifinals.

The physicians' team, led by Gray, had scored enough wins this season to go on automatically. But the nurses needed a win to make it to the next round. Beckett was their ringer. Too bad she didn't know how to dress herself.

"It can't be that bad. Let me see," Annie said, her puckered face filling the screen when Beckett flicked the camera view to face the camera at her mirror. "Is that one of your work shirts turned inside out?"

She flicked the camera back. "It's the only newish thing I own that's clean. And doesn't have buttons."

Thomas hated buttons. On his good days, he could deal with seeing them in public, but if one was visible in the house, especially around food, he became physically ill. It made dining out impossible.

"What about that cute green sundress you wore to my birthday dinner?"

"It's April. In Rhode Island. The dress is thin and silky, and I can still smell the frost in the air. Even with tights, I'd freeze."

"Write this down," Annie said seriously. "Never wear tights with that dress. Understood?"

"Great, so we've agreed the dress is out." She held up a baggy, soft green sweater. "How about this?"

"You're filling in for someone on maternity leave; that doesn't mean you have to dress like you're on maternity leave."

Beckett didn't even pretend to be offended. The sweater had been a Christmas present from her great aunt, who was more of a one-size-fits-all kind of knitter.

"What about my maroon sweater?"

"The one with moth holes in the armpits?" Annie scrunched her nose. "How about the pretty black shirt with the cutouts across the belly? Paired with dark jeans and your red leather boots. You'll look hot."

"Shirt's dirty, and you borrowed my boots." Beckett reached into the cleanest-looking pile and randomly selected a shirt. "How about my blue-and-white-striped long-sleeve tee?"

"I love that top. It's very nautical. Might even make Levi think you're asking to be his skipper."

"Never wearing that in public again." To bed was a whole other story.

"You'll look great in whatever you wear," Annie said sweetly. "Just avoid tights, work shirts, and anything that looks like maternity clothes."

"So you're good with my 'real cocks have feathers — everything else is just a dick' shirt?"

"Your boobs look great in that shirt!" Annie laughed. "I still vote for the dress, because it makes your eyes pop, looks great with your complexion, and would be worth the frostbite. Plus, if you get too cold, I'm sure some handsome sailor would offer you his coat."

"Are you setting me up to take home the win or setting me up on a date with your fiancé's friend?"

"Can't it be both?" Annie asked sweetly.

If the cake tasting had taught Beckett anything, it was that no, some people can't have their cake and eat it too. The other thing it had taught her was that she was in danger of forming a serious crush on Levi. So tonight, she'd go to the game and have fun, but she'd keep the talk about the bowling, her eyes on the ball — no matter how amazing Levi's butt looked in denim — and above all else, she'd keep her distance.

"It's not the right time," she confessed. She had a lot on her plate and some big decisions ahead of her. Even rearranging her schedule and figuring out a family solution so she could go bowling turned into an ordeal.

More than ever, Beckett needed to remain focused, not get all girly over being set up by her friend with a guy who was distraction personified.

"How long do you think it will be until it's the right time?" Annie asked.

"I don't know," Beckett admitted, her palms going damp at even the thought of letting someone into her life. "Why?"

"I mean, you're not the least bit excited he's going to be there?"

"Would you believe me if I said the idea of seeing him landed somewhere between 'sticking my fingers into dark, unknown holes' and 'playing with strangers' balls' on my list of reasons not to go tonight?"

Annie snorted. "No."

Beckett plopped onto her bed and let her head hang over the side. "Me either. He's growing on me, and I'm not sure how I feel about that."

"When I was going from man-free living to living with a man, I had to force myself to stop thinking about how I felt, and just *feel.*"

"When was the last time you saw me *feel*? In case you haven't noticed, me and the feels aren't close. In fact, every mistake in my life came from the freaking feels."

Annie laughed. "Maybe tonight, start with one of the easier emotions."

"Emotions come in levels?" When had that happened? As far as Beckett knew, they were all equal-opportunity home-wreckers. Sure, she knew there were the big ones: love, hate, heartache. But misplaced happiness could create as much havoc in someone's life as sorrow or anger.

"All I'm saying is try to go into tonight with the goal of having fun." Annie's voice was soft with understanding. "Can you do that?"

Beckett thought about leaving Thomas and Gregory in the ill-equipped hands of Jeffery and groaned. Jeffery said he'd handle things, that there would be no calls from home — and no calls to the cops. Then again, he'd said that before.

She hadn't believed him then, and she didn't believe him now, yet she was still willing to risk coming home to a disaster so that she could go bowling.

Why? She could have used her busy day as an excuse to wiggle out of playing. Annie was pushy, but she was also a good enough friend to know when to back off. Beckett could blame her earlier acquiescence on temporary chocolate drunkenness. But when it came down to it, she didn't use any of those excuses, because she wanted to go.

She wanted to see Levi again.

Over the past several days, Beckett had worked hard to maintain perspective, limit her communication with Levi, and keep things professional. All she'd accomplished was adding to the anticipation of their next

233

meet. Which, had she been given a choice, would have happened at a more convenient time, when she was dressed like an adult. Not last minute, while looking like a pizza delivery coed in an inside-out work shirt and day-old jeans.

Beckett swung her legs off the bed to look down at herself and smiled.

She'd already found matching socks — the hard part was over.

"I'll try." Those two words kickstarted her stomach into a spin cycle of nerves — the good kind. She couldn't remember the last time she'd been so excited about going out. Usually, the stress of leaving overpowered the giddiness. Not tonight.

Tonight was all about fun.

Her doorbell rang. "Someone's at the door. I'll see you there," she said. "Oh, and Annie, thanks for being such a great friend."

"Back at ya." Annie blew her a kiss and hung up.

"Dad, someone's at the door," Beckett called down the hallway, then slipped on her REAL COCKS T-shirt. Annie had agreed it made her boobs look great, and when paired with her black skinny jeans and leather jacket, she looked old enough not to be carded.

Confidence bubbling, she added a little

makeup — not so much as to appear that she thought this was a date, but enough that he would wish it was. Giving herself a once-over in the mirror and deciding Annie would approve, she puckered her lips, swiped on her tinted lip gloss, then decided it was too light and mixed it with another lip gloss.

She was about to wipe it off and start over when the doorbell rang again.

"Dad? Can you answer the door?"

Met with silence, she grabbed her purse and rushed to the front door. A little winded, she glanced through the peephole, and her breath stuck in her lungs.

"Sweet baby Jesus," she whispered, going up even farther on her tiptoes to take in the hunk on her front-porch step.

Mouth dry, breathing a little heavily, she took in the sight of Levi, resting a hip against her porch rail, arms crossed to further define his already defined biceps and chest, and exuding enough testosterone to seep under the door and make her woozy. There were also the dark jeans that clung to his thighs, a crisp blue button-up that he hadn't bothered to finish buttoning, and a really warm-looking coat that had her second-guessing her fashion-over-function leather jacket.

And if that wasn't enough to have her wondering if she should open the door or hide in a closet and pretend she wasn't home, there was that bad-boy grin, which always managed to make her stomach do silly little flips.

The man looked so at home in his own skin, it made her wonder what that kind of confidence even felt like.

Good lord, he must think she was a certifiable nut. First, she rewarded his sweet offer to help defuse The Cocky-Inquisition by screaming at him to leave — which had more to do with Pete being at her house than Levi. Then, too embarrassed to explain the situation, she'd ignored a good portion of his texts. And now she was spying on him through the peephole in an outfit that promised things she could never deliver on.

What was she even supposed to say when she opened the door? "Sorry I kept you waiting for ten minutes in the freezing cold while I applied lip gloss. I asked my dad to let you in, but he didn't hear me. Oh, and by the way, in case you ever want me to play skipper to your captain, we'll have to go to your place, because I live at home with my dad and sleep in my childhood bedroom."

"If you're angling for a better look, just

say the word, and I can turn around," he said.

Beckett leaped back, her hand over her mouth. How was it that despite being left to wait in the freezing cold, he was still flirting? And how was it possible that he could see her through a closed door?

She glanced at the mess behind her, then at herself in the mirror, before silently going up on her toes to peek through the hole again. Only a few seconds had passed, but he'd managed to look even better. In fact, the longer she stared, the hotter he became, and the more convinced she was that agreeing to go bowling had been a mistake.

"Your breath is steaming up the peephole, Girl Wonder." His deep, sexy chuckle came through the wood door. "Are you going to keep me waiting out here in the cold all night?" When she didn't answer, he said, "I've got a camping chair, a subzero-rated sleeping bag, and a box of granola bars. I'm good for the long haul."

Beckett didn't want to read too much into those words, but she smiled all the same.

Telling herself to get a grip, she zipped her jacket over her offensive tee and opened the door, not as wide as to showcase her dad's equipment strewn around the front room, but enough so she could look out.

"Hi," she said with a smile. It was a goofy smile, but she couldn't help it.

"Hi, Beck."

"Hi," she said again, as if her conversational skills were those of a toddler. "What are you doing here?"

"I was in the neighborhood and figured I'd offer you a ride to the bowling alley."

"You didn't have to do that," she said. He raised his brow, and she realized she'd sounded accusatory. "Thank you, but I can drive myself."

"I know you can, but you'd be a Popsicle by the time you arrived."

"You live near Bowl-A-Rama. If you drove me, you'd have to bring me all the way back across town after. That would add like an extra hour to your trip."

He shrugged. "I don't mind."

Beckett couldn't tell if he was being serious or sarcastic, and she instantly felt uncertain about this whole night. She'd never had a guy pick her up at her house before, always opting to drive herself. She met her dates at a pre-arranged location, and left her phone on in case her family called and she needed to cut out early.

But tonight wasn't a date. Her dad had promised there'd be no hysterical calls from home. And Beckett was supposed to have fun. She'd really thought over what Levi had said about putting herself first every once in a while. Tonight was her inaugural run.

"Okay, let me just change out of my work clothes," she lied. She was about to close the door when his foot slid into the small opening.

He pushed it back open a tad. "You want to invite me in first?"

It wasn't that she didn't know basic etiquette; she simply didn't know how to tell a guy who'd just offered to go an hour out of his way to drive her home that she didn't want to invite him in. His seeing her daily reality wasn't how she wanted to start the night.

But if she was going to do this, then she was going to be honest about who she was and how she felt. It was a risk, but she'd rather know what she was walking into before she let even one more feeling escape.

"Would it be okay if I said no?"

Levi pushed off from the railing, his boots clicking on the wood porch, not stopping until he stood so close, she smelled the frost on his skin. "I showed up unannounced, so you can tell me whatever feels right. You aren't going to get any pressure from me, about anything."

"Thank you," she whispered, trying to remember the last time a man had been so unfazed by her tics and quirks. "Would you mind if I shut the door for a moment while I tell my family I'm leaving? I don't want the animals to get out."

Those beautiful blue eyes softened with understanding, and Levi took a step back. "Like I said, I'm here for the long haul."

Beckett slowly closed the door, her eyes on Levi, until it clicked shut. Then she sprinted down the hallway. By the time she reached her room, she was sweating through the armpits of her shirt. Tossing it onto the dirty pile, she pushed way back in her closet, where she kept all the clothes she wished she could wear but never had a place to wear them to.

And there it was.

The slinky, stiletto red shirt she'd bought to wear to a party. She'd spent a pretty penny on it, but it made her waist look a size smaller and her boobs two sizes bigger. More importantly, it made her feel sexy in that confident, self-assured way of women who have it together. Which was why she'd bought it.

The purchase was a challenge, issued to herself, to be bold and prove she had it together. It was only a silly shirt, but to

Beckett, it represented so much more. All the missed opportunities — road trips with friends; sneaking out to go a boy's house; flipping through a college catalogue and deciding where she wanted to go in life, what she wanted to be.

One shirt couldn't give her all that, but it went a long way toward saying she was the kind of woman who went bowling with friends on a weeknight.

Slipping on a leather jacket that had zippers on the cuffs, she found her dad in the studio, lifted his earphones to tell him she was taking off, then raced back to the door in under two minutes.

She found Thomas in the entry and Levi still on the porch, foot tapping hello. The sight would have been endearing had Beckett not been so focused on the fact that the door was wide open, and Hurricane Jeffery was on display for the whole neighborhood to see. The only person she cared about was Levi. What did he think about the state of affairs behind the Hayes's front door?

Her confidence shaken a little, she zipped her jacket to the neck, then walked to the door. "Sorry I kept you waiting. I had to find my dad."

"No, you didn't. You were changing shirts." Thomas tugged the red hem out

241

from under the black jacket. "This was not the shirt you had on before."

"I wasn't finished getting ready," she explained.

"Yes, she was. She had on a T-shirt. This shirt is red and has buttons. Lots of buttons, even though zippers are more efficient."

"I'm more of a zipper man, too," Levi agreed, while eyeing her zip-up jeans.

"She was nervous," Thomas said, focusing on the porch rail directly behind Levi.

If the lack of eye contact bothered Levi, he didn't show it. In fact, when he spoke to Thomas, he kept his gaze on Beckett. "Nervous, huh?"

"I'm not nervous," she said with a nervous laugh.

"Yes, you are," Thomas said, each word receiving the same emphasis. "You changed your clothes a lot of times."

"A lot?" Levi teased gently. "What's under the jacket, Beck?"

"A few," she corrected. "And none of your business."

"Interesting," Levi said, and she could swear he purred. "How many times did she change clothes?"

Thomas clapped, thoroughly enjoying this fun game with his new buddy. "Eleven, not

242

including shoes. And she checked herself in the mirror before answering the door and then straightened her shirt. Grooming for one's mate is the first step in fornication."

"Thomas!" She put a hand over his mouth.

He pushed it away. "It's Tommy."

Levi lifted a brow. "You thinking about fornication, Beck?"

"No, I'm not!" She forced annoyance into her tone to distract herself from the intense sexual awareness bubbling up inside.

"You wore a new top," Tommy — aka Traitor — informed the group. "You applied makeup. You keep licking your lips. You found matching socks. You want to fornicate."

"Eleven changes is a lot of primping for someone who isn't thinking about fornicating," Levi gently teased.

"And that is not including shoes," Thomas reminded them.

"Okay, fornication expert, time to say goodbye. I set the alarm for dinner. If it goes off and Dad doesn't hear it, then go remind him." She kissed her finger and pretended to touch his nose. "And be good for him tonight. You can play video games until nine, no later."

"I will try," he said, and Beckett knew

that, unless she wanted a meltdown, it was the best she'd get. "Bye, Levi."

"Bye, Buddy." Levi waved and stepped back to allow Beckett out.

"I like Buddy better than Tommy," Thomas said as he disappeared down the hallway.

"I'm so sorry about all that," she said, closing the door behind her. "I caught him looking at porn the other day and realized he'd googled fornication."

"I'm not," he said. "But you should know I'm not that kind of guy. I need to be wined and dined before I fornicate. It's important that you respect me for my mind and soul, not just my body."

"I'll keep that in mind." She searched his eyes. "Do you know anything about a mysterious pair of flip-flops that arrived in the mail for Thomas?"

He grinned. "They fit okay?"

"They could have been ten sizes too small, and he would have shoved his feet into them like Cinderella's stepsister," she said. He looked so proud of himself, she had a hard time keeping a stern face when she said, "Levi, they were way too expensive, overly generous, and if I could have sent them back, I would. But he made sure to wear them through the mud before showing them to me."

"So he liked them?"

"Loves them. He's the flip-flop king around the house." She sighed. "So thank you."

"Then my job here is done." His lips curled softly at the corners. "You have a pretty smile. You shouldn't hide it so much." She tried to suppress the urge to smile even wider, but her will was no match for Levi and his "it's Friday somewhere" personality. He was always smiling and having fun, two things she needed more of in her life. Why fight when giving in seemed so much more enjoyable?

"I'll remember that when I'm wiping the floor with you."

Instead of a trademark comeback, he jammed his hands into his pockets and rocked back on his heels, as if suddenly nervous. "It sounds like you haven't had dinner. Do you want to stop and grab something to eat beforehand?"

As if on cue, her stomach growled. She hadn't eaten since lunch, and with Levi showing up unexpectedly, she hadn't had time to make her usual dinner of PB&NCD. Peanut butter and Nacho Cheese Doritos.

"Are you hungry?" she asked.

He gave a small shrug. "I ate at my mom's, but I can always eat."

It was tempting. But they had to get across town for bowling. She didn't want to keep the team waiting, and if he'd already eaten, it would be awkward. "I don't want to be late. I can grab a hot dog at the bowling alley."

"Or we can stop and get you something to eat that hasn't been sitting in a heater since the place opened."

She rolled her eyes, not that he saw, because the porch light went out, plunging them into twilight. She could make out nothing but his big, gleaming white smile. "Trying to get me alone in the dark?"

"Thomas doesn't like the way the light hums." She went about the task of finding her keys. Not so easy when her bag doubled as purse, glove box, home office, and vending machine.

"How do you see when you get home late?"

"I have a flashlight." That was attached to her keys.

She was reconsidering her logic when a click sounded next to her, and a light, bright enough to be seen from Mars, illuminated the inside of her purse. Not to mention the cockiest grin this side of reentry.

246

"Thanks." For the light and for reassuring her that she'd picked out the right shirt. She found her keys and wiggled them to show how capable she was. "I got it."

He turned his light off, and she grimaced. Why was it so hard to accept help from him? She wasn't exactly eager to sit in the passenger seat, but she wasn't rude about letting people know.

Except for Levi. When it came to him, she would rather fall on her face than appear weak. He was one of the few people who didn't walk on eggshells around her — and now that he'd seen her house, she didn't want him to start.

"I know I must come off like a borderline crazy person control freak," she said, purposely taking her time as she locked the house, so she wouldn't have to look at what she assumed would be his shell-shocked expression. "Sometimes I even think I sound like a warden at Alcatraz, but if I don't lay out the rules and set alarms, then disaster often strikes. And yes, in case you thought you heard wrong, I do live with my dad and brother. Not because I'm incapable of living on my own, but because it's easier."

"Beck," he whispered, his warm breath against her ear causing her to shiver. "You are the most capable person I know."

Even though her eyes still hadn't adjusted to the dark, she turned. "Really?"

"Really."

Beckett felt her chest tighten. "I get that it's a lot, my life, so if you decide you'd rather let me drive myself, it's no big deal. Because if *I'd* walked into this, I'd probably —"

"I like your brother," he said, and just when she thought he couldn't get any sweeter, two large hands settled on her hips and slowly turned her until she was facing the most gorgeous man she'd ever met. "And I'm sure, if your dad is anything like you, I'll like him, too."

"He's more like Thomas. I'm kind of the odd one in the family, if you can believe that."

"I like how you care for your family," he whispered again, and again she shivered at his nearness.

"You cold?"

Nervous. Feeling shy. Thinking about fornication. "I'll be fine."

But he'd already slid off his coat and slipped it around her shoulders, the inside still warm from his body heat.

"Tonight we're aiming higher than fine."

Grabbing the lapels of his coat, he gave her a lingering sweep with his gaze. Then he zipped it up until she was surrounded by a cozy cocoon that smelled like yummy man and romantic spring nights.

Beckett wondered what he saw. A bold and put-together woman, or the big mess under the designer top? She knew no matter what he thought, he'd be polite and pay her a compliment. Hadn't he implied that his mom had raised him right?

To her surprise, instead of saying she looked pretty, or any of the other throwaway lines guys used that always made her uncomfortable, he leaned down and whispered in her ear. A few simple, lighthearted words that meant more to her than any empty platitude.

"Matching socks, huh? I hope I'm worth it."

CHAPTER 11

Levi knew what it had taken for Beckett to leave her scooter at home and carve out a night for herself. He was coming to understand the unusual amount of responsibility placed on her shoulders. In the early years, Michelle had been a hardworking single mom, raising Paisley and running the Crow's Nest. But she'd always had people around to help out when times were hard. Or when she just needed a free night to herself.

At first there'd been Levi and his mom, then Gray had come along, and finally Emmitt, rounding out what had become the most unlikely family. They didn't always agree, and they knew how to push each other's buttons, but they always had each other's backs.

Levi wondered who, if anyone, had Beckett's.

Tonight, he wanted to be that person for

her. He avoided involving himself in other people's family issues because, well, he had enough on his own plate. But Beckett deserved to have a night of fun to herself. And he was going to make sure she got it.

Christ, what was it about Beckett Hayes that reeled him in?

Levi went for stacked, sophisticated, and no-strings. Beckett was willowy, perpetually frazzled, and becoming more and more intertwined with his world. And judging by the nervous way she clutched her phone, she was as close to having a fun evening as a DC politician was to crossing party lines.

He'd noticed that the farther from her house they drove, the higher the tension in the cab became, until they were a mobile powder keg, her cell was the fuse, and they were one call from blowing the whole night to hell. She had a definite handle-with-caution vibe going on, which he believed stemmed from her worry over what was going on back at home.

With a resigned sigh, Levi pulled into the bowling alley and parked toward the back. Instead of shutting off the engine completely, he left the heater running. "You want to talk about what happened back there?"

"God, yes." She released a sigh of relief so

large, the window momentarily fogged up. "I just wasn't sure how to broach it."

He unbuckled his safety belt and turned toward her. "I want to make sure you have fun tonight."

"I do, too," she said. "Just like I want you to have fun."

"Good. Then we're on the same page," he said, but the fleeting, sidelong glance she gave him implied otherwise. "I just mean, I understand family dynamics and how stressful they can be. One time, my mom pretended her back went out so that she'd have an excuse to stay on my boat. After three weeks of sleeping on a lawn chair, the kind with slats, I woke up to find my mom and her water-aerobics friends doing synchronized swimming dives off the back of my boat. They had on matching suits, those decorative hats with rubber roses on top, the whole nine yards."

Beckett laughed. "What did she say when you caught her?"

"She said as long as I was there, I could judge," he said. "So, I don't want you to get stressed about leaving your scooter at home. If you need to cut out early, just say the word, and we'll head home."

"You thought I was stressed about home?"

"You went quiet after we left your driveway. You keep checking your cell. And you've avoided eye contact. What else would you be stressed about?"

Curiosity had him leaning on the center console at the precise moment Beckett turned to face him. Her lips parted on a gasp, and he forgot what they were talking about, because he was a breath's distance from discovering what flavor lip gloss she had on — with his tongue.

At her house, he'd picked up hints of spice, but after sharing the cozy cab of his truck for fifteen miles, he'd narrowed it down to cinnamon. From this distance, he'd bet what was left of his mom's galaktoboureko that his stunning copilot had a thing for horchata.

"That I somehow gave you the wrong impression of what tonight will entail," she whispered, looking up at him, and *holy fuck.*

"You might want to clarify what impression you'd hoped to give. Because you're looking at me like you want the grand tour of my boat — starting with the master cabin."

"Pretend that I don't," she said, her gaze zeroing in on his lips. "That's what I do."

"Ever since seeing you at the beach in that white two-piece, I've tried pretending," he whispered. "It's getting harder."

"You remember what I was wearing last summer?" Her eyes became two big circles of wonder, and Levi's chest ached.

He wasn't sure what kind of assholes she'd dated in the past, but the Steves and Bruces of the world needed a serious ass-kicking if a woman as gorgeous and incredible as Beckett found it surprising that she was memorable.

"Beck, I can't keep my days straight, but there isn't much about you that I don't remember." And that was the truth. He tapped his temple. "It gets stored up here in my Dolittle box." At her snicker, he raised a brow. "Try me?"

She crossed her arms and leaned back. "Okay, what was I wearing the first time we met?"

"That, Girl Wonder, is a trick question." He waved a stern finger her way. "The first time you came into my bar, you were wearing a pretty blue top that had two tiny strings holding it together, jeans, and these black steel-toe boots that made you look like you wanted to bash in your date's teeth."

"My date was Zane, and no, he was not a Zamboni driver, he was a college music professor, with the attention span of a fly and the arms of an octopus. While he kept his teeth, his shins will never be the same." She gawked. "That was eight years ago."

"As for the first time we met and exchanged more words than 'a pint of whatever IPA you have on tap,' that was at the annual Bonfire Days. You showed up in the aforementioned slinky white two-piece, a green wraparound thing that knotted above your breasts, and these sexy sandals that crisscrossed all the way up your calves."

"That sounds more like your other head talking." She glanced down, then back up at him through her lashes. "What else do you remember?"

"I was watching over a bonfire, making s'mores for a group of kids, when I spotted you walking a herd of dogs. One of them broke free, his tiny legs moving like lightning, and he snatched the marshmallow right off my roasting stick. The thing was still smoldering from the fire."

"That was Diesel. He smelled the melting sugar and couldn't help himself."

"So you remember, too." He placed way too much hope in the way her cheeks flushed. "That night, he was my wingman. I'd been dying for an excuse to talk to you away from the bar. And there was my chance, only I'd barely said hey when a beefy guy with oak trees for arms appeared out of nowhere."

"That was Pete," she said, and now he had a name to go with the meathead. "It was our first date."

"Hell, he was acting like he was about to put his ring on your finger." He shook his head. "Had I known it was a first date, I would have made a move."

He didn't think she was aware, but she leaned forward and placed her hand on his forearm. "What would you have done?"

"Honestly, back then I probably would have said something stupid, and you'd never have given me the time of day again."

"And now?" she breathed.

"Now, I'd take my time. Ask the right kinds of questions and really get to know you, because why rush a good thing?" he said, looking into her eyes. "And I'd tell you how rattled I am around you and all the things I don't know about you and find myself wanting to learn."

"What do you want to know?" she asked, tucking her hands inside his coat sleeves. *I can't tell if he's being serious or not, and that makes me nervous,* her tone said.

Levi was more serious about getting to her than he'd been about a woman since Vikki. But that was where the similarities ended. Vikki was refined, accomplished, and summered on her family's yacht at every luxury resort from Maine to Miami.

Beckett was too genuine to be polished, her accomplishments too selfless to be counted, and she knew more about human kindness than the most revered philanthropists. He'd spent time with his share of pretty women, but Beckett had the kind of beauty that lingered long after she'd left the room.

"Are you any good at bowling?" he asked.

She laughed. "You can ask me anything you want, and you want to know if I can bowl?"

"For now." He had a hundred other questions, but a parking lot wasn't the right place to ask them.

"You scared of losing to a girl?" she challenged, her eyes lit with excitement over the idea of making him eat dirt.

"Not scared. Just curious."

She gave a noncommittal shrug. "It's not really my strong suit, but I do okay. Good enough to beat you."

"Do I sense a bet coming on?" he asked. "We talking teams or individual scores?"

She didn't look intimidated in the slightest. "This is between you and me, sailor."

He liked the way she called him sailor, in that smart tone she adopted whenever she issued a challenge. He'd like it even better if she were screaming it from the bed of his cabin.

"Winner gets to name their spoils," he said, and when she didn't answer, he leaned over and whispered in her ear. "It'll give me the chance to see what Girl Wonder wears under her cape."

"I didn't bring my cape. And I'm still going to kick your ass."

"I hear you've been putting a little unwelcome pressure on the whole overnight experience," Emmitt said, handing beers to Levi and Gray, who were sitting at lane six, lacing up their bowling shoes.

Levi frowned. "When did she say that?"

Gray and Emmitt exchanged confused looks, then started laughing.

"I was talking about Paisley and the ski trip," Emmitt said. "But I'd rather talk about who you thought I meant."

Levi spotted Beckett by the counter, testing out bowling balls with Annie. She'd handed back his coat the second they stepped inside — which was a damn shame, because she looked good in his clothes — but she hadn't removed her leather jacket. Which left his mind to fill in all the possibilities of what could be beneath those million-and-one zippers.

If it was anything close to those ass-shaping jeans and sexy ankle-high boots she had on, he'd die a happy man. He'd never been a fan of those crazy printed socks that were sold at the tourist shop downtown. But his gaze kept being drawn down to the dancing flamingos and just how far they went up her leg.

"I'd rather not," he said, knowing how uncomfortable Beckett would be if she overheard them talking about her.

"I'd rather. How about you?" Emmitt looked at Gray.

"Rather."

"That makes two against one," Emmitt said. "You lose."

The idiots laughed over how clever they were, and Levi went back to inputting names in the automatic scorer. He could feel the looks behind him, knew the guys were smirking.

"Stay out of my business," Levi said.

"Did you stay out of my business when I was making a complete ass out of myself over Annie?" Emmitt asked.

"If it wasn't for me, there wouldn't be a you and Annie."

"And if it wasn't for me, you'd still be spinning your wheels with Beck." Emmitt laughed, and Gray toasted him with his beer.

"I do fine on my own."

"Says the guy who took a girl to a cake tasting, and now the whole town thinks they're getting hitched." Emmitt grinned.

"How're the wedding plans coming along?" Gray asked.

"Good. We've got the cake, the venue, and the ceremony site locked down," Levi said.

"I think he was talking about the other plan. The one that involves using my wedding to get you laid," Emmitt said. "I know it's customary for someone in the wedding party to hook up, but the invites haven't even gone out."

"He needs all the time he can get," Gray said.

Levi leveled them with a look. "You want your wedding at the justice of the peace? Then you should be thanking me. Beckett already had a ton on her plate without adding planning a surprise wedding."

Emmitt watched Annie testing bowling balls at the counter. "Annie's afraid that she pushed Beckett too hard and that she'll put her own plans on hold again. Work so hard to make Annie's dream perfect, that she'll neglect hers."

Levi was afraid of that, as well. "Why do

you think I'm overseeing everything?"

"Because you want to get in her pants?" Emmitt said.

"Because if I didn't, your wedding would be: A, held at the justice of the peace. Or B, rival Prince Harry's, and Beckett wouldn't have a single client left."

"I still think it's C, you've got a thing for Dolittle. But Annie and I appreciate it all the same."

"Yeah, well, if Paisley's inheritance goes belly-up because my staff robs me blind while I'm picking out floral arrangements, remember this conversation."

"Now I know why you asked me to plan the bachelor party," Gray said.

"Wait, what?" Levi asked. "You asked *him* to plan your bachelor party?"

"You're already doing so much with the wedding."

"But you asked *him.*" Levi pointed at Gray. "To plan your bachelor party?"

"Why do you keep saying it like that?" Gray smacked Levi's hand aside. "I'm the only one who's actually been married before. I think I can plan a bachelor party."

"What the actual fuck?" Levi said to Emmitt, who was smiling like an unapologetic asshole.

It was bad enough that Levi was already

sharing the role of best man. But now the good ol' doc, who didn't know a gentleman's club from a geriatric pole class, was recruited to plan the bachelor party. *The* same bachelor party Levi and Emmitt had been planning since they'd found his dad's *Playboy* at the bottom of his toolbox — Vanna White was on the cover, and Levi's fondness for blondes was cemented.

He wasn't ready to go all girl on Gray and play the besties card, but he and Emmitt were old-time bros. Had been since elementary school. If anyone was planning the bachelor party, it should be him!

"Vegas. Palms Resort. Secret suite on floor 54. Thirty-six hours Bro-athalon. That's the party you handed over to mama's boy here?" When neither guy looked properly concerned, Levi snapped his fingers at Gray. "First thing that comes to mind. Vanna White. Go."

"Wheel of Fortune."

"Wrong," Levi said, enjoying the sight of Emmitt's shit-eating grin fading into abject horror.

"What?" Gray asked. "She's on *Wheel of Fortune.*"

"Said every high school virgin ever," Levi responded. "The correct answer is . . ." Levi pointed to Emmitt.

"Cover of *Playboy*. May of '87." Emmitt rattled off her stats like any hot-blooded teenage guy who hadn't been too much of a golden boy to search out his dad's stash.

Gray's fingers slid over his phone's screen; then he held up an image of the vintage magazine cover. "Says right here, 'Before *Wheel of Fortune*.' "

"Sorry, no points for remembering the fucking article names," Levi pointed out.

"I have to agree, man," Emmitt said. "Promise me I didn't make a mistake asking you?"

Gray shoved Emmitt. "It's not like I was your first choice. You asked me because you felt bad. It was a pity pick."

"Pity pick? No way," Levi argued. "And for the record, I didn't need anyone's help with Beckett. I was doing just fine on my own. I didn't need you throwing me a bone by putting us in each other's path. And if you want him to plan your party, by all means."

Emmitt snorted. "Before you get your panties in a bunch, I asked last week at bowling. I asked Gray because he doesn't leave me hanging. If you can't keep bowling night straight, I don't want to run the risk of you getting the date wrong and us spending it at the Holiday Inn down the street with a llama for a stripper. And since I didn't want to end up at the Ice Capades, I was going to ask you to co-plan it tonight."

"I wouldn't take us to Ice Capades," Gray said, and they both glared at him. "Different situation. It was my birthday. And for the record, I bought those tickets for Michelle, Paisley, and me."

"Even Michelle knew Aquaman on Ice is lame. Frozen on Ice is the way to go," Levi said, managing to still sound like a guy who knew all about Vanna White.

"So do I need to get down on a knee, or will you be the co-host?" Emmitt asked.

"If G does all the legwork, I'll oversee to make sure it's a bring-your-man-card kind of place," Levi said. He and Emmitt bumped fists.

"Just remember there's an actual bride in the equation this time."

"Don't worry, Wally." Levi clapped Emmitt's shoulder. "The Beav's afraid of Annie, too. Which is why we will scratch any destination that requires a thousand dollars in singles. But seriously, don't worry. Anything too crazy is out, because work is crazy."

And because strippers had lost their appeal when Levi became an uncle. Even lingering second glances at women who hadn't made the first move wasn't his idea of fun. Which was why he was taking cues from Beckett. With Beckett, he'd had to modify the rules. She'd never make the first move, but he paid close attention to her body language to know when to push a little and when to back off and let her get used to the idea of a relationship.

Only she'd showed him a few new sides of her in his truck earlier. Flirty being the most surprising. He'd never anticipated a good-night walk to the door so much.

"What are we talking?" Emmitt asked. "A long weekend?"

Levi choked. "I was thinking an overnight. Some upcoming Monday between now and the wedding," Levi said.

"The rest of the world works Monday through Friday," Gray pointed out. "So unless you think an arcade is bro enough, it's going to have to be a weekend."

Levi let out a tired sigh. "Let me see if I can get Gus to cover the bar for a night."

"What happened to the new bartender you were training last week?"

"He's not working out."

"Dude," Emmitt said. "Stop firing the kids for not getting it right day one. I get that this is your dad's bar, and you can't stand to see anyone but him behind it. But if you're going to make this trip of yours, you need to keep someone around longer than three hours."

"If I'm leaving for six months, it can't be just some kid. It has to be the right kid."

"I guess that's one way of seeing if the kid can handle it."

"You guys going to sit around gabbing like biddies at bingo, or are you ready to play?" Beckett asked, holding a bright, sparkly yellow ball.

But what had his blood pumping was Beckett's lack of jacket. She'd gone to the counter zipped to the collarbone and come back sporting a red shirt that was silky, curve-hugging, with these tiny buttons than ran from neck to navel. Levi usually preferred the ease of a zipper, but the way those buttons gently tugged at the seams in silent challenge made his fingers itch to prove they were up to the task.

Oh, she'd unbuttoned enough to keep things interesting. And Levi wasn't one to stare, but that shirt racked her pins up something special.

"That looks like a custom ball," he said. "I thought you weren't a ringer."

"I said it wasn't my strong suit. I used to play on a league, but it's been a while. Charlie keeps it behind the counter for me, so I don't have to lug it on my scooter."

She handed it over for him to inspect, and that's when he saw it. In big silvery letters, inlayed into the surface of the ball, were the words HOW BIG IS YOURS?

He smirked. "If you win, you can find out."

"I am going to win. And why waste my bet on something I can learn from the stall in the lady's room?" She gave a toothy grin. "Now who's up?"

"Ladies first," Levi said, stepping back to watch as she strutted to the line and, *damn,* she filled out those smarty pants spectacularly well.

She stepped onto the polished wood floor and gave a little wiggle of that heart-shaped ass. Her arm went down, and she glided forward, and . . .

"Shit," Levi said, and all three guys stood to watch as the ball slid right down the middle of the lane, the spin too fast to be seen by the human eye. It arched right and back left, and before anyone could blink, Beckett was walking back, a loud resounding crack cutting through the air.

Gaze locked on Levi, she smiled as the pins flew every which way, one landing in the neighboring pit. Her smile wasn't overtly sexy or even smug. She was smiling because she was enjoying herself, letting go and having fun. And it was the sexiest thing he'd ever seen.

Levi stepped onto the polished wood floor to wait. Confidence lit her expression as she strutted toward him, not stopping until she was inches away.

"Girl Wonder, if bowling isn't your strong suit, what is?"

"Wouldn't you like to know?" she asked, and he had a hard time answering.

Her hair hung in loose waves, her brown eyes sparkled with humor, and she radiated this gentle sweetness that attracted people to her like bees to honey. Beckett looked carefree and happy. Two things he wanted to make sure she felt all the time.

"I've wanted to know for a few years."

CHAPTER 12

Beckett thought about those words for the rest of the night. She hadn't known how to respond when he'd said it, and she didn't know how to respond now that they were heading home. She'd been so busy trying to decipher what he'd meant that she didn't notice they'd pulled off the freeway until all the streetlights had vanished.

"Where are we going?" she asked, looking at the highway disappearing in the rear window.

"Surprise."

"I don't like surprises."

He flashed her one of the easygoing grins that made her heart skip a few beats. "You'll like this one."

The tires spun beneath them, and Beckett yelped, jerking up straight to look out the side window, then down at the road. "We're no longer on pavement." The car bounced, and trees flew by. "We're not even on a road."

"If surprises were clearly marked, then everyone would know about them." He placed a hand on her thigh, and a small spark ignited.

"What was that?"

"Chemistry. Something that shouldn't come as a surprise. Now, hold on." With a laugh, he gunned it, and they sped up a winding gravel track. The sky was black, the wind whistled past them, and Beckett took his hand and didn't let go until they pulled through a clearing and stopped.

Beckett wasn't sure where they were until he shut off the engine and she could hear waves crashing on the rocks below.

"Did you bring me to Make-Out Point?" she asked, a small thrill bubbling up like she was sixteen and about to sneak out to meet a cute boy.

"In Rome, it's called the Cliffs," he said. "But Make-Out Point is a little south of here."

"I bet you spent a lot of time there with the cheerleading team, growing up?" she teased.

"Not as much as you'd think," he said, but she didn't believe him. "I was more into the swim team. How about you? Let me

270

guess — you were into college guys in high school."

"No. I was pretty shy growing up and could barely talk to guys my own age," she admitted. "More animal friends than people."

It hadn't helped that her mom was long gone by then, so Beckett came home after school to help out with Thomas. She never went to a school dance, let alone on a date that ended at Make-Out Point.

"What kind of idiots did you go to high school with? I'd have sweet-talked you up here first day of freshman year."

"I grew up outside Trenton, New Jersey. So that would have been quite the commute for a teen. Plus, when I was a freshman, you would've been" — she did some quick calculations — "nineteen or twenty. Off at college, and you already know how I felt about college guys."

"I'd kick any twenty-year-old ass who came sniffing near Paisley," he said, and she wondered, not for the first time, how being responsible for a teen girl affected his outlook on dating. He flirted with anyone who had boobs, but she had a hard time placing the last woman he'd dated. "And no, Michelle got pregnant my sophomore year of college, so I would have already been back in Rome."

Beckett thought about twenty-year-old Levi, off at college on a sailing scholarship, the parties, the girls, every night a new fun adventure to be had. His whole life ahead of him, then deciding to walk away from that freedom to help his sister. There weren't many men who'd do what he'd done. Instead of feeling bitter or robbed, he'd embraced being an uncle and given it his all.

"You got quiet," he said, giving her knee a squeeze.

"I was thinking about how lucky Paisley is to have you for an uncle," she said quietly. "And that I'm pretty lucky you don't scare easy. Think of all the fun I'd have missed out on."

"The fun's just getting started," he said. "Now, put my coat back on, and don't get out until I come around and get your door."

"But you'll get cold."

"No self-respecting Rhode Island man leaves the house to pick up a beautiful woman without bringing a spare." With no warning, he lifted her hand to his warm, full lips and blew on it before placing it back in her lap. Then he shrugged out of his coat and handed it to her. "There are gloves in the pockets."

Beckett was glad it was dark in the cab, because she was at least a dozen different shades of charmed.

He reached behind his seat and came up with another coat and a cloth bag, then opened the door and climbed out. It took her eyes a moment to adjust to the dark after the overhead light had come on, but she was able to make out his shadow in the moonlight as he walked around the back of the truck.

And what an impressive shadow he possessed.

Tall, broad shoulders, big hands, and an even bigger chest — so solid and stable, a woman could easily lean on it. Those words pretty much summed up his character, as well. There was nothing about Levi that scared her — except her feelings for him.

Her door opened. "Careful, it's rocky out here."

He offered his hand to help her out of the truck. But when she was safely on the ground, he didn't seem in a rush to let go. Which was fine with her, since she liked the feel of his skin against hers.

The cold air stung her nose and turned her breath to ice, but the rest of her was toasty from his body heat, which still clung to the coat. He walked her to the back of the truck, then lifted her onto the tailgate, which was padded with that subzero sleeping bag he'd mentioned.

"Put on the gloves while I bundle you up."

She'd only put the first glove on when he grabbed a puffy blanket and wrapped it around her like a burrito, then hopped up next to her. Even through the triple layer of blanket, she could feel his thigh pressed against her, his shoulder brushing hers as he dug through the cloth bag.

When it became clear he wasn't finding what he wanted, she reached over and slid his flashlight from his front pocket. He hesitated for a moment, long enough for her to know he was acknowledging her handiwork, then went back to the rustling.

She clicked on his handy-dandy flashlight and aimed it at the bag, which she could now see contained a Thanksgiving-load of Tupperware.

"What's that?" She reached into the bag, and he closed it around her hand.

"Be patient," he said, and only when she removed her hand did he go back to work. He pulled out a few containers, opening each one and sticking in a plastic fork, then handed her a bottle.

"You brought wine? How about a wine opener?"

He flipped over the flashlight. The bottom was a wine opener. "Handy. You know, you don't strike me as the kind of guy who prepares moonlight picnics."

"You need to get to know me better," he said, then handed her one of the containers. The delicious scent of fresh herbs and tomatoes greeted her. She put it to her nose and sniffed.

"Oh my god," she moaned. "What is this?"

"Dinner. I noticed you never had that hot dog."

"Thankfully I didn't, or I wouldn't have this in my hand." She took a bite, and her mouth exploded with the most amazing flavors. "I've never had this. Why have I never had this?"

"It's moussaka, which is kind of like Greek lasagna, only with eggplant and potatoes instead of noodles. It's my favorite recipe from my grandmother."

"And you're sharing it with me?"

"My mom baked it tonight to tempt me into having dinner at her place. It worked so well, I figured I'd do the same."

"What would happen to the great Levi Rhodes if it got out he stole moves from his mom?"

"My mom would get bumper stickers made. Then tell whoever would listen about

275

the mind-altering powers of her moussaka. It's already rumored to be the cure for finicky-kid syndrome."

"Maybe I should send Thomas her way. He won't eat anything green, mushy, or with nutritional value. So different from when I was young. My mom didn't do picky. You ate what was served or went hungry. By served, I mean what was delivered. She was more of a takeout kind of cook." She took another bite and moaned. "You seriously grew up eating like this every night?"

"My mom shows her love through food, which is why I was a chubby kid."

"I need to see pictures to believe it. Best surprise ever," she said around a mouthful. "I recognize the name from your menu, but I had no idea what it was, which is why I never ordered it. I will next time."

"Don't. Gus is a great chef, but he can't hold a candle to my family. Next time you want some, I'll make it for you."

"You cook?"

He released a very male-sounding laugh. "Since I was old enough to reach the counter. I deliver, too, if you're lucky."

Realizing she had polished off a big portion, she offered him the container. He merely took the fork — the same one she'd been using — and had a bite.

She sipped from the bottle and offered it to him. He waved it off. "I'm driving. But don't let that stop you."

Beckett took another swallow and laughed. "What?" he asked.

"I'm sitting on a tailgate, eating Greek food, and drinking wine from a bottle. On a weeknight."

"You need to hang with me more," he said and had another bite.

Something she was beginning to seriously consider. If he could make her feel this special hanging out, what would it be like to go on an actual date? And how hard would it be when it ended?

"No wonder women can't leave you alone," she said, leaning back against the side wall to sip the wine.

"Funny you should say that, since the only woman I'm interested in keeps ghosting me."

"I wasn't ghosting you," she said, and he shot her a disbelieving look. "Okay, fine, I was ghosting you, but only because I was embarrassed of the epic display of crazy when you dropped me off."

"I grew up in a Greek home; embarrassing each other was our way of showing affection," he said. "Just tonight, my five-foot-nothing mom sent me to my room because

I took you wedding cake tasting before bringing you home to meet her."

She tried to sit up and choked on her wine. "What did you tell her?"

"That I'll bring you over for dinner before the wedding." With a wink that stirred her insides, he took one last bite, then put the lid on the container and stored it back in the bag.

"What are you doing?" She reached for the moussaka, and he gave a low chuckle.

"There's still dessert."

She stretched, gauging how much room was left in her stomach, then factored in the kind of dessert that was likely to follow up that meal. "Is it as good as I think?"

"Better."

"Fine, but I reserve the right to go back to the moussaka after dessert."

"Deal." Keeping one container out, he set the bag behind him. "It's kind of messy, so open up."

She considered calling bullshit, but the sweet vanilla teasing her nose had her opening wide. The moment her lips closed around the fork, she melted into a delicious, heavenly sugar coma. "That is the best thing I've ever tasted."

"So far," he said in a tone that had her swallowing her bite whole.

278

He set the dessert aside and pulled out a small stack of cards. "Before we finish, I wanted to give you this."

She glanced at the four-by-five card and lifted a brow. "It's a scorecard. You do know that I won."

"Honey, the whole East Coast knows you won." He clicked on the flashlight. "Turn it over."

She did, and on the back was a handwritten list of terms, between her company and his. When she got to the end, she reread the whole thing over again, but it was hard to make out the words with the grateful tears swelling in her eyes. As the content began to make sense, she looked up at Levi, and his expression made her heart turn to mush.

"You want to hire me?" she whispered.

"I know it's not official," he said. "But it's a starting point. There are two things in there. First, I want to put you on retainer to help me handle my staffing needs."

"There's more?" she asked.

He chuckled. "There's another card." She pulled the cards apart to find another offer. "I want to do a six-month contract between Consider It Done and the Crow's Nest. I thought about what you said, and you're right, with the proper planning and partner, I can expand my client base with delivery.

After the six months are up, if both parties agree it's beneficial, then we can talk about a long-term agreement."

Beckett stared at the contract and didn't know how to respond. She'd been hoping for a sixty-day trial run but had prepared herself to settle for thirty days. "This says that if both parties find the relationship beneficial, then Consider It Done will be the exclusive delivery service for the Crow's Nest."

"One delivery service is all I can handle," he joked. "Plus, Gus doesn't play well with others, but for some reason, he likes you. Why jinx it by adding an unknown?"

"This is more than generous." She met his gaze. "But why? I know I said it was my Must Have, but I would have agreed to your micromanaging as long as Annie got her wedding."

He leaned in. "And I would have agreed to host the wedding even if you didn't let me . . . oversee."

She was speechless, because the walls were down, her armor on the floor, and she was as vulnerable as she'd been the day she'd let Pete in. "Why are you doing this?"

He looked confused. "Why wouldn't I?"

"You barely know me."

"I know everything I need to. You're a

hard worker, you're honest, and you made so many spot-on calls about my business, I'd be an idiot not to hire you." When she started to speak, he held up a hand. "Before you give me an answer, I want you to go home and think about what terms you want added to the contract. Make sure you add in your policy for cancellations, overtime fees, and being-an-asshole tax. You can use it as a boilerplate for your other clients."

"What happens if I don't meet your expectations?"

His expression turned soft. "I have no doubt you'll meet my expectations."

Beckett wished she felt as certain about the arrangement. The quickest way to complicate a professional relationship was to make it personal. The harder she tried to ignore the chemistry between them, the more aware of him she became. They hadn't even been on an official date yet, and already the lines were becoming blurred.

"Oh," he said when she failed to express the same enthusiasm. His expression was serious. "Unless you have concerns about working with me?"

"No. I mean, maybe." She shook her head. "I hadn't thought I did, but now I'm not so sure."

He chuckled. "I'm glad we got that cleared up."

"Being around you, the way we were tonight, confuses things for me," she admitted quietly, thinking back to the sweet way he'd catered to her every need, checking in several times to be sure she hadn't had a call from home, sending her secret glances when no one else was looking.

And he wasn't the only one succumbing to the attraction between them. Beckett was just as guilty — if not more. Indulging in secret glances, breathy laughs, and using any excuse to touch him. And that was before she'd revealed her sexy red top.

"How can I help clarify things?"

"That's the problem. Once you do, pretending to be friends will be hard."

"Pretending we're not already more than friends is harder." He tucked a strand of hair behind her ear, and she leaned into his hand.

She forced herself away from his soft touch. "Not as hard as it will be when our best friends get married, our merged social circles are authenticated by the state of Rhode Island, and things between us go south."

"This thing between us started long before our friends became engaged. And it's not going away any time soon." He placed her hand on his chest and held firmly. "That, right there, is chemistry. Plain and simple."

"Maybe, but our situation has never been more complicated." There were so many things that could go wrong, and too many people a falling-out between them would affect. "The adult thing to do is ignore it."

"I can think of a dozen other adult ways to handle this situation," he said. "Want to hear my top ten?"

CHAPTER 13

Beckett would be surprised if even one of his top ten involved clothing of any kind. And while the possibility of them sleeping together wasn't as alarming as it once had been, she'd have to be crazy to entertain the idea with any real seriousness.

"I'll pass," Beckett said. Then she added with a touch of sarcasm, "Plus, it's not like sex has ever messed up an already complicated situation."

"I was talking about going on an actual date, just you and me with none of the outside baggage, but I'm willing to try your idea."

Her nipples were more than onboard. In fact, the only part of her that still thought this was a bad idea was her head.

"I don't do relationships so well," she said quietly. "Which is why I date guys who live out of the area. That way, when it becomes too much for them, we go our separate ways, and there's no awkward run-ins around town."

"Don't lump me in with those idiots from your past, who were too stupid to realize what they had. I'm a man who knows what he wants." He reached out and, before she knew what was happening, he lifted her up and placed her on his lap. "And I want to see where this goes."

And by *this,* he had to be referring to the chemistry between them. Anything more was out of the question. Beckett didn't do serious, Levi was leaving for the summer, and neither of them had much luck in the relationship department.

"I still have concerns," she said.

"Fair enough," Levi said. "And you won tonight."

"That I did." Though it had nothing to do with the final score.

"Then the floor is yours. Name your terms," he whispered, his lips against her earlobe sending delicious shivers down her back. "Let me warm you up while you think."

Warm? The moment his hands slid down her back, beneath the blanket, to her thighs, she went from warm to surface-of-the-sun hot. Her hormones felt like mini furnaces racing through her body. Then he pulled her against his chest, and she had to reevaluate her earlier assessment.

He didn't just feel solid; he felt secure. And when his arms came around her, all the stress drained from her body, leaving her relaxed and content. Safe. Three feelings she hadn't let herself experience in a while. But in his capable embrace, she couldn't resist.

"I'm all ears. Tell me what you want."

So many things. Nearly all of them she was too afraid to say aloud for fear of jinxing what was happening. But each and every one, she wanted with Levi. And there he was, inches from her. All she had to do was go for it.

Be bold. Be bold. Be freaking bold!

But no matter how many different ways she told herself to go for it, making that first move was paralyzing. Because if this attraction was half as powerful as she anticipated, one kiss and they'd both ignite. And hadn't they both fought enough fires for one lifetime?

From the outside, it was easy to mistake Beckett for someone who needed saving, when in reality she'd been saving herself since she was a kid. A guy like Levi, with his loyal heart and need to protect others, might mistake her private nature for weakness. She wasn't interested in becoming another one of the people Levi worried about.

"I know what I want." She slid her arms around his neck. "But before I tell you, I need your word that whatever happens between us, it will never become awkward."

"You threw your cock in my face, and mine's been pushing up against your backside for the last few minutes. I think we're long past the awkward stage."

She barked out a laugh and covered her mouth. She had no idea how he managed it, but around Levi, she waffled between laughing at him and cussing him out.

"I like that just when I think I have you figured out, you do something that surprises me," she admitted, because he most definitely surprised her — tonight and at every turn — in the best ways possible.

His gaze turned so serious her chest tightened. "There's a lot about me that might surprise you, if you give me a chance." He looked her in the eye. "You willing to give me a chance, Beck?"

She had long thought she was missing whatever elusive quality it was that made someone lucky in love. It had affected her relationships with men, friends, even her family. At this point, she wasn't even certain she was capable of giving a guy like Levi the kind of chance he deserved. But, God help her, she wanted to try. So badly, her body quivered with anticipation, while her heart rolled over to show its soft underbelly.

Levi was kind, funny, sweet, and so giving of himself. He had this capable way that drew her to him, a contagious confidence that made her want to say yes. But it was the small things he did for others, going out of his way to make their lives easier and happier, that challenged everything she believed about Levi — and what dating could look like with the right man.

She wasn't saying Levi was her Mr. Right, or that she was even looking for Mr. Right, but she'd be a fool to pass up the chance at an affair with a guy she'd been crushing on from afar. What was the harm in enjoying the time they had, then going back to her regularly scheduled life after he set sail?

"I'd like to try," she said honestly.

"I like the sound of that," he murmured, as his hand cupped her jaw and his fingers slid into her hair. His thumb lagged behind, languidly tracing down her cheekbone to lightly graze her lower lip.

"I like playing hooky with you," she said, feeling suddenly very shy. "And I'm realizing that I like being with you. A lot. I'm just working up the confidence to say it."

"I think you just did." He tucked a strand of hair behind her ear. "This is new to me, too. You're not on the edge alone."

"Who says I'm on the edge?"

He chuckled and placed her hand against his heart. She could feel it pounding through all the layers of fabric. "Then how about you be there for me, because I'm on the edge looking over."

"Levi," she whispered thickly.

She didn't know who made the first move, but one minute she was telling herself to be bold, the next their lips brushed in a kiss that was so tender, so perfect, she never wanted it to end. She would be content to sit right here, on his lap, and kiss him until the sun came up.

His mouth slowly moved against hers with devastating care, and a seriousness that shook her to the core. An inferno of lust ignited in her belly, expanding in all directions with such speed her head spun.

His fingers gently tightened in her hair, tilting her head to the side as he kissed his way down her neck, his breath hot on her skin. To say his lips were experienced was like saying Jimi Hendrix was good at guitar.

"Levi," she groaned. "Who kissed who?"

He smiled against her skin. "Does it matter?"

"Well, if I kissed you, good on me. If you kissed me, then I'd like to be the one to initiate the next one."

He looked up, staring at her for a long beat, then shrugged. "Okay, you caught me. I kissed you. Your turn."

"My turn?"

"Yup." He leaned back against the truck bed wall, all casual like, his arms folded behind his head.

She bit back a smile, then rested her hands on his chest, one on each pec, and leaned in. And this time, when their lips met, there was no doubt who'd kissed whom. And since she was being bold, she wasted no time tracing her tongue along the seam of his lips.

"God, Beck," he groaned, giving her the confidence to deepen things — on every level.

Gently sucking his lower lip, she ran her hands up from chest to jaw, holding him exactly where she wanted, then covered his mouth with hers. She wanted to cover a lot more of him, but the blanket bag was acting like a slinky, coiled around her lower half.

She shifted; he moaned. She twisted, and things got interesting. Laid-back Levi lost some of that trademark control and pulled her all the way against him, then took over. Which was fine by Beckett, since she was having a hard enough time remembering to breathe. Levi was a master kisser, with the kind of well-honed skills that made Beckett wonder if she'd been stuck on the bunny slopes of dating.

Speaking of slopes, Levi might not be on the competitive sailing circuit anymore, but his body hadn't suffered one bit. He was all sinew and muscle, from his pecs way down to his abs, and he had six, well-defined, well worth the hype, packs to explore.

"Beck." His groan sounded husky, and his hands captured her wrists. "A few inches farther, and it's game on."

"I'm sorry." She tried to snatch her hands back, but he held them in place. "I just meant to kiss you and end it there. But —" She shrugged.

"Your hands didn't get the memo?"

"My head's having similar issues."

His eyes heated. "What does that mean? Again, asking for a friend."

"That I'm beginning to wonder if you're right," she said, trying not to stare at his mouth and failing horribly. "Maybe the best way to figure this out is like two adults and face it head on."

"That's the smartest idea I've ever heard." His eyes were dark. "Go on, I'm listening."

Only he wasn't. He was too busy sliding his hands up her sides, slowly closing in on her lace bra, to be paying attention.

"Well, we could set some guidelines, so we each know where the other stands."

"Rules like: If I lick it, then it's mine?"

Heat pulsed low in her belly. "More like, managing expectations so no one ends up confused."

He lifted his head. "Do I look confused?"

"No." She swallowed. He looked a little wild, and on edge, like a big, beautiful turned-on man who wanted to rip each little red button off — with his hands tied behind his back.

"Why don't you start with the first rule." He dipped his head until his warm breath tickled her throat, and his lips were so close that when he whispered, "While I try to clarify things for you," each word danced off her skin.

Beckett smiled as Levi kissed his way up to cover her mouth with his, then kissed her with a seriousness that made his position on matters crystal clear. Gone were the gentle exploration and teasing nips, and in their place was an urgency that swept over her like a storm in July.

"Rule number one," she said, suddenly understanding Thomas's need for rules. "No sleepovers."

"Not a problem," he said, rising up on his knees. In one fluid motion, Beckett was lying in the truck bed, the sleeping bag under her, and Levi on top of her. "When I get you in bed, there won't be any sleeping." He gently sank his teeth into her earlobe, then sucked it into his mouth. "Next?"

"Um." She had a hard time concentrating with his mouth on her. "Rule two. What happens between us stays between us."

The last thing she needed was Annie getting it into her matchmaking mind that there was long term potential here.

"Fine by me." He lifted his head. "I'm not into sharing. Plus, that falls under the 'If I lick it, then it's mine' rule."

"Shhhh," she said, pulling him back to her. "I can't think with you talking."

Apparently, that worked for him. With a bad-boy grin that stole her breath, he devoted his entire focus to applying kisses — hot, teasing kisses — down the column of her neck, paying special attention to the curve. When her layers of clothing obstructed his path, he peeled open the coat, then took his sweet time inspecting all one dozen of her jacket's zippers.

"Sexy," was all he said before she felt a confident tug at the base of her throat.

As he slowly worked the zipper lower and lower, his work-roughened knuckle against her skin had her pulse racing higher and higher.

His hands were masterful, one sliding under the back of her jacket, the other parting the front, while his heated gaze locked on hers. With a final slip of the zipper, her jacket fell to either side, allowing a rush of cool air to travel along the freshly exposed skin. Any chill quickly vanished when Levi bent his head, his lips whispering over the gentle hollow above her breastbone.

Lying beside her, he came up on his elbow to watch as his knuckle followed the path of tiny buttons on her silk shirt, from her belly to the front clasp of her bra. With a masterful flick of the wrist, the first button was toast. Much like its owner.

He moved the silk aside to bare the edge of the black lace hidden beneath and let out a groan that had a slow burn starting deep in her belly.

"Stunning," he breathed, sending a little thrill through Beckett.

Never in her life had she been called something so fairy-tale as stunning. That he'd said it with raw male appreciation in his gaze only added to the anticipation as his fingers fiddled with the next button. This one didn't come undone as easily.

"Rule three," he said, his brow puckered in concentration. "If the buttons are too small for my hands, they end up on the floor."

"Or, practice makes perfect," she teased, reaching up to easily flick the bottom button free. Levi shoved her hands out of the way to try again.

Beckett laughed; she couldn't help herself. Levi went about the task with such determination, his forehead furrowed, his lips forming a thin line. And as he grumbled over all the places the designer could shove his buttons, his expression resembled someone trying to defuse a bomb, not attempting to unbutton a blouse.

"You think this is funny?" he asked.

"Very." She leaned back and took a moment to watch him. The careful way his fingers moved over the delicate silk, how his broad shoulders blocked the moon as he leaned closer, his gaze flickering to her every few moments as if gauging how she was feeling.

Alive was the first word that came to mind. Actually, *cherished* was the first, but that felt a lot scarier than *alive,* so she stayed with the safe choice.

A smug grin lit his face right as she felt the fabric give. He looked so proud of himself as he pushed the silk aside and the lace trim on her bra peeked out. His gaze dropped to admire his handiwork, his thumb brushing over the lace, and a flash of sheer male appreciation lit his eyes.

She watched breathlessly as his gaze slid ever-so-slowly from her breasts to her lips, and by the time he reached her eyes, there was a tenderness in his that melted her insides.

"You going to finish what you started?" She toyed with the neckline of her blouse. "Or do you need some help?"

"I always finish what I start." He captured her hands in his, bringing them to his mouth to give her fingers a playful nip. "The question is, will you be able to handle it?"

She teasingly rolled her eyes. "Which brings us to rule number four. No calling, texting, sexting, or otherwise communicating about your alleged sexual prowess."

"There's nothing alleged about it." When she chuckled, he added, "Do I sense another bet coming on?"

"Didn't go so well for you last time, big guy."

He gave a low, sexy laugh. "I'm having

one of the best non-dates of my life with a woman whose lips taste like horchata. And she just issued a challenge I'm dying to accept."

Without warning, Levi covered her mouth with his. No hesitation, no tentative brushes this time. Oh no, Levi kissed her with single-minded purpose: to show her just how hard he was going to rock her world.

Note to self: Never, ever, ever challenge Levi.

Because, *oh man,* was she ever in trouble. He teased and kissed, one hand fisted in her hair, the other roaming down her back to her bottom, languidly taking his time until she was quivering beneath him and he'd proven his point.

And when he pulled back, they were both breathing hard, and Beckett was clinging to him like a koala to a eucalyptus tree.

"You warm enough?" he asked.

"If I say yes, will you finish helping me out of my clothes?"

"There is nothing I want more than to know if you match up your lace as well as your socks," he said gruffly, spanning a hand over her hip, making her feel petite and incredibly feminine. "Except to know what makes you . . . you."

"Are you trying to figure me out?" she

asked. "Because that could take a while."

"What's the rush?"

Biting her lip, she spoke softly. "You're leaving in a few months, remember?"

"Doesn't mean we can't enjoy the time we have."

"Those are big words for a first non-date," Beckett joked, hoping he'd laugh and stop looking at her as though she were special. He didn't laugh, and the flutters got worse.

"This is an important first non-date. And you're worth big words." And if that wasn't the most romantic thing in the world, he added, "You're worth a hell of a lot a more than the Bruces and Steves of the world."

"What's wrong with the Bruces and Steves?" she asked.

"I can make a list for you later. That you had to ask will be at the top." His fingers slipped over her hip to her lower back. "When I get you naked, it won't be a guessing game. I'll know what you like, what you love, and what you'll want for breakfast come morning."

She liked how up front he was, loved how his fingers slid under her shirt to the bare skin beneath, and as for the breakfast — she hoped he'd be on the menu. But he seemed to have a set pace and plan in mind, which was great, since her plan hadn't extended past the red top and boots.

"The matching socks," she whispered. "They were worth it."

"And I haven't even hung the moon yet," he said with a boyish smile that sparked a giddiness inside, a bold recklessness that fueled the hope that maybe she could have something of her own. Something that was all hers, even if only temporarily. Despite all ginormous signs that this was an incredibly idiotic idea. But that was a problem for another time. Right now, she wanted to be present and enjoy what had turned out to be a wonderful night.

So when he rolled onto his back and pulled her close, she snuggled into the crook of his shoulder. Face tilted skyward, she watched the stars overhead, millions of them flickering in the otherwise black night.

"There are so many stars," she whispered.

"It's not as beautiful as being in the middle of the ocean, but it's a close second," he admitted. "If I close my eyes and listen to the crashing waves, breathe in the ocean mist, I can almost feel the boat sway beneath me."

Beckett closed her eyes and breathed in deep, letting the steady pounding of the surf lull her into deep, rhythmic breathing. Levi's arms slid around her, pulling her close, and she threaded their fingers together.

"Do you miss it? Sailing?"

"Yeah." She felt the word rumble through her. "Out there, time slows down until it's just you and the water. The farther you get from shore, the more the noise and confusion fades, until it becomes quiet enough to think. About important things."

"That sounds like heaven."

"Don't get me wrong — I love Rome. I love time with my family and friends, and knowing if something happens, I'm here to take care of them," he said. "But sometimes I need the quiet. To process or reflect. It's difficult for me to do that when my world's so loud and demanding."

"When was the last time you went sailing?"

"For more than a long weekend?" He chuckled. "How long have you lived in Rome?"

She shifted to rest her cheek on his chest, looking up at him. "That long?"

"Longer." He sounded tired, as if he were emotionally running on empty. "Which is why I come up here when I can."

"I thought you came up here to make out."

"Beck, the only person I've ever brought

here is Michelle." He slid his hand along her back and over her nape to play with her hair. "And now you."

Beckett didn't know why she had such a hard time believing that. Maybe because it didn't fit the play-it-fast-and-loose ladies' man she'd made Levi out to be. Then again, nothing she'd learned about him over the past few weeks had supported that image.

"I'm not saying I didn't spend time at the Cliffs," he joked. "But after my dad passed, this was the only place I could come to be alone and think. And I came here every chance I got. I'd bring a six-pack, a sleeping bag, and a journal. Then I'd sit on the tailgate and list all the things I was going to do once Mom and Michelle were settled."

"Like a bucket list?"

"Are you a fellow bucket lister, Beck?"

"Yes," she admitted. "Although I'm better at making lists than actually checking anything off."

"I'm not much better. I was getting ready to take the trip my dad and I planned when Paisley was born." He smiled. "That girl inspired a list all her own. And I have checked off nearly every milestone in that journal."

She shifted to rest her cheek on his chest. "What's left to check off?"

"On my Paisley List?" He considered that for a moment. "Walk her down the aisle, keep her away from boys until she's thirty, teach her how to drive before I go completely gray." He sobered. "Right now, my focus is on helping her to handle Michelle's death. She puts on a brave face, but I know she's shattered inside. Ditto my mom."

"Is that why you changed your plans around? So Paisley's time in Europe with Annie will coincide with your trip?" It didn't take a mathematician to explain why the countdown clock above his bar had a tendency to jump ahead.

"It's not that I think Gray couldn't handle anything that might come up, but —"

She looked up at him through her lashes. "But you don't think Gray can handle whatever might come up the way you can."

"I must come off as an overprotective parent with a God complex." Chagrin lit his cheeks. "I promise you, out of the three dads, I'm the only one who didn't get a Proud Helicopter Papa ball cap for Christmas."

"I didn't imagine you would. And for the record, you come off as a devoted and loving uncle." She lifted her head slightly. "I'm not sure how valid my opinion is, since I have the home number of every one of

Thomas's teachers, and I still make my dad bag lunches when he goes to Boston for work."

"I take my mom to all her doctors' appointments because she's afraid of hospitals," he said, his hand abandoning the nape of her neck. "I've also been known to drive across town just to start her fire when it snows."

"If I was sent home with a container full of that flaky, buttery, phyllo dough with custard dessert, I'd start her fire every night."

"It's called galaktoboureko, and if you play your cards right, I'll send you home with the rest."

Glancing at the stars overhead, Beckett closed her eyes and made a wish that one day she could play cards at the same level as Levi. His game was so flawless, she almost believed that he wasn't playing a game at all.

"How long will you be gone?" It was more a reminder for herself than a question.

"Six months is the plan."

Those words functioned as the wakeup call she desperately needed. He might find her interesting now but, while Beckett led an unusual existence, his interest in her would quickly wane. That was assuming they even made it to summer.

"I'll miss the beginning of her senior year," he continued. "But be back for the big stuff."

"College trips, prom, graduation. All so exciting." And all things she wished for Thomas's future. But those milestones wouldn't have the same trajectory as Paisley's or her classmates'. While Thomas might be able to live on his own one day, that day was a long way off.

"Terrifying, you mean. I'm still coming to terms with leaving this summer when Paisley decides she suddenly wanted to go on this upcoming school ski trip, which I had actually encouraged her to go on. Don't know what I was thinking there."

"That going on the trip with her friends and being excited about something new shows that she's moving on with her life. I think it's a good idea."

"I did too," he said. "Only now, all I can think of is what if something goes wrong and I was the one who pushed her to go. And if Gray gets his wish, I won't even be a chaperone. I'll be at some bachelor party."

"Earlier you said I was capable —"

"I said you were the most capable person I know," he amended.

A warm tint crept up the tips of Beckett's

ears — and spread to places she usually kept locked away. Dark places that she was afraid to shine a light on.

"I'm capable because at one time I felt powerless," she said, hating the sour feeling that burned in her stomach whenever she spoke of her mother. "When I was a little younger than Paisley, I found myself in a situation I was completely ill-equipped to handle. I promised myself I'd never let that happen again. And it hasn't, but constantly battling everyone and everything for power is exhausting."

"And I imagine lonely."

"It can be," she said, her voice thick with emotion. "It can also be healing, if handled correctly. And with you in Paisley's corner, she might win a little freedom to leave the nest. It could be a good thing."

"Somehow I don't think that's how it happened for you," he said. His blue eyes, now stormy and deliberate, never wavered from hers.

"No. Mine was more of the 'aim for the leaves on your way down' kind of experience," she said, hiding behind humor.

Levi didn't let her. His arms came all the way around her so he could lace his fingers with hers. "I love that you're strong and resilient, but I can't help but worry about

305

the woman inside the tough-girl jacket."

"Me too, sometimes." Her throat closed, because she'd never admitted that aloud to anyone. Including herself.

Maybe it was that she was staring at the sky, or the intimate way the night had settled around them, but there was an easy calm about Levi that soothed her fears and made her feel safe.

"A few months after Thomas was diagnosed with autism spectrum disorder, my dad was in New York scoring a soundtrack for a movie. Leaving my mom alone to raise two kids over summer vacation. Judy did her best to keep us entertained, lots of day trips and hiking, but I think the reality of what life was going to be like eventually wore her down.

"One day, after hiking, we stopped by the grocery store on the way home. Thomas was asleep in his car seat, and she said she'd only be a minute. Only it wasn't a minute, and the longer I waited, the more anxious I became and the hotter the car grew, until I knew I needed to find her. But she'd left me in charge of Thomas, so I couldn't leave him alone. He was only three. Plus, if I woke him up and put him in a bad mood, it would only cause more stress for Judy. I didn't know which decision was right. So I waited."

"She just left you in the car with a toddler?" He sounded horrified. "Didn't anyone passing by stop to help?"

"Not until Thomas woke up and started crying. That got some attention, but when people asked if we were okay, I said we were fine. Partly because Judy always told me that Tommy's condition was no one else's business, but mainly I wanted them to leave, because I was embarrassed. About his crying, my inability to soothe him, and that someone in my family had ASD. Judy was in such denial, words like 'autism' or 'spectrum disorder' weren't allowed."

She took a painful breath as the sensations from that day came rushing back. The suffocating heat filling lungs, panic and the sweet floral scent of her mom's perfume, the haunted look in Judy's eyes before she climbed out of the car. Mostly, though, she felt the burn of embarrassment, which had since turned to shame.

"I was more embarrassed by my baby brother's behavior than my mother's," she admitted roughly. "How messed up is that?"

"You were a kid yourself."

"I was old enough to know better. And old enough not to let Tommy sit in the hot car for over three hours, while I waited for someone who knew about him to exit the store." It was one of Judy's friends, who wasn't all that surprised when the store manager confirmed Beckett's biggest fear, that her mother wasn't inside. "By that time, Judy was well on her way to Florida."

"Jesus, couldn't she wait until your dad wasn't gone?"

"If it makes you feel any better, my dad was always gone back then. He was a pretty crappy husband, always working or in his head. She's a decade my dad's junior and was barely twenty-one when they got married. Jeffery was already a successful musician who promised her a life full of travel, movie openings, and pampering. Then she got pregnant with me, and Jeffery stuck her in a small house in suburbia, while he went to the openings, and didn't understand why she was miserable."

"Then she should have divorced Jeffery. Not abandoned her kids in a parking lot."

"I don't think Judy was cut out for motherhood, especially to a special needs kid."

His deep blue eyes never left hers. "That's not an excuse."

"When Thomas got older, I realized that she'd done us a favor, leaving before he became attached," she said. "Because she would have left eventually. Looking back, I think she was trying to keep it together until Jeffery got home from his trip. The night before she left, I overheard her talking on the phone. She said Jeffery had added another week to his trip. She feared that he'd go on one of his trips and decide never to come back, leaving her alone to deal with everything."

"So instead, she left you alone with Thomas? To deal with everything." He kissed her forehead. "I can't even imagine what that was like for you."

Those first few years, balancing high school, Thomas's needs, and her dad's depression over losing his wife, had been stressful, triggering a lifetime of panic attacks. Terrified her dad might leave, or Thomas would be taken away by the state, Beckett had picked up whatever slack necessary to keep their family together. Eventually, the Hayeses moved to Rome, and they found a new rhythm, but glitches from the past still haunted her.

"Let's just say, long car trips have never been the same."

"Did she ever apologize?"

"Not since that day." Moving only her head, she looked up at Levi. "She did call, though. Once, on my sixteenth birthday. She didn't say anything, but I knew it was her. There were so many things I wanted to ask, but I was afraid of saying the wrong thing, scaring her off. So we just sat there on the phone, neither of us speaking, listening to each other breathe." She shrugged. "Then she hung up."

"Beck." His gentle caress wrapped around her as his lips pressed healing kisses in the hollow behind her ear. "Nothing I can say could make that right."

"You don't have to make it right," she said quickly. "Listening is enough."

"It doesn't even come close." He sounded angry — not at her but for her.

Possessive guys had always been a hard pass for Beckett. But with Levi, she couldn't decide if his protective nature pissed her off or turned her on.

"It means something to me," she said, surprised at how true that was.

It had only been a few weeks since that stormy night Levi had offered her a ride home, but it felt as if they'd known each other forever. Beckett knew from her studies that the amount of time two people spent together wasn't nearly as important as the quality of the time spent. And Levi was the kind of person who looked for meaning in every moment.

She didn't know the full affect Michelle's

death had had on his family, but she could sense something had a hold on Levi deep inside, something that he was afraid would never let go. Beckett suspected he was the one holding on, which resonated with her on such a primal level, it drove her to want to help. "What about you?" she asked gently. "Are you comfortable with where your family is in their grieving process? Are you comfortable taking time for yourself, to process everything that's happened in the past year?"

"The guilt makes it hard to tell," he said, absently playing with her hair again. "My family needs me here. To run the bar and grill, the marina, keep things going. But I need space to come to terms with losing Michelle. She wasn't just my sister or my best friend, she was . . ." Beneath her, she felt his chest collapse on a sigh.

She tilted her head to look up at him, and the grief she saw etched in the lines around his eyes and lips broke her heart.

"If this is too personal or hard to talk about, you don't have to answer," she said, even though she desperately wanted him to.

Beckett's gut told her the key to understanding the outgoing and elusive Levi Rhodes was going to be in his answer. He was the friendly bartender who took care of everyone but belonged to no one. A man who loved his hometown but called a boat home. A man who treated her as if she were the kind of woman who deserved romance and devotion.

"She was my responsibility. When my dad died, I promised him I'd take care of the family. Only I was working on my boat when my sister died. Just some freak accident, and she was gone. How will I ever explain that to my dad?"

The twisted guilt in his eyes broke her heart. Even though Michelle had been married at the time of her passing, Levi still claimed responsibility. Beneath all the flirting and laid-back swagger, Levi was struggling with demons of his own, a history of loss and misplaced guilt that stood between him and what he desperately needed.

Genuine happiness.

Reassuring him that he wasn't at fault wouldn't make a difference. Beckett had learned early on, when it came to the complicated matters of the heart, forgiveness had to come from within.

Cupping his face, she whispered, "You're a great man, Levi. I can only imagine how hard it was to lose as much as you have. I hope you find what you're searching for this summer. You've earned a little peace and quiet."

"What if I've changed my mind about what I want? What if I get all the way out there and realize what I'm looking for is here?"

A thrilling shot of panic, and a little bead of stupid hope, expanded in her chest, because he was gazing at her as if she were what he was looking for.

Second note to self: Not ready for prime time with Levi.

Because she'd been there and done that — was forced to pick up the pieces when "things" got too complicated. And if there was one word to sum up her life, it was complicated.

Her ex had even bought her a COMPLI-CATED AF pajama set for her birthday one year. And he was tough enough to carry a badge and gun. But as she looked at Levi, thinking about what he'd been through, he seemed tougher.

And wasn't that a terrifying thought.

"I need to be honest with you," she said, because he deserved to know what he was getting into. "This, nights like tonight, is all I can give right now. My life is so crazy, I can't promise any more."

"Beck, whatever it is you're afraid of, I

can handle it."

"You can until you can't," she whispered. "And in my experience, most people can't. So I need you to promise to be honest when it becomes too much."

"Try me," he said, his expression full of compassion. But it was the certainty in his voice that made her want to believe. Allow herself to be seduced by the possibilities, to let go and see if maybe, just maybe, she had a real shot at being part of something amazing — something that was just hers — even if it was temporary.

"Okay, for starters, I like coffee cake and bacon for breakfast."

He laughed. It was a good laugh, and it transformed his entire face. A hum vibrated through her entire body.

"Noted."

Chapter 14

Typically, when Levi wanted something, he made a plan, then went after it. And he wanted Beckett. Bad. He'd bet the boat she wanted him back, but neither of them was ready to take it too fast.

Beckett had a habit of dating forget-me-tomorrow kind of men. Which boggled the mind, because she was in no way close to a forget-me-tomorrow kind of woman.

Levi slid her a glance as he pulled into her driveway, noticing she was wearing a grin about as big and dopey as his. When he flicked off the engine, they stared at each other as the dome light faded and the cab grew cozy.

"I wanted to thank you for tonight," he began, taking her hand. "I know how hard it is for you to find time for yourself. That you chose to spend it with me is pretty humbling."

She glanced his way. "You *were* blocking

my escape."

"That was a pretty desperate move on my part," he admitted.

She snorted. "You haven't had to make a desperate move in your life, Levi Rhodes."

"I'm about to make one." He leaned across the cab and gave her the kind of kiss she deserved. Tender and warm, a gentle invitation with a finish that hinted at possibilities.

Naked and panting possibilities.

Before he lost himself again, he pulled back and rested their foreheads together. Slowly, Beckett's lashes lifted to unveil a pair of big, whiskey-brown eyes and — *Christ almighty* — he saw more than he'd anticipated.

Beckett's normal sharp edges were softened, her mascara slightly smudged, her nose pink from a night under the stars. She looked adorable, windblown, and completely carefree. It was a good look on her.

"Can I take your sweet smile to mean that you had a good time tonight?"

Her eyes widened into matching circles of surprise. "Are you fishing for compliments, or is the great Levi 'Lady Whisperer' looking for reassurance?"

"How about we go with the latter."

She snorted. "I had a great time. I'd

hoped the laughing and ear-to-ear grin were enough, but next time I'll be sure to pat you on the head."

"Next time, huh?"

"You did invite me to dinner at your mom's house. That's some pretty strong game," she teased. "Should I relay the invitation to Annie, as well?"

"Only if you want the guys to give me shit from here until eternity." As if his previous line of questioning hadn't already made him look like a total fool, he found himself saying, "After the quiet ride home, I may or may not have started second-guessing my approach."

That sweet smile faded into a single, tight line of reproach. "I don't play games, Levi. Just because I'm quiet doesn't mean something's wrong, or that I'm tentative or unsure. And don't mistake my shy side for me not knowing my mind or — why are you smiling?"

Levi framed her face. "Your shy side is one of my favorites. Right behind your feisty side. As for knowing your mind, that was never in question. I just can't always make out what you're thinking, and that makes me nervous. You make me nervous." He paused at her smile. "Oh, you like that you make me nervous, do you?"

"You're always so confident — it's a nice change."

"Confident?" He was amused, if not a tad moved, by her assessment. "That's complete and utter fear you're seeing."

"Then you wear it well."

Loud music sounded in the distance. It was difficult for Levi to make out the song through the truck's cab, but Beckett didn't seem to have any trouble. Apology, mixed with tired resignation, flickered in her eyes as she glanced over her shoulder to the front door.

"I also like that you can't guess what I'm thinking, because the inside of my mind usually sounds like the trading floor on Wall Street."

She was trying to make light of all the balls she was juggling and the snap decisions people in her life made that affected her ability to keep her word. But he'd already looked past the tough-girl exterior to the fragile woman who was fueled by constant fear of disappointing others.

"And now?"

"Now it sounds like the trading floor during a flash-crash?"

"I may have been on that exact floor a time or two." He brought her hand to his mouth and delivered a kiss. "If you need to send a representative in your place, I'm your man."

Loud voices erupted from inside the house. With a resigned sigh, she looked at him over her shoulder. Her expression of unyielding determination hit him like a cement truck. She'd already decided to face the music alone. For some reason, that didn't sit well with him.

"Nah," she said, reaching for the door handle, then hesitating, her back to him. "Thanks for tonight. It was sweet of you to make it such a special evening."

"Any time." Not wanting to let her go quite yet, he said, "And Beck?"

She looked back, and he doubted that she realized just how dejected she looked. He wondered what she'd do if he offered to whisk her away, for the night, a week — a trip around the southernmost tip of the Americas. Would she flip her neighborhood the finger and tell him to gun it? It wasn't as if the universe were about to give her a pass on the drama for the night.

Based on the ruckus coming from inside her house, he didn't think her family would, either. And wasn't that the heart of the problem? As long as Beckett's loved ones needed her, she'd continue to put her own needs on the back burner.

Levi didn't want to let her go — he'd done too much of that lately. But he also didn't want to be one more person, in an already long list, asking her to choose between conflicting loyalties. She had enough demands on her time.

With a playful wink, he said, "When you relay this story to Annie, could you maybe replace the sweet with something more manly, like studly or smooth?"

"Only a stud could pull off such a fun and righteous night out. Oh God, Levi is one smooth operator." She tried to bite back a smile and failed miserably. "Better?"

"You can save the 'Oh God, Levi' for when it's just us two."

Before she could respond, chaos broke free inside her house. The piercing beep of a smoke detector cut through the night, shouting ensued, and her phone immediately started ringing.

She cringed. "That's my signal."

"Time to turn back into a pumpkin?"

Dealing with her phone, she distractedly looked up. "I was never really into the princess thing."

Too bad. If there was one person who deserved a little happily ever after, it was Beckett. Not to mention, she'd look amazing in a corset, glass slippers, and nothing else. Well, maybe those thigh-high stockings naughty Cinderella wore.

"I see it now."

"See what?" she asked self-consciously.

"That." He reached past her to point to the sky above her house, purposely nudging her shoulder with his, waiting for her to move close and look out the windshield.

"What am I looking at?"

"The Girl Wonder signal. See, right there, big as can be."

She realized he was pointing at the moon and nudged back. "Ha ha."

"I'm serious. Capes are way hotter than crowns."

She grinned, and since her cheek was right there, so close he could smell the sea mist on her skin and watch as her good mood was snuffed out by the escalating disaster — he closed the distance between them. Applying a big, wet smacker to her cheek — right above the dimple that formed when she smiled — and another, softer one, to her lips when she laughed.

The last peck though, that was all Beckett, he was proud to report. She cupped his face and delivered a sweet, sexy, and way-too-short kiss that had his mind spinning.

When he pulled back, he noted that the music had lowered. A loud whacking, which sounded like a piñata getting beheaded, ensued until the alarm bleeped to a stop. She glanced over her shoulder at the neighbor's front door, which now stood open, silhouetting a pacing figure that bore a striking resemblance to Karen waving a rolling pin.

There were no silhouettes on her porch, because all the exterior lights were off. An ax murderer could be hiding in the shadows, and she'd be none the wiser.

"I'd better get going." With that, she grabbed her bag, shut the car door and, with a wave, headed toward her house, his coat dwarfing her tiny frame.

There was confidence in her steps, in the way she held her shoulders; she was acting for all the world as though she weren't walking into a crazy house — alone.

If that last part didn't have him opening his door and walking up her drive, then the way she disappeared into the darkness did.

Flashlight set to blind any would-be attacker, he aimed it at her porch, not surprised to find her rummaging through her bag.

"Please tell me you're looking for the charged taser you keep in your bag of tricks?" he called after her. "And not your keys."

322

She glanced up from the bag, her eyes squinting into the light, before sticking her head back into the purse. She didn't come back out until he was standing behind her, shining the light over her shoulder and into her bag. Sensing she needed both hands to search, he palmed the bottom of the bag.

"Thanks," she mumbled, not bothering to look up. Even when the slamming of cabinets sounded from inside.

She handed him a wallet, which required him to put the flashlight between his teeth. Next came her giant calendar, three packs of gum, a library book titled *Animals of the World,* and a dish — which looked a lot like the ones in his truck.

"Did you steal my leftover galakto-boureko?"

"You said you'd send me home with some," she said into her bag. Suddenly, a hand shot out, keys dangling from the fingertips, and she followed this with a smug smile. "Found them."

She stuffed everything back in, took the bag from him, slipped it over her shoulder, and then lifted his flashlight to light the door lock.

He gripped the back of his neck. "Here I thought Paisley was going to be the one to send me into premature grayness."

Ignoring this, she stuck her key in the door, twisted, and the lock clicked. She opened the door, peeked in, and slammed it closed. She spun to face him, her look expectant.

"Everything okay?" he asked.

"Yes," she said as the door flew open.

They were greeted with the sound of Beethoven, the scent of burnt ashes, and Thomas. "No. Everything is not okay. Dad called me Thomas."

"Your name is Thomas," Beckett said patiently.

"Not anymore. It's Tommy. T-O-M-M-Y, Tommy," he said loudly.

"Your sister told me to call you Thomas," an older male voice said from somewhere in the bowels of the house.

"School says I get to choose what you call me. I choose Tommy. T-O-M-M-Y. Tommy," her brother repeated over and over again.

Tommy began walking tight circles around the front room, following a set of muddy footprints that appeared to have already dried. Every so often, he'd step on one of a hundred or so Lego pieces — all red — with his rain boots, smashing it deeper into the carpet. Behind Tommy, doing his best to keep pace, was a dog with tree stumps for legs.

Beckett took one look at the scene and sighed, her head dropping to meet her chest. "Where's Gregory?"

"In his cage," the same voice bellowed from inside. "I didn't want him to eat the jellybeans."

"What jellybeans?" she asked.

A man in a charred apron, with professor glasses and the hair of a Muppet, came into view. He pointed to the "Lego pieces" Tommy was stomping into the carpet. "I lost track of time, and Thomas fed himself dinner."

"Jellybeans?" Beckett's head jerked up. "They make him sick."

The dazed Muppet scratched his head. "About that. Don't worry, I cleaned it up. Mostly."

"I did not eat the red ones," Tommy explained, without stopping. "Red food coloring increases hyperactivity."

It also increased the odds that Beckett would be stuck with a cream-and-pink-colored area rug.

"Why don't you sit on the couch before you wear Diesel out?" She walked her brother to the couch and placed the dog in his lap.

"Can I play videogames?" Tommy asked.

"Not after dinner. You know the rules."

"I haven't eaten dinner. Just jellybeans."

Beckett spun around, sniffing. "Dad, is that smoke?"

Only Dad was gone. He'd disappeared into the kitchen the second he saw she wasn't looking. Hands dug into her hips, she looked off to the left. "Dad?"

"The pizza's a little overdone, but definitely edible," came from the kitchen.

"Describe edible?" she called into the house; then she, too, disappeared after her father, dropping her bag on the tile and leaving the front door wide open.

Not wanting to let the heat out, Levi stepped inside and closed the door behind him. Sticking to the promise he'd made earlier to wait until she invited him in, he didn't go farther than the entry. Not that he needed to in order to see what was happening.

From his vantage point, he could look right into the kitchen. The lights were on, the table was set, but that's where the dinner's-ready picture ended. The fridge was wide open, one of the chairs was turned over, and salad fixings were strewn from the table to the counter. A crispy black pizza sat on the stovetop, still smoking. Another lay cheese-side-down on the floor in front of the garbage can, red sauce and pepperoni splattered on the wall behind.

It looked like a crime scene. A pizza burglary gone wrong.

"What happened?" Beckett gasped.

"I put the pizza in the oven, went back to the studio. By the time I got back, the pizza was on the floor, and Thomas was upset because —"

"T-O-M-M-Y. Tommy," came from the front room.

"— it wasn't the right kind."

Christ! How could Mr. Hayes keep missing the point? Was he riling up his kid on purpose? How fucking hard was it to use the name Tommy? Especially when the alternative was clearly pissing his son off.

Beckett acted as if it were no biggie, even encouraging her dad to walk her through what happened next, when she would be within her rights to strangle him.

"I must have accidentally grabbed a pepperoni instead of plain cheese. Honestly, honey, I don't know what happened."

Neither did Levi. Jeffery was looking at the red smears on the walls, as if he hadn't the faintest idea what had transpired. Tommy was on his feet again, going in circles and spelling out his name, like a jellybean-fueled NASCAR driver. And Levi was dizzy just listening to the conversation.

He could only imagine what was going through Beckett's mind. Then she took in a deep breath, which lifted her shoulders, her chin, and that "so this is life" bravery she clung so tightly to, and suddenly he got a clue as to what she dealt with daily.

"Hey, Tommy," Levi said quietly, afraid the kid would spin himself sick again. "Why don't you help me pick up those jellybeans before the rug is just one big red circle."

"I don't like the red ones. They make me hyper," he said, moving to circle Levi. "Dad burned the pizza. The alarm was loud."

"I know, I heard it," he said calmly. "But it's over now."

"It hurt my ears."

Watching Beckett deal with the aftermath of what he'd promised would be a fun night out hurt Levi's heart. She'd tried to explain things, but he'd selfishly dismissed her concerns.

Remembering that redirection was a parent's greatest tool, Levi said, "Do you think it was too loud for Gregory Pecker?"

"Yes." Tommy stopped on a dime, the dog collapsing at his feet. "Chickens hear better than humans. They even regrow damaged hearing cells, so their hearing remains top-notch throughout their lives. It is their keen sense of hearing that alerts them to predators so loud noises can make them stressed or anxious. Yes. The alarm was too loud for Gregory."

"Do you want to make sure he's okay?"

"I do." He smiled and then led the dog into his bedroom.

Levi scraped a few jellybeans off the tile by his feet, then placed them in a vase on the entry table. He was about to gather the ones in the front room when Jeffery said, "I must have lost track of time. The next thing I knew, someone was pounding on my studio door, the smoke detector was going off, and smoke was coming out of the oven. I hit the detector with the broom until it was on the floor, but there was no saving dinner."

"Why didn't you set the timer to remind you?" she asked.

"I don't like the sound of it going off." To prove it, he picked up a small plastic bug-shaped timer from the back of the stove, walked to the garbage can, and stepped on the release lever, then tossed it inside.

The action wasn't so much aggressive as it was a tantrum. But it was concerning enough to have Levi ready to abandon his post to put himself between father and daughter. Not only did Jeffery have a good six inches and sixty pounds on his daughter, he also didn't appear to handle stress all that well.

Beckett, on the other hand, was dialing it in at cucumber-cool, her emotions completely in check as she retrieved the alarm from the trash.

"That's why I got you a new timer, remember?" Her voice was soft as she wiped the timer on her jeans, then gently placed it in her dad's hands. She twisted the bug's head, and a soothing acoustic guitar began playing.

"Here Comes the Sun." Jeffery closed his eyes and smiled. "I used to play this for you when you were little and didn't want to go to sleep."

"I remember." She went to place the timer on the counter, but Jeffery wouldn't let go.

"I don't like things cluttering the counter." As if a five-inch timer was the issue with that kitchen. "And Beatles or not, I don't like timers. They break my concentration."

Instead of telling him, "Too fucking bad," Beckett stood back, leaving the entry to the kitchen unblocked. "Why don't you place it where you want. We'll only bring it out when I'm gone, and you need to use the oven."

"I guess that can work," he said, even while making it clear he didn't like her solu-

330

tion. Not one bit.

He took his time considering all the different options, wrinkling his nose when he saw a splatter on the wall or the slice of pepperoni clinging to the vent. Finally, he chose the drawer farthest from the range, dropped the timer in, then closed it with his elbow.

"Good choice."

"I'll try to remember to use it so I won't burn the pizza," Jeffery said, his gaze just to the right of meeting hers. "I was going to clean the mess up before you got home. But it's hard when you're not here and things go wrong."

"I know," she whispered.

Completely oblivious to how he'd just made his daughter feel, Jeffery went on. "You're so much better at this kind of thing than I am."

"Nothing a sponge and soap can't fix," she said, and that's when Levi finally understood.

Why she kept her phone close, always checked in with home, and avoided long-term commitments. How a hard, scrappy worker had managed to lose so many jobs around town. And why she let clients walk over her.

Her relationship with her father reminded him of Emmitt's problems growing up. His father, Les, was ten years sober, but Levi didn't think attending meetings and finding a sponsor would help this family.

At some point, the Hayeses had undergone a major role reversal. With no mother figure in the picture, a father who had trouble parenting, and a brother to raise, Beckett wouldn't have hesitated to step up. It couldn't be comfortable or natural for her, being her brother's parent, her dad's keeper, and the sole responsible party in the house. All at the expense of her own happiness.

Beckett swept her hair into a ponytail and surveyed the damage. The kitchen alone would take her hours to clean.

Doing it with her dad's help? She might as well burn down the house and start over.

So when her dad reached for the broom, she intercepted. "Why don't you let me do this, so you can finish up whatever you were working on in the studio. I'll call you when dinner's ready."

"If you're sure," Jeffery asked, but he already had one foot out the door.

Groaning, she slipped off her boots, irritated over how her night was going to end. It had been so amazing up to now; she was determined not to let a little burned pizza ruin her mood. Bowling with friends, a romantic tailgate picnic, followed by an even more romantic make-out session with a man who thought her beautiful.

"You need to match your socks more often, Jasmine Beckett Hayes," she said to herself.

"Jasmine, huh?" asked an unexpected male voice.

"Oh my God!" she gasped, spinning around while holding the broom like a javelin.

Levi stood at the entry, boots off, arms crossed, a shoulder resting against the door, looking big and badass. "That's a princess name if I ever heard one."

"You're still here?" She blinked. "Why are you still here?"

"And you go by your middle name."

She ran through every scenario that might end with him being in her house and came up blank. He'd walked her to the door, helped her inside, and then — *ohmigod.* The broom slipped from her fingers.

"I left you waiting on the porch." She cringed. "Again. Damn, I'm not so good with this whole man-in-waiting thing you've got going on."

"You were met with a lot when the door opened." He lowered his voice. "Are you okay?"

"As long as you didn't see or hear any of that, I'm okay." She walked closer and looked up at him. "Please tell me you just now walked in."

"I followed you inside."

She looked at the ceiling. "Can we pretend the night ended with that kiss in your truck, you drove off, and we forget the rest?"

"Not sure I can." He pushed off the wall. "Definitely not comfortable driving off until I know you're okay."

"Is this your way of angling for another kiss?" she teased. When he didn't so much as grin, she went still. "You're serious?"

He stood with his feet shoulder-distance apart, his arms crossed so tightly his biceps bulged, and a stubborn set to his jaw. He was dead serious.

"You're worried because of what happened with my dad?"

"I'm not going to lie — there were moments."

She wasn't sure how to respond. Levi was, by nature, a fiercely protective man when it came to those closest to him. That he placed her in the same category as Annie or Paisley was touching. That he thought her dad could ever hurt her was frustrating, if not a little embarrassing.

She could only imagine what had gone

through his mind watching everything unfold. The assumptions he must have made about her dad, about her family . . .

"Levi, my dad would never hurt anyone. He's the gentlest man I know," she said. "Just because he suffers from Asperger's doesn't mean he's a bad dad or violent."

"Of course it doesn't." Levi reached out and took her hand, slowly tugging her close. "But I heard the sadness in your voice when he blamed tonight's problems on you."

"He didn't —"

"Mean to," he said softly, wrapping his arms around her. "I know, but the result was the same."

"You don't understand," she whispered into his chest.

He tilted his head down, meeting her gaze. "Then help me understand, because it bothers me that you've been conditioned to believe your needs aren't as important as other people's."

"They're not more important than mine, they're just more immediate. There's a difference," she tried to explain, a familiar and unwelcome awkwardness pushing her buttons and twisting her tongue.

There were a lot of ridiculous myths surrounding autism, which made it difficult for some to understand how an autistic person could be a good parent. Normally, she wouldn't care what anyone thought, but with Levi, it was different.

He was different, so she desperately wanted to extinguish any myths he'd heard. Fortunately for Beckett, myths were, by definition, untrue. And while her dad might hit on a sensitive spot from time to time, if he had any idea that he'd hurt her feelings, he'd feel awful. And while he might not show it like other dads, he loved her.

Why it was so important that Levi understood was still a mystery, but her need to explain away his fears went bone-deep. "Imagine growing up in a house with two people who weren't born with a filter," she began. "There's a misconception that people on the spectrum don't feel emotion — that's so far from the truth. They experience things on a level we can't even imagine, emotions, sounds, energy. They just don't use the same words or outlets we're used to. Tonight was a toxic combination of no schedule and overstimulation. What they said —" She took a breath. "They don't mean to be dismissive or hurt my feelings."

He tipped up her chin. "But they do. I can see the hurt in your eyes, and it breaks my heart."

She was a little breathless over his words.

"My dad's an amazing musician who pays his bills on time, owns his house and truck outright, and puts every penny I pay in rent into an account for me that he thinks I don't know about. His reason? When I move out, I'll have a nice nest egg to put down on a place of my own. He helped me start my business, never complains about the animals I parade through the house, and cries when we watch rom-coms. He can't help it if cooking and helping around the house just aren't his strong suit."

He cupped her chin and tilted it up to meet his gaze. "A smart and very sexy woman recently told me that practice makes perfect."

"Sexy?" She nuzzled closer, loving how she felt in his arms.

"And caring, special, and so incredibly deserving." He kissed the tip of her nose. "Make sure people treat you accordingly."

She placed her hands on his chest. "You're just saying that because you saw me get my ass handed to me by red jellybeans and a Beatles timer."

"I said that because it's the truth. You deserve a little of that peace and quiet, too." He studied her with those assessing eyes. "Now, I promised you a fun night, and that doesn't include you cleaning the house by yourself. So how about you order up some pizza, while I start on the kitchen."

"I don't need to be taken care of, Levi," she said.

"I like that about you." He wrapped his arms around her. "But needing and wanting are two different things. And there are times I'll want to take care of the woman I'm with. Not because I think she's weak, but because I want to make her happy."

"You want me to be the woman you're with?" she asked, finding it hard to breathe.

"Remember that ledge, and how I asked you to be there for me? It's only fair that I get to be there for you, too."

"For how long?"

"As long as we make each other happy." When he said it like that, unapologetically, it sounded so reasonable. Because as long as they made each other happy, they'd continue on, until one or the other changed their mind.

"That sounds like a perfect rule number five."

CHAPTER 15

Beckett took the highway off-ramp a tad too fast. The worn shocks on her dad's pickup groaned, and the truck bobbed and jerked, mimicking the victory dance Gregory was doing across the headrest of the bench seat. A backseat driver with the lock-picking skills of a seasoned criminal, he'd enlisted his beak and talons to free himself from the confines of his cage minutes into their trip across town. And hadn't shut up about it since.

A distraction she could do without.

Beckett hated driving vehicles with doors. Almost as much as she hated driving in the snow. It was about as comfortable as base jumping with four skis while wearing a straitjacket.

Thankfully, Main Street had been plowed, creating a snowbank that ran the length of downtown. Today's forecast called for clear skies and sun, but Jack Frost was standing his ground, whipping up temperatures so low that even the marine layer blowing up from the south couldn't budge the snow, which stubbornly clung to the crape myrtle trees and lampposts lining the wharf district.

"Cluckidy cluck cluck," Gregory cursed when Beckett downshifted, causing the truck — and her passengers — to jerk forward.

Her dad still drove the same 1978 cherry-red Toyota pickup he'd purchased from an avocado farmer in college. It was a POS when he'd bought it to lug his grunge band's equipment, and it drove with all the ease of a tractor in rush hour. But it was familiar, reliable, and still running — three reasons Jeffery would be buried in it.

Fitting, Beckett thought, since the tiny cab gave off a coffinesque feel. Especially when the entire Hayes clan crammed in for a fun family trip — where Beckett was cast in the role of middle sardine and knocked knees with the oversized Magic 8-Ball gearshift knob.

Taking the truck wasn't Beckett's first choice, but with the chance of black ice and her day's schedule — which included transporting Gregory, Diesel, and eventually Thomas when school let out — it was the safe choice.

Her two current passengers didn't seem all that put out by the arrangements. Diesel's front legs were on the door rest, his nose pressed through the slightly cracked window, his tongue and Dog Wonder cape billowing behind him.

Gregory's steamy affair with the truck began the day he realized he could escape his carrier. He loved the freedom to roam, the feel of the cracked dash against his beak, and the wind in his feathers — especially when the wind originated from pressure-controlled vents.

To combat the chill from the open passenger window, the heat was cranked to high, the airflow full-blast, making it perfect conditions for pilot Gregory Pecker to take to the air.

Getting as high as possible on the seatback, Gregory dropped his head low and fully extended his wings, moving them up and down as if they were flaps on a F-15 fighter jet, soaring through town at g-force speeds, divebombing every time they went under a large street sign or overpass.

The faster Beckett went, the closer he positioned himself in front of her vent, as if using the wind necessary to increase his speed.

"Can you flap those somewhere else?"

Beckett downshifted, and the Magic 8-Ball landed on MY SOURCES SAY NO. "You're going to get feathers in my hair."

Pilot Pecker didn't seem concerned in the slightest, cooing loudly as his wings darted this way and that, whipping up enough loose feathers to make a boa.

The next meeting on her agenda was with the savvy and sexy owner of the sailboat *Rhodes Less Traveled.* When they signed the legally binding contract between their businesses, feathers would not fly. Not when it was the first time they'd seen each other since their tailgate picnic.

"Last warning," she said, with no real bite. Gregory was as excited about today's outing as Beckett.

In fact, when she pulled into the employee parking lot that separated the Crow's Nest from the marina and caught sight of Levi's truck near the back entrance, her lips tingled, and elation swelled like a helium balloon in her chest.

She squinted through the windshield, trying to make out whether his boat lights were on. They were not, but she still managed to locate *Rhodes Less Traveled* without any problem. Not because of the name, but because she'd spent many a summer coffee break watching him work on his boat —

hands dirty, shirt off, board shorts slung dangerously low.

Beckett was so busy checking out Levi's mast, she failed to spot the snow-covered speed bump in time to slow down. The first two tires went over and up, getting enough air that when they landed, the pickup bottomed out, and complete chaos ensued.

The steel undercarriage met the pavement with grinding force, the screech loud enough to be heard a mile away. In the passenger's seat, Diesel braced himself on all fours, eyes extra-bulgy, tongue panting, and let out a nervous fart when the back tires cleared the bump. From the floorboard, Gregory ran in circles as if he were being chased by Karen and her pickax, finally settling down when Beckett pulled into a parking spot.

Gregory squawked disapprovingly at Beckett, then went about grooming himself with his beak.

"It's okay, kiddo. I'll groom you before our next stop."

She certainly wouldn't be making a smooth entrance. Nor would she be getting a moment to herself to calm her nerves over seeing Levi again for the first time since their date. More importantly, since the kiss that shook the eastern seaboard.

The memory still made heat burn her

cheeks, not to mention other parts of her body she wasn't ready to recognize.

Still, after a quick check in the rearview mirror for stray feathers, she grabbed her bag and hopped out. Her breath crystallized on contact, and the blast of frigid air stung her nose. She clapped her hands together to get the blood flowing, then fished through her bag for her rainy-day gear.

Locating two sets of rain booties and matching red ESA vests, she reached into the cab to slip them on both passengers. When they looked cozy and cute as could be, Beckett stood aside to make room for them to exit. Diesel moved from the passenger's seat to the driver's seat, but was intercepted by Gregory, whose flapping feathers gave him just enough lift to land on Diesel's back before he popped to the ground and shook himself to reposition his ruffled feathers.

Diesel followed, as tranquil as Gregory was melodramatic.

Beckett bent into the cab of the truck to grab the pink pastry box she'd picked up on her way over. It had slid all the way forward. Beckett lay on the bench, using all sixty-and-change inches to tap the corner of the box with her fingers. She'd just wedged

344

the tip of her pointer under the flap when a deeply amused chuckle came from behind her.

"Is that your way of asking if those pants look good? Of if you have feathers stuck to your ass?" Levi said. "Either way, I'm going to need a closer inspection."

She straightened and dusted off her butt; three feathers drifted to the ground. Not bothering to hide her grin, she turned to face Levi and nearly dropped the pastry box.

He stood in the open doorway of the bar, gray Henley stretched across his shoulders, ball cap turned backward, wiping his hands on a rag. And smiling. One of those "Hey babe, remember that kiss" smiles, which clenched her stomach and tightened her throat even from thirty feet away.

Without waiting for her, Diesel wandered straight to the door, passing Levi on his way in, closely followed by Gregory, trotting behind.

"Sure," Levi said, watching them as they went by. "Come on in, guys."

As she approached, his warm gaze traveled over her. "You're lucky I'm too distracted by the way those leggings fit to notice not one, but two health-code violations in my bar."

"You can always kick us out," she teased.

His gaze moved over her again. "I'd rather face the health department shutting me down. Plus, Girl Wonder needs her trusty sidekicks."

"I do. I'm headed to the hospital. One of their long-term patients is turning thirteen, and her birthday wish is for Dog Wonder to pay a visit."

It wasn't the first holiday Samantha had celebrated at the children's hospital, but hopefully, it would be the last. After being diagnosed with a rare blood cancer, Samantha had undergone a series of painful treatments, which required an extended stay in the long-term-care unit, spanning the holiday season. Her letter to Santa had but one thing listed: to see her pet, Wonder Dog.

Rome General's policy was clear: Only service animals were permitted on the premises. Frustrated that the hospital board wouldn't make an exception, Samantha's mom did the next best thing and reached out to Fur-Ever Friends — who put her in touch with Beckett.

Diesel might have flunked out of service-dog school, but he'd completed the right training and certification to be acknowledged by the hospital as a therapy dog. So while Beckett couldn't train Samantha's Wonder Dog in a day, she could bring a newly renamed Dog Wonder in his place.

Some glitter glue, a handmade cape, and a couple of dollar-store Santa hats later, Beckett took Dog Wonder on their first tour through the pediatric ward. With bat ears, tree-stump legs, and the overall shape of Mr. Potato Head, Diesel was born to make people laugh. What she hadn't anticipated — hell, what no one had anticipated — was how easily Samantha's treatment had gone while Diesel stayed by her side.

The difference was so astounding, the nursing staff asked if Dog Wonder could come back for Samantha's next treatment. Moved by Samantha's story and her courage, Beckett brought Dog Wonder to every treatment until Samantha was given a clean bill of health and able to go home to her own dog.

This past Christmas marked Samantha's six-year anniversary of being cancer-free. It also marked the Dynamic Dog Duo's decision to visit the pediatric ward regularly. Because for every child sent home, another one was waiting to fill that empty hospital bed. And if there were even a chance, no matter how small, that a visit from a funny-looking dog could make a difference in a child's hospital experience, then Beckett would be there.

Samantha's treatments hadn't been so reliable. The cancer was back. And Beckett would be there with Dog Wonder to help her get through the new therapy.

Levi reentered the bar and looked down at the only occupants. "Dog Wonder. Girl Wonder." Levi's gaze turned to Gregory. "Peck and Beck. Or does Pecker have a superhero name, too?"

She laughed. "He isn't allowed in the hospital."

"He isn't allowed in here, but that hasn't stopped him."

She set the pink pastry box on the bar top. Then heaved Diesel onto one barstool, settled the chicken on another, and sat in the middle. "Annie's going to watch him."

"So, Annie plans to meet you here, then cock-sit while you're making the rounds at the hospital?"

"Don't worry, I'm meeting her at the hospital when she gets off. I'm going to get a list of guests so I can start on the seating chart, and she's going to take Gregory to the outpatient clinic for some socializing."

"Or you can leave him here with me. It doesn't get more social than a bar at happy hour," he said. "You can pick him up after you're done."

Surprise stalled her breath and made her

refocus on the hunk in front of her. "You hate him — why would you offer to keep him?"

"Hate? This guy and I are old mates. Aren't we?" He picked up Gregory and scratched him under the wattle, and the traitor started cooing. "Plus, when you come back, we can go over the seating charts on the deck and watch the sun set."

She looked up at him through her lashes. "That sounds more like a date than making a seating chart."

"You could write it in that book of yours as seating arrangement and food sampling. That it happens under the setting sun doesn't make it any less professional."

"We do need to arrange a time to pick the menu." And her week was filling up. She glanced down and groaned. "But I'm dressed like an action figure."

"If action figures looked like you, I'd have never left my room when I was a teen."

"Are you asking me to play hooky again?"

With a grin that had her inner bad girl wanting to come out and play, he said, "I can think of some more descriptive names, but for the purposes of this conversation, 'hooky' works."

Temptation zinged. Escaping with Levi, even for an hour, sounded deliciously sinful. Plus, they did need to put a check through those tasks, and soon. The wedding was only a little over a month out.

She pulled her schedule out, flipped to today, and groaned. "I have a client after the hospital, and I won't have time to swing back here and still pick up Thomas from school on time."

He shrugged and moved behind the bar. "Paisley's got her driver's test later today. I can drop Thomas off when I take her home."

"That's a lot of driving around for you. Don't you have a ton of work?"

"If it means I get to see you again." He shrugged. "Plus, I've hired this company to take some of the load off. It's run by a brilliant and sexy woman who's assured me I'm making the right choice by outsourcing my staffing issues."

He reached under the counter and slid a stack of official-looking papers onto the bar in front of her.

"What is this?"

"I lined out a rough proposal for you to look at."

A bubble of emotion expanded high in her chest; she felt as thrilled by the gesture as she was when he'd first offered the opportunity.

"You are making the right choice," she told him, drawing up all her self-confidence so she would sound 150-percent certain. "In fact, I've begun planning out my strategy for you to look at."

She reached into her big bag and pulled out an official-looking proposal of her own. Secured in a sleek folder, it was professional, organized, and, she hoped, impressive.

"Look at you," he said with the lilt of approval in his tone. "All official and organized." He opened the folder and turned the glossy colored pages, studying the color-coded tabs, charts, and steps she thought they should take. "You clearly spent a lot of time on this."

"You're entrusting your family's business to me when you had no reason to. I'm going to do everything I can to prove to you that your confidence in me isn't misplaced."

"Beckett, you didn't have to —"

She held up a silencing hand. "But I did. For me, this opportunity is huge. That it's coming from someone so successful means even more." The sensations roiling inside her were complicated and difficult to identify. This chance meant so much more to her than she could explain. But, since crying wasn't exactly professional, she swallowed and went on. "By Monday, I will have a list of solid office-manager candidates for you to interview."

"Of that I have no doubt."

"Once you make your choice, I will work with the new hire to address the rest of your staffing issues. My goal is to make sure you are properly staffed by the bachelor party."

He made a face. "Emmitt and Gray have big mouths."

"Don't be mad at them. It was my idea to use them as resources to better understand where you needed the most help."

"I can only imagine what they said."

"Nothing I didn't already know. That you're a sweet guy with a huge heart who works tirelessly to make sure his family is happy and cared for. At his own expense, even. That man deserves a few days to relax with his friends."

"I'm sweet?" His brows snapped together. "I can't picture Emmitt or Gray using that word."

She smiled, pressed her elbows on the bar, and leaned toward him for a kiss. "Very sweet."

His eyes hazed over with heat as the knuckles of one hand slid down her cheek. "Go on."

Her smile grew. "And caring." She kissed

his cheek. "And hardworking." Then the cleft in his chin. "And deserving of being someone's top priority." The final kiss captured his lips and lingered so long it made her belly flip.

He pulled back with a grin. "You applying, Girl Wonder?"

"That's what it says in this contract."

"That's not what I'm asking."

"I know." But that felt like a really big thing to admit after one date and a few kisses. Even if those kisses were molten.

To turn the conversation in a more comfortable direction, she slid the pink pastry box from Holy Cannoli toward him.

He leaned away and looked at the box. "What's this?"

"It's a thank-you for the other night."

He grinned. "I've never been thanked for taking a girl to Make-Out Point."

Then he opened the box and laughed.

"What? You said you liked cream puffs."

"Oh, I do. But after today" — he let out a low whistle — "they're my all-time favorite."

Beckett went up on her toes to look inside the box and burst out laughing. The two cream puffs were stuck together, and each was topped with a slice of candied cherry, making them look like boobs.

"For the record," she said, "I ordered a

cream puff. The rest was Cecilia's doing. Now I know why she offered me a two-for-one deal."

"Shhhh," he said, dipping his finger into the whipped cream, then placing it on her lips. "You're ruining the moment."

He leaned over the bar and kissed the frosting off her lips, and the deep groan in his throat made something happen low in her belly. That same hot and tingly sensation his kisses created.

He pulled back, eyes hot. "I think we should finish these in my office."

"I can't. I want to" — she was a little surprised she actually meant that — "but I only have a few minutes."

"And you decided to spend them with me?" he asked.

She smiled, still feeling a little shy about the whole thing. "After the other night, I've been looking forward to spending them with you."

"It was pretty epic on my end, too."

His flirtation was easy, smooth, but it still created discomfort in her chest. "I'm trying to thank you for how you treated my family. It got crazy, and you just rolled with it. That means more to me than you'll ever know."

"Beck, everything about the other night was honest and real, and my big takeaway is how much you care about your family. In my book, that makes you a pretty special lady."

"I think our feeling about the importance of family is one thing we have in common."

"We have a lot more than that in common. And we barely touched on them the other night."

No matter how much she wanted to pretend the magic had been nothing more than a romantic moonlight setting, and the emotions he'd evoked would fade, she knew that would be a lie. They might not have had sex, but what they'd shared had been even more intimate.

Levi's willingness to be open and vulnerable with her, to share his dreams and tragic losses, had, little by little, chiseled away at the barriers she'd erected between herself and the rest of the world. He'd managed to slide right past them and into her heart.

His determination to follow his dreams, to make his trip a reality, reminded her how it felt to be excited about life, to find the silver lining in even the darkest of situations.

"I bet we do," she admitted.

He slid his hand across the bar. It was big, warm, and gentle as it settled over hers. "Which was why I was hoping you'd be open to a real date. Wednesday night. You, me, and another of my grandma's recipes?"

"I can't Wednesday. Thomas has art class, and I'm this week's parent helper. How about this weekend?" She shook her head. "That's a long time to wait to select the wedding menu."

He leaned against the bar. "How about tonight?"

"Don't you work?"

He shrugged. "I think my staff can handle a few hours without me."

"Well . . ." She wanted to explain that she hadn't prepped to be gone for more than a couple of hours, then caught herself. She'd promised to try. This was her chance to really be bold and take a risk. Plus, how risky could it be? It was just dinner. She took a deep breath to push the nerves away and gave a single nod. "I'll bring the cake."

He smiled. "As long as it's iced."

CHAPTER 16

Levi took the last turn toward the marina with Paisley sitting beside him in the truck, frustration wafting off her in waves. Her arms were crossed tight, her gaze out the window, her jaw clenching and unclenching, a glimmer of tears in her eyes.

He groaned internally. He should be used to tears by now, but he wasn't sure a man ever got used to seeing the women he loved hurt.

Parking near the dock leading to his boat, he shut down the engine and looked at Paisley. "Honey, it's not the end of the world. It's not like you'll never get your license."

She shot him a side-eye glare, reached for the handle, and pushed the door open.

Levi got out and met her in front of the truck, where they opened a locked gate and continued toward Levi's slip. "You told me yourself that a lot of your friends didn't pass."

"The first time," she said. "After today, this is my fourth time. That testing guy, he had something against me. I could tell as soon as I met him. He didn't smile or anything. I mean, who doesn't smile when they're about to usher a teenager into the next phase of adulthood?"

Levi bit the inside of his cheek to keep from laughing, but that didn't stem his smile.

They slowed when they reached the boat.

"What are we doing today?" Paisley asked.

"I'm going to replace a few parts on the engine, and you're going to start sanding the steps into the cabin so we can refinish them."

"I get to pick the music," she said as she stepped onto the boat.

"Within reason. None of that high-pitched stuff that makes my ears bleed."

"Whatever."

Levi pulled all the supplies together while Paisley chose a station on the radio that only made him grind his teeth half as hard as usual.

He knew how devastating this fourth failure was to a kid Paisley's age, and it wasn't all about not getting her license. The embarrassment of it was equally — if not more — painful.

He set the sander and sandpaper near the teak steps, and Paisley got right to work. He guessed the sanding might even help her work out some of her frustration.

Levi sat nearby, opened the engine compartment positioned below deck, and unpackaged the new parts. "So, what's this I hear about you reconsidering the ski trip?"

"I thought about it," she said, the earlier annoyance in her voice almost gone now. "You were right."

"Whoa, what?" When he turned to look at her, the clamp he was holding fell into the compartment, and he swore under his breath. "Look what you made me do."

Paisley's giggle lightened his heart as he fished out the clamp.

He knew this was another sore spot in Paisley's young life. She'd done her level best to pretend she wasn't interested in the trip, that it wasn't cool, but he knew that the real reason Paisley had tried to get out of it was because her mother was supposed to have been a chaperone. Going on the trip would mean having to face her mother's loss all over again. He didn't blame her for doing all she could to avoid it. He was more surprised to hear that she'd changed her mind.

"So, the ski trip?" he asked again. "Something big must have changed for you to admit I was right."

"Maybe I'm maturing."

"Pffft. You might be able to get that past your dads, but you aren't fooling me. In fact, I know you're lying."

Paisley stopped sanding and met his gaze. "Why would you say that?"

"Because your voice just rose into an octave that only dogs can hear."

She smirked. "I'm getting a cold."

"Now you're just compounding lies. Your mom used to do that whenever she got caught in a lie."

"According to her, she only got caught because you ratted her out. Are you going to rat me out?"

Bingo. Right on target. Again. Gray and Emmitt really needed to take daughter-reading lessons from him. "As long as you always tell me what's going on, and stop hiding things, my lips are sealed." When she sighed with relief, he asked, "So, who is he?"

"Oh my god." Her eyes went wide. "You do know everything."

Not really, but he had been a teenager once upon a time, and he could vaguely recollect what motivated him to change his mind back then.

"This is true," he lied. "Plus, I used to be the guy who convinced the girl to go on the overnight field trip. So I know exactly what's behind your sudden change of heart. What's his name?"

She opened her mouth, then closed it and refocused on attacking the stairs with the sanding block. "I never admitted there was any guy."

"You might want to work on that innocent routine before you talk to your dads about the trip again, since it's on the same weekend as the bachelor party."

"All the better," she said. "They'll be forced to let some other parents chaperone for a change."

"I don't see that happening."

"You guys are so overprotective." The earlier whine reentered her voice.

"We're involved, not overprotective. There are a lot of kids who would give their right arm to have parents as involved as us."

"And kids are starving in other countries — I get it." She looked up and met his gaze. "But I can handle this, seriously. I just want to go skiing with my friends. And yes, one of them is a boy. And he's age-appropriate. Not that it matters, since boys and girls have to sleep in different cabins."

"Same rules as when I was a junior. And

guess what, all I had to do was go around back and tap on the girls' window."

"I won't do that, I promise. And it's only one night. For gosh sakes, I'm going off to college in another year. This would be a chance to let me get the feel of it."

"To see how you handle it?"

She snorted. "No. To see how you guys handle it. I'm going to handle it just fine."

Levi laughed, and they both got lost in their work for a while.

"Some of my friends are getting jobs this summer," she said, and Levi knew she'd just dropped the bait.

"You're about that age," he said, knowing where this was going. Knowing why that uneasy feeling settled in his chest, as if he were losing something precious but gaining something more.

"I thought it might be fun. Getting a summer job."

"You've got that trip to Europe in July. And then there's also club soccer." Which he'd coached since Paisley was six. It was the one place he still had some relevance in her world.

"I don't have to do club soccer to play. I've been playing on varsity since I was a freshman." She squinted into the sun, her hair coming loose from her ponytail and blowing in the wind. No longer the little niece who always loved to tag along. "I'm helping Yiayia with this scrapbook she's making. It's mainly pictures of Mom. Did you know that she backpacked across Europe the summer before college?"

"You're going to Europe, this summer. With your dad and Annie."

"Which will only make it easier when I go with Owen," she said. "We both know he's MIT bound, and I don't know what I want to do yet. So we thought it would be cool to take one last big trip together. Like Mom did."

"Have you told your dads this?"

She sighed. "Not yet. But I was hoping you'd be there when I did."

Oh, Levi wouldn't miss that conversation for the world. They were going to lose their shit. Gray's trigger would be "backpack across Europe," and Emmitt's would be "with Owen." Gray couldn't stand the idea of Paisley being far away and needing him, and Emmitt didn't care if Owen was gay, straight, or sexually fluid: The kid had a penis, and therefore needed to keep his distance from Paisley.

Surprisingly, Levi was eerily calm. Maybe it was because he shared that same urgency to visit a new place, make new memories that didn't have any connection to old ones.

"Instead of soccer, I want to work at the boat rental and bait shack. I saw a picture of you and Mom running the shack when you were my age. It looked like fun."

"And this has nothing to do with the stream of college guys who spend their summer hanging around the harbor?"

"A perk of the job?" She gave a cute shrug. "If I work there, it will make it kind of a family tradition. Plus, you'd be my boss, so it's not like I could get into trouble."

He laughed. Working a summer job by the marina was the definition of trouble. He and Michelle got into more trouble working the boat and bait shack in their teens than he did in college. All under their parents' noses. But it was the kind of trouble that makes growing up fun. And if any kid deserved a summer of sun and fun, it was this kid.

"I won't be here this summer. I'll be somewhere in the Gulf of Mexico."

"Right." She went back to sanding. "Being a shack girl is still a family tradition. Plus, Annie said I won't know what I want to do with my life until I live a little."

Levi had to chuckle, because that sounded like Annie. And he couldn't wait for Emmitt to realize it was his fiancée who sanctioned Shack Girl Paisley.

Levi paused what he was doing and looked up. "Preseason starts in March. I always hire help from the junior college to get the boats and kayaks ready. It only pays minimum wage, and it's hard work, checking the hulls for damage, replacing parts, inspecting the rigging. But it's yours if you want it."

Paisley's face lit up. "I want it. I can work after school and weekends. And maybe by summer, I can work the boat and bait shack."

And while she was enjoying one of the best summers of her young life, Levi would be on the other side of the hemisphere. Just him, his mast, and the wide-open ocean. Paisley's wasn't the only life he'd be missing out on. The more time he spent with Beckett, the lonelier the wide-open sea started to sound. A thought that, just a few short weeks ago, never would have entered his mind.

A lot had changed since that night Beckett walked into his bar and, with a single conversation, sent his compass spinning off its axis. He needed to be sure that it was more than animal magnetism at work, because his internal guide had never steered him wrong. And now it seemed to point in just one direction.

Beckett.

Levi was already in so deep, it made the Mariana Trench look like a tide pool. Before he got ahead of himself, he needed to know if Beckett considered him more than a fun escape from her day-to-day life. Which was why tonight was so important.

When Paisley stopped to replace the sandpaper with another sheet, Levi closed the engine compartment and grabbed a rag to wipe the grease from his hands. "Don't need to load that up again. We've got to get going."

"Already? Why?"

"I need to swing by and pick up Beckett's brother before I drop you home."

Her expression was part panic, part plea. "I can't go to the school. What if someone sees me?"

"Then you wave." He joked, but she didn't laugh. "No one will see you; the special ed classes have an early release. We'll be out of there before the final bell rings. And after I drop him off, I'll take you home."

"I can't go home!" Paisley stood, arms out to the sides. "The minute I get home, everyone is going to ask how I did. I don't want to admit I'm a four-time loser any sooner than I have to. Can't I stay with you to-night?"

"You're not a loser. You just need a little more practice to build your confidence."

"I suck at driving." She piled the sanding supplies in a corner and put her hands on her hips. "I'm never going to pass."

"Your mom sucked at driving, too, but with practice, she got better."

They strolled along the dock toward the car, and Levi was already thinking about seeing Beckett at the marina once she was done with her client.

"Dad yells at me, and he's always hugging the armrest like he's expecting me to drive off a cliff. Annie is always using the imaginary brake."

"I have lots of practice sitting in the car, because your mom needed a *lot* of practice to pass."

She turned to him and said, "Really? Why didn't you tell me before?"

A pang squeezed his chest.

"Did I ever tell you about the time your mom was learning to drive in Grandma's car? Grandpa was explaining how to react if someone coming from the other direction crosses into your lane, then a squirrel ran across the road, and she jerked the wheel so hard, she landed us in a ditch."

"Oh my god." Paisley laughed. "Did she hit it?"

"Thump, thump."

Paisley tented her hands over her mouth. "Did she cry?"

"Okay, she didn't hit the squirrel, but yes, she did cry. She wailed so hard, Grandpa had me drive home, and I didn't even have my license. She refused to get behind the wheel for a month." He hooked his arm around Paisley's shoulders and gave her a side hug. "You may have failed four times, but your mom failed seven. Or it might have been eight, I forget."

"No way."

"Sorry, kiddo, you not only inherited her bad taste in boyband music, but her test-taking skills, too. On the upside, you've also got her resilience and strength. You just need practice."

They reached the truck, and Paisley leveled that grin at him, the one he could never refuse.

"Then, can I drive us home?" When he hesitated, she said, "Come on, I've done it before. Plus, how am I going to get better if I don't get to practice?"

Levi tossed her the keys and started toward the passenger's side. "Once we get to the high school and pick up Tommy, I'm

368

driving the rest of the way home."

It would give him a chance to pick Paisley's brain. There was a lot more to Beckett than pie, scallops, and moussaka, and he needed to find out before tonight. Levi wasn't looking for someone to play hooky with, he was looking for something a little more serious. And he was looking for that with Beckett. So creating the right tone for their meeting was crucial.

When they got into the truck, he asked, "What are the most romantic things on my menu?"

"Mom always said, 'Anything made with love.'"

CHAPTER 17

Beckett was headed for some serious heart-break, and no amount of pie could fix it. Not that she wasn't going to try.

While she and Dog Wonder were at the pediatric ward, she'd received a call from Fur-Ever Friends, who were excited to relay that it was time to make things official. Gregory was scheduled for his final certification test, and if he passed, he could be reunited with his family at their earliest convenience.

She'd banked on the testing schedule being backlogged, to give herself the time she needed to prepare for goodbye, but a last-minute cancellation had left an opening for Gregory to slide in. With only an hour to drop off Diesel and drive to the shelter, there was no time for just Gregory and Beckett.

When they arrived at the Fur-Ever Friends training barn, Katie and her family were waiting at the curb to walk Gregory inside. Before Beckett could gather her wits, the test was over, Gregory passed his ESA certificate with flying colors, and he was handed over to his fur-ever family — who invited Beckett to a celebratory dinner after.

She politely declined, telling herself the cleaner the break, the faster she'd heal. She'd always been spectacular at denial, constantly in forward motion so she wouldn't have to look back. It had gotten her this far, but the weight was getting harder to carry alone.

Which was how she found herself at the marina, dressed in a cape and space-girl buns, with three different kinds of cake and a half-eaten carton of ice cream. Determined to make it to the boat before she took another bite, she made her way down the dock and around the pump station, heading toward Levi's berth. Only when she reached the back of his boat did she notice someone waiting.

Levi stood on the deck, and he'd clearly come straight from work. He was wearing dark jeans, a white dress shirt unbuttoned at the collar, and a navy crew jacket that added a touch of sailor-boy swagger to the businessman. His elbows rested on the deck railing, two beer bottles dangling from his fingertips. He looked strong and capable, like a big, sexy shelter from the storm. He walked toward her, his feet eating up the distance, until he was standing close enough to touch. Close enough to smell — she sniffed again. "Is that bacon?"

"Bacon-wrapped scallops." He took her by the hand and led her across the glossy cedar flooring to a sophisticated semi-circular seating area. In its center sat a welcoming blue-glass firepit and a table set for two. "They're on the grill."

Only the best item on the Crow's Nest menu. They were listed as an appetizer, but Beckett ordered them every time she ate there. Topped with a heavenly green sauce made from garlic, fresh herbs, and diced jalapenos, the dish was Beckett's personal favorite.

"You sure know how to make a lady feel special," she teased.

Levi's eyes ran the length of her, paying careful attention to her leggings, her cape, and her space-girl buns. By the time he made it back to her red-rimmed eyes, he took the cakes from her hand, set them on the table, and pulled her against him.

"I'm sorry about Gregory," he whispered into her hair.

"Me too." She wrapped her arms tightly

around him and buried her face in his neck. Breathing in his strength and listening to the soothing beat of his heart, she finally admitted to herself that this was what she'd come here for.

Her friends would want to talk about Gregory's adoption, and her family wouldn't know what to say. But Levi, he just held her while she pretended those weren't tears on her cheeks. The boat swayed gently beneath them, and she gave herself over to Levi's capable arms and tender embrace, not in any rush to move.

"He had to leave sometime," she finally said.

He brushed the tear away with the pad of this thumb. "I'm sorry that sometime was today."

"This is ridiculous," she said, trying to stop the tears without much success.

She was ridiculous. Standing in front of the sexiest man she'd ever seen, who'd arranged the most romantic date in the history of first dates, and she was dressed like Punky Brewster and bawling over a chicken.

"It's not like I'm never going to see him again." She sniffed. "He lives a mile from my house."

"It's how you feel. That's as real as it gets," he said, zero judgment in his voice.

"When Michelle and Paisley moved in with Gray, it was only a block over, but it could have been on the other side of the country. It felt like my heart had been shattered. Not seeing Paisley every morning when I woke up, knowing some other guy was tucking her into bed. Sure, Paisley was happy to see me when I dropped by, but to me it felt as if I'd been replaced. I couldn't deal."

It was that same fear that kept Beckett so involved with her family. She knew they needed her around, but that didn't mean they wanted her. In fact, when she came home after a long day, she rarely got the feeling that she'd been missed. Her answer was to carve out a place in their lives that no one else could fill, but even that security didn't reassure her like it used to.

"What did you do?" she asked, self-consciously fiddling with the hem of his jacket.

"Found a new rhythm. Started renovating the boat where my dad and I let off, joined a softball league, anything to pull me out of my misery. Happy distractions, I guess." He stilled her hands and pressed them against his chest. "Not that I didn't eat breakfast at Michelle and Gray's for the first few years, but I knew the only way I'd get through that feeling of loss was to find my own space.

Hell, I even started dating."

"Was that when you moved onto the boat?" she asked casually. "When you started dating?"

Dipping his head, he looked at her. "Actually, I moved onto the boat after Vikki left. I sold the house, fit everything that mattered into the bed of my truck, and crashed on that hammock" — he pointed to the reef-green hammock on the port side of the boat, swinging gently in the breeze — "while I made the master cabin habitable."

"With its calm and soothing shades," she teased, taking in the masterfully redone upper deck.

Unlike the dark wood and masculine design of the restaurant, his boat was bright and warm with an understated ruggedness. The modern lines of the boat were softened with round throw rugs and plush fabrics, dividing the large upper deck into several smaller, more intimate areas. Everything looked custom but not ostentatious, built with purpose.

"Well?" he asked. "What do you think of *Rhodes Less Traveled*?"

"Your boat feels like you."

"What exactly do I feel like?" His hands slid down to her ass.

"Warm, cozy, fun," she whispered. "Like home."

He pinched her butt. "You just described Diesel."

"Not the kind of fun I'm thinking of." She went on her tiptoes to kiss his lips. "And I don't feel at home when I'm home."

"But you feel that way with me?"

"I feel a lot when I'm with you," she admitted, and Levi pressed a whisper of a kiss to her lips.

Around them, thick clouds soaked up the setting sun as the tide rolled in and seagulls circled the marina. Vibrant hues of orange and pink reflected off the massive glass doors that separated the outdoors from the interior galley, the warm light turning his eyes a tropical blue. But neither of them moved. Just swayed gently in each other's arms.

She didn't know how long they stood there, gazing into each other, both aware that something significant was happening, and neither pretending to fight it anymore. It was as if only the two of them mattered in that moment — and then her belly growled.

"Come on," he said, laughing and giving her a playful smack to her butt, "let me show you what we will be dining on this evening."

She grabbed the cake boxes and followed him to the barbecue, where he lifted the lid.

A warm blast of broiled bacon teased her senses, and the possessive way he claimed her hand, as if she were his, teased a whole lot of other things. She peeked over his shoulder into the grill and gasped, because in addition to the bacon-wrapped scallops was a feast for six. Slider-sized patties; crab cakes; a stainless-steel steamer filled with clams, garlic, and simmering white wine. But what had her heart skittering to a stop were the two gigantic artichokes, halved and placed facedown on the hot grill.

She breathed in the savory mesquite scent and groaned. "What's all this for?"

"I may have heard that you had a rough day. Annie called."

"So you decided to raid the restaurant freezer and cook me everything?"

"Actually, the plan was to make a few of my favorites, a few of yours, and see what crosses over." He looked at the boxes and half-eaten ice cream on the table. "But now, I'm wondering if this is more of a straight-from-the-cake-box kind of house visit. Should I grab a couple of forks and pour the ice cream into glasses?"

"And waste perfectly good scallops and

artichokes?" She took a seat at the bar, which overlooked the barbecue, and sipped her beer. "Did you know that I happen to love artichokes?"

He met her gaze over the grill's lid. "I did."

"Honestly? Or did you get lucky?"

"I never leave things to luck. She's more temperamental than chance." He skillfully flipped each scallop, then squeezed lemon over the artichokes. A blue-and-red flame sparked, licking the sides of the artichokes, curling the leaves and blackening the tips before vanishing beneath the grill.

"You don't even serve artichokes at your restaurant."

"Remind me to rectify that oversight." He placed the artichokes on a white plate, then made a big show of squeezing the charred lemon over the top, and slid it across the bar.

"Levi Rhodes, are you trying to impress me?"

"Desperately." He looked up from plating. "Is it working?"

She looked into his eyes and saw a hint of vulnerability, as though he were willing to work as hard as it took, and Beckett felt everything inside of her shift. He might want to impress her, but she was desperate to be a part of him. To be the kind of woman he'd work hard to impress always, and that's when it hit her.

She was in serious trouble. This wasn't some silly attraction or hormones talking. Her heart was involved, and she wasn't sure how she felt about that.

He was leaving in six weeks, and if she wasn't careful, he'd take her heart with him. But as she looked around his boat, she couldn't help but wonder: Did Levi realize, while he was searching for a happy distraction and dreaming of a solitary life at sea, that he'd managed to build a homey retreat with all the makings for family fun? The seating for ten, industrial-sized grill, excess snorkeling gear, and water toys — none of that spoke of a man embarking on trip-for-one around the continent.

Then again, the serious and vulnerable man who sat in front of her now was nowhere near the same flirty, life-is-one-big-party guy she'd met all those years back. Just like she was no longer the shy and uncertain woman who was willing to settle.

None of that changed the fact that he was still leaving, and her life was in Rome. He wasn't in a position to give what she knew her heart needed. So she changed direction to something she could handle. Flirty, funny Levi didn't make her feel things she was foolish to feel.

Flirty, funny Levi she could handle.

"Depends." She took a swig of beer. "Do you take your artichoke with mayo or butter?"

"Honestly, I'm an artichoke virgin. So you'll have to take your time with me." He grinned, erasing every ounce of vulnerability and replacing it with testosterone-dripping swagger. "But since a Boy Scout is always prepared, I have both. Plus, some lemon-garlic aioli."

A plate with three blue bowls, expertly arranged and garnished, appeared. Next came the scallops, and the steaming clams, which he poured into a big, shallow bowl.

"If your goal is to make it hard for the next guy, you're doing a good job," she said.

"Lucky for you, I already have your next guy in mind." He walked around the bar, bracing a hand on either side of her, and leaned in. "He's about six-two, dark blond hair, blue eyes, a real dreamboat, and manly as hell."

"I hear he can be a bit of a braggart, though."

"It's not bragging if it's the real deal." He nipped at her lower lip. "And for the record, it's the real deal."

She laughed, and the release felt good.

Being in his arms felt even better. She didn't know how he did it, but the man had a knack for turning her world completely upside down and sideways — in the best possible ways.

"For the record," she whispered back, "I'm more of an experience-it-for-myself kind of person."

"What are you looking to experience tonight?"

All her life, Beckett made the "responsible" choice, put others' needs before her own, even at the expense of her happiness. Went out of her way to avoid rocking the boat. But with Levi, she believed things could be different. That responsibility and happiness weren't mutually exclusive, but in fact, usually came as a package deal. She was on the verge of something amazing and wanted to reclaim the parts of her life that she'd lost.

Starting with incredibly hot boat sex.

Beckett wanted to know what it was like to be wanted with a certainty. She wasn't greedy; one night would do. Maybe they'd even make it to breakfast. And maybe, if she was lucky, he'd even help her figure out what she liked and what she loved. But one thing was for sure — she was ready to rock the boat.

"Everything you have to offer." She locked her arms around his neck, then slowly drew him closer until he hit the edge of the barstool, her legs on either side of his. Her mouth a scant inch from heaven.

"That's a tall order," he murmured, peeling the coat open, his hands wasting no time sliding inside and around to cup her ass.

Her breath caught. This was what she wanted. "Good thing you're six-two."

"Don't forget manly as hell." His grip tightened and, in a move so manly her panties went damp, he engaged her in a sexy little game of musical chairs. At the end of round one, Levi was sitting on the barstool, Beckett was straddling his lap, the coat was puddled on the floor, and her T-shirt was doing little to conceal how much she enjoyed the game.

"How could I?" she said, deciding she was ready to advance to round two, and gripped the hem of her shirt to pull it up, up, and over her head, dropping it to join the coat.

And like every manly-as-hell guy, Levi was rendered silent by a pair of boobs.

She could never be called curvy by any means. On a good day, she was a full and respectable B who, with her miracle bra, could hold her own against the over-frosted cupcakes from Levi's past.

His breath caught when her nipples beaded under the cool night air, telling him she was having a good day.

"You good?" she finally asked.

"Just taking a moment." He ran a hand over his jaw.

"Beck, I might need some help here," he finally said. Palms flat, fingers splayed, he took his sweet time smoothing his way over her hips and up each rib, his thumb grazing everything in between. "Because I feel like I haven't eaten in months, and I'm standing in front of an all-you-can-eat dessert buffet, suddenly realizing I should have grabbed a bigger plate."

Beckett started to argue that she could feel his real deal, and it was more than big enough, but then he was kissing her. Hot and frantic, skipping right over the niceties, and getting her worked up in record time.

"I thought you didn't know where to start," she said.

"I figured it out," he said silkily, his mouth brushing her ear.

The low rasp in his voice ignited a hum of anticipation under her skin. So did the way he abruptly stood, plopping her ass on the bar top and stepping between her legs.

"Let me know if you approve." Her bra slid to join the pile on the floor, exposing her bare breasts. "I guess practice does make perfect," she breathed, because she hadn't even felt him undo it.

"We haven't even gotten to the good stuff."

Beckett watched breathlessly as he dipped his head lower and lower until his hot mouth settled on her bare breast, sending her hopes for the night soaring. Man of his word, he didn't rush, didn't let up, took his time to learn what she liked, methodically nipping and kissing, worshiping her into a frenzy, before gliding to the other and back again.

By his third pass, Beckett's body was on fire, shaking with want and desperate for more. So much more that her eyes burned.

"Feels so good," she groaned, her hands in his hair, locking him to her.

Other than smiling against her skin, he didn't respond, except to place an open-mouthed kiss right above her belly button.

Then one below.

And another even lower.

Then those very deft fingers were on the move again, tugging at the waist of her leggings until — *bingo.* He put his mouth right where the lace met skin. And when her leggings wouldn't go any lower, he gave her butt a little pat.

Eager to get to the *screaming his name* part, Beckett did her best to assist, lifting her hips so he could slide her leggings off. Which he did, right along with her boots, stripping her down into nothing but teal panties, her red cape, and space-girl buns. Amazing what the proper motivation could do.

Properly motivated herself, she hooked her thumbs into his front pockets, pulling him close enough to reach his jeans zipper.

"Uh-uh." He stopped her. "Tonight is about you enjoying some of that me-first time you never get."

"But what about you?"

"To the winner go the spoils." He kissed her cheek, then her nose. "Now lie back and let me spoil you."

She did as told, and when his mouth came down on hers, it wasn't sweet or warm. It was inferno from the word go. His kisses went deeper, became hotter, and Beckett couldn't keep her hands off him.

Sliding her palms down his chest, she blindly found the hem of his shirt and tugged it up as fast as she could. Only he was faster. Laughing as he leaned back.

"Please?" she asked. "Otherwise I'll feel underdressed."

"You are in the perfect state of dress," he

385

said, looking at her as if she were the milk and he was the tiger ready to lap her up. She watched breathlessly as his gaze slid ever-so-slowly from her breasts to her stomach, and by the time he reached her panties, she was shaking all over.

She reached again, and again he leveled her with an authoritarian look. "Just your shirt?" she asked sweetly.

She knew the moment he gave in, because he sighed one of his "what am I going to do with you?" sighs, which always felt more like an endearment than a rhetorical question. "Why do I feel a rule coming on?"

"No rule. Just the shirt?" She held out her hand, and he obliged. Smiling, she tossed his shirt over her head and leaned back on her palms. "Let the pampering commence."

"Now lie back and enjoy."

Who was she to argue? Especially when a sexy and shirtless Levi had his magnificent torso on display. When she leaned back on her elbows, he took a seat on the barstool, as if getting comfortable for the duration. His palms slid down her bare thighs, gripping her from underneath and tugging her so she was teetering on the edge of the counter.

The lower he went, the closer his shoulders moved, and the farther apart her leg moved to accommodate him. And accommodate him, she did. All the way down to where her skin met lace, and the sheer anticipation of the next stop on his journey had her back arching off the counter. Only instead of kissing her where she wanted — no, where she needed it — he skipped over her hottest button to nuzzle her inner thigh.

"To the left a little," she groaned.

"Here?" he asked, kissing up the seam of her panties.

"That was right. Left." She shifted her hips to the side, trying to be helpful as he licked her inner thigh. "Higher."

"Is that you relaxing?"

"Yes." She bit back a smile. "I'm completely relaxed. Scout's honor."

She held up her best Scouts sign, and Levi sucked her fingers into his mouth and slowly released them. "Good. I'd hate to have to make a new rule."

He lowered his head, then paused to give her a pointed look. She laughed, and he picked up where he'd left off. Slowly kissing her insane, his hands and mouth lavishing every inch of her skin, raising the tension until she was certain she'd shatter, then slowly backing off.

"Levi," she groaned. "I need to come."

"And I need you to relax."

"But only if you get to the good parts."

He went back to teasing and licking, and just when she thought he'd back off again, he said, "Beck, you might want to keep your cape on for this." And licked her straight up the center.

"That was a good part," she moaned.

And that's when the good became amazing, and when his finger got involved, it became a religious experience. He tugged her thong to the side and dipped his tongue in the holy water, and sweet baby Jesus, she pushed into him and groaned out his name.

He seemed to like the sound of it, because he dipped again, and again, not giving up until her thighs burned from clenching so hard.

"Almost," she moaned, trying to press herself against his tongue. "Just a little more."

"Be careful, I'd hate for you to get all tense. I'd have to start all over again."

Her eyes snapped open, desperate. "I can't start over. I can barely handle continuing."

"Then relax," he said against her inner thigh. "Or I'll invoke rule three." This was whispered against the topmost inner curve of her leg.

"Rule three?" she asked.

"Oh yeah. If I lick it, then it's mine." The

last word vibrated through her core, as he claimed her with a lick that had her sex-shocks bouncing in anticipation of what had to be the world's most overdue man-given orgasm. But he didn't stop there. Levi showed her exactly how talented of a multi-tasker he was, and just how much she'd been missing in life.

The man was a sex god, taking his time as if every move, every kiss, every lick was an event unto itself. He approached foreplay the same way he approached sailing — he was methodical, disciplined, holding back, making sure that when he crossed that finish line, it was to fanfare and explosive applause.

He wanted people cheering his name, and she desperately wanted to cross that line. She could see it, building in front of her. All Levi had to do was give one well-placed flick, and fireworks would explode skyward. Only he was teasing her, dancing around the sacred spot for what had to be hours, it seemed.

"Levi, please."

"Since you asked nicely," he said, and before she could strangle him, he launched a full-fledged attack on her body. There was nothing nice or polite about the way he was touching, kissing, pampering her until they found the kind of rhythm with each other it took people years to fall into.

"More," she said, even as her head thrashed.

"You're there, you just have to let go." He pulled her panties aside, and his tongue did a little one-two action, right up the center, lingering until the pleasure built and she felt everything inside tighten to the point of snapping. But no matter how far she stretched, it was always just out of reach.

"I can't."

"Beck," he soothed. "Remember that edge I told you about. You're there, but you don't have to be there alone. If you let me, I'll catch you when you fall. But you have to choose to let me, that's how this works."

Beckett had found herself in one of those "leap, and the net will appear" situations. She couldn't even run a block without becoming winded; how was she supposed to leap?

But as she stared into his eyes, an overwhelming sensation of being safe wrapped around her, and her walls started to crumble. Her muscles uncoiled, her eyes drifted closed, and she felt herself climbing, higher and higher, above the fear and uncertainty, above the doubts and disappointments, to a place that was safe to consider the possibilities.

"That's my girl," he said, gently coaxing her.

Those three words slid past what was left of her armor and settled in her chest. She wanted so badly to believe them, believe that she was his girl, that she gave up fighting and leapt.

And even as she let go, she felt Levi's strength take hold. Bracing her as the biggest orgasm of her life raced toward her, straining her body and short-circuiting her brain. Her lungs burned, her breath came in painful bursts, and Levi met her every need.

"You might want to keep your eyes open and cape on for this, Girl Wonder," he said.

Her stomach trembled with anticipation as they locked gazes, and if the fate of the world depended on her looking away, she decided they'd all die. Because without breaking eye contact, Levi pulled her panties all the way off — with his teeth — then sat back to admire his handiwork.

Beckett didn't move, let him look his fill. There was something incredibly erotic and empowering about being stripped naked for his viewing pleasure. But it didn't come at the expense of her pleasure. Oh no, Levi kept the pace steady, purposeful, taking her higher and higher without rushing her.

"I got you," he whispered one last time, with a final swirl, combined with just the right amount of pressure. Beckett didn't care how far she'd eventually fall. Her orgasm hit hard, and she flew apart like a mountain stuffed with seventy-five tons of dynamite. For a moment, she could have sworn she left her body, but Levi made sure her landing was just as pleasurable.

He gently coaxed her down, whispering sweet words and giving her tender kisses.

When she could draw in a breath, she found herself staring up into the bluest eyes. The way he looked at her, and the reverent way he held her hip, his thumb sliding back and forth over her stomach, offering her comfort and connection, as though she were precious.

As though she were his. She didn't mean to fall; she knew better. But the warm ache in her heart told her that she had. Totally and completely.

He'd said he wanted to discover what she liked, and then what she loved, but in true Beckett fashion, she'd jumped right over the first part. Old Beckett would be throwing her clothes back on, making an excuse for why she had to leave, and overthinking everything to the point of a nuclear-scale meltdown.

But bold Beckett was done with excuses and overthinking. Levi said he had her, and she was going to give him the chance to be the man he promised. Not because she was testing him, but because she was trusting him.

So without asking what was next on his list, she tugged his belt and said, "I think I'd like that tour of your cabin now."

Levi couldn't decide if he was the luckiest son of a bitch to walk the earth or the stupidest. Because only in his wildest dreams would there be a reality where Beckett Hayes was kissing him, naked on his deck and asking him, no, *begging,* for a grand tour.

Or maybe he was the one begging. It was hard to tell when she slowly sucked his lower lip into her mouth and released it with a sexy fucking *pop.*

She was hot, naked, and — there went his belt buckle — he was hesitating. Not on the kissing — he could do that all night, and ditto with the touching. And didn't he want to see just how good she looked in his bed, then compare this to how she looked in his bed when the sun came up? Fuck yeah, he did.

But Levi had a hard time envisioning a tomorrow where Beckett didn't harbor some regrets. Hell, he'd convinced himself that the time they had together would be worth it. Even worse, he'd convinced himself Beckett was on the same page. A see-where-this-goes expiration-date-looming kind of relationship. But there was nothing expiration-date-looming about her.

Beckett's nature veered toward selfless and caring. It didn't take a relationship expert to see that her emotions didn't turn off when the clock ran out. Oh, she played the impenetrable superhero well, but beneath that cape and armor was an empathetic and nurturing woman whose capacity to love astounded him.

Then there was the way she arrived to-night, all soft and pliant and so damn sad over a chicken, so maybe the right thing to do would be to take a breather, clarify where everyone's at emotionally, and avoid any potential regrets.

"Beck?" he asked against her lips. "Are you sure?"

He could have sworn she said yes, but it was hard to tell with her tongue in his mouth. Plus, there was her sexy little mewl-ing that was doing a great job of distracting him from the question at hand.

Oh, and her hands? They were flat against his abs, pressing him back into the seat, and just like that she was straddling his lap, her cake coming in complete contact with his éclair. Normally, he'd take that as two big green lights, front and center, but with Beckett, he wasn't taking any chances.

"Was that a yes?" He hoped to God it was, because he needed her like he needed his next breath. And breathing came high on his list, right after tasting the sweet spot right behind her ear.

Still no word from her, but then, miracle of all miracles, it happened. She made a condom appear out of thin air. One minute her hands were unbuttoning his jeans, the next they were holding a condom — strawberry-flavored and ribbed for her pleasure. Which he'd remember for next time.

And in case *that* wasn't crystal fucking clear enough, her slim fingers delved beneath his jeans, skin on skin, as she got a hands-on experience that, based on the way her breath caught, put any and all questions to bed that Levi was not, in fact, a braggart.

Those toned legs wrapped around him, and Levi did his part to ensure her comfort, sliding his hands down; as though they had built-in GPS, they located her ass in a millisecond. Silky-soft and completely naked. He went to work supporting, exploring, cupping until he had two palms full of that heart-shaped backside — and life was suddenly wonderful.

She was squirming, trying to climb up his body, so he obliged, lifting her until all their good parts were in line. It got a little crowded in his pants with her hands, his raging hard-on, and their suctioned bodies, but he made it work. When her legs locked behind his back, he stood with her in his arms, wrapped around him like a pretzel.

"Wait," she said, her breath coming in choppy gasps. "Not yet."

Levi waited. "Was that a 'not yet, I'd rather walk to your cabin'? Or more of a 'not yet, I remembered I said I never, ever, *ever* want a tour of your cabin'? Because if it was the former, I'd like to point out that I admire your independence. But if it was the latter, and this was a 'caught up in the moment, might be feeling regrets,' just say so. Second thoughts happen."

He might shed a tear to two, but he'd understand, whichever way she decided.

Beckett silently watched him, and he wasn't sure what to make of it. Then a small smile started at her cheeks and lit her big brown eyes, and it had a good portion of hunger and need.

"No second-guesses. They only thing I regret is not going home with you that night at the bonfire."

Levi's chest felt tight over that amazing and terrifying admission. His lungs seized up when he realized she meant it. He could see the truth in her eyes. This insane pull was definitely a double-sided situation. They were finally both on the same track, barreling toward each other at a speed of two-hundred-and-sixty-eight miles per hour. And when their paths finally intersected, it was going to be catastrophic.

"And I said 'wait' because" — she reached over and pulled two more condoms from her bag — "I figured we'd need these."

Catastrophic or not, that was what he was looking for. A sign that this wasn't some spontaneous hookup. She'd thought this through, made her choice, and *hallelujah,* she'd chosen him.

"Now about that tour." She slipped down his body, took his hand, and gave it a gentle squeeze that he felt all the way to his soul.

Silently, she led him through the galley, and he couldn't help but follow as she took him down the stairs to the lower deck and into his master cabin, the same master cabin he'd pictured her in a thousand times over.

And when she reached his bed, she climbed in and lay back against the headboard. And what a sight she made. Her hair spread out on his sheets, her lithe body completely bare. Her eyes looking at him as if he really could hang the moon.

"I've been thinking." She offered up a sweet smile. "Maybe we should get rid of a few rules."

Depending on the rule, he was game. Unless it was rule three, because she was already his, and he didn't feel ready to give her back. Now rule one, he could get behind. How else was he going to see if she looked better naked under moonlight or sunlight?

For the record, she looked beautiful in the moonlight. The soft glow on her skin; the way the light reflected off her shiny, wet, full lips.

She patted the bed. "I feel content to stay here all night." She reached out her hand to him. "Join me."

Those two simple words slayed him. He wasn't chasing her, sweet-talking her, or charming her into his bed. She was meeting him halfway, reaching out, showing him that she, too, could be vulnerable.

For him, she could be vulnerable. And wasn't that the most beautiful thing he'd ever seen.

"If I have my way, you won't be leaving my bed until next week," he said, crawling up her body to take her mouth.

She took his right back, further confirming why he couldn't stop thinking about her. Her hands fisted in his belt loops, and she yanked him on top of her.

"Too many clothes," she said. Her hands sliding beneath his jeans once again, over his ass, and with the help of her feet, taking his jeans all the way off.

"You found out what I liked; now it's my turn," she said, her hands giving a delicate squeeze that made his eyes roll to the back of his head. He'd barely regained consciousness when she bent over and covered him with her sweet mouth.

"Jesus, Beck," he groaned, resting his arm over his eyes. But he glanced down at her, because he couldn't help himself. Watching her slowly drive him out of his mind with her gentle licks and sucks was the sexiest thing he'd ever experienced.

"Too many more turns like that, and it will be game over." He rolled her over, pinning her beneath him. "And when I cross the finish line, I want to do it with you. Okay?"

She beamed up at him. "Okay."

"Okay." He kissed her gently, then not so gently, running a hand down her stomach and between her legs. He danced around the edges until her body was quivering beneath him, and her breath was coming in short gasps.

A second finger joined the party, making sure she was wet and ready. It didn't take long until the moans started, and he felt her hips push against his hand, straining for more friction.

"I see the finish line," she panted, the small of her back arching off the bed.

"Already?" he asked.

She nodded. "And if you want to join in the celebration, you'd better suit up."

Never one to keep a lady waiting, he slipped on the condom, and just as he had it secure, she lifted her hips, and talk about hole-in-one.

"Oh God," they sighed in unison.

Levi may have chanted it a few times, because she felt that good. That perfect. Like everything in the universe came together for this one moment. That's when Levi realized he didn't just want her to stay the night. He wanted her to stay. Right here, beneath him, in his arms.

Then she started moving, and he was pretty sure his heart lodged itself in his lung, because he became light-headed and stopped breathing at the same time. And when she buried her face in his neck and moaned his name, a mindless whisper, he felt like his heart would beat right out of his fucking chest.

"Do you see it?" she asked, and he realized he was doing more feeling than work, and she was a few notes ahead of him. Rising on an elbow, he pulled her against him until their bodies were slick with friction, and his pulse was spiking like he was in the race of his life.

Then he looked down, their eyes locked, and there it was, the finish line. In all his years of sailing, and all the titles he held, it had never been so clear.

"I see it." He took her mouth, moving inside her with strong, deep thrusts and feeling her body tightening around him. She rose up to meet him, every fucking time, never shying away, stripping him down until he couldn't hide anything.

And he didn't want to. For once in his life, he wanted it all out there. Wanted to see how she'd react, if she'd run or if she'd take a chance on him. And then her hands came up to lace with his and she said, "I got you."

And hell if he didn't cry a little. Putting

everything he had into those last few moments, he withdrew all the way, then slid back in, meeting her on the return. They both groaned and repeated the motion, over and over again, both giving everything they had.

"I see it, too," she moaned, and in a final push, she shattered around him. Back arched, head thrown back, riding the high. And when she hit the top and he felt the tremor, he tumbled over with her. The pleasure and loss balling tightly in his chest, then exploding with the force of a semi going headfirst into a concrete wall. The power took him out at the knees, and he pulled her to his side right before he collapsed.

Levi concentrated on pulling air back into his lungs. Beckett hadn't moved, hadn't tried to slither away, just lying there, a content ball of sated woman. He tugged her against him, her back to his front, nuzzling into her hair so he could breathe her in. To his surprise, she just melted into him with a dreamy sigh, and Levi knew right then that the peace and solace he'd been searching for was right there in his arms.

CHAPTER 18

"I need to know that you can handle this," Beckett said, throwing on Levi's coat and grabbing her keys.

"By the time you get there, it will be nine," Jeffery pointed out, as if Beckett wasn't aware of the time. "What kind of emergency could there be this close to closing?"

"It's a bar, not just a restaurant. And I don't know."

When she'd been at the Crow's Nest earlier that day, things seemed fine. She and Annie met for an early dinner, speculated over how the bachelor party was going, and Beckett naively joked that everything at the restaurant was smooth sailing, even without its captain at the helm.

"Maybe you should call back and get more information before you go all the way across town," Jeffery said, blocking the front door. "It's dark out. Too cold to be riding around on your scooter."

"Which is why I was hoping to take your pickup." When he didn't move, she said, "Dad, can I take your truck?"

"Of course. It's just —" He looked at Thomas on the couch, apprehension creased into his forehead. "I go to Boston tomorrow to meet with a new client. I need to make sure I'm prepared."

"I'll be back before you have to leave tomorrow. I'll probably be back before you go to bed."

"Okay," Jeffery said and handed Beckett the truck keys.

"Thank you." She kissed him on the cheek and ducked under his arm to get out the front door. But her dad was right behind her.

"Maybe you should call Levi."

"Already tried. And if he could be reached, they wouldn't have called me."

Jeffery looked ready to swim to Nantucket to bring Levi back if necessary. Tommy rubbed his eyes as he came out on the porch. "Tommy, it's cold. Get back inside." To her dad, she said, "I'll be back as soon as I can."

"There's got to be someone else you can call."

"I've called everyone." She jogged down the steps. "But I'll try again." She stopped to open the truck door and found her father right behind her, in his pajamas and bare feet. Oblivious to the frost on the ground. "Good God, Dad, get inside."

"I can't," he said, voice low and desperate. "Tomorrow's a big day for me. I've been working on this score for months. Plus, Thomas has that field trip to the museum."

"The field trip is Monday, and Tommy and I have walked through everything. No surprises."

"This is a surprise," Jeffery said. "What if something happens? He's already upset about the chicken going. Now you're leaving so suddenly. What if he starts asking about the field trip?"

"You remind him it's not until Monday." She nudged her dad back so she could open the truck door, then squeezed between him and the door to slide behind the wheel. "You were there for me through tough nights. And you were great. You don't give yourself enough credit. You're going to be okay." She met his gaze directly. "But I need to hear you say it."

"We'll be fine," he said, gripping the top of the door.

Beckett felt like Gumby, pulled in every direction. But one responsibility stood out above all others, and for the first time in longer than she could remember, it wasn't her responsibility to her family. It wasn't to Levi, either. Not exactly. It was to herself. She'd made a promise she would grow her business, and if she didn't put herself first for a change, nothing would ever get better.

Things *had* to change. In the end, it would benefit everyone.

"Dad?" The word came out as a reprimand. She caught herself and checked her frustration. Honestly, it sometimes felt as if her father were harder to reason with than Tommy. "Move your fingers so they don't get caught in the door. I made a promise to a client. This is my business. This is important to me. I have to go."

He let go, but his gaze remained locked helplessly on hers. She shut the door and hit the lock. Sure enough, her father grabbed the door handle.

Beckett felt awful, but for the first time, it wasn't because she'd failed her family. It was because she knew exactly how her dad felt right now, and she wouldn't wish that stress on anyone. But tonight, he had to figure it out for himself, or ten years from now, she'd still be figuring it out for him.

Stomach in knots, she eased onto the road, making sure her father's feet were clear of the tires before pressing on the gas.

She gave him a reassuring wave as she backed out of the drive.

Once she was on the street, she exhaled a long breath, but that didn't make the sight of her father, still standing in the road behind her, any easier to process.

In truth, she was a little sick over how good it felt to hand off all the responsibilities that really shouldn't have been hers in the first place. She felt guilty over this tiny sensation of freedom.

Beckett positioned her phone in the holder attached to the dash and said, "Okay, Siri. Call Captain Cool."

Her call went directly to voice mail, and Beckett's shoulders slid a little lower. This time, she decided to leave a message. When the voice mail prompted with a beep, Beckett forced her voice into that not-a-care-in-the-world octave.

"Hey, it's me. Uh, Beck." She rolled her eyes. "I just wanted to touch base and see if you had any other backup numbers for Gus. I got a call that he came down with food poisoning" — she pushed an unconvincing laugh from her throat — "ironic, right? Anyway, I'm on it. You don't have to worry. I guess you don't have cell service out on the ocean, huh? Well, if you get this and happen to think of someone I could call to fill in, let me know. If not, no biggie. I'll handle it."

At the stop sign, she squeezed her eyes against the burn of tears, cleared her throat, and said, "Hope you're having fun. I hear Nantucket is cold enough to freeze your nuts this time of year."

She disconnected, then continued toward the bar while speed-dialing Gus to get the numbers of anyone she might have forgotten. When he didn't answer, she thought about what her father had said and dialed the restaurant.

Eleven rings later, she slammed her finger against the disconnect button. "Is today some freaking holiday I don't know about? Where is everyone?"

Panic perked in her belly like one of those old-fashioned coffee machines. "I'm fine." She wrung the steering wheel with her hands. "I've got this, because that's the kind of person I am. The kind who can handle anything. No matter what."

She down-shifted, and the fortune inside the Magic 8-Ball spun and spun before landing on DON'T COUNT ON IT.

Beckett did what any grown woman would do — she used her last lifeline.

"Okay, Siri, phone a friend," she said, and nearly wept when Annie answered on the first ring.

"Did you butt-dial me?" Annie teased, the warm giggle in her tone pricking at Beckett's eyes. "Because my butt misses you, too."

"Gus has food poisoning, one of the waitresses is a no-show, apparently everyone in Rome decided to dine at the Crow's Nest, and the situation must be so dire that they called me," Beckett rushed out in a single breath. "Oh, and Levi's at sea, and I swore on my business that I'd take care of his restaurant. Only no one's answering to tell me what the fuck is going on!"

The desperation in her voice sounded an awful lot like her father's a moment ago.

"Okay, take a breath. Let's think this through," Annie said, her bedside manner as a physician's assistant kicking in. "What do we know? You're down a cook, server, hostess, and the owner. No need to freak out."

"Your saying that makes me freak out." Beckett paused. "I never said I was down a hostess."

"Whoever's job it is to answer the phone, they either are completely inept or a no-show," Annie reasoned.

"You're not making me feel better," Beckett said.

"Symptoms, prognosis, treatment," she

409

replied. "And as a medical practitioner, I can promise you that you will survive this. In fact, you're going to rock this. You've been training for this moment for weeks. It's no different from planning a wedding."

"I would argue it is completely different," she said. "And planning weddings isn't a task we've proved I excel at."

Annie ignored this. "Creating menus, seating charts, organizing a staff, partaking in a happy-hour cocktail when the occasion arises. You specialize in getting shit done. You got this."

Beckett didn't share her confidence, and that was before she turned the corner and saw the massive structure flickering in the distance. Twinkle lights outlined the four-thousand-square-foot open-concept eatery, and the two floor-to-ceiling glassed-in decks, which spanned the entire length of the curved sea wall, connecting the marina and harbor.

Cars circled the parking lot. People stood huddled in their coats on the outside terrace, waiting to be seated. Inside, a tide pool of activity surged, as people mingled in the bar area and around the fire pits on the upper lounge.

She realized that the level of activity and number of customers wasn't all that unusual for a weekend night at the Crow's Nest. Located off the cobblestone streets of the historic fishing district, and butting up to the picturesque wharf, it offered spectacular water views, and locals expected a wait. A booth, the central dining area, or even the bar — a seat in Levi's place was prime real estate.

People could point to the location, the panoramic views, or even the award-winning menu to explain the restaurant's popularity. But Beckett was beginning to learn that it was Levi himself who kept people coming back. He had this relaxed way about him that immediately put people at ease. Had them laughing as if reliving a pleasant memory from another time.

Levi created space for people to be happy. He'd created a special space for her to find happiness. And she wanted to do the same for him.

"I've got this," she said, in the *fake it till you make it* tone she used on her dad. "I have no idea how to run a restaurant, but it can't be harder than running my house. Right?"

She double-parked behind a black Jeep she knew belonged to Seth, one of the servers Beckett had interviewed for the wedding. He was a local who'd been waiting tables at the Crow's Nest since he graduated high school, and he always worked the dinner rush to closing shift.

She should take comfort in that, except he was the one who'd called her to report the out-of-control shit show, his words, that Beckett was somehow supposed to fix.

"Or house-training a chicken," Annie said.

At that, Beckett smiled. "I'd better go."

"Call if you need backup. I get off in two hours and know how to make some mean dumpling soup. Jewish and Vietnamese."

"Thanks." Beckett disconnected and climbed out of the truck.

She was immediately hit by a blast of sea air and echoes of chatter and laughter coming off the terrace. It wasn't just crowded; there was a restlessness among the crowd, a growing impatience that could lend itself to a rowdy Saturday night. Because on a cold Saturday night, where else would people go but the local watering hole?

Not wanting to push through the crowd at the entrance, she cut around the back of the building and slipped through one of the massive sliding glass doors, which in the summer months opened to merge the bar and outdoor terrace. Tonight, the door was only opened enough to allow the sound of the waves in the dining area — which was full to capacity.

Across the floor, she spotted Marie, the floor manager, standing at the hostess station and talking with a customer. When Beckett approached the circular podium, Marie's eyes lit with relief.

"Oh, thank God you're here." Marie patted her chest. "Seth said you were on your way."

"I came as soon as he called."

"My daughter came home from a sleepover with a fever. Not high, but enough to make me concerned."

"I'm so sorry."

"There's a cold going around her school, and I've been praying it would miss our house." Marie let out a long sigh. "Gus said he'd find someone to cover the rest of my shift, but —"

"Gus is sick, too. Which is why I'm here," Beckett explained. "How can I help?"

Marie pointed to a group waiting near the front door and waved them over. "Winters. Party of seven," Marie confirmed when they approached the podium. "Beckett here will show you to your table."

"Wait, what? I have to go check on the kitchen," Beckett said quietly so that the customers couldn't overhear her.

"You need to seat these customers first.

Table seventeen." She pointed to the location on the seating chart — which was about as useful as taking a trip across the country with only a coloring map from elementary school as a guide.

"Where are you going?"

"Home," Marie said.

"No, no, no." She reached out and gripped Marie's forearm. "You can't go. We're already one manager down. I can't afford to lose you."

"If I could stay, I would, but my husband works the night shift at the docks, and I don't have childcare. If I'd known about Gus earlier, I could have arranged for my mom to sit. But she'll be asleep by now, and my husband leaves for work at ten. I have to get home before he goes."

"Is there anyone else you can call? It's going to be a nightmare without you."

Beckett suddenly had the most bizarre déjà vu sensation — probably because she'd just watched her father beg the same way.

"It's my kid. I'm sorry."

How could Beckett argue with that logic? She was guilty of doing the very same thing, prioritizing family over work. She just wasn't used to being on this side of the equation. And it sucked. Big time.

"I hope she gets better." Beckett plastered

on a smile and said, "Winters party, right this way, please."

Beckett led the group of seven, which happened to be a birthday party, to one of the big, high-backed booths by the window. She took their drink orders, which she scribbled on a napkin, then headed to the bar.

She'd relayed the drinks to the bartender when Seth, the most senior staffer left in the restaurant, came out through the kitchen's swinging doors with plates piled on both arms. He caught sight of her. "I called Gus — he said to talk to you. Don't go anywhere."

He disappeared to deliver the plates, and Beckett leaned against the wall. It was almost ten at night, for crying out loud. How could the place still be this busy?

Beckett's heart skipped, then dropped. A cold, sticky sensation crept along her hairline, around the back of her neck, down her spine. For a confusing moment, her vision dimmed at the edges.

Panic entered her bloodstream, and her mind numbed around the edges. If Levi knew the gravity of this situation, he would come unhinged. Damn, she wanted to be the hero here. For Levi. He was so amazing in so many ways. She really wanted to have his back here, even though she couldn't fathom what she could do to salvage the situation.

"You okay?" Seth asked. "You look like you could use a drink."

"A big one. But I'm betting it's against company policy to drink on the job?"

Seth flashed her a smile. "I bet Levi would let it slide. I mean, this is a complete shit show," he repeated for the second time. "I didn't mean to drag you into it, but when I looked at who the next emergency contact was, I saw your name."

"Calling me is exactly what you should have done." A waitress passed by with two armloads of plates. "How are you serving food without a chef?"

"Gus stayed as long as he could and hammered out a few orders before he left. But that was the last of it. What do you want to do?"

Marie grabbed her purse from beneath the bar. "Good luck, guys. See you tomorrow."

Beckett had to curl her fingers into her palms and dig her nails into the flesh to keep from grabbing her by the arm, dropping to her knees, and begging her to stay. This had to be some type of cosmic payback for abandoning her father with Tommy.

Fine. She'd have to handle this the way

416

she knew her father would have to handle Tommy.

Beckett grabbed a menu from the bar, a marking pen from a cupholder, and scanned the offerings. "Point out anything that's mostly pre-made. Anything that can be heated up or thrown together."

Five minutes later, they'd cut the menu down to half a dozen appetizers and a few salads. She promoted one of the bussers to waiter, Seth to chef, and herself to chief shit-catcher, moving wherever she was needed — behind the bar, in the kitchen, at tables.

When Beckett took a second to breathe, she realized two hours had passed in a blur. She glanced at her phone and found four missed calls from her father, two from Tommy, and a slew of texts she couldn't bear to read. But nothing from Levi.

The bar was still busy, but the dining areas had started to empty out. They'd finally caught up with the front of the house, and things were quieting down. She wasn't out of the woods yet — the bar had been known to go full-tilt until last call.

Beckett checked her watch and sighed — she still had three hours to go. She dropped a scribbled note for drink orders before disappearing into the kitchen to check on Seth.

He stood at the stainless-steel counter, his apron resembling a modern art splatter piece, his shoulder-length hair pulled into a makeshift man-bun. He was humming while chopping ingredients and completing prep for the next day.

"You really came through tonight," she said.

Seth flashed her a crooked smile. "No problem. And maybe you can mention that to the boss man for me?"

She laughed. "I'll see what I can do. And thanks for stepping up. You were a lifesaver. Do you know where Levi put the close-out procedures? I looked in his office and couldn't find it."

"Gus moved it." Seth pointed to a folder on the top shelf in the kitchen that Levi had put together before he left. It outlined every detail that had to be attended to before the last person set the alarm and closed up. With Marie at home, that honor went to Beckett.

Beckett opened the folder and had started reading down the checklist when her cell rang with an incoming call. The screen showed her father's number. Again.

She looked at Seth, and he nodded. "Take

it. We're starting to slow down."

"Thanks," she said, then walked into Levi's office to answer the call. "Hey, Dad. Sorry I didn't check in. I just now had a chance to breathe."

No response prompted her to check the connection; then she plugged her free ear and raised her voice. "Dad? You there?"

Instead of her father's voice, she heard leaves crunching, as if someone was walking at a steady pace. The sound made Beckett's stomach clench and her heart hurt. "Dad? Can you hear me? What's going on?"

"He woke up and was upset that you were gone." His breathing got louder, but the crunching grew intermittent, as if her father was slowing down. "He wouldn't go back to sleep."

"Tommy? Dad, are you outside? It's forty degrees out." She closed her eyes and rubbed at the fatigue.

"I told him to go back to bed, but he only wanted you. And you know I have to work on my presentation."

"Where is he now?"

"I don't know." The sound of crunching glass coincided with her dad's voice becoming ragged — more frantic.

"Okay, take a deep breath, we got this," she said, taking a deep breath herself. "Did

419

you check the basement? You know how he likes to hide in the Batcave."

"He was in his room," he said, his words nearly drowned out by the crunching.

"Is that glass?"

Her question was met with an eerie stillness that slid down her spine and prickled her skin.

"Dad?" she asked. Silence. "What are you doing?"

His breathing was heavy and distraught. Then the sound of metal on metal knocked in Beckett's ear.

"Dad? *Dad.*"

"I told him to stay put, but he just ran from me," he whispered.

Realization spread over Beckett like an icy blanket. "Dad, are you back in your studio?"

"He won't come to me."

The line went dead, and the eerie iciness leeched deeper, into muscle, into bone. Beckett called her father back, but got no answer. Trying her damnedest to keep her shit together, she dialed Annie, relieved when she finally got a sensible adult on the other end of the line.

"Hey," Annie said, her voice thick with sleep.

"I know you pulled a double, and you must be exhausted. I'm so sorry to ask, but can you swing by my house and check on my brother?" she said, then offered the short version of the story.

"Absolutely. I'll call you as soon as I get there."

Beckett knew that Annie could handle whatever she found, but the wait to hear back from her felt interminable. Where time had flown by earlier in the evening, now it crawled. Where the business of the bar had initially kept her mind busy, now nothing distracted her from a sick feeling in her gut.

Something was wrong. Really wrong.

When Annie finally called back, twenty minutes later, her first words were, "You need to come home."

Levi had to hand it to Gray — sailing to Nantucket for beer tasting and whale watching made for a damn fine bachelor party. There was no Vanna White or need for dollar bills, but then again, they were no longer those guys.

One by one, each of them had started a new chapter, and damn, if Levi wasn't excited about where this new one was headed. And it had everything to do with a certain sexy little complicated and compassionate concierge, who, in a month's time, had Levi seriously reconsidering postponing his summer sailing trip to embark on a more personal one.

Which was the only thing that could explain why, instead of taking advantage of some bro-time belowdecks with friends, he was pacing from the bow to the stern and back again, in nothing but sweats and a sweatshirt, freezing his nuts with a beer in one hand, his phone in the other aimed toward the sky as if that would help him catch a signal.

Instead, he was the one caught. At first, he thought it was Emmitt's dad stretching his legs, but before he could lower his phone, he realized it was the groom-to-be. Who took one look at Levi, perched off the bow like Rose from *Titanic,* and grinned. "Whatcha doing?"

"Just wanted to check in at the restaurant," he lied. Between his time with Beckett and these last couple of days with the guys, the last thing on his mind was business. He felt rejuvenated, and his brain had actually slowed down enough for him to think clearly.

Only the more he thought, the clearer it became just how screwed he was. The clock in his bar was steadily ticking down the days until he left, and the clock in his chest was collecting all the things he wanted to experience with Beckett before time ran out.

This was a discrepancy that couldn't be rectified.

"Sure was a big smile for work."

"You know me." Levi pocketed his phone.

"I do. Almost as well as I know myself." Emmitt leaned a hip against the railing and glanced down at his phone. "So if I were to offer you my cell, I wouldn't see Beckett's number on the call history?"

"Why are you getting signals and I'm not?"

"Because you use that shitty second-rate cell company," Emmitt said, without looking up from his phone. "Kind of stupid, since you live on a boat. Reliable service is hard to find out here, especially with all the fog out tonight."

"Fine. If I admit I wanted to call Beckett, can I borrow your phone?"

"Depends. Why do you want to call her?"

To see if she's open to a repeat of last night's Goodnight Moon.

Last night, Levi had asked Beckett what she was wearing, and her reply was a photo. Nothing too racy but showing enough skin to make him want to turn the boat around and exchange a proper, in-person, goodnight that would make for a very good morning. Beckett reminded him that this trip was about Emmitt — the lucky son of a bitch with a working phone — and promised him a bedtime story tonight, under the same moon.

So there he stood — same bat time, same bat channel — with Girl Wonder armed in nothing but her cape and go-go boots, and he was being cock-blocked by his wingman. Which left him with three options:

1. Tell Emmitt the truth, and break rule number two — *what happens between us stays between us* — and risk Emmitt telling Annie, and Annie telling Beckett, which was a guarantee since, when it came to Levi's personal life, those two acted like a bunch of gossipy high schoolers. Or:
2. Lie, and risk Emmitt not handing over the phone, which would mean standing up Girl Wonder and her cape of wonderment. Which left:
3. Shove Emmitt overboard.

"Whoa." Emmitt took a step back. "Back off, lover boy. I go overboard, and the phone goes with me. Plus, it isn't working. That's why I was out here, trying to get a signal to call Annie." He held out the phone. "See, no signal."

"You fucking with me?"

"Check for yourself."

Levi snatched the phone. "Shit." No signal.

"How about your satellite phone?" Which Emmitt had dragged to some of the most remote shitholes, so he wouldn't miss a call from Paisley while chasing a story.

"The one Annie made me leave behind because of your whole 'You guys are missing the point of being out on the open sea'?" Then the fucker sucked in a mocking lungful of salty air. "Thanks for making me see the error of my ways."

Unwilling to admit defeat just yet, Levi walked down into the galley of the boat, where Gray, Emmitt's dad, and two of their buddies were engaged in a high-stakes game of Monopoly: Star Wars Edition — because that's what happened when a *Wheel of Fortune* fan is tasked with organizing a bro-party. With Levi in the master, Emmitt's dad playing the cancer card for Paisley's bunk, and the Smug SOB of the Hour claiming the top bunk, it left only a couch large enough for one. Meaning the loser was sentenced to sleep on the deck loungers, with only a blanket and disgrace for warmth.

"Anyone have a working phone I can borrow?" When the reply was some noncommittal shrugs, Levi added, "Whoever gives me a working phone can take my bed."

There was a second of silence, and then four sets of eyes locked on his, gauging the seriousness of his offer. "It expires in thirty seconds."

The men were out of their seats, pockets were being padded, duffels emptied, phones held toward the ceiling. Gray looked the most desperate, probably because he'd spent last night on deck and wasn't interested in a replay. Especially with the temperatures being ten degrees lower.

"You're serious about your sat phone?" Levi asked when most of the guys disappeared up top with their respective phones, stomping and arguing.

"If I had it, don't you think I'd have given it to Gray just so we wouldn't have to endure another night listening to him bitch over how cold his delicate doctor hands are?"

"I'm going to make sure no one goes overboard," Emmitt's dad said, throwing a coat over his wiry frame and heading outside.

"Yeah, it'd be a damn shame if someone *accidentally* went overboard," Emmitt mumbled.

A moment later, Gray entered, wearing a blanket fashioned as a wizard's cape over his head and dragging at his feet. He went to the stove and put on the teakettle. "I've got nothing. How about you?"

"Not even enough to log in as HitMe-UpHarry," Emmitt said, referring to the fake Instagram account he'd created after catching Paisley with a senior a few months back.

"If Paisley comes home with a hickey, it's on you," Gray said to Levi.

"I suggested Atlantic City; you chose my boat."

"That was before you talked her into going on the school sex trip." Gray poured himself a cup of tea like a proper grandpa, then plopped down at the end of the circular bench that spanned around the table.

"I'm on a text thread with some of the moms from my parent group, who are chaperoning the ski trip. Hoping for a four-one-one on the situation."

"It will have to do," Gray said, moping. "Were there any new posts when you last checked?"

"Nah, but I'm betting she's got a secret account. One where she posts all the good stuff."

Paisley did, in fact, have a secret account,

427

which Levi had unintentionally discovered. He did not make a fake profile of a cute boy-bander wannabe to friend her and troll. And he did not tell the dads. At first because he hadn't had the time, but now because they were talking as if he were no longer in the room.

"Maybe it's time to cool it with the cyber stalking, give the kid some space," Levi said, thinking back to what Beckett had said, that what Paisley needed right now was a little freedom to explore. "She's with over a dozen qualified parent chaperones. Everything's fine."

"As if you didn't just sacrifice your bed for the chance to check in," Gray accused, while counting his stakes in the game — mostly fives and ones, with the only matching properties in his possession being light blue.

"Oh, that was about a different female. Cute enough to cause a man to throw his best friend overboard for a phone." Emmitt laughed.

"Ah, the reason he bailed on poker?" Gray held the tea bag by his thumb and pointer, his little pinkie in the air, and steeped his tea. "And we know it wasn't because you were working. You had a visitor."

"Who's cuter than you."

"She knows you're leaving in a few months, right?" Gray's gaze pulled from the game board for a second and met Levi's. "Are you still leaving?"

"Of course I'm leaving. This trip is already fifteen years late." But even as he said the words, his heart clinched. He'd considered asking Beck to join him, but that was crazy. They'd only been dating a few weeks, and sharing a sailboat with someone long-term was an even bigger commitment than getting married. There's nowhere to run on a sailboat. Besides, she couldn't get away. Not with her responsibilities.

And how fucked-up was that? Levi hadn't had a spare second to himself in fifteen years, and now that he had the time and freedom to take this dream trip, the only person he wanted to share it with was a woman who didn't have time or freedom.

"You didn't sound so sure there," Gray said.

"Just thinking. I don't have to leave the first day of summer, you know. I was actually thinking I'd wait until you and Paisley left for Europe in July," he said to Emmitt. "She'll need someone to train her how to manage the kayaks and canoe rentals."

"Do you remember the Shack Girl when we were her age?" Emmitt asked with a shake of his head. "Whose stupid idea was that?"

Levi and Gray both looked at Emmitt, who groaned.

"Right," Emmitt mumbled. "My beautiful fiancée. What the hell was she thinking?"

"That giving Paisley some space and a summer flirting with boys isn't the worst thing in the world," Levi said, spinning the beer in his hand. When both men looked at him as though he'd suggested stripping naked and diving into the cold ocean, he shrugged. "She was just reminding me how we're all going to have to get used to her growing up and going away. Better to know if she can handle a summer on her own before college starts, isn't it?"

"Hell." Emmitt pocketed his phone and took a drink of his beer. "When did this happen? Yesterday she was a feisty five-year-old throwing a tantrum; now she's leaving for college. *College.* Christ."

"Where do you stand on all this?" Levi asked Gray.

"Does it matter?" Gray leaned forward, elbows on knees, and started peeling the beer label. "The first part of the summer, she'll be working; then she'll be in Europe. Where the fuck will I be? She's been my whole life."

A heavy silence settled over the group, as the conversation took on a serious weight. This talk was a long time coming, but it was the first time Gray had initiated the topic. And by the way he shredded the beer label, there was some anxiety floating beneath the surface. Completely understandable. He'd only lost Michelle a year ago. Now Paisley was spreading her wings.

Levi's chest ached for his friend.

"You've got your work," Emmitt said. "And if you'd ever look up from your medical files, you'd see a line of ladies wanting to check out Dr. Doable's stethoscope."

Gray shook his head. "They're not Michelle."

"If there was one thing I learned from Michelle, something she made me promise when you proposed, is don't wait for Paisley to leave to start rebuilding a life of your own. It's only going to make everything harder when she goes."

"I know. I just need a little more time."

Levi shrugged. "I don't have to leave this summer. I could wait until Paisley's off at college. Be around to hang out. Bar can always keep me busy."

Emmitt laughed. "You're in such deep shit, man. The funniest part is you don't even know it. You're worse off than Gray."

Gray dropped his play money on the table. "My hands are never going to work again."

Emmitt looked at Levi. "Now do you believe me about not having my other phone?"

Les appeared, holding his side and out of breath.

"Dad?" Emmitt stood. "Are you okay?"

Les nodded. "I was trying to give you space for your Kumbaya moment when I heard someone on the radio. It was your security company," Les said to Levi. "I guess the alarm went off about an hour ago. The cops arrived to find the back door unlocked."

"Was anyone hurt?" Levi asked, then remembered putting Beckett's name on the emergency list. "Jesus, did they call Beckett? Is she okay?"

Because he could just picture her getting the call and charging down there like a loose cannon, with complete disregard for her own safety. Her fearless nature was impressive, but in this situation, it fueled a million different scenarios — none of them good, and all of them what his nightmares were made of.

"Your tall friend, the one who holds his liquor like a girl, is talking to them now. But from what I understood, when the cops arrived, no one was there. Which is why they need you or your mom to come and see if anything is missing and file a report."

The cops? Jesus.

"Tell them I'll be there in a few hours," he called over his shoulder as he raced to the helm, his legs nearly buckling under the heart-pumping panic. "And under no circumstances is anyone to call my mom."

Levi hadn't been there when his mom and niece found out about Michelle. No way in hell was he going to allow the police to drag his mom down to what sounded like a crime scene. And Beckett, *Christ,* Beckett. What if they'd called her first, and she'd gone to the restaurant to check on things?

It was like reliving that night of the accident all over again.

CHAPTER 19

Beckett's toes were numb, her nose frozen, and she was trembling from the leftover adrenaline.

It had taken the local fire department, fifty-eight search- and-rescue volunteers, and more than an hour to locate Tommy. With his father MIA, he'd been desperate to find Beckett. So desperate that he'd punched out a window and left the house in the middle of the night. Searchers had walked past him twice, because when he heard them yelling, he'd hidden behind a cluster of boulders.

It wasn't until Beckett arrived that they understood his inclination would be to run from strangers yelling his name. After getting her dad settled, she convinced him to take his guitar and play some of Thomas's favorite songs. They'd nearly exhausted the entire Beatles library when Beckett heard a humming in the distance.

The moment she saw his little body, curled into a tight ball with Diesel cuddling him for warmth, she wanted to pull him into her arms to be sure he was all right. But touching Tommy wasn't an option, so she slowly approached him while singing the song.

She wrapped him in a warm blanket one of the firemen had provided, and after a trip to the emergency room for stitches in his arm, they'd returned home to get some sleep.

To Tommy's delight, he was given an honorary fire hat and badge. Beckett was given a few sympathetic looks, but Jeffery was given the best gift of all — being the hero who'd found his son.

The nightmare was over, everyone was in bed, and Beckett was too drained to even cry. She just lay on her bed, staring out the window at the stars, wishing she was with Levi.

It bothers me that you've been conditioned to believe your needs aren't as important as other people's.

It was starting to bother her, too. It struck her as she watched the volunteers search the woods, seeing the number of people caught in the Hayes vortex, putting their lives on hold to deal with a fallout they'd had no part in making. If that wasn't a metaphor for Beckett's life, a sign for her to make some changes, then she didn't know what was.

As it stood now, her future had all the appeal of juggling chainsaws in the middle of a freeway.

Something had to change — Beckett felt it in her bones. She didn't know how yet, but being an army of one wasn't all it was cracked up to be.

She pulled the blanket up around her neck, closed her eyes, and tried to stop the shivering. Her toes were finally coming back to life when she heard something small bounce off her bedroom window.

A small *ping,* quickly followed by another.

With a groan, Beckett slid out from under the warm covers and grabbed the sniper-scope Nerf gun she kept under the bed. The last time someone had come knocking at her window in the middle of the night, it had been the neighbor's boyfriend, looking for a booty call and getting the wrong window.

Instead of a seventeen-year-old prom queen wearing his jersey, he'd come face to face with an overworked almost-thirty-year-old wearing a flannel nightgown and overnight foam curlers she'd bought after bingeing *Shark Tank.*

Beckett looked out the window. Not a teenager, but someone booty-call-worthy. Levi. He stood in her side yard, feet in a wide stance, arms crossed, looking at her. All the earlier drama and chaos faded, and Beckett found herself smiling.

After everything that had transpired in the past ten hours, he could still make her smile.

She slid open her window, and a cold burst stung her lips. "What are you doing here? You weren't supposed to be back until tomorrow."

Without a word, he lifted his phone and tapped the screen. Oh, he was sending her a text. How modern of him.

With a quick "be right back" finger, she ran to the bathroom to unplug her phone from where it had been charging, then raced back to the window, holding it up to show him she had it. He tapped his cell again, and hers lit up.

Oh my. She had dozens of missed calls and texts. Not surprising, since her phone had died during the search. She opened the most recent thread from Captain Confident. Two simple words that brought on a whole different kind of shivers.

Come out.

Be right down

Sensation trilled down her spine, but she couldn't tell if it was relief or excitement.

Beckett wrapped herself in his coat, because why not, pushed her feet into Uggs, and opened the front door to find snow falling. Levi had moved to stand by his truck, hands on hips, head down. It was a posture she wasn't familiar with and one that put her on edge, but her brain was so fogged from stress and fatigue, she didn't understand her body's reaction.

"Levi?" she asked, rushing her steps to meet him on the driveway. "Are you okay?"

He lifted his head and met her gaze. The look on his face froze her stomach solid. His expression was hard, his eyes piercing — and not in a good way. Levi was throwing off a tsunami of emotions, with anger and disappointment jockeying for the lead position.

Before she could ask what was wrong, he said, "You first."

"Am I okay?" Confusion complicated what she was feeling. "Yeah, I'm fine."

"Is your dad okay?"

"If you ask him, he's a hero." She gave a half-hearted shrug, still upset by her father's irresponsible behavior. "I think he's lucky

438

to have me as a daughter."

"What about Tommy?"

She tightened the cross of her arms. "That's a whole different story." She took a beat. "What's going on? You're scaring me."

"Welcome to the club." He ran a ragged hand down his face. "Jesus, I need a minute." He paced the length of his truck, his hand gripping his neck, anxiety pouring off him. "What happened tonight at the bar? You just disappeared."

"I didn't disappear."

"Then what the hell happened?" His earlier concern morphed into anger. Scalding hot, and aimed at her. "And it better be a good fucking story to justify leaving the bar the way you did."

"An emergency came up at home, and I gave Seth exact instructions on what to do, how to set the alarm; he even did food prep for tomorrow. He texted me when he closed up and assured me it all turned out fine."

"Glad he's assured everything's fine." The force of his censure landed squarely in the center of her chest and dragged her heart to her feet. "Jesus, for all I knew, you were on the road somewhere dead."

"Yeah, Tommy and my dad had one of their things. Tommy decided to go looking for me and —" She waved a dismissive hand. "He's home now. I'm more worried about what's going on with you."

"Was it life-threatening?" His expression remained rock hard, and the look made her feel as if she'd swallowed a beehive.

She exhaled. "Levi —"

"Was it?"

"Well, it —" She took a step toward him, and he held up a hand. She swallowed. "What's this about?"

Levi opened his mouth, then closed it and looked at the ground. "I had an emergency, too, tonight. Got a call over my boat's radio from my security company, informing me that the alarm was tripped."

She pulled in a sharp breath. "Oh no."

"I called you a dozen times, but you didn't answer."

"I panicked and left my cell on the bathroom counter. Someone lent me a handheld radio —"

"By the time I got there . . ." He stopped short, jaw clenching. "The bar was robbed."

She covered her mouth with both hands, eyes wide, stomach sick. "Oh my God."

"Several cases of beer and wine are missing. The cash from tonight's sales. Vanished."

"I don't know how this happened. I went through everything with Seth. But I promise you, I'll fix this. Even if I refund you the lost money."

"It was over six grand," he said, and Beckett felt the blood leave her face. That was two months' salary for her, easy. "And I already talked to Seth. He didn't know where the safe was — I purposely hadn't told him, because I still don't have a clue as to who's been slowly ripping me off — so he put the cash and receipts in a bank bag and left it on my desk, thinking locking the office door would suffice."

"Shit." Tears crept into her eyes. She couldn't believe this was happening.

"Oh, and the best part. A set of gold-leaf champagne goblets my yiayia brought with her from Greece, then passed down to my mom as a wedding present, are missing."

"The ones in your office?" she asked, remembering the beautiful antique wedding glasses prominently displayed in the locked glass case behind his desk. "Are they valuable?"

"Maybe a couple hundred bucks at a pawn shop. To my family?" He shook his head and kicked at the ground. "My mom's going to be devastated."

"I'll fix it."

"That's not the point. Seth is a kid. If I wanted a kid closing up my bar, I wouldn't have hired you."

"I know, I'm sorry. I thought everything was covered, and when Annie called —"

"Stop. This isn't about your dad or Tommy. This is about you. Christ, Beck. Don't you see that you're so busy helping everyone, you're not helping anyone."

"I told you upfront how crazy my life is," she said, slow and even. "You walked in with your eyes wide open."

"I'm not asking you to pick me over your family. I'd never do that. But when you put yourself in a position where you have to choose between two people who are counting on you, we all lose." He looked at her for a long, agonizing moment, then shook his head — as if shaking her off. "You knew how hard it was for me to leave the bar — my dad's place — to anyone, but I trusted you. Trust doesn't come easy for me. You knew that. I trusted you, and you fucking bailed."

That was a direct hit. Guilt and disappointment pushed at her chest. But also, a good dose of anger. She was mad at herself, but she was mad at Levi, too.

"That's not fair!" She bit the inside of her lip to keep the tears at bay. "I didn't bail. I walked into a shit show. An honest-to-god shit show. The only employee who could find his head from his ass was Seth. The rest of them floundered without you at the helm to micromanage. But I stuck it out. I worked my ass off for hours before I left. Then I gave one of your *senior* employees all the information he needed to lock up right. I called and checked in to make sure everything was okay. Considering the mess I walked into, I'd say I handled myself pretty darn well." Her voice cracked with emotion. "And for the record, this is why I said we'd never work."

"You never gave it a chance, Beck," he whispered.

"Maybe not, but that's because for this to work, you'd have to give up so much. And you would, because that's who you are." She clutched her arms around her stomach as if it would hold back the pain. "And I can't ask you to do that."

"No, you wouldn't ask. That's the real problem. You just make up your mind and go. Love is a two-way street, Beck. You have to take a stand; you can't just walk the line." He moved a step closer, and she could see the snowflakes clinging to his lashes. "Do you do this because you don't think you deserve to be happy? Or because you don't think you deserve to be loved?"

"Both," she whispered, her emotions

burning so high, tears pooled on her lids.

"You know the crazy thing? I'm pretty sure I love you, but I don't know if you're brave enough to step into the ring with me."

Her heart ached at how easily he said those words. It ached even more because he deserved someone who could believe them.

"Rule number six," she said, the pain slowly spilling down her cheeks. "We agreed, love was never on the table."

"We never had a rule six." He shoved his ball cap back on. "But clearly, you did. So I'm calling rule five — this isn't making me happy." He opened his truck door and gave her one last look. "Bye, Beck."

CHAPTER 20

Levi sat on the couch in his office, staring at his parents' wedding picture and the empty case next to it. Nothing left but two circles on a dusty shelf.

He rested his head on the couch back, wondering how in the hell he was going to explain to his mom that he'd lost her dowry. Even worse, how he was going to explain that, between planning a wedding and the bachelor party, he'd lost the woman he wanted to bring home to meet his family.

He and Beckett had gone about things ass-backward, but for them, it had worked. Until it hadn't. And now he had a gaping hole in his chest and ironclad proof that his family's tradition of finding true love had skipped him over.

He believed that Beckett could have been his great love. All she had to do was meet him partway.

"I'm fucked." He ground his palms against his lids.

"More than you even realize."

He opened his eyes to find it was Emmitt who had spoken. He'd seated himself at Levi's desk, flipping through the inventory log and making himself right at home. Gray was across the room, inspecting the empty display case while nursing a cup of tea.

"I've got a call in to local pawn shops," Levi said.

"Good luck with that." Emmitt leaned back in the chair and kicked his feet up on the desk, showing off a pair of god-awful pangolin-hide boots that some Colombian drug lord had given him in return for doing a story on his missing daughter.

"With any luck, my mom's glasses will turn up before she catches wind of the heist."

It had been a day since the break-in, and Levi was still trying to make sense of the situation. Besides the money, some alcohol, and the glasses, he couldn't seem to find anything else missing.

The going theory was a crime of opportunity. With no sign of forced entry, the sheriff suspected the door hadn't been properly secured, someone let themselves in, and had accidentally activated the alarm.

Panicked, they grabbed what was visible and took off.

It didn't account for the two previous thefts, but now that the cops were involved, Levi knew solving those mysteries wasn't likely.

"I think he was talking about Beckett," Gray said, sipping his tea.

Yeah, he knew that, too. He'd spent all day going through inventory, trying to forget the small, defeated expression on her face when he'd taken off, leaving her in the cold driveway with nothing but a robe and a broken heart to cling to.

She'd hurt him. But he'd hurt her, too. Badly.

"How is her brother?" he found himself asking, because it was easier than asking about Beckett.

"I checked on him this morning," Gray said. "I prescribed some pretty heavy meds. He got twelve stitches from punching through his bedroom window."

"I punched an exploding concrete factory with my forehead. Why didn't I get the good meds?" Emmitt asked.

"Because you're an asshole." Gray looked from Emmitt to Levi. "Apparently, you were too."

"She didn't tell me Tommy had to get

stitches," Levi said. "Just that he'd gone on an impromptu walk after a blowup with his dad."

"Did you ask her?" Emmitt asked bluntly.

"Didn't really get that far." Levi rubbed his hand over his chest, trying to ease the raw ache that had been gnawing at him since yesterday. It didn't help. Nothing he seemed to do helped. "I was still freaked over what happened at the bar . . ." He stopped. "We didn't get that far."

"Did you not think that maybe she was still freaked over Tommy, her dad, her business, the wedding? Then she had to deal with the fact that she let you down?" Emmitt said. "That's a lot, bro."

"Exactly what I've been telling her." Levi sat forward. "She's so busy giving everything to everyone, she doesn't save anything for herself."

Curly and Moe exchanged amused looks. If Levi wasn't so bone-tired, he'd kick both their asses to the curb and lock the door.

"Herself? Or you?" Gray asked.

"Her!" he snapped, and another silent conversation was exchanged between his uninvited guests. "Maybe me a little, too. I just needed to know if I even rated a blip on her radar." Levi didn't know where that last part came from — or the way his heart dipped when he said it. "I guess I got my answer."

"What? That her family is as important to her as P is to you?" Emmitt asked quietly. "Isn't that a good thing?"

"It's not that simple." The complicated knot of emotions in his stomach multiplied.

"Why not?" Emmitt asked. "We all know that, regardless of the 'give Paisley space' BS you were spouting the other night, if it came down to her needing you, your decision would be simple."

"What else do you assholes know about my life that apparently I'm missing?" Arms crossed firmly, he pushed back into the couch. "Go on, explain this huge cosmic joke that everyone but me seems to know the punch line to."

Emmitt looked at Gray, who gave an elaborate you-handle-this-idiot roll of the eyes.

"Whatever you think you know about women, you're wrong. Not when it applies to the *the* woman." Feet on the floor, Emmitt leveled Levi with a serious-as-shit look. "You keep thinking if it comes easy, it isn't worth it. But when it's worth it, it becomes easy."

"Did you read that in a fortune cookie?"

"All I'm saying is that the outside bullshit

is just that, bullshit. What's going on between the two of you — that's what matters. The rest you deal with together."

"She isn't really into the whole tackle things together."

"Okay. So that's outside BS she brought to the table. Your inability to deal with it is yours." Emmitt shrugged. "Why does your baggage take precedence over hers?"

Levi opened his mouth to argue and snapped it closed. He couldn't answer that. More like he didn't want to, because Emmitt's assessment shed a whole new light on things.

He'd promised to keep things light. Coaxed her into opening up with promises of no pressure and no drama. And when she'd finally felt safe enough to drop her walls, let someone in, he turned her world into his own personal emotional dumping ground.

"Man." He dropped his head into his hands. "I just wanted to make her happy, and instead, I made her miserable."

"Nothing can make you as miserable as running from love." Emmitt stood and came around the desk to sit on the couch next to Levi. "I had to lug all my sorry-ass misery to India before I'd had enough."

"I hope you admit you've had enough

before your chance passes you by," Gray said quietly.

"What if I fucked up worse than going to India?"

"Fix it. Isn't that what you do?" Emmitt asked without a trace of humor. "You stand behind your bar and dole out more advice than a motivational coach in a group session. Why don't you step into the trenches with the rest of us and apply some of that wisdom to your own life?"

"Because if I get this wrong, I'll never forgive myself."

"Why, though?" Emmitt asked. "Gray, here, gets it wrong all the time. And you keep forgiving him."

"Only because Michelle was so happy to provide me with a brother I never wanted. She'd kick my ass if I tried to return him," Levi joked, but he didn't feel like laughing. "Plus, Paisley's kind of taken a shine to him."

"Tell me about it," Emmitt grumbled, then put his hand on Levi's shoulder. "And the only way you could get this wrong is to do nothing. So if you love her, then do something, bro. Whatever it is will be the right move."

Levi found his focus going back to the collection of wedding portraits in the glass case. The only difference between Levi and what those photos represented was that they hadn't stopped until they earned their great love story.

He and Beckett had only just begun theirs. And he was not going to leave the story unfinished.

"I love her." He looked at Gray. "So, how did you make yourself unreturnable?"

"For starters, you might want to check with your mom before you start accusing innocent women of getting your family heirlooms stolen."

"You said I was going to get to tell him," Emmitt whined.

"My mom has the glasses?" Levi asked.

"Oh, more than that." Gray laughed. "She's got enough alcohol in her garage to open a distillery, and six-grand worth of new scrapbooking supplies. Seems she's been storing up for an upcoming wedding."

Beckett came awake with the distinct feeling she was being watched. Her head ached, her lids were scratchy from crying, and the cold, empty feeling, which only disappeared when she slept, poked her between the ribs. It was following the same rhythm as the finger poking her arm.

"Tommy." She put the pillow over her

head. "We talked about coming in my room before seven."

"It's nearly noon," Jeffery said.

She threw the blanket back and sat up, then immediately slammed her lids shut. The sunlight was just too bright for her to handle.

"Noon?" Blindly, she grabbed for her robe. "Thomas's field trip is today. If he misses the bus . . . It won't be good."

"He prefers Tommy." Jeffery put a hand on her shoulder and pushed her back down. "And he's already on the bus. I dropped him off after we had breakfast."

"He's what?" She shook her head to help lift the sleep-induced fog that was clearly affecting her comprehension. "Wait, you're supposed to still be in Boston."

"I came home early. What? Why are you looking at me like that?" He got quiet. "Are you still angry with me?"

"I'm not angry, Dad. Just really, really sad," she admitted.

Jeffery studied her, then shook his head. "Nope. Your nostrils are flared, your fore-head furrowed, and you're doing that thing with your hands." She looked down to find them strangling the sheet. "You're angry."

"Okay, fine, I'm angry."

"With me," Jeffery prompted.

"You're high on the list," she said.

Guessing by the way her dad forced himself to maintain contact, he knew this. And it made him uncomfortable, but if things were going to change — and, God help her, things needed to change — then there would be a lot of uncomfortable talks in their future.

"I needed you to be the parent this weekend, Dad. So did Tommy. But instead, you got in your own head and hid in your studio."

Wasn't that the same thing Levi had accused her of doing? Getting into her head and, instead of being the person he needed her to be, hiding behind her family dynamics.

"I needed a moment," he admitted. "It wasn't right, but there it is. I needed a moment."

"He punched through a window!"

"I didn't know that. Until later. I just assumed he walked out the front door."

"Because you locked yourself in your room. So when he couldn't get hold of you, he went looking for me. And my whole life blew up, because I dropped everything, like I always do, and this time it hurt more people than just me."

Jeffery leaned against the headboard next

to her, his expression sad yet hopeful. "I need to stop doing that then, don't I?"

Beckett felt fresh tears forming. "Yes, you do. I need to stop letting you do that. It's not all on you."

"Actually, it is. I'm the parent. It's time I acted like it." He took her hand in his. "So I came home early, made my son breakfast, and took him to school. I turned the radio to the ballgame highlights, and Tommy told me he'd prefer to listen to the Beatles. My son prefers the Beatles."

Beckett's throat tightened. "You're a good dad. And I know what I'm talking about, because you raised me."

Jeffery leaned down and kissed her on the forehead. "We raised each other, kiddo. But you're grown up now. Ready for a life of your own."

She wasn't sure if she was ready, but if her dad could find the strength to try harder, then so could she.

"Yeah, Dad," she whispered, hoarse with emotion. She rested her head on his shoulder. "But you don't need to rent out my room just yet. I've decided to expand my business, hire an assistant, and the rent here is pretty hard to beat."

"Thank God," Jeffery said. "I might look wise and capable in my new slacks, but I'm

455

going to need help brushing up on my adulting skills. We can start with how to use the stove and work our way up, because I don't think frozen pizzas are going to cut it."

For the first time since waking up, she really looked at her dad. Dressed in slacks, a sophisticated sweater set, and . . . She rubbed her eyes. "What happened to your hair?"

"Tommy and I stopped by the barber on the way to school. We both got a trim, and I let him pick my new cut. Do you like it?" He beamed, and Beckett felt her chest squeeze.

"You look great, Dad," she said quietly.

"You mean I look like a father who's got this whole adulting thing down." Jeffery winked. "And if I could offer some fatherly advice to my strong, self-reliant, and sometimes prideful daughter, it would be that the best parts of life are rarely lived alone. Where I've relied too much on others, you've gone the opposite way. Maybe we can help each other find a healthy balance."

"I'd like that," she whispered, knowing that was exactly what Levi had been trying to give her. Balance. Support. The space she needed to find her way.

He'd been willing to be patient with her

situation, take what she could give, and not pressure her for more. So she took, and the moment he needed something in return, she'd used his understanding nature against him. Blaming a conflict in priorities was easier than risking him walking away, because she wasn't special enough to stay. She'd been there before and barely found her way back. Convinced herself that she wouldn't survive that kind of blow again. Not from Levi.

But she didn't want to just survive. She wanted to live. And she wanted to live her life with Levi. All she needed was to be bold enough to find out if he felt the same.

Oh, and to admit that she needed his help. Again. Only this time, that didn't seem so scary.

Last note to self: Erase never, ever, ever from your vocabulary.

CHAPTER 21

Levi skidded off the highway onto Beckett's street, kicking up slush and sending his truck sideways. Not wanting to go another moment without her knowing how he felt, he didn't slow down, even though he couldn't see more than five feet in front of him because of the snow.

The moment he'd left the restaurant, he understood just how wrong he'd been about everything. A phone call to his mom about the missing items put everything into perspective.

"Better to ask for forgiveness than permission," had been her explanation for why she'd been sneaking into the bar after hours to do a little wedding shopping. "Didn't want the wedding to sneak up on you, so I tucked a few things aside. And the money's in my safe. Minus a few scrapbooking purchases."

He'd been so busy looking for someone to

blame, he'd never considered someone was looking out for him.

"Why didn't you tell me?" he'd asked.

"Last I checked, my name's still on the business license, under owner and founder. If anything, you should be asking my permission to hire a new staff," she'd chided. "And why you're looking for a new office manager, instead of coming to me, makes me wonder how many times your dad dropped you on the head."

He not only owed his mom an apology, he owed her the respect she deserved as a partner. But first, he owed a special lady in his life some big words. He gunned it through the snow, his truck coming to an abrupt halt as he threw it in park.

His breath caught in his chest as he looked through the windshield. Because kneeling on the front porch, surrounded by the entire contents of her bag of tricks, as if she'd been in such a rush she'd dumped it upside down, was Beckett. Snow stuck in her hair, scarf dragging on the ground, her hands in constant motion as she searched through her belongings. She was so focused on finding her keys, she didn't hear him until he reached into the bag and pulled them out.

She froze, her gaze running from his hand to his arm, and finally, her mouth formed a perfect O of surprise. "Levi? You can't be here."

She was flushed, her nose pink from the cold, and her eyes looked as if she'd been crying all night. But she wasn't cutting him any slack. He loved that about her.

Scratch that: He loved her.

"Actually, I can't leave," he said, his eyes calm and on hers. "Not until I tell you something."

"What?" she said, and he could hear her heart beating as if it were his own.

"I was wrong before. And I wanted to set the record straight about —"

"Shhh." She put her gloved hands over his mouth. "Before you say anything, I want you to know I was coming to see you. Only now you're here, and I won't have the car ride to get this right, so if I mix things up, remember that." She took a big breath. "I don't know if you could ever forgive me, but —"

"You've already apologized," he said.

"But —" Her hands went back over his mouth, and he smiled.

Taking her wrists, he brought her hands to his chest. "I want to revise rule five."

"You do?" She looked so small and defeated.

"Yes, I do." He gripped her hips and

pulled her close. "You asked for how long, and I said as long as we're both happy. That doesn't work for me anymore."

"This is why I wanted to come to you. I got all frazzled and —" She frowned when he smiled. "Stop doing that — you're making it worse. And this is important. You're important. To me," she whispered. "You're important to me. And before you revise rule five, I'd like to call in my spoils."

"Actually, you did, that night of our tailgate picnic."

She shook her head. "I never said the words, so it doesn't count. So, I'm saying them now. I've always wanted to learn how to sail, and it just so happens that, starting today, my dad is making sure I have every weekend off. So I want you to teach me how to sail. After that, if you still want to revise rule five, then we can talk about it."

She was wearing a pretty blue sweater, messy ponytail, no makeup. And he couldn't take his eyes off her.

"Is it my turn now?" he asked, and after a moment, she nodded. "First, you never, ever, ever have to apologize to me for being there for your family. Second, swallowing my pride isn't my strong suit, and I'm sorry for being a dick. Thirdly, I won't change my mind about rule five. Because I'm no longer okay with the time frame. When you asked me for how long, I should have said forever. Because you make me happy, Beckett, and I want to feel like this forever. With you." He leaned down and kissed her gently. "I love you, Beckett. And wherever you are is where I want to be."

Going up on her toes, she took his face and whispered, "I love you, too."

And when their lips met, he knew that he couldn't make a wrong move, because any move with Beckett was the right one. Slowly, she pulled back and blinked up at him.

"Did you kiss me, or did I kiss you?"

He laughed. "Does it matter?"

"No," she said, wrapping her arms around his neck. "I'm wearing matching socks, so that proves intent."

He looked into her eyes, and the love he saw shining back was the kind people wrote stories about.

EPILOGUE

Beckett still wasn't sure if Cupid was to blame, but Rome's most cynical romantic officially believed in everlasting love. She wouldn't go as far as to say she chased rainbows, but she never missed a chance to wish on a shooting star.

Levi had given her that. And so much more.

A gentle spring breeze settled around Annie and Beckett as they stood at the end of the marina, watching the sun make its final descent into the horizon.

"Now?" Annie whispered.

"Almost," Beckett said, giving Annie's hand a squeeze. The sky was still too pink, and Beckett was going for a blush.

After weeks of planning, her best friend was about to walk down the aisle and marry the man of her dreams.

Candlelit paper lanterns lined the dock,

463

with twinkle lights twirled through the rope railings. Then there was the arbor, constructed of white birch and covered with so many hydrangeas, it looked as if Martha Stewart herself had designed it. Strings of fairy lights cascaded down from the top, mimicking a million stars, brilliant enough to make a wish.

"My bouquet," Annie gasped. "I forgot my bouquet." She frantically searched the ground around her feet, then lifted her silk dress, as if the flowers could possibly be hidden beneath the mermaid-cut gown.

"It's right there," Beckett said, pointing to Annie's hand, which was strangling the stems of the four-dozen coral-colored peonies.

"Oh." Annie laughed. "I'm just a little nervous. I would have forgotten my dad if he . . . Oh my God. I forgot my dad." She cupped her mouth. "I can't walk down the aisle without my dad."

"One father of the bride, delivered on time and as promised," Paisley called out, nearly jumping the curb as she pulled up in Beckett's Vespa. On the back, clinging to the seat like a koala, was the father of the bride. Looking quite pale himself.

"Dad, I forgot you," Annie said, running

464

to the bike and throwing her arms around him.

"I'm here now," Marty said, climbing off the bike to give his daughter a kiss. "Had to show those yahoos how to tie a proper bow tie."

"Emmitt couldn't tie his tie?" Annie paced. "This is a bad sign."

"Just nerves," Beckett assured her.

"What if he doesn't show? What if he saw the tie problem as a sign too?" Annie took the helmet from her dad and instead of placing it back on the bike, she stared at the scooter as if contemplating a hijacking.

"Looks like we got a runner," Paisley said. "I've got my license now, so you just say the word, Mom Two, and we're out of here."

Shooting the teen a glare, Beckett stepped between Annie and escape. "Annie, if you want to Thelma and Louise this shindig, just say the word. But before you do, I need you to do one thing for me. Can you do that?"

Annie looked at the bike, then back to Beckett and nodded.

"Look down that dock and then tell me what you want."

Annie slowly turned her head and looked down to the end of the marina to find Emmitt looking back. Strong, confident, his

465

eyes promising love and ever after. A small smile tugged Annie's lips, followed by a glow that could only be love.

"I want him. I want to spend every day of my life feeling the kind of love I feel now, with Emmitt." Her eyes never wavered. "I want to get married. Today. In this dress. To that man."

"Thank God. Do you know how many paper lanterns I assembled?"

"And they looked perfect. Everything looks perfect." Annie paled. "Not too perfect though, right?"

"Just the right amount of perfect," Beckett assured her.

"You're the best friend ever." Annie threw her hands around Beckett and squeezed. "And I'm ready. Now."

The sky turned magically coral as Beckett spoke into her secret service earpiece, an essential accessory for every maid of honor slash wedding planner. "Cue music."

The gentle strings of the harp began to play, and the procession lined up.

"No, I mean now. I don't want to wait another minute." Annie took her dad's hand and stepped into the aisle.

Caught off guard, the crowd was a little slow on the uptake, but Emmitt didn't blink, just smiled and said, "That's my girl."

"When you and Levi get married, I'll throw you the best wedding ever," Annie said and, without another word, walked as fast as she could down the aisle to the man of her dreams. The audience finally caught on, standing as the bride glided by, well ahead of her wedding party. And when she reached the arbor she kissed the man of her dreams.

"I don't mind her planning the wedding, as long as I get to plan the wedding night." Two strong arms wrapped around Beckett's waist and she tilted her head back to find Levi standing right behind her, staring down at her with so much love in his eyes, Beckett's heart slowly rolled over in complete surrender.

This, right here, was the man of *her* dreams. Beckett had been so busy running from love, she'd crashed right into it.

Into Levi.

"I hope it involves a tour of your cabin."

"Oh, it will be the grand tour, followed by an around the world tour." He leaned down and kissed her. "And I'm serious. Marry me, Beck."

"We're at Annie and Emmitt's wedding," she said.

"If you want to get technical, it's our wedding. Right down to the lemon cake with limoncello buttercream frosting." He walked around to face her. "We planned it before I got to propose."

"Propose?" She laughed, a bit hysterical. "We drive each other crazy. I'd drive you crazy. I do drive you crazy."

"In the best possible way."

"My family."

"Would be our family," he assured her.

"But we went about all of this backward. It would never work." But even as she said it, she wanted it to work. So incredibly badly.

"We went about this our way." Levi dropped to one knee and a flock of flutters took flight in her chest. "Marry me, Beck."

She pulled her hands away. "You're just caught up in the moment. It's an overdose of bliss talking."

He took her hands back. "It's my heart talking. And you're worth more than any moment — you're worth forever."

"Forever is a long time. Plenty of opportunities to screw up," she admitted, her knees wobbling. "I mean, there'll be times my family will need me, at a moment's notice. And I won't be able to keep myself from running to the rescue."

"Then I'll go with you. Be right by your side," he said. "Have I mentioned I look damn sexy in tights and a cape?"

She laughed but inside she was melting. There was her man, kneeling before her, offering to take her exactly how she was. And if that wasn't proof that romance existed, then what came next did.

Levi pulled out a box, which contained the most beautiful ring she'd ever seen. "Marry me, Beck."

She waited for panic to set in, for the little voice to whisper that it would never work, but instead felt a warm rush of love and certainty wash over her. She wanted him. Not just for today, or next week. She wanted her happily ever after. With him.

She dropped down to her knees and cupped his face. "Only if you'll marry me back."

ABOUT THE AUTHOR

Marina Adair is a #1 nationally bestselling author whose fun, flirty contemporary romances have sold over a million copies. In addition to the When in Rome series, she is the author of the Destiny Bay series, the Heroes of St. Helena series, the Sugar, Georgia series, and the St. Helena Vineyard series, which was the inspiration behind the original Hallmark Channel Vineyard movies: *Autumn in the Vineyard, Summer in the Vineyard,* and *Valentine in the Vineyard.* Raised in the San Francisco Bay Area, she holds a MFA from San Jose University and currently lives in Northern California with her husband, daughter, and two neurotic cats. Please visit her online at MarinaAdair .com.